WHERE PIGEONS DON'T FLY

WHERE PIGEONS
DON'T FLY

Yousef Al-Mohaimeed

Translated by Robin Moger

دار بلومزبري - مؤسسة قطر للنشر
B L O O M S B U R Y
QATAR FOUNDATION
PUBLISHING

مؤسسة قطر
Qatar Foundation

First published in English in 2014 by
Bloomsbury Qatar Foundation Publishing
Qatar Foundation
PO Box 5825
Doha
Qatar

www.bqfp.com.qa

First published in Arabic in 2009 by the Arab Cultural Center

ISBN 9789992179161

Typeset by Newgen Knowledge Works (P) Ltd., Chennai, India
Printed and bound by CPI Group (UK) Ltd, Croydon CR0 4YY

It is the severest of torments to be granted a mind that protests in a society that does not

Abdullah al–Qaseemi

Part 1

A neck, a sword and leaden air

Riyadh:
Shepherds
Driving the flock
To the wolves.

Ali al-Amri, *The Widows' Sons*

As the train moved out of Liverpool Street station at sunset on that mild July day in 2007 and headed north towards the coastal town of Great Yarmouth, Fahd al-Safeelawi felt happy.

He had granted himself a two-day break from his exhausting job at the print and copy shop in order to wander the streets and parks of London, taking up residence in a modest hotel in Queensway near Hyde Park. He had frequented a small Lebanese restaurant where he tasted white rice again after a long abstinence and an unassuming Iranian place where the tubes from *shisha* pipes crept like serpents between the cane chairs scattered about the entrance. He had discovered a little pub with a wonderful Victorian atmosphere called *The Happy Lion* and spent his time roaming between Oxford Street and Trafalgar Square and sitting in new bars and cafés down by the river near London Bridge.

I

Once inside the carriage he found a seat by a table on which he placed the backpack that had become part of his body and from its side-pocket pulled out a bottle of water and a box of Panadol Extra bought from a chemist's on Edgware Road. He pushed a tablet to the back of his throat, followed it with a swig of water, then did it again. From the bottom of the bag he took out *The Painted Kiss* by Elizabeth Hickey, a novel about the relationship between Gustav Klimt and his young lover, Emilie, whose name Klimt had uttered as he died. Grown old, Emilie looks back over her life, from when she was a twelve-year-old schoolgirl taking art lessons from Klimt to the moment she moved his paintings from Vienna to the Austrian countryside. The book reminded Fahd strongly of a film he had seen a year ago, *Girl with a Pearl Earring*, adapted from a novel about the life of Dutch artist Johannes Vermeer, who painted a portrait of the same name. There was a delightful interplay between the two great novels.

Fahd followed the flocks of words and then rested his head against the cold windowpane. He almost immediately dozed off and while he slept the train began to move. He woke suddenly, to find himself confronted with an elderly Englishwoman, sitting in the seat opposite and smiling at him. She was turning the pages of an interior décor magazine with a fascination only broken by his startled coming to. He began looking out at the greenery, the tiled houses, the cows and sheep as they passed before him like a rapidly spooling film reel.

He thought of his close friend Saeed, who had called to check up on him three times in the nearly eleven months he had spent in Britain. Fahd considered rewarding him for these phone calls and his rare loyalty by surprising him with a call of his own from 'the lands of the Franks' as Saeed called them. There weren't many names in his mobile's address book: Hank, his friend Badr al-Ha'ili, a young Frenchwoman called Linda, Santia, his girlfriend and fellow student at the Spanish language school, and Neil, the young accountant who ran the print shop. And then there was Saeed, his friend from childhood and his shameless, wild youth in Riyadh.

When he dialled the number and put the phone to his ear it wasn't the standard ring tone that he heard but a song: a song that wiped out everything that had become his world and hurled Great Yarmouth into the sea, as though this unexpected song had the power to shove the peaceful town, with its old buildings, churches, pubs and promenade of white sand, its funfair and kind-hearted people, into the North Sea. And not only had the town flown away, but with it all the language, companions and contentment of his new life.

Fahd felt a great yearning squeeze his neck and set his eyes streaming. At the same instant he was possessed by fear, a terror of the sheikhs—the fat men with long black beards he always saw at night, advancing with sharpened lances with which they pierced his pillow and riddled it with holes, the white feathers flying out until he couldn't breathe, and he would awake in a panic, feeling that he was choking.

He put the mobile down in front of him and, resting his elbows on the table, he held his head in his hands and began to cry, his slender body shaking with a strange hysteria. The elderly Englishwoman started towards him, gently touched his arm and murmured, 'Are you all right?'

'Yes,' he said, mortified, 'I'm fine,' and turned his tearful eyes to the window.

3

T ARFAH AL-SAMITAN DIDN´T LIKE books that much, though she read crime stories and romances; she much preferred music and dancing. She loved Khaled Abdel Rahman's melancholy voice, just as she loved Snickers and the Hilal football team and was obsessed with fashion accessories and sex.

Late one morning in July 2006, Fahd had pulled over to wait for Tarfah outside Jarir Bookstore on King Abdullah Road, and she emerged at her slow, assured pace carrying a red carrier bag and a handbag. She got into the little car and as always, warned him not to set off until she had settled comfortably in the passenger seat. He turned the key and said, 'Where to?'

She didn't have much time; she had to be back at the Academy in an hour.

'Shall we get a coffee at Starbucks?'

'Sure, but I thought Java Café had nicer coffee.'

Raising her *abaya* over her head she said, 'As you like, sweetheart!' He went with her suggestion, though he didn't agree that they should take the coffee with them as they drove around in the Riyadh morning.

At the Starbucks in Wuroud he veered right towards the entrance to the family section.

There was nobody about that morning other than a solitary van with an Indonesian driver sitting inside. Fahd parked next to him and turned off the engine. Tarfah hesitated.

'Do you still want to do this?' she asked.

'How do you mean?'

'Wouldn't it be better to bring the coffees to the car and go?'

He pulled the key from the steering column. 'It's better that we sit down, so I can get a look at you.'

She glanced over at the Indonesian. 'I don't know. To be honest, the morning is a scary time.'

'Don't worry yourself; it's all fine,' he said confidently, opening the door.

He got out and she calmly followed holding her carrier bag and the handbag embroidered with shield-bearing horsemen. They entered through a door on which swung a sign: *Families Only*. The place was filled with the invigorating smell of coffee. The glass door slid open and as the door glided slowly shut she held her forefinger to his mouth, touching it then taking it beneath her veil and giving it a kiss.

'Honey!'

Casting his eye over the partitioned wooden rooms with their hinged doors, he chose the furthest and held open the door, stepping back to make way for Tarfah, who brushed past, her eyes on his.

'Cappuccino?' he asked.

'Anything from my sweetheart's hand is sweet.'

Fahd stood facing the Filipino employee while a young Saudi with his back turned scoured a milk jug with steam. He ordered a large cappuccino and a hot chocolate and had just glanced at the doughnuts and cookies behind the glass when he felt a draught brush him from behind. He wasn't sure: had the outer door to the family section opened? Was it the wind of some ancient angel, lying in ambush? Was that the odour of Friday prayers? Of a damp toothpick? Was it agarwood oil, perhaps, or Indian incense from a Friday night wedding? Perhaps it was all of these. But one thing it most certainly was not, was the scent of a female body preceded by her perfume.

'Peace be upon you and the mercy of God.'

'And upon you be peace.'

Fahd's hand was pointing at a cookie decorated with pieces of chocolate but the moment he turned it began to tremble. He saw a face staring at him, a cream *mashlah*, delicate and striped, and a carefully groomed beard. The man said only, 'Peace be upon you and the mercy of God,' and left the rest to Fahd's terror and his fear, which were more than enough to expose him. The sheikh was like a wily fox, startling his prey with his flashing eyes.

Fahd's shaking hand betrayed him as the man waited for him to fold without need for further questioning: *That's right, she's not my wife, nor my sister, my mother, or one of my close female relatives: she's my friend. In fact, I'll be completely honest and up front with you: she's my girlfriend, my lover. We came here to drink cappuccino and hot chocolate together while she consoled me over the death of my mother, whose passing has left me utterly alone. I can't be sure, sheikh, if I would have kissed her today, or rather waited until the sadness had lifted from my wounded heart. But she may well have comforted me by hugging me and stroking my hair, might even have granted me light kisses.*

The mellifluous voice broke in on Fahd's thoughts. 'How are you, brother?'

'Praise be to God.'

'Your good name?'

'Fahd.'

'Are you here with anyone, Fahd?'

'Yes,' Fahd said, and, flustered, pointed to the last booth at the back.

'Who is she?'

Here he was, aiming his lance at Fahd's eyes and pricking them out, as Fahd thought of all the stories he had read in the papers of people trying to make a run for it. A man in his forties tried to sneak out of a fourth floor window and was smashed to pieces when he fell ... A young man fled with his girl and driving wildly they collided with a reinforced concrete barrier and died ... Two men and their female companions drove the wrong way down the road in a bid to escape, hit an oncoming vehicle and all four died ... A story from Tabuk, another from Sharqiya, a third from Ha'il, and now ... This time the papers would write of a young woman from Starbucks who committed suicide by throwing herself into the roaring torrent of King Abdullah Road, the car wheels grinding her to paste in her black *abaya*, her beautiful shoes sent flying.

'Who is that with you?'

'My wife.'

He could only lie and Fahd was certain the sheikh had seen the lie for what it was. There was even a small smile forming around his eyes as he said, 'She's not your wife, young Fahd. Tell me, and don't be frightened. All we do is look after people and correct their behaviour.'

Fahd recalled an interview in the newspaper *Ukaz*, in which the head of the Committee for the Promotion of Virtue and the Prevention of Vice had said they covered up over ninety percent of cases of illegal association between the sexes. Would Fahd and Tarfah be part of the ninety percent? The man's face overflowed with sympathy and compassion, comfort and certitude. With his tall and slender body he was like a man standing

7

by his son at the edge of a swimming pool, persuading him to take the plunge: right there beside him, ready to rescue him if it comes to it.

'She's not my wife. She's my girlfriend.'

Just like that he took the decision not merely to dive in but to strip off his swimming trunks and hurl himself at the water's surface.

'Don't be worried. Come along with me. Just a few simple procedures and you can go on your way with the protection of God.'

'But what about her? How can I leave her on her own?'

He had scarcely finished the sentence before the man set off, saying, 'Don't worry, don't worry: this is our job.'

They were joined by a short, plump man with the eyes of a hawk and no *mashlah*.

'Go with him, my son,' the sheikh said.

The man encircled Fahd's wrist with an iron grip and tugged and it was at that precise moment that he realised today, Wednesday, 13 July, was to be his Day of Reckoning. There was a Day of Reckoning for everyone in this city: you died instantly, or passed safely across its threshold and were saved, or you carried it with you wherever you went, never to be forgotten, like a thief's brand on your face.

The sheikh left them, heading over to where Tarfah was sitting unaware, removing the red rose from the carrier bag where she had put it. She was sniffing it and waiting for her cappuccino, waiting to talk about the terrible week Fahd had spent following his mother's death and his attempts to move her from the emergency ward of King Khaled Hospital to the department of forensic pathology at Riyadh Central Hospital. Now Tarfah would never get to wash away his sadness with

8

her laughter and chatter. Instead, loathsome black ants would scale her ripe body and enter the chambers of her living heart. Her heart, her love and her life would die, the music and the gentle Gulf dances would die and the sash about her hips would become a hangman's rope.

As Fahd left the coffee shop the yellow sun was beginning to grow harsher and a thin policeman in baggy trousers, belt sagging beneath the weight of his holster, stood waiting by the door of a GMC SUV. He opened the two rear doors and indicated to Fahd that he should climb into the third row of seats. The policeman got in and was followed by the short, plump man who inclined his bulk towards Fahd and opened a bag under his nose: 'Put your things in here. Everything in your pockets.'

'Why?' asked Fahd stupidly, then, seeing the man's irritation, added, 'The sheikh told me it was just a few basic procedures out by the car, and now you're putting me in the car. Where are we going?'

He spoke like a child refusing to go in on his first day at primary school. He put the bag down in front of him as the soldier looked over with evident distaste and shouted in a reedy voice: 'Do what you're told, boy.'

Fahd took out his wallet and keys and placed them in the bag.

'Your mobile,' the plump man said coldly, without looking at him.

Shit, he thought to himself. What would he do if they opened the phone and searched through the names, the messages, the swapped pictures, the Bluetooth records, the …? Why hadn't he asked to go to the bathroom in the coffee shop and chucked it down the lavatory?

Taking the phone from his pocket he made an attempt to at least remove the SIM card. His hands were concealed behind the armrest but the man caught him at it and with unexpected strength plucked the phone from his grasp and put it in the bag. The man opened the ID and read out the name: 'Fahd Suleiman al-Safeelawi …'

'Nice to meet you,' he added, with mocking relish.

He opened the wallet and found a photograph of Fahd's father in his forties, just before his death. *That's my father, may God have mercy on his soul.* He switched on the mobile phone and paused at the password. He handed Fahd a pen from his pocket and the folder he was carrying.

'Write down the password.'

'No.'

Surprisingly, the man didn't become angry; he didn't slap Fahd or set the skinny cop on him. Instead, he said quite simply, 'No problem: it's up to you.'

Tarfah emerged following the sheikh, stumbling in her *abaya* as she wept and pleaded. From the other side of the window Fahd saw the hands he had kissed so often lifted to the sheikh's face as though she were begging.

She would be kept waiting outside the Starbucks for half an hour, even after the Committee's vehicle carrying Fahd had left. Every luxury vehicle that passed by would slow down, the young drivers peering curiously out, while some of the café's customers turned to the window to enjoy the show as though they were watching some drama from the natural world on the Discovery Channel. The lioness stalks her unsuspecting prey through the bush, moving her paws very slowly so as not to make the grass rustle, and thus did the sheikh move his paws, quiet and assured, as he guided his quarry to the ambush.

Fahd put his head between his hands as he sighed and said, 'There is no recourse nor strength save through God.' Then, firmly and with a faint tremor, he muttered, 'Oh Lord! Oh Lord, help us!'

The short man with the eyes of a hawk and a brown spot on his forehead rebuked him. 'You discover God after you've committed the sin.'

With no apparent humility he recited from the Qur'an: '"Now, when they embark upon a voyage, they call on God and worship him alone, but when He has delivered them to dry land, they give a share of their worship to others."'

On the verge of tears, Fahd said, 'Protect us, God help you! At least keep her from harm!'

And so it was, in this country of fear and confusion, that Fahd was transformed in an instant from confident and collected to flustered, uncertain and defeated. Perhaps it was the sight of Tarfah weeping that so affected him, and then again, what might her brother Abdullah do, he who had so very courageously defied her desire to enrol at nursing college before finally surrendering to her limitless obstinacy? What would her poor mother do? How would her little girl, Sara, sleep at night? What embrace would compensate Sara for the warmth of her mother's arms? *What embrace will comfort me?*

–2–

W ITH HIS EXAGGERATED AIR of exquisite dignity and grace, the sheikh with the cream *mashlah* looked exactly like the man who had whispered in the ear of Fahd's father, Suleiman, twenty-five years before. As Fahd climbed into the back seat of the Committee's GMC he couldn't help thinking of his father getting into the secret police jeep in Buraida's Jurida market all that time ago. His father had told him the story many times.

The morning of 3 November 1979 was mild and a light breeze bathed the faces of the rural vendors spread through the marketplace. Fahd's father noticed two men dressed in black winter clothes. One had his *shimagh* wrapped across his face and the other wore a black overcoat and dark glasses—and it was this man who approached him, whispering in his ear in front of the customers that he wanted him for a moment. So, leaving his neighbour Ibn Qanas in charge of the crates of courgettes and tomatoes, he walked off with them. He would never return to his crates.

Fahd learnt later that the journey his father endured was exhausting. He was sat before an investigating officer who interrogated him bluntly and unnervingly about his role in the Salafist group whose ambitions had extended to overthrowing the country's rulers. Smelling of fresh vegetables pulled from the fields of Khabb al-Muraidasiya, his sleeves rolled up and his *shimagh* cocked back like a truck driver, a worried Suleiman sat there and answered the questions honestly and clearly while the clerk beside the officer wrote it all down.

Suleiman had explained that all he cared for in the world were his crates of courgettes, tomatoes and beans and that for over a year he'd had no connection to the group which two days before had assaulted the Grand Mosque on Mecca. The interrogation ran for six hours and when he asked if he might perform the afternoon prayer the scowling officer only asked him if he thought he was on holiday.

'Don't assume you'll be going home to your mother any time soon.'

And indeed, he didn't return for four years, during which time he was moved from Buraida to Riyadh, Jeddah and Mecca. He entered a temporary prison on Airport Road in Riyadh, then a new facility outside Mecca where he made friends. There was Mushabbab the Southerner, Salah the Egyptian, Bandar Bin Khalaf and Deifallah, and there were the guards, whose shifts might change, though their eyes, frozen like the eyes of the dead, never did. They were like those who ready bodies for burial, who wash the corpses indifferent and inured, and so they never knew his woe and his regret at having turned down his father's plea that he do as his brother did and continue his education in Buraida, taking himself off instead to a run-down house in the Riyadh neighbourhood of Umm Sulaym.

How small and tame Umm Sulaym had been in the 1970s. From the roundabout to the old neighbourhood facing Al-Jahiz School it was a considerable distance, the whole way lined with street-vendors and students. He did not enjoy studying at the Imam al-Daawa Institute in Deira: studying Ibn Malik's *Alfiyya* in his grammar classes rattled his brain and left him dizzy and he was encouraged to rebel when they taught him that studying in government schools was dishonourable and that he must seek true and lawful knowledge from sheikhs and scholars in the colonnades of mosques and the galleries of Mecca and Medina.

That afternoon, as their son Suleiman quitted the Jurida market for the last time, his mother, Fahd's grandmother, was in the village of Muraidasiya setting down the coffee pot and a few sugared dates in front of her husband. Throwing her shawl over her head and shoulders and sitting before him to pour the first cup, she thought nothing of her striped green *thaub*, but he flung the dregs of the coffee behind him in the direction of the old mulberry tree, and cried, 'Your *thaub*'s on inside out, woman.'

At this, the grandmother was perturbed and examined her sleeves, muttering, 'God, make it well.'

The following day they sent Suleiman's brother Saleh to the market to ask after him and Ibn Qanas told him that two strange men had turned up and spoken with him. Suleiman had gone with them and had not yet returned.

Suleiman reached Riyadh cuffed hand and foot and accompanied by a young policeman, returning once more to the accursed city that had destroyed his modest dreams of learning and wealth and introduced him to a strange world of religious groups and parties.

It had been a simple enough beginning: murmuring invocations after the afternoon prayers and listening to the silken voice of the imam as he invited anyone who wanted to take part in a retreat that coming Thursday to register his name with the muezzin. So it was that his name first found its way into the records of a small mosque in Umm Sulaym.

They left for the Hassi River in two cars, Suleiman riding in the Volvo belonging to the mosque's imam, an upright young man from Beir. When they arrived they set up a tent, cooked some food and formed a *dhikr*. Then they listened to selections of the prophetic *hadith*, played a bit of football and returned home the next day. After two months of these trips a benefactor from the congregation sponsored an *umra* to Mecca and taking the decision to abandon the Imam al-Daawa Institute and the hated *Alfiyya* of Ibn Malik, Suleiman's arduous journey began. He dropped in on the owner of the petrol station where he worked and handed in his notice, saying that he was going to travel in search of knowledge, and received one hundred and fifty riyals, two months wages, which he put in his pocket and departed with the others in a small microbus.

Inside the Grand Mosque, making his way to the ambulatory around the Kaaba, Suleiman passed a gallery where a sheikh was debating with his students and, joining them, heard the name of Sheikh al-Albani for the first time. He hunted for his writings in the bookshops around the mosque, read up on the prophetic *hadith*, both authenticated and doubtful, and studied the prayer habits of the Prophet. He had no idea what Divine Reward Salafism meant, but was embarrassed to ask the Brothers. He read a lot and understood little. He pored over his two-part study of *hadith* authenticity, *Instigation and Dissuasion*, and leafed through *The Night Ride to Jerusalem and the Ladder* about the Prophet's miraculous flight from Mecca to Jerusalem and his ascent to the heavens. He loved the books of Nasser al-Deen al-Albani and little expected that one day he would meet him face to face, so the first time he saw him in the flesh within the Grand Mosque, his astonishment was considerable: his mouth gaped and he was rooted to the spot. He had felt much as his son, Fahd, felt when he was joined in the lift at Mamlaka Tower by the singer Rashed al-Fares with his brown skin, long black overcoat and manager, to whom he chatted away. Each of them was encountering his idol: Suleiman had read much of Sheikh al-Albani and loved his ideas, while Fahd listened to al-Fares and adored his rapid music, a taste he tried to impose on his girlfriend Tarfah.

On the back seat of the Committee vehicle Fahd watched the drivers hurtle down the roads in their cars and thought of his father's ordeal. Suleiman had been questioned interminably until it was finally established that he had not taken up arms to hijack the Grand Mosque when they stripped his clothes off and one of them examined the front of his shoulders to determine if the butt of a Belgian rifle had jarred against them and left a bruise.

He was sentenced to jail then transferred to a new prison outside Mecca whose walls gave off the smell of fresh paint. He and his companions were the first guests to enter that now venerable building. How Fahd wished that his father had not bequeathed him this part of his life and revealed to him his secret papers.

Suleiman left a part of his secret life to Fahd for one reason: his fear that his son might become embroiled in the activities of extremist groups and that he might not stop at distributing pamphlets in the court of the Grand Mosque, as his adolescent father had done back in the dying days of Ramadan in August 1979, but take up arms or strap an explosive belt to

16

his body. Fahd came to understand that Suleiman had been afraid, that his fear became an obsession, and before he passed away he set aside a few possessions for his son, instructing his wife to hold them in trust and hand them over when he had grown, as though anticipating a sudden death in the midst of his young life.

So it was that Fahd got his hands on his father's old books: *Apprising the People of the Signs of Discord and the Portents of the Hour, A Vindication of the Religion of Abraham, Upon Him be Peace*, and pages written in a shaky hand, memoirs and diaries. There was a small and dirty string of prayer beads made from olive stones and a blue biro with a grubby plaster stuck on for a grip. There was a photograph of Suleiman and a man with long hair sitting together in the terraces of Malaz Stadium, another of him with a group of young men around a fire on a sand dune in Maizeela outside Riyadh, and a third and final picture in black-and-white of Suleiman alongside his father, Ali, old and oblivious of the camera, and his brother Saleh.

As he sat in the back of the vehicle looking out of the window, Fahd recalled when his sister, Lulua, had handed him a leather bag, black, ancient and falling apart. Their mother had asked her to give it to him as a bequest from his father. Inside he found the timeworn, personal effects that his father had insisted be handed over to him only once he had come of age. Why his mother had waited until he was in his early twenties he didn't know. Maybe because of their relationship, which for the last three years had been bleak. He had opened the bag in a fever of excitement. There was no money, no treasure, just his father's stupid journals: his years in prison and words of wisdom for his son.

THE GMC WITH THE Committee's logo on the driver and passenger-side doors moved off and headed down a side street in Wuroud, the driver looking to skip the traffic on King Abdullah Road. Fahd thought of how many times he had crossed this road with Tarfah, the two of them staring at the vast advertising hoardings by the corner of the Ministry for Municipal and Rural Affairs and laughing, their fingers entwined.

'Remember your aunt's house that's up for rent in King Fahd?' he had asked her one night. They had gone to the house and stretched out naked in a sitting room devoid of furniture, the echo bouncing from the bare walls parroting their voices, their laughter and their moans.

He twisted about, looking for Tarfah. *Where have they taken her? Where will they take me?* His fearful muttering was interspersed by the hawk-eyed man's directions to the driver.

At the Owais Markets traffic lights the driver crossed straight over instead of turning left into the King Fahd neighbourhood. The streets were very quiet; there was none of the usual bustle around Haram Mall, which lured shoppers in with its cheap, low-quality goods.

Fahd sighed and muttered a prayer; perhaps these moans and murmurs might move the hawk-eyed man to pity him. But it was no use: the man was like a butcher at Eid al-Adha, dragging the animal by its foot, the handle of a sharpened knife clamped between his teeth as he listened to the latest joke from his colleague.

'It's just a few papers to sign and you'll be on your way.'

That is what the man had said, encouraging Fahd to talk briefly and clearly. Fahd sighed and directed his gaze to the street, thinking again of Tarfah. *What are you doing now? Where are you? Has the sheikh in the cream* mashlah, *his eyes full of calm and warmth, taken you off in his colleague's car to the Committee or the women's shelter? Don't put your faith in his deceptive courtesy, his claims that it's just a few official documents, just a signature on a pledge and you can go home. They'll tell you that they are looking out for you, but they lie. He'll trick you as he tricked me. He'll lock you up or ask your family to collect you.* The scandal!

Fahd imagined Tarfah bobbing on the back seat like a freshly slaughtered pigeon, her door secured with a safety catch that could only be opened from outside while doubtless the sheikh in the cream *mashlah* rode up front, reciting *hadith* on the virtues of the chaste, inviolable woman who stayed at home. He longed to call her and make sure she was all right, but they had taken away his phone and all his papers.

The GMC stopped outside a building. The man with hawk-like eyes opened the door and glared at Fahd, who remained inside with the policeman and the driver. There was a short delay then he emerged from the building accompanied by a bulky man, a toothstick poking out of his thick lips, which he bit on every now and again as he muttered and spat and looked over at Fahd. The short man gestured at the driver, who got out with the bag containing Fahd's possessions and stood next to them. Then the big man came forward, opened the rear door and took Fahd to the building while the bag swayed in his other hand.

He sat down facing the men. There were three of them, waited on by an Indonesian, who brought them tea. The big man came over and stood in front of Fahd.

'Stand up. Lift your hands in the air.'

Fahd raised his hands as though he were at a custom's check or airport security and the man began to pat down his pockets and body, front and back; he even felt beneath his balls. The hawk-eyed man gave a shout, springing towards Fahd and yanking at his upraised left hand.

'What's this?'

He removed the prayer beads that had been left to him by his father, a small string of beads that he had wrapped twice about his wrist the week before: olive stones that had been stored in his father's bag for nearly twenty-five years.

In his diaries, his father had told him that he had kept the beads as a reminder of the long prison nights and their boredom: the darkness, the isolation, the sadness. He wanted to remember how he had passed the time fashioning prayer beads from olive stones or breeding cockroaches, letting them multiply before destroying them all.

My son, keeping hold of that which reminds you of tragedy will prevent you forgetting it, and so you will be able to avoid the things that led me into its trap. All I ask of you is that you keep it safe after I am gone and remember that the ultimate destiny of the political parties and religious groups that vex the government is extinction, failure and psychological torment. While your contemporaries are seizing their opportunities and succeeding, you will have wasted the best years of your youth chasing after lost dreams.

–4–

THE MEN WHO WERE artfully guiding Fahd into the Committee's detention cells reminded him of his grandfather, Ali. These men took him into their snare where they unleashed accusations like maddened horses and set about destroying his life with malice and spirit. But had he been alive, his grandfather might have done worse: he might have flogged his grandson before the people in Tahliya Street for consorting in private with a strange woman, he might even have approved of beheading him with a sword.

When his grandfather had been sent the news of a baby boy he didn't go straight home to his wife's family after evening prayers. Instead, he stayed in the mud-brick mosque with the congregation, praying through a watch of the night until his misgivings had abated and the moon had reappeared, for that night, fifteenth of Shaaban, 1379 AH, there had been an eclipse.

Ali was miserable, distraught and full of foreboding. An eclipse of the moon as a child entered the world! For a newborn to arrive accompanied by the wrath of God was terrifying; the baby's whole life and future was in doubt.

'I said he was defective from the day he was born.'

Words he repeated throughout his son Suleiman's life, until the boy's childhood became filled with injustice and misfortune and he lived all his days with a sense of guilt for what had befallen his family.

At first Suleiman's mother, Noura, told her husband, 'Seek protection from the Devil and stop prophesying like a pagan!' But just a week later she herself was shouting in fear and every member of the household wailing when they were told that her younger brother, Ibrahim, and his school friends had been seized by the police outside Muhanna Palace and taken to Riyadh, where he remained for two whole months before returning to Buraida to be flogged before the crowds with his companions. Only then was Noura persuaded that her son Suleiman truly was a curse on her family.

Noura's family in Buraida maintained a somewhat open-minded household, unlike that of her husband's family in Muraidasiya, who were said to be so excessively credulous and superstitious that they gave their cockerel a ritual washing to cleanse him of impurity before he mated with the hens. Her father was one of the great itinerant merchants of the Nejd, who had spread out to Egypt, Iraq and Palestine in the early twentieth century, while in the early 1920s her brother Ibrahim and his friends had despaired of the extremism of the parliamentary deputies who walked the streets carrying long staffs made from the branches of the *shauhat* tree, white turbans on their heads. The deputies exhorted people to pray, warned against gatherings of young people, denounced the wearing of the white *ghatra* and *aqqal* and decried the spread of cafés serving tea and *shisha*. They banned the motorbike, which they referred to as 'Satan's steed', and whenever they found a young man in possession of one, they would confiscate it.

At this, Fahd's Uncle Ibrahim and his friends, nineteen young men all told, decided to march in a demonstration to Muhanna Palace, the residence of the city's governor, Ibn Battal, carrying on their shoulders a young man acting the clown and dubbed the *akia*. They came to a halt outside the palace shouting fearlessly and wildly, 'Down with Ibn Battal! Long live the youth! Down with the deputies! Long live the *akia*!'

Seven years passed, during which the heart of Ali and Noura's youngest child, Mohammed, was weakened by measles and he passed away aged four. 'If death let me choose between them, I would ask he take the bird of ill omen,' Ali muttered bluntly, pointing to his middle son, Suleiman.

Ali's face never brightened again. As everyone in Muraidasiya knew, Mohammed was the apple of his father's eye, while his eldest, Saleh, was his right hand, his tongue and his support.

Fahd had been told so many stories about his grandfather. Who could forget Ali's opposition to the village muezzin? Ibn Dakheel had mounted the first-ever loudspeaker on the village mosque, his voice ringing like thunder when he cleared his throat at dawn. Ali tried urging the congregation to reject this heretical innovation on the grounds that all innovation is deviance and all deviance leads to hellfire. He went further: 'To remain silent over the truth is to be a devil without a tongue.'

The loudspeaker was affixed to the roof of the mud-brick mosque, facing out over the houses and farms of the village. After dawn prayers the men parted ways, shuffling homewards with drowsiness hovering over their heads, Ali amongst them, leading his sons, Saleh and Suleiman, like two befuddled puppies. No sooner had he stretched out his legs in the breakfast room, sipping at his morning coffee, than Suleiman fell asleep in a warm corner, while Saleh slipped outside carrying the hunting rifle, the .25 calibre pellet gun.

23

It was his habit to surprise birds in their nests at first light, but now he passed Abu Rashed's fields, ignoring the calls of the songbirds in the massive thorn trees. He broke the gun's barrel and taking a small wetted pellet from beneath his tongue, blew hard to remove the last vestiges of his spit and thumbed it into the breech. He clicked the barrel straight as he approached the mosque, took aim at the loudspeaker for a few seconds, then, whispering 'God is great' over and over, he pressed the trigger and struck it dead centre. He repeated the dose three times.

The afternoon prayers came and went with no terrifying thunder and no heretical innovation that leads to hellfire. From that day forward, Saleh became a family hero and champion of the Faith, acquiring both social standing and an enormous confidence in himself and his actions, no matter how wrong or reckless.

Suleiman, meanwhile, was little more than a heap of tattered summer clothes bundled up by his mother's side, confused and uncertain and beset by a sense of injury, injustice and ill-treatment. No sooner had he finished his basic education than he decamped to Riyadh to complete his studies. He did not go to Buraida where his brother had been for years, living with his uncles and studying at the National School—'the Brothers school' as it was known—until his father finally moved with his wife and three daughters to Quwai in West Buraida, escaping before God could wipe the village of Muraidasiya from the map. After the business with the loudspeaker, there could be no remaining amongst a people who, as the Book said, 'have changed what is in their own souls', for now God would surely change the grace he had bestowed on them with a mighty flood to drown the village, with an earthquake to shake it and turn it on its head, or something similar.

The well dried up and the date palm in Ali's wall died. Then, a few years later, Ali died as well, proud that no man could accuse him of neglecting the good cause, and proud of the stand he and three other men from Quwai had taken against moral corruption in the winter of 1966, travelling together to Riyadh with a great crowd of citizens from Buraida to stand outside King Faisal's palace and denounce the opening of a girls' school, setting up a tent by the main gate until they were chased away.

How proud Saleh was of fighting heresy in Muraidasiya in the 1960s! How proud, too, to breathe into his father's ear the damaging allegation that his maternal grandfather hid a transistor in his bedroom in Buraida on which he listened to the *Voice of the Arabs* radio broadcasts. Ali al-Safeelawi, however, held his father-in-law in great esteem, so despite his burning desire to denounce his use of the radio and decry it as a heresy and a deviancy and a blasphemy on a par with harbouring a prostitute, he held the knowledge close and condemned it in his heart.

How Fahd longed for the bravery of his Uncle Ibrahim and his friend the *akia*, to be able to scream at the Committee man and the thin policeman with his belt and revolver dangling like the head of drowned child, to snatch back the bag of his possessions and demand: 'When did you presume to own people who were born free?'

What freedom? he asked himself. When his own father tasted the bitterness of long years in jail just for being careless enough to pass out pamphlets to worshippers in the Grand Mosque? Was he dreaming of being a leader in the fight against corruption and the collapse of our values and moral code?

Did he dream of silencing song and stilling the instruments, of preventing women and female singers from appearing on television? Were he and his comrades going to fill the earth with justice after it had brimmed with injustice and tyranny? Or did he just want to say to Ali, his father: *Here I am! Here I am. The one you mocked and whose fate you saw in the moon! I came to show you that this is more than a childish game, more than a paltry rifle that young boys use to hunt sparrows or, like my older brother, destroy with its puny pellets a loudspeaker in some remote village west of Buraida.*

Father, did you want to make them pay attention to you? Did you? Then may you go to hell, you and your senile father and your outdated, backward ideas, for you will bring this ignorant country nothing save more ignorance!

Apologies for this anger, Father. It makes me sad to think you lost your youth when it was you who later taught me the joys of literature and the arts, to watch the films of Walt Disney. You looked after me with love. Saeed, too, son of your friend Mushabbab, who was executed at the dawn of a new year; Saeed, my closest friend who, when confronted with tragedy would always find the strength to burst out in laughter, creating a flagrant, riotous uproar in Tahliya Street.

5

S O PAINFUL, THAT MOMENT, long ago, when they shoved Saeed's father, Mushabbab, into the cell. Suleiman al-Safee-lawi didn't recognise his friend, though they had met at the farm a year before to pick up the secret pamphlets. When Mushabbab entered the cell his clothes were torn, his hair was wild and his face covered with dust. Barefoot and utterly exhausted he threw himself down and slept for five hours like a dead man. Suleiman tried to rouse him for sunset prayers but he did not wake, turned on his side like a corpse.

Years later, Suleiman was to wonder why Saeed's father had deceived his pregnant wife and mother and brought them north on a journey to disaster, to a doomed war in the Grand Mosque. Suleiman hadn't told his young son, Fahd, a thing. *Saeed's father has gone on a long journey*, he'd said. *He's entrusted us to look after his son and keep him safe.*

Every Friday morning he would ready himself early for prayers, then Fahd would sit alongside him in the wine-red Caprice as they drove to the neighbourhood of Jaradiya, south of Central Hospital, where he would park in a narrow road and order Fahd to get out and knock on a small steel door beneath a concrete awning. The roar of the air cooler mounted on two pipes in the street would suddenly cease, then the door would open and out would come Saeed in his wrinkled *shimagh*, his face still drowsy despite the droplets of water that clung to it.

He would get in and they would drive to Ulaya, to pray at Sheikh al-Islam Mohammed Bin Abdel Wahhab Mosque near the house.

After prayers, Suleiman would go to the Afghans selling toothsticks and buy a long stick, which he broke into three. He would sharpen each piece and hand one to Saeed, one to Fahd and silently chew the third as he walked to the car, the two boys scurrying behind him like tame kittens. He would drive to nearby Urouba Road, pulling over just before the Layla al-Akheliya traffic lights outside Alban Zaman dairy to purchase a five-litre container of sour drinking yoghurt and milk, before going in to the Sulaimaniya supermarket and picking up a copy of *Sharq al-Awsat*, while the boys, beside themselves with joy, got a cold can of Pepsi each.

Holding their cans, the paper tucked beneath Suleiman's arm, they would climb to the second floor of their small rented flat and after lunch the two boys would stretch out in Fahd's bedroom to watch cartoons—*Lady*, *Sally* and *Falouna*, and occasionally, *The Iron Man*—though Fahd, making sure Saeed didn't notice, would move his pillow from beneath his head and hold it in front of his face to hide his eyes, frightened by the creatures that he feared might reach out through the screen and attack him.

Just before sunset Suleiman would take them with his wife and their little sister, Lulua, to Sindbad's Toy Town next to King Fahd Library, or to Marah Amusement Park on King Fahd Road, where they placed woollen blankets beneath their bottoms and shot with heart-stopping speed to the end of the long, undulating slide before panting back up. No one panted more than Lulua, who suffered severe asthmatic attacks that sent the whole family on frequent journeys to the Children's Hospital in Sulaimaniya which left Suleiman dizzy, the spinning of his head made worse by the wails of the sick children sat waiting on plastic chairs. The moment Lulua emerged from the oxygen chamber he would hurry away before Fahd could make him stop at the man selling snacks and toys by the large glass door.

Whenever Suleiman was busy, or wanted to meet one of his friends, he would offer to drop the family at the entrance to the Khaima Funfair for women and children then take himself off for two hours or more. Fahd hated this funfair: the vast building and dimly lit halls. He would lose sight of his mother, sometimes for half an hour or more, and when she finally found him, dragging Lulua behind her, she would grab him viciously by the ear and angrily demand, 'Where have you been, you clown?'

Those times when he was lost, he felt destined to live his life far from his family; he feared a swarthy woman would snatch him up and run off and he would go to live in a gloomy house that never saw the sun. Any mention by his parents of the municipal workers who stole children would set Lulua and him trembling and whenever he caught sight of cleaning staff or the like he would shut his eyes until they had passed by.

'The *ziyoud* will get you!' his mother would tell them.

When he was small he assumed the *ziyoud* were the men in Punjabi outfits, Afghans or Pakistanis he guessed, but once he was older he realised that they were Yemenis. Every time his father parked outside the supermarket and went in alone, he and his sister would hide beneath the seats in the back, curled up in the footwells out of sight of the thieves.

Could this fear of his date back to the silly rhyme he heard when he was five?

Mummy and daddy loved me,
They went to Jeddah and left me ...

He felt that his parents really would abandon the two of them without warning, a fear that grew when they went out at night, leaving them with Asiya, their Indonesian maid. They wouldn't leave until the children were asleep, but if either woke unexpectedly it was torture. At around ten or eleven Fahd would be thirsty and get out of bed muddle-headed, keeping his eyes barely open, not enough to banish sleep but just sufficient to see his way through the living room to the small fridge in the kitchen. On his return, his anxiety would take him to the door of his parents' bedroom, which he would open without knocking to find them gone. Was it then that his instincts told him that he would, in fact, lose them at an early age and at more or less the same time?

When Fahd was fifteen, his father had been obliged to travel to Qaseem, a matter of signing court papers to do with Ali's will. Fahd had woken early, before Suleiman, hoping for a final chance for his father to change his mind and take him along, even though the night before he had stressed to Fahd that it was more important that he remain at home with his mother and sister, tucking a fifty riyal note into Fahd's top pocket as he smiled: 'When I get back we'll go to Thamama so you can learn to drive!'

Suleiman drank two cups of coffee standing up, refusing Soha's invitation to eat the breakfast she had prepared and telling her he had to make the second court session in Buraida before noon. She handed him a cloth bag with a zipper, containing two thermoses of coffee and tea and a cheese and jam sandwich wrapped in cling film, which he placed in the footwell of the seat next to him before his wine-red Caprice moved out into Zuhair Rustom Alley. Fahd stood there waving goodbye, gazing at the red glow of rear lights as his father tapped the brakes just before Sayyidat al-Ru'osa Street.

Fahd shut the door and returned to the living room and, as he busied himself searching for something entertaining on television, his mother groaned, 'Your father's forgotten his bag!'

She phoned him and he came back, turning around on Quwa al-Amn Bridge. Fahd waited for him on the doorstep, the Samsonite suitcase beside him, and when the car pulled up, he opened the rear door, put in the case and jokingly said to his father, 'Welcome home, Dad.'

Suleiman chuckled and asked for some water. His mother gave him a new bottle of mineral water and as he rushed back down the steps she shouted for Fahd and handed him a glass of water from the fridge in the kitchen. Suleiman drank, his eyes stern.

'Look after yourself, my man,' he said. 'And your mother and sister, too.'

Then he moved off.

These were his last words. Off he went, rushing to make the second court session, but he never arrived. Soha called him half an hour later on his mobile phone as she usually did.

'The number you have dialled is currently unavailable, please try again later.'

The recorded message was slurred, heavy and menacing. Ten minutes later she tried again and she kept trying until just before noon.

Panicked, Fahd phoned his friend Saeed and asked him to come over right away. Disoriented and anxious he climbed in next to him.

'Where to?'

'The highway to look for my father!' Fahd snapped.

Saeed hesitated and then made a call that lasted for a few minutes. He suggested they ask at the accident and emergency departments of the major hospitals to find out if anything had happened—God forbid.

Saeed's Honda Civic gradually descended to King Fahd Road and from there to Khazan Street, taking a left on to Assarat Street and passing through the lights outside the gate to the Central Hospital, before they came to a stop beneath the bridge that led to Aseer Street, where the trees slept still as stones. Trembling, Fahd got out and followed Saeed to the entrance of the emergency ward. They questioned a young man at the reception desk and he directed them to another building that dealt with traffic accidents.

The Sudanese receptionist had a paper cup of tea in front of him, a Lipton label spilling from its edge. He was sprawled out, yawning violently in the summer's noonday heat. They made their request and he coldly opened a vast leather-bound ledger and turned the pages until he came to the day's entries, then ran his finger down the morning's accidents as though scrutinising a menu at a restaurant.

'His name's not here.'

Seeing that they hadn't moved away he returned his gaze to the ledger and asked about the make of car. Fahd told him and the Sudanese placed his finger next to an incident that had taken place that morning on Qaseem Road involving a red Caprice. Fahd's blood surged, turning to boiling water that flowed down over his feet.

'Red or purple?'

'Says red here.'

Saeed inquired about the name of the victim and he spun the ledger around to show them the space reserved for the name, *Unknown*, then beneath that in the box for the victim's condition, *Injured*, which had been scratched out in red pen and next to it added the legend: *Deceased*.

When Fahd's eyes fell on the word *Deceased* his tongue froze, a lump of wood wedged in his throat. Fighting his desire to collapse he asked, 'Fine, so how do we check this person's identity?'

Giving a luxurious yawn, the man said indistinctly, 'See this number? You can go and check in the morgue.'

It was terrifying for these two teenage boys to contemplate going to the morgue with nothing more than a number—No. 67. His imagination ran away with him: the guard examining the number then heading over to one of the drawers and yanking it out as though it were a carpart or some file in a government archive. He breaks open the tape around the head of the cadaver, wrapped like *eid* candy, and the fabric loosenens. Bit by bit he pulls it back to reveal hair, plastered down like the hair of a mummy, then a face, peaceful and serene.

'This yours?' he'd ask, nonchalantly.

They wouldn't be able to move, their feet paralysed.

How can we bear to see our father, whose laughter, smile and mockery we worship, become a wreck of a corpse. How? The same thought occurred to them both, for Suleiman was not just

Fahd's father; Saeed, who had had no one else to raise him, thought of him as a father too.

Without entering the morgue they lurched woozily out of the door and Fahd almost fell as he stumbled against a street vendor. A white ambulance drove by without sounding its siren: just a sullen light flashing in the glum afternoon. Two women spread out their wares on the pavement facing the accident ward while a lone woman sat in the shade of a small tree by the hospital's steel wall, latching her child to her breast beneath her *abaya*. A boy led an old man who was inching his stick along the pavement and a young man emerged from the accident ward followed by a Filipino nurse who guided a drip stand alongside him as they headed for the emergency department.

'There is no god but God! God willing it isn't your father! Just the same make of car.'

Saeed was consoling Fahd or maybe he was searching for a small chink of light in the darkness on behalf of them both, because he added, 'Anyway, there's a difference between red and purple. I'm sure it's just a coincidence.'

Suddenly Fahd collapsed, sobbing crazily as his eyes flickered back and forth between the people and cars around him. 'My father's dead! My father's dead, people! Dead!'

Saeed embraced him. 'Seek refuge from Satan!' he scolded. 'You should be ashamed of yourself. First we have to make sure it's him, not someone else, and secondly, you're a man and you have to act like one in a crisis and make things easier for your mother and your sister at home.'

He got Fahd into the car and sat in his seat, thinking hard and repeating, 'There is no power or strength save through God.'

As they were about to set off for the mosque and the washing of the body, Fahd's mother came up and pushed a small bottle of agarwood oil into his pocket, saying that his father had been fond of it and liked to use it when he went to Friday prayers with the two boys. When Fahd opened it, taking the small glass stopper from the bottle with trembling fingers and put it to his nose, his father appeared in front of him, walking two or three paces ahead of Fahd and Saeed, his fragrant scent vanishing between the columns of Mohammed Bin Abdel Wahhab Mosque in Ulaya as he selected a place wide enough for Fahd to sit on his right and Saeed on his left.

After the body had been wrapped, Fahd took out the agarwood oil and thought of wiping the stopper against the cotton but Ibrahim took the bottle from him and sprinkled dark drops on the corpse.

Fahd could not believe that his father had really done it, that he had closed his eyes forever. How miserable he felt! He wished that Suleiman had given in and taken him with him, that they might have gone together to the heavens.

But who can be sure? I might have been saved only to suffer even more. How often I imagine myself sitting next to him as the Caprice veers from left to right across Qaseem Road then plunges off in the blink of an eye to smash into the iron fencing that stops the camels wandering on to the road. The body of my father, who never wore a seatbelt, leaps up and strikes the ground, leaving nothing but a small bruise at the base of his skull. Did he die of fright, or did he bleed for the hour it took someone to come to his aid, like the accident report stated? If I had been alive alongside him I might have saved him, stood my dusty, dizzy body on the tarmac and held out my arm in front of the first car to pass and forced it to stop. We could have taken my father to the nearest emergency ward and saved his life!

Faced with the male mourners his young eyes welled. He hated their makeshift tenderness as they pityingly stroked his head. A boy of fifteen has a real need for a proper father like Suleiman, not just a paterfamilias who commands and denies, but an intimate friend in whose embrace he could find refuge.

How hard it had been, accompanying them in the hearse to Naseem Cemetery, driving in awful silence from Rajehi Mosque on to the Eastern Ring Road then into East Riyadh and through the long wall around the graveyard. A sob rattled in his chest and his Uncle Saleh drew his head towards him and said, 'You're the man of the house now.'

Fahd gave a sudden groan and Saleh stroked his hair.

'Take refuge from Satan, Fahd.'

How hard it was to be surrounded by men, most of whom he didn't know, as they singled him out with their consoling words. One, the stupidest of the lot, put five hundred riyals into his top pocket. Was this the value placed on the departed? How hard it was to return home with his Uncle Saleh and cousin Yasser, carrying his father's brown *mashlah* that had covered his coffin. How hard for a fifteen-year-old boy to come home to find his mother and sister weeping together and be scarcely able to make them out through the cascade of tears veiling his eyes and drowning his heart in precocious, merciless sorrow. How often after that did Fahd lie in bed at night hugging his father's *mashlash* and breathing in its scent, berating himself and muttering out loud, until the tears drenched his clothes and he finally fell asleep at dawn?

I have not had my fill of you, Father! How could you go and fulfil the prophecy of that stupid rhyme? Why did you leave me all alone and naked? You never lived: just an outcast childhood, a youth spent

36

imprisoned and in exile and finally a grown man denounced by his own family. No one would welcome an old ex-con until fortune finally favoured you with a wonderful Jordanian woman, Soha, my mother. But your luck was cursed, scarcely baring its teeth in a false smile before you were whisked away in the blink of an eye. I miss you, Father, now more than ever before. I miss you most in my youth. I miss you even at the dead of night as I ready myself for sleep and feel the loneliness, desolation and interminable tears. A night without end.

Do you know what it means for a fifteen-year-old boy to go out to Zuhair Rustom Alley every afternoon and sit waiting for you on the doorstep? Can you understand the depths of his despair, his wailing sobs, every time he sees a car that reminds him of your wine-red Caprice. I swear that if you knew how my heart trembled, how my groans betrayed me as I circled your car like an imprisoned puppy longing to escape from its shadowy seats, you would have sprung from your grave in an instant and sprinted from the cemetery, your hair unkempt and covered with the coffin's dust, traversing the streets like a man possessed to clasp me in your arms, pulling my little head to your chest and sobbing in remorse, 'Never again, Fahd. I swear to you I shall not die again so foolishly.'

It wounded me to hear Saeed say, 'You're lucky! You saw your father and spent your childhood with him, while I was born to find mine already gone!'

Saeed, can you know what it means to see if you were born blind? Of course you can't, you could never see: your understanding of the world around you came from your other senses. But to lose your sight aged fifteen means that you have experienced the world and the pleasure of gazing upon it, only for everything to turn a misty white like milk. That is how I feel, my friend. That is how I came to see my father on every corner, on every street in Riyadh, to hear his unmistakable laugh in the shops. For years I woke terrified, as though his *hand had fallen on my head to rouse me, gentle and calm: 'Come on, Fahd. Time for school.'*

You knew a little happiness, Father, living with my mother for a decade and a half. Then your dream passed away and you departed early. I, too, have known happiness for fleeting moments. But in this country they're too sharp to let joy bloom unchecked. The guardians of twisted virtue, the guardians of the imprisoned breeze, leapt to pluck out my joy in its first year of life. I wonder, why do these severe and grim-faced men invade the precious privacy you have with your beloved?

6

LEFT ALONE IN THE detention cell without being told why, Fahd had no choice but to entertain ghosts from his own memory who insisted on visiting him. Entering Shalal Café one summer's night, for example, Fahd was looking for Saeed in their usual spot in the seats furthest to the right, over where the air was a little warmer and away from the clamour of mobile phones, but couldn't find him. Then he saw him a few seats further on, unsmiling, taking a pull on the mouthpiece of his *shisha* then raising his face to the heavens and noiselessly blowing out the smoke. Fahd descended on him boisterously.

'Where's Uncle Saeed got to?'

Saeed was in no mood for fun and laughter. He answered as though he were someone else, struggling to drag his words out from inside him. 'I'm thinking about my strange life, Fahd. I'm thinking about a life with no childhood, about days with no flavour to them.'

'Fear your Lord, sheikh! You're doing fine. Be happy that you're free: no mother or father to chase you around.'

'I wish I had a father to chase me, one who I could take to the internal medicine specialist at Abdul Aziz Hospital, to the ophthalmologist at King Khaled Eye Hospital. I wish I had a father to take care of, to sit up with when he needed company. You know, people sometimes say it's more painful to lose a father when you're a child or teenager.'

'Of course it's more painful: you knew him and got used to him and you see him everywhere you go. Saeed, you can't imagine how it feels to see my dad in the street. I see him on Urouba Road, going into Panda supermarket, standing outside Al-Ahnaf Bin Qais School with the other fathers, walking into Blue Diamond Video with me ...'

Waving at a waiter who rushed past without noticing, Saeed interrupted him. 'Sorry Fahd, but what you say is wrong. Real suffering is to enter the world without a father, to find yourself confronted by some husband of your mother's and have to call him "Dad".'

He was silent for a while, letting his bare head sink back like a man recalling his past. 'My mother no longer trusts any man alive. All men are swindlers in her eyes. She thinks I'm always lying and cheating. My father, God have mercy on his soul, lied to her. Just imagine: when she was five months pregnant with me he came to her and said that he was going to take her and her mother to Mecca for the *umra*. My poor grandmother: she was so happy, dreaming of visiting the Grand Mosque again, a quarter of a century after she made the pilgrimage with my grandfather, who died a decade before I was born.

'My mother never had the slightest idea what my father planned to do that day, the first of Muharram, 1400 AH. I was still in the womb. Maybe I could sense something, could hear what was going on in the Grand Mosque? Perhaps I heard the first shot that killed Muhsin, the one they called the first martyr to fall? My mother and grandmother were shut up with the other women and one of them convinced the rest that the Mahdi would fill the earth with justice and that the army of the oppressors would set out from Tabuk as foretold in the *hadith*. God would make the earth swallow them up, she told them, and the victorious Mahdi and his forces would set out for Medina followed by a great throng of people acclaiming him as their leader. There he would pray before leaving for Damascus, where he would lead the prayers following the return to earth of the Messiah, Eissa son of Mariam. That's how they brainwashed their tiny minds.'

The waiter was standing in front of them. Fahd ordered a pipe with apple tobacco and a pot of stewed black tea, and Saeed a coal to replace the one that had turned to ash on top of the tinfoil cover pierced with tiny holes.

'For my father and his group, there was an abundance of signs to show the Final Hour had come. One of them was that Pharaoh would possess the gold of the earth. Now the doctor's son and former minister Rashad Pharaoun had invested in the village of Mahd between Jeddah and Medina. There was gold there. The place later became known as Golden Mahd and attracted government money, so of course in their eyes this man was the Pharaoh and was harvesting gold from the earth of the Hejaz. You see how naïve my dad and his group were, Fahd? How they shaped reality to suit their whims until they'd built their ridiculous myth?'

'Myths. That's just about right,' Fahd replied.

Saeed puffed experimentally at his *shisha* on to which the waiter had placed another two glowing coals.

'I can never forget my first days, Fahd,' he went on. 'Imagine my mother's womb as a prison inside another prison halfway between Mecca and Medina, where she'd been taken, inside a still larger prison that was the country itself, inside the prison of this hateful planet. Sometimes I'm just speechless. Years before this all took place, my father used to frequent Ruwail Mosque in Bateeha Street. This one time, the man giving the sermon was the Mahdi himself. He used to meet them at Dar al-Ilm behind Amira al-Anoud Palace in Khazan Street. Of course, these guys weren't Muslim Brothers, or Qutbis, as they were known, the ones who followed the teachings of Hassan al-Banna and rejected the idea of opposing the traditional religious hierarchy; the doves, in other words, as opposed to the hawks who believed in violence and force of arms. So why did my father turn against the authority of the Supreme Imam and take up arms in search of a stolen dream? What did he want? I've no idea!'

Saeed was talking, sobbing almost, as they sat in Shalal Café. Amidst the bubbling of the *shisha* pipes he went on as if speaking to himself. 'My father threw it all away, success, ambition, a family and a life, and galloped after a mirage dreamt up for him by a diseased mind.'

He turned to Fahd, the beginnings of a small smile taking shape above his small moustache.

'Know what, Fahd? If he could hear me talk, he'd say you're the sick one, you're the one that's lost, that it's you who's galloping aimlessly after your desires. Yeah, and he might be right if he did. I'm fundamentally unhappy with my life, but he's the one who made it like that. He's the one who created this future for me. I lived with my mother and my grandmother. While I was learning my first life skills, developing my first view of the world, His Honour was basking in death. For long years my mother wept through nights of loneliness on his account, remembering how he had caused her to go to prison. My mother, who had never clapped eyes on a soldier in her life. My grandmother too. She absolutely loathed him, of course. He had deceived her at the end of her life and got her locked up. She may even have hated my

42

mother and me as well, even though we had nothing to do with the mess.'

'Saeed,' Fahd said, 'You're doing so well at the moment. You finished your studies and got yourself a respectable job. Isn't that enough? Thank God for what you have!'

Saeed sipped at the cup of dark brown tea in his right hand while his left gripped the *shisha*'s hose, and smiled. 'Some things are hard to make up for. You lived your whole childhood with your father. You felt secure, in other words. I never had that feeling. A few months later my uncles tried to marry off my mother and a new chapter of my painful life began.'

A Bengali hawker passed by and offered them small bags of pistachios and almonds. Saeed lifted a hand in refusal and went on. 'You know, Fahd, one of these days I'll introduce you to a colleague of mine from work. His name's Rashed. He's around forty and a real bookworm. He was the first person to encourage me to read up on Islamist groups. My friend, after reading about these guys, I truly wished that my father had been a Sufi. I wish he had been a *tablighi*. Those extremists think they're good for nothing but contemplating the world and the possessions that surround them. Some may say that their beliefs are wrong. Well, what's right then? Brandishing guns in the House of Calm? Killing worshippers, soldiers, women and pigeons? What did my father want? Do you know what they used to say and dream about, because these were essentially people who were driven by confused dreams? They would say that we shall come together in the Grand Mosque and pledge allegiance to the Mahdi and on the third day the infidel army shall set out from Tabuk and God will make the earth swallow them up without us having to kill a single person in the mosque.'

Smiling, and shifting the coal that had settled on the ash-smeared head of the *shisha,* Fahd said, 'Just think of it: they really believed that the military base in Tabuk, which for them was the infidel army, was going to move against Mecca to fight them and that God was going to make the earth swallow them up on their way over.'

Saeed let out a short laugh that fought back a tear.

7

S OMETIMES FAHD FELT SAD to be all alone with no brother, but Saeed's presence in his life gave it some warmth, especially once they were living together at the flat on the Northern Ring Road in Maseef. Before they lived together Saeed would drop by Fahd's at least once a week and the two would go out to Shalal Café on Dammam Road, or the Qif in Salah al-Din, having first taken a turn around the wall of the Ministry of Education, stealing delightful glances at the girls who hid their jeans beneath *abaya*s. Saeed would send a trial balloon towards them, a flirtatious word for the girl to engage with or ignore, then decide whether to try further or give up. Fahd would giggle in embarrassment and keep quiet, sometimes turning round to watch the reaction of the girls they had just flirted with.

Among the girls he hunted down on their jaunts was young Nada, and this despite the fact she was out walking with her brother and sister, the latter becoming a stand-in girlfriend to Fahd. But Saeed soon discovered that she had to climb mountains and descend valleys if he wanted to meet her, as an entire army of relatives was constantly in attendance.

Fahd and Saeed would sometimes agree to meet up at sunset or evening prayers when all the cafés closed their doors, getting together in the lobby of the Salahuddin Hotel. If they were in the mood to revisit childhood memories they would head to the nearby Abu Baseel Restaurant and order two loaves of *tames* flatbread and a couple of bowls of stewed beans or bean paste.

If Saeed didn't want to go out he would ask Fahd to bring over *fateer* from the Damascus Fateer House or hummous with olive oil and falafel from Abu Zaki Hummous, and the two of them would stay up until midnight, when Fahd would make his way home, muzzy-headed and melancholic. Following the death of his father, this happened more than once. He needed something to help him forget what had happened, because the death felt like a betrayal and he was struggling to forgive his father for suddenly vanishing from his life and leaving him all alone with his mother and little sister, Lulua.

Fahd was haunted by the memory of the tortuous evening when his Uncle Saleh had come over bringing with him his son, Yasser, his mother's brother, Ibrahim, and his two great-uncles on his father's side. Fahd was sitting in the small *majlis* whose window looked out over the passage by the side of the house, sprawled out in the light of a green lamp revising his chemistry syllabus. He had grown used to the silence, broken only by the sound of the Bangladeshi who delivered orders from the supermarket, and the moment the doorbell rang he went to open the dining room window and looked down into the street. All he could see was red light from the back of a car stopped next the front door and when he made to go downstairs, a worried Lulua blocked his way.

'Who is it?'

'Don't know,' he answered as he went downstairs over the cheap black carpet.

He opened the door. There were five of them and they greeted him. Ibrahim gave a smooth apology. 'So sorry for turning up without an appointment or a phone call.'

'This is your house, Uncle,' Fahd said politely. 'You don't need to call ahead and make appointments.'

Yasser stared at the poster of a Paul Klee abstract depicting a fisherman in his boat then looked over at his father. 'Representations of living creatures aren't permitted, nor is glorifying them and hanging them on walls.'

Fahd longed to scream in his face: 'What's it to you, scumbag? Is this house yours or ours?'

As Yasser's father nodded his agreement, Ibrahim deftly took up the conversation. 'It's none of our business. Is that why we're here, Yasser? Fahd,' he continued, 'you know that the fingernail never leaves the flesh: you're part of us my boy and there is no one closer to you and your sister than your Uncle Saleh.'

The fan in the ceiling turned sluggishly as his words took flight, sometimes settling on Fahd's ears and sometimes floating through the *majlis* window to the alleyway outside.

Yasser stroked his forked beard with his long fingers as he watched out of the corner of his eye from behind his spectacles, his loosely draped *shimagh* pulled back to show the front half of his white skullcap and a set of coloured pens proudly arrayed in his breast pocket. How Fahd would have loved to see Yasser turn up with his white doctor's uniform and (why not?) a stethoscope hung around his neck or carried in his breast pocket.

Yasser was in his fourth year studying medicine at King Saud University. His enrolment there had been enough for his father to leave their home in Buraida and move to Quds in East Riyadh. No sooner had Yasser's feet stepped over the threshold of the College of Medicine than he fell in with some religious students, standing shoulder to shoulder with them as they set out to put heavenly reward before earthly success and battle with the dean of the college to prevent male and female students mingling in the laboratories of King Khaled University Hospital.

They wrote one complaint after another and faxed them off, once to the rector, another time to the governor of Riyadh, a third time to the Interior Ministry, and occasionally to the king himself, while they fanned the flames on Islamic websites.

Yasser had not wanted to study medicine but his father had forced him so he could show off to people about his son. After completing his first year, he planned to transfer to study *aqeeda* at the College of Sharia in Imam Mohammed Bin Saud Islamic University and asked an ultraconservative sheikh for his opinion. Instead of telling him to study medicine and use his knowledge to benefit the *umma*, the sheikh declared that it was a worldly and useless subject, and that God had not included it amongst those branches of learning extolled in the verses of the Qur'an.

'There's mixing of the sexes, as well, sheikh!' Yasser added, to ensure the sheikh would make him abandon the sins and studies of the unbelievers. Instead, the sheikh fell silent for a moment then surprised him by insisting that he continue with his medical studies to fight against the corrupting influence of co-education.

'There is more than one type of *jihad*, my son,' he said, 'and the *jihad* of you and your fellow students, the struggle against mixed classes and moral degeneracy, is the greatest of them all. Your duty is to fight the hypocritical secularists wherever you find them, for as you know, moral degeneracy is one of the causes of the collapse of societies and states.'

And so Yasser stayed on at the college, inciting his fellow students against the university authorities, groups of them walking in on the dean and occasionally making official complaints about the department and the dean to the rector himself. If necessary they would collaborate with others outside the university and send telegrams to the king and crown prince, warning of the problems created by allowing students of both sexes to study side by side in the university's laboratories and dissection classes, in operating theatres, hospital corridors and common rooms.

So he fought, as his sheikh had suggested, withdrawing from his studies and striving hard in the distribution of little booklets and cassettes that warned young Muslim women of the dangers of mixing with men, expounding the religious rulings that forbade it and talking of the threat it posed to the *umma*.

Saeed knew Yasser. He would sometimes run into him at biology lectures in the College of Science. More than once he had seen him leading a bunch of students through the reception hall of the university's administration building, sprinting towards the lifts on their way to see the rector.

'Sometimes I wonder how he manages to pass in a difficult subject like medicine when he's so busy with complaints and statements,' Fahd said one day at Saeed's flat.

Saeed gave a mirthless smile, leaping towards the kettle in the kitchen area in the corner when he heard the sound of boiling water and the pop of its automatic switch. He started preparing two cups of tea.

'You know that they've got doctors with the same extremist beliefs? They fix their marks, even if they don't deserve them. I heard worse than that: they've got extremist friends in the IT department who can access student records and their grades, pass and fail and so on.'

'But how?' said Fahd, astonished.

'It's no problem. They'll change an F to D, or even higher. Helping those Brothers who are distracted from their studies by the war on corruption and temptation and the battle against the secularists in the university brings them heavenly reward.'

Then Saeed laughed, and, stirring the tea, shouted, 'Long live the Arab nation!'

'And the Islamic nation,' he added, bringing the cups over.

Some months later they were back in the flat flipping through the papers. Fahd was reading a long article in *Riyadh* about the imposition of a uniform dress code for all female Saudi employees in the health services. Doctors, pharmacists and nurses were forbidden from wearing jeans, were required to cover their hair, must have no gold or other jewellery on them, nor wear nail polish or make-up, and had to use rubber-soled shoes that made no sound when they walked, with heels less than five centimetres high. Fahd was reading these details out loud to Saeed, and they both thought of Yasser and his *jihad*; Yasser, the holy warrior doctor who championed his Faith in the College of Medicine.

'I can understand everything except for this business with the rubber soles.'

'So they don't make a sound when they walk,' said Saeed sagaciously.

'Well, I realise that, but so what if they do make a sound? What could possibly happen?'

'Sound, my friend, attracts attention to the seductive motion of the female form!'

'I don't get it,' Fahd said.

'Anyone who hears that sound, even if they don't actually see the lady doctor, will still picture her in their mind—her buttocks, her swaying breasts—and he'll desire her.' Saeed laughed.

'What? So even the click of a heel is shameful, now?'

'Of course. It leads to temptation.'

Saeed dropped a Lipton teabag into one of the cups.

'Know something, Fahd? Sometimes I think we're lucky to be living in a time like this, and in this place in particular. Bizarre things like this could lead to the creation of bitterly dark art and theatre. Unfortunately, art itself is also under attack and outlawed.'

Fahd let out an uncharacteristically loud laugh and said, 'Just imagine: every female doctor and pharmacist will put a little ruler in her bag and when she gets a new pair of rubber-soled shoes, out with the ruler to check if the heel's higher than five centimetres.'

'No,' replied Saeed, more earnest than ever. 'The real disaster is that breaking these rules might lead to someone losing her job. A doctor's heels clicking over a hospital's marble corridor could put her on the unemployed list. What a country.'

A moment's silence passed and then Fahd shouted, 'I've got an idea!'

'Let's hear it, genius.'

'Why don't they lay carpets in the hospital corridors, so the doctors' and nurses' shoes don't make a sound?'

Saeed groaned. 'I swear to God you're the most brilliant man I know, more brilliant than all the holy warriors in the hospitals.'

He took a sip.

'Why don't you register that idea with the patent office?'

8

Darling: don't miss page 5 of Riyadh.

T ARFAH RECEIVED FAHD'S MESSAGE and her laughter washed the night. His message was the fourth she had received since the decision to impose the dress code. The rest of the messages had been from her friends at the Academy for Health Sciences, mocking the idea of the shoes, jeans and accessories. Tarfah thought of the students who wore jeans in class beneath their *abayas* and then a second *abaya* on top.

Sameera, or Sameer as the other girls called her, would dash from her family home in Shubra, a full-length *abaya* draped over her head, and as the Palestinian bus driver set off down King Fahd Road, she would take it off and stow it in her capacious bag to reveal another *abaya* covering her shoulders, the garish silver embroidery on its sleeves gleaming against the black cloth. Another embroidered panel spread down her back and over her buttocks. She would put on a pair of large pink sunglasses and, from her seat in the back of the small bus, would turn her gaze to the cars moving past them on the road.

From her first day at the Academy this young woman in her twenties had strutted the corridors dressed in dark blue jeans and a white shirt with a drawing of a huge eye over her small breasts. Her stride was broad and manly and she never stopped chasing after the soft, brown-skinned girls.

When Tarfah saw Sameera for the first time she felt rooted to the spot and started to stare at her as they sat facing each other across the corridor. Sameera took the cushion from her seat and hugged it, its corner between her open thighs as she twirled a pen around her mouth in a quite blatant fashion. Tarfah couldn't tell if she was looking at her or the window behind her, because the sunglasses completely hid her eyes.

She wasn't the only one at the Academy: there were five girls, 'boyettes' as they were known, who wore jeans, baggy shirts, trainers and sunglasses and roamed the courtyard hitting on girls. One would put her hands in her jean pockets and walk along with a male self-confidence, arm-in-arm with a soft white girl on whose shoulder she would sometimes drop her head. She was away in another world, insensible to the glances and sly comments of the others. They would go to the bathroom together, the open-topped partitions unable to muffle their fevered panting.

It was terrifying to watch them argue with their girlfriends, swapping filthy phrases and accusations back and forth because the girl had seen her 'boyette' come on to some young woman who had responded to her advances. For Tarfah and her friend Nada there was nothing funny about it; it was strange and painful.

When Sameera tried it with Tarfah the time they found themselves alone together beneath the stairs, Tarfah could only pretend to ignore Sameera's flirtatious comments about her eyes. She pleaded with her to give it a try for a few minutes: just a hug and a clinch, and if she enjoyed it then she would kiss her a few minutes more. But Tarfah's response as she charged up the stairs in fright was that she would be unable to oblige: 'I hate girls!' she shouted.

Sameera left her to vanish on to the second floor, but she didn't give up hope.

Tarfah had told Fahd that she would never work as a nurse, anyway, since her brothers had strongly opposed the idea and decided she would either become a laboratory assistant or a pharmacist. Then she laughed out loud as she told the story of Nada's cousin who worked as a pharmacist at a government hospital.

It was midday when a Bedouin with a thick upswept moustache stood up carrying a little tousle-haired girl, red-cheeked with fever. The cousin fetched the medicine and placed it over the prescription lying on the table—Fevadol for the temperature, an antibiotic called Augmentin and a strip of suppositories just in case—and started to write out instructions for their use. She took the bottle of antibiotics and made a mark with the pen above the level of the white powder inside, saying that he must add clean water up to the line then shake the bottle. Her white hand squeezed the bottle tight and shook it up and down in front of him as she said, 'Shake it hard.'

The Bedouin's gaze devoured her.

He took the bag of medicines and walked a few paces then stopped and put the girl on the floor, removing the antibiotics from the bag and returning to the counter. Watching him as he walked towards her she noticed that he was aroused. Embarrassed, she averted her eyes. 'Do I put the water in this bottle, or another one?' he asked. She answered with a shake of the head and fled to the shelves at the back of the pharmacy.

Tarfah laughed noisily. 'Just imagine! Can you believe this society? These people? That's real frustration...' she added sadly. 'Is it this hard for people to have sex?'

'What do you mean? You're not saying that these directives are right?' Fahd asked.

Her voice a little calmer, Tarfah replied, 'No, sweetheart, you know my position, but I can't imagine what it will be like to work there.'

He told her that if the legislator who drew up the directives had thought a little differently, he would have issued severe laws that would commit anyone convicted of harassing women to years in prison, enough to make the Bedouin hesitate a thousand times over before exposing himself to her. But the punishment was always borne by the poor woman because she was the one who provoked his pole.

Fahd did not entirely trust his lover. Despite the fact she worshipped his very eyes, as she was always telling him in her texts, he would have his doubts whenever she called him and he heard the racket and wicked laughter coming from her friends at the Academy.

'Where's Tarfah got to?' a girl might ask.

'Over there, breastfeeding,' another would answer and they would burst out into wild laughter. Tarfah would laugh, too, and shout at them to shut up so she could hear him.

'"Breastfeeding" means talking on the phone,' she would explain.

Her friends would try to make him overhear their jokes or mocking comments, then attempting to persuade Tarfah to let them say hello to her sweetheart. Tarfah told him that they also tried to make her talk to their boyfriends but she absolutely refused to do so. He wasn't convinced that she spoke to no one else apart from him, especially since her friends would encourage her to live 'free' as they called it, simply and happily. 'The world isn't up to your complications!'

One message in particular had left him wracked with doubt:

I send you a bullet of love, an artillery shell of desire, a bomb-belt of tenderness and a booby-trapped car of roses and jasmine.

What do you think of this?! she had added at the bottom, then told him it had been sent by a Palestinian driver to a friend of hers who took his bus from Suwaidi to Mugharrazat. Fahd asked her how the Palestinian could send her friend a message like that unless she was having an affair with him. She stammered and snapped, 'Believe it or not I didn't look at it like you!'

When Tarfah sent him a video clip of herself gazing from the bus window in her sunglasses, occasionally raising her uncovered hair with her right hand and sorrowfully singing along with Abdullah Ruwaished, *If I had another life, by God I'd live you twice*, he asked, 'How did you manage to film a clip like that in the bus? Did the driver see you as you drove through the streets?'

She swore that there was a closed curtain between them and the driver, but some mischievous students liked to hassle him and would sometimes lift the curtain and talk to him, though he remained extremely respectful and courteous.

At first it would irritate Fahd when she talked to him like this, and her stories of Sameera—or Sameer—and the other 'boyettes' would leave him unsettled, but occasionally he would feel that he was taking things too seriously, in a society that was unsmiling and tragic on the outside, but playful and cynical from within.

What could be more cynical than Sameera bumping her hand against Tarfah's bottom as she walked past her, only for Tarfah to turn round angrily: 'Yes?'

Sameera wiggled her hand and eyebrows in astonishment as though she had done nothing wrong.

'I told you. I've got no time for girls' silly games!' said Tarfah in vexation. She twisted her mouth in disapproval. 'Silly groping.'

'Dear God,' answered Sameera mockingly. 'If only I had you trapped under the stairs or in the bathroom.'

Life in Riyadh was full of contradictions. No one cared how you were: your poverty, hunger, sufferings and woe; yet at the same time everyone thought that you were easy, that anyone could do with you as they liked.

9

F AHD RETURNED TO IT, again and again: his uncle's visit. When Fahd's mother knocked on the salon's inner door her son politely excused himself to his guests. Soha handed him the tray of coffee, cups and dates, whispering, 'Who is it?' and, when he had told her, 'What do they want?'

Fahd shook his head, professing ignorance. When he poured the first cup for Ibrahim, the man took it, saying, 'Live long, my boy!'

The man talked for a long time about decency, about protecting women and their dignity and satisfying their needs, until he finally got to the point, to wit: for the widow to stay single was damaging to her.

Fahd broke in. 'But my sister and I live with her.'

'Your sister is a young girl, Fahd, she needs care and attention, and you'll get married eventually.'

Had his uncle heard something? Had his mother complained to someone, and word got out, as it always did with the inhabitants of Buraida? Had his uncle got wind of her dissatisfaction, or her dreams? It was as though the man's words contained some mystery impenetrable to the boy, who sat listening politely before the shocking sentence hit him.

No one had any inkling of the terrible impact of this shock; the last sentence his Uncle Ibrahim uttered was like a cannonball crashing through the wall of a perfectly quiet library, a volcano obliterating a world at peace, an earthquake in the upper reaches of the Richter scale demolishing a sad and humble dwelling, a shark's sudden leap splitting the quiet surface of the water. How can one convey the blunt force of that sentence? That an uncle with two wives should come and rescue Fahd's mother, the widow Soha, from her loneliness and protect her two children from hunger and corruption.

'Your Uncle Saleh is a safer bet than a stranger to keep the family safe and protect his niece from strangers entering the house.'

'So that's how it is. I don't think so, Uncle,' said Fahd, adding sharply, 'My mother won't find it easy to replace my father's memory with another, whoever it might be.'

When the men had left, Fahd crept to his room, closed the door and wept until his soul grew still. He addressed his innermost self like an old man standing on the smouldering ruins of his house remembering happier days.

In the early morning, mother would wake me to go to school, while little Lulua was still sunk in sleep. I would sit drowsily in the living room as my father had his breakfast of a fried egg and a dish of Wadi al-Nahl honey. The voice of Fairuz, discovered by my father courtesy of Nabeel Hawamla, his Palestinian colleague at the newspaper distribution company, issuing from the kitchen:

I yearn, but for who, I don't know;

At night it snatches me from amongst the revellers.

How Fairuz used to upset me when I was seven, my mother standing in front of the kitchen sink and opening the north-facing kitchen window, the March breeze buffeting her voice, low, effortless and sad:

The breeze blew upon us at the valley's mouth

O breeze, blow, and take me to my country!

I used to believe that I would come home from school one day to find my mother gone, especially when her family had left for Amman after Saudi Arabia threw out the Jordanians, Palestinians and Yemenis. Jordan's announcement that the war against Iraq was a war on the Arab nation was, we sensed, the reason my family were expelled, and I only saw them again a few years ago. My mother was miserable, silent and tearful, but she rinsed her sadness and loneliness in song and night time excursions with my father to cafés and restaurants. On Thursdays and Fridays they would take us with them, while the rest of the week they would go out by themselves after we were asleep.

Will Fairuz continue to pour out her voice over the walls of our house? Will the aroma of the Turkish coffee to which my father and mother were addicted still ascend? Will the smell of oil paints waft from my room while I paint a portrait of a three-year-old Lulua, her mouth smeared with ice cream? Will my sister ever play again on the little piano my father brought back from Dubai? Will the Paul Klee and Gustav Klimt posters stay on the walls of the salon and the sitting room? Will life carry on in the corridors of our top floor in Ulaya, that life my father made, or will my uncle occupy our house on the pretext of protecting the poor widow and her two little orphans? He will come, and death shall come with him. Fairuz will die; her voice will be choked off, and in her place, Sheikh al-Hazifi reciting surat al-kahf. The Turkish coffee will go, its aroma fading in the face of Arabic coffee and sugared dates. The little piano will be destroyed, its white and black keys flying to the vast rubbish skip at the end of Sayyidat al-Ru'osa Street. My little sister will die and in the portrait that I painted her playful eyes will be ruptured, but the ice cream shall remain about her mouth, a witness. The head of her cotton doll will be severed because it is haram and all the videos put to death; Falounu and Sally will go to meet their fate.

What was it that Uncle Ibrahim was after? When he came to broach the idea of my uncle marrying my mother, did he mean it? Was it to be an atonement for taking part in a demonstration outside Ibn Battal's palace against the deputies and the pious, to show his relatives in Qaseem that it had been the error of a teenage boy?

At the end of that long day, night finally fell and Fahd went out, frustrated and sad. He drove towards Pizza Hut, passing the generator where the black cat hid. He had never liked cats. A shudder would run through his body whenever he caught sight of it hidden away, its eyes staring at him.

As soon as he was past the restaurant, Sulaimaniya supermarket and the petrol station, he stopped at Tareeqati Café and felt his way into the dimly lit interior. He ordered a bitter Turkish coffee and pondered his life, which since his tenth year had rushed by with frightening speed.

When he left the café he did not return home but aimlessly roamed the streets.

Back at the house, at the bottom of the four steps leading up to the front door, he passed the tub full of small roses that he had planted with his father the year before and he recalled his uncle commenting on the flowers: 'You should grow something useful instead. Courgettes. Tomatoes.'

The man still thought he was in Muraidasiya; anything related to beauty meant nothing to those villagers. What's the use of looking at something that you can't eat? That was how they thought. Why remain a widow or divorcee, stuck at home without a man to put food on the table or share your bed?

When Fahd came inside, and while he was climbing the stairs with downcast eyes, he was surprised by his mother, who was sitting on the top step waiting for him. She looked at him. He told her nothing of what they had said. 'They were just asking about the inheritance and dad's car, whether we were going to sell it or not.'

She withdrew to her bedroom without saying a thing, but he sensed that she had detected his lie. Perhaps she had been eavesdropping from behind the wooden partition. She would do that a lot and often surprised her children by knowing what they were up to, astonishing them with her insight and teasing them by saying that a gazelle passed on everything they said and so they should never lie to her. It was certainly too embarrassing for his mother to tell him, 'You're a liar: they came to ask for my hand in marriage,' and perhaps it was too embarrassing for him to tell her that as well. His mother was shy and unsure, and it was easy to convince and influence her.

'But no,' he muttered to himself as he went to his gloomy bedroom. 'I will lie, Mother. And as for the gazelle, I killed it when my father died.'

Part 2

Sandals emerging from the darkness

10

B URAIDA WAS UNFAMILIAR TO young Fahd, despite having
lived in the city for months during the Gulf War in the
early 1990s, and despite his father's former life there. Shortly
before his death, Suleiman had told Fahd tales from his
youth.

Ali had insisted Suleiman study at the National School and
Suleiman had kept resisting, but in the end he had consented
because it was an opportunity to escape the village of
Muraidasiya.

For a while he read Ibn Hajjar's *The Attainment of the Goal*
with Sheikh al-Duwaish. The sheikh, he told Fahd, had been
an extraordinary man with an astonishing memory: he could
listen to more than one student reciting the Qur'an at the
same time, correcting their errors of pronunciation and intonation even though they were reading separate verses. Even
Sheikh al-Albani, who occasionally returned to the text beside
him to prompt him as he talked, sought help from al-Duwaish,
consulting his computer-like memory. God have mercy on his
soul! He died young, in the prime of life.

After sunset, Suleiman studied inheritance law with Sheikh
al-Kaleeli, the imam of a mosque close by the home of his
friend, al-Ulayti. The first time he went to see him, Suleiman
sat flustered before the sheikh, who cast a keen and mistrustful
eye over him, then said, 'You studied at a government school?'

'Yes.'

He gazed at Suleiman for a moment, closely examining his face as he prepared to hurl his first fatal arrow towards those boyish features. 'Does the earth revolve?'

'Yes, sheikh,' Suleiman replied, confident and candid.

'There is no power nor strength save in God!' the sheikh said, then rose to his feet, pulled out a book and handed it to him.

'Read this book, my boy, and then come back.'

Suleiman read the title: *Heaven's Potent Rage Against Followers of the New Age* by Sheikh Hamoud al-Tuwaijri.

He read it in days and understood that it disputed heathen astronomers who believed in the spherical nature of the earth and its revolution and refuted their claims.

The sheikh didn't dismiss Suleiman as he had expected, but showed him sympathy instead, feeling it his duty to take him by the hand and lead him from falsehood and bewilderment on to the path of righteousness and truth. The earth is flat, as the Lord tells us in His Book, and, contrary to the theories of heathens and atheists, does not revolve about itself or circle the sun. No: it is the sun that turns about the earth.

Suleiman loved these ideas, but quickly moved beyond them. He discovered that the Salafis of Buraida were in fact just doctrinally observant Hanbalis. He felt that he shouldn't ally himself with any particular doctrinal school, and he found what he was looking for with the Divine Reward Salafist Brothers in Riyadh. He spent hard days of hunger and deprivation with them and suffered through Riyadh's long winter nights, to the extent that when he accompanied the leader of the group to Buraida and visited his old school, he dropped in to see his family for a day in Quwai then slept for several nights in a classroom. He felt proud when he saw the looks of envy and jealousy from his peers in Buraida. He had begun to move with a commanding, disciplined air and could finally dream of restoring his ruined self-confidence.

The trip was the occasion of the final meeting between the Brothers in Buraida and the Salafist Group that would continue on the path to the Grand Mosque. There was affection and dialogue between the two parties before it turned into hostility and mutual loathing, the conversation gradually metamorphosing into a call to actively bring about a radical change, to do away with corruption, sin and doctrinal constraints. The inhabitants of Buraida followed the Hanbali rite, and the Hanbalis' severest defeat had come when a group of them debated a Zaharite sheikh in Mecca, who brought them to a standstill with his proofs and logic. Suleiman had witnessed this event and it was then he realised that life and ideas might exist elsewhere, in places other than Buraida. Adventures, fraught with dangers, followed one after the other until he found himself behind bars in Mecca where, one day, he was joined in his cell by the young Mushabbab.

Mushabbab told his friend some of what had taken place the day of the Grand Mosque's occupation. He didn't see it as a takeover, but as the only proper way to acclaim the Mahdi, and the most appropriate place to do so.

Their arrival with their weapons had been a somewhat bizarre affair. It began just before dawn when their men carried in the bodies of four women inside coffins. In the Grand Mosque the body of a deceased woman wasn't simply covered with an *abaya* (lest her body be visible to the worshippers) but was placed in a coffin with an arched wooden lid. The Prophet's wife Aisha had been the first to buried in this domed coffin and now it was being used by the Brothers to smuggle guns.

The first dawn of the new century crawled slowly by, the group hefting the coffins with cool detachment while the weapons, hidden with their ammunition, almost seemed to come alive with longing for the bodies that surrounded them. By the Imam and the cloth coverings of the Kaaba the four coffins were laid in a row. Imam al-Subayil gave his usual calm and reassuring recitation, ushering in the dawn and stupefying the Meccan pigeons that strutted happily over the white marble.

No sooner had he performed the two dawn *rakaas* than ten men rose to their feet behind him, some wearing brown *mashlahs* beneath which they hid their pistols, and one took hold of the microphone that linked the prayers to a live radio broadcast. The Imam snatched it back to perform the prayer over the coffins, but the man drew his dagger and brandished it in the face of al-Subayil who cried, 'Fear God!' and backed away.

When the prayers were completed the Imam crept away to his room by Safa hill as the lids were lifted from the coffins and the Belgian-made automatic rifles distributed amongst the members of the group, some of whom spread out to the mosque's gates, locking them one after another. By one small door a guard in civilian clothes objected: 'Why are you locking the gates?'

'None of your business!' Muhsin shouted in his face.

They argued and Muhsin pulled out his revolver and took aim. The bullet flew out, a messenger of death intent on its victim, but not towards its intended target: cleaving the cold dawn air with a penetrating, vicious whine it struck the domed bronze head of a nail sunk in the metal plating that covered the wooden door. The wayward bullet gave a violent clang, ricocheting back towards the breast of the bearded young man and striking him dead: the battle's first martyr. That is how they thought of their dead: martyrs.

The sound of the shot reached the ears of the worshippers and the other members of the group, and the first spark of the conflict flared.

Muhsin fell, twitching a little before his corpse lay still. The last gate hadn't been closed and so those who could fled before the members of the group could shut it, while two lorries reversed towards the moat by the outer entrance to the underground cells. One carried weapons and ammunition, the other boxes packed with dates and sacks of cottage cheese.

The Grand Mosque was surrounded by cells, each one a small square room no more than nine metres square with a door consisting of a plate of reinforced steel a metre high, topped with iron bars as in a prison. Any passer-by could thus see into the cells, discouraging visitors to the mosque and worshippers from using them as places to rest or sleep. The young men of the group used these tiny cells to store guns and ammunition and their dates and cheese.

The preacher shouted to the mosque walls, and the hills of Mecca thundered and echoed back his words: 'My Brothers in God, the Prophet, may the prayers and peace of God be upon him, said that in the last days God would send a man to set the *umma* back on the path to righteousness; He would send the Mahdi, Mohammed Bin Abdullah, to fill the earth with justice after it had been filled with injustice and tyranny.'

The leader of the group suddenly snatched the microphone off him and addressed his followers: 'Seif! Seif! The north gate!' before the preacher resumed his account of the Mahdi's prophesied return at the start of a new century and exhorted the worshippers to acclaim him between the *rukn* and the *maqam*.

The leader took the microphone a second time: 'Brothers! The government's soldiers are yours for the taking!'

And so the two voices of the preacher and the leader mingled in a distant dawn, the flocks of pigeons fleeing, hearts quaking as the sniper climbed up towards the soaring minarets.

Eid was a skilful sniper. In the days that followed he relentlessly picked off any soldier who invaded the court of the mosque or descended from the sky beneath his parachute. Suleiman remembered their time together in Sajer, chambering a bullet and preparing to shoot a bird swimming through the sky. As it approached the tree to land on a branch, the bullet zipped, lodging in its little heart, and it tumbled to the ground a motionless corpse.

'The true marksman,' Eid would tell Suleiman, 'is the man who can hit the target on the wing, the moving target, not the stationary one. There's no glory in a sitting target: that's for women!'

The same was true of life: the moving target is seductive, hard won. Any man can claim the prize that sits there, the whole world's for the taking, but not everyone has what it takes to seize the fleeting chance, the fleeting moment, and turn it into opportunity.

In jail, Suleiman recalled a young man called Salah, one of a group of Egyptian pilgrims. The Egyptians spent days in anticipation of the confrontation, inspired and impatient and listening to tales of *jihad* in the way of God. These feelings were completely new to them, and when the actual moment came it affected them so forcefully that some snatched up guns and began chasing after the soldiers and guards and shooting them dead.

Amongst those roused to action was a youth by the name of Abdullah. He wasn't granted the chance to enter the Grand Mosque, but he was member of the group and lived in the suburbs of Mecca. He took his vehicle and a machine gun and headed out to Sajer to inflame his comrades out there and lead them back to occupy the Prophet's Mosque in Medina, drawing the world's attention to a second target and perhaps relieving the siege around his brothers in Mecca. Chased by the police and the army, who tried to make him surrender and hand over his weapon, he instead turned his car about and sent a shower of lead in their direction. They responded in kind. Their bullets broke the rear window of his truck and successive rounds slipped through, penetrating the flesh and sinews of his neck until his head lolled forward against the steering wheel, a fat fruit fit for picking.

The days passed slowly in the Grand Mosque and one by one they fell. Helicopters fired down from on high while teams of police and National Guard troopers took aim from the Ashraf building. Towards the end, the leader was hiding behind the Ismail *maqam*, his back to the Kaaba and his light automatic rifle trained at the Ashraf building. He was screaming at his men, asking them to supply him with a Belgian-made gun so that his rounds might reach a more distant target. But after ten days under siege the place was closing in about them and the volume of fire was too great for them to handle.

In those final days the police attempted to bring tanks in through the gallery, so the members of the group drew off petrol from the lorries and began to pour it into the earthen-ware pitchers intended to hold the *zamzam* water, then sealing them with scraps of cloth and setting them alight, they hurled them towards the tanks' tracks to explode like Molotov cocktails.

Incessant bombardment forced the group down from their elevated positions. The artillery was bombarding the high minarets where the snipers sheltered, the shelling so severe that the towers shook. The snipers began to descend to the rooftops. Most of the bodies there were headless. The bullets had ripped open skulls and blood mingled with brains on the sloping tiles. The survivors descended to the second floor and tried to flee or surrender, most of them ending up sneaking down to the storage rooms underground, where they were eventually choked with tear gas. Those who still could, emerged dishevelled, dusty and wild-eyed, their clothes in tatters. The papers were filled with their images, some sitting with thick grimy hair, others bowing their shaven heads. The mellifluous tones of radio announcer Hussein Najjar commented on their humiliation and defeat.

Suleiman never thought he would return to Buraida, especially with the wretched memory of his detention there, but return he did one dawn in January 1990 with his little family in tow, fleeing the indiscriminate Russian missiles that could flatten his house in a heartbeat and because, following his experience in jail, he had come to believe more than ever in his father's judgment that he was 'defective'. He asked his wife what would prevent the erratic and unseeing missiles from turning away from the airbase and the vast fortified palaces in Maadhar and landing on a rented top-floor flat in Ulaya, home

73

to an exhausted father, a miserable mother whose happiness was already deserting her at a young age, and a pair of children like pet kittens who knew nothing of life other than the fantastical, dreamlike stories they watched on a small screen.

The family stayed for several months with Uncle Saleh, in the big house in Buraida's Bashar neighbourhood where he lived at that time. He had three sons, the eldest of whom, Yasser, was ten, while Fahd was six and his sister, Lulua, three. How different their house was! Extremely spacious, with a courtyard where the children played football, a small cornershop that sold ice cream on the street outside, and in a secluded corner of the building next to a bedroom for female visitors, a guest room set aside for the Riyadhis—Suleiman and his family.

Soha would quake when Fahd went missing for more than an hour, maybe because he was young and pale-skinned with an eye-catching coppery tone to his hair. She feared for him in the streets and alleys and from the attentions of her uncle's children.

When the children were standing in front of the tall, hand-cranked washing machine, Yasser would play a game that Fahd found hard to understand, or rather he understood it, but enjoyed it, and so pretended he didn't.

Yasser would try to pick him up from behind, lifting him so he could see his face in the mirror as he roared gleefully. But it was more than childhood fun and games. At noon one day, while the men snoozed before the afternoon prayer, Yasser led Fahd up to the roof to 'fly pigeons'. He laughed when Fahd said, panic-stricken, 'I'm scared!' He assumed Fahd was scared of him, but what frightened him were pigeons, cats and any domesticated animal. Yasser pointed through the coop's netting to the nest boxes.

'The one with the fat breast: see her? That's Velvet. The one standing over there is Fickle and next to her is Dancer. Look at her chick inside the shelter.'

'Where?' cried Fahd, backing away from the netting. 'I don't see it.'

Yasser followed him, throwing his dirty white *ghatra* on the ground.

'You're a dwarf. You'll never grow,' he said, and started pulling at Fahd from behind, lifting the little feet in their Riyadhi shoes off the ground so he could see the tiny fluffy chick. Fear started to prick at Fahd's young heart, not only because of the pigeons, but also because of his cousin's pigeon, which stirred wildly and hungrily rubbed against him. Fahd stood there silently then climbed downstairs, alarmed and bewildered.

His mother was not asleep like he had thought, but had put on her headscarf and the hooded robe she wore to pray and was standing by the door that opened on to the courtyard. The instant she felt him enter the room where his father was sleeping, she crept after him and beckoned him outside. He came out of the room and she led him to the empty women's bedroom and started to interrogate him. 'Where have you been?'

He lied to her for the first time in his life, telling her that he had been in the men's *majlis* waiting for a guest of Uncle Saleh, but she looked for a moment at his green woollen *thaub*. He was wondering what she was looking at when she surprised him by asking, 'Who were you with on the roof?'

Then suddenly Fahd broke down and wept and told her what had happened. He felt guilty, scourged by sin, as his mother plucked up a small white feather stuck to the bottom of his clothing.

11

T HE AFTERNOON OF THE day after his uncle's visit, while Lulua lay on her back watching *Sally*, Fahd was in the men's *majlis* with his schoolbooks, revising for his end of year exams. His mother slipped silently into the room so as not to break his concentration, placing a pot of tea on the table next to him, and before she could leave he invited her to sit for a while.

He had no idea how he would tell her what had happened. She might feel guilty herself for upsetting him and involving him in her problems, she might not be the slightest bit bothered, and she might lash out at those around her. He had no idea how she would respond. She had been suffering bouts of breathlessness since Suleiman had passed away three months previously.

'Do you know why my uncles came yesterday?'

'You lied to me, Fahd? My heart told me you were hiding something!'

He started to tell her what the men were planning: how her well-being had become a legal duty, as though they had evidence of her conducting secret liaisons with strangers, or someone had said that they saw strange men entering the widow's house at noon, while her children were at school.

There was a long and dreadful silence, as though she were looking back over her life and what had happened to her. Her

distracted air was intensely provoking to her son, and whee-
dling suspicions began to circle his heart, goading him like a
switch on a stubborn donkey: Was there something linking
her with a man other than his father? Had she been so sad
and silent these last few years because she was torn between
his father and another? Was it possible that his uncle had won
her heart, and she his, all those years ago when they were staying in his house in Buraida, fleeing the madness of war? Fahd
raised his face to the ceiling: *No. I take refuge with God from
doubt and uncertainty!*

After a full minute of silent contemplation Soha suddenly
started to wail. How could they think of this with her husband
so recently laid to rest, the soil over his grave not yet dried
by the sun? How could she forget Suleiman's smile, his playfulness and his laughter? How could she forget his voice as
he read her verses by Abu Tammam and al-Mutannabi and
the poems of Mahmoud Darwish, especially *Ahmed the Arab*
and *Praise for the Lofty Shadow*, which he had memorised from
a cassette tape given to him by Nabeel Hawamla? And how
could they forget how they had mistreated Suleiman from the
day of his birth to his death? Were they intent on wronging
him even after he was gone?

After Suleiman left prison and was back in Buraida, and once
Eid al-Fitr had come to an end, his family arranged a job
for him as a correspondent for a small contracting company.
Ali al-Safeelawi dashed round to all the families he knew
and whose men he trusted in order to get his son engaged in
quick order, lest he be drawn after some new dream and lead
his family into even more trouble than before. Ali wasn't that
worried about Suleiman going to jail, or even being killed, but

he did fear the scandal that had caused one man in Buraida to mock him in a packed *majlis*. He had walked out and now avoided male company.

The families did not answer his plea. A very few confronted him with reality: the reality of the jail in which the expectant groom had languished and the fact that people like that never gave up their ideas, which flowed from them like blood.

'We don't want our grandchildren to become orphans with no one to provide for them,' said some. Those who were more diplomatic and considerate of Ali's feelings said simply, and with blatant dishonesty, 'The girl's taken.'

And so Suleiman left his family and his two-faced city forever. Sensing his father's frustration and his concern for the family's honour he decided to relieve him of the burden of his presence and asked his permission to seek a living some-where else. He returned to Riyadh to work as a driver for a press distribution company, where he had the job of deliver-ing newspapers to government offices. The streets of Riyadh were not as wide as they are now but nevertheless he spent his whole day trekking back and forth between various govern-ment agencies, sometimes forced to wait at this building or that because the guard wasn't around to receive the stacks of six daily newspapers. He would spend a few minutes perus-ing one of the papers as the voice of Umm Kulthoum swelled inside the car, sedate and pleasant in the early morning.

Sometimes he would go for a stroll with a middle-aged guard from Jazan, who worked at one of the agencies and would tell him what went on in this ministry or that institu-tion; how the employees fought over the newspapers and the minister himself had to distribute them himself in instalments. With his yellow teeth and creased orange headscarf the guard would chuckle, 'The minister and his deputy have given up public affairs and are working as newspaper boys.' Then he would withdraw to the stove in his room to make tea for himself and Suleiman.

'They all go home at midday.'

On more than one occasion as he stood outside the Presidency for Girls' Education near the television building, waiting for someone to open the door, Suleiman had seen a middle-aged man dressed in a smart suit, tie-less, with sparse hair and a thick blonde moustache sprinkled with white, adjusting his spectacles as he sat on a sheet of paper on the edge of a plant pot that held an ancient thorn tree. He had a small paper bag, out of which drifted the smell of fried falafel, and he turned the pages of *Sharq al-Awsat* with interest. At first, Suleiman assumed he was some sub-editor who came early for some complex reason of his own, but after an entire month had passed he was certain that the man worked in the Presidency.

One day Suleiman got out of his van carrying some newspapers, and, shaking the man's hand, asked if he was an employee. He was, the man replied in a lovely accent; he had been under contract with the Presidency for twenty years, an accountant responsible for the daybook, the general ledger and the department's expenditures, and an occasional supervisor for inexperienced young Saudis. He asked Suleiman about his job and qualifications. Suleiman told him that he distributed newspapers and that he loved his morning work because he came from a rural family that liked to get up and start work early.

The next day, the man told Suleiman that he, too, was a country boy, a Palestinian, who had emigrated with his family as a young man to study accountancy at the University of

Jordan in Amman before the Presidency had hired him more than twenty years ago.

'Which city do you come from, sir?'

'From Qaseem,' Suleiman replied.

'We've got three from Qaseem, one from Bakeeriya and a couple from Buraida.'

He amazed Suleiman. He knew the people well and he knew the country. He could list the prominent families and their leading men and could reel off the history of Riyadh. This foreigner was an embodiment of the city's memory, a witness to what had taken place here.

Some days later, he invited Suleiman to his office to drink coffee before he continued his morning rounds. Suleiman came in hesitant and shy and the man asked him if he drank Turkish coffee, apologising because he had no Arabic coffee: the employee who made it didn't come until nine o'clock. Suleiman thanked him and turned the coffee down, so he made him a cup of tea and they talked for a while about everything under the sun.

The Jordanian would drop his sons and daughter off at school and would then have to come to work very early to go through the official accounts and expenditures in peace and quiet before the noisy young employees turned up. His son Essam was studying law at the University of Jordan and Soha, his daughter, was in middle school. Twins Ammar and Nabeel went to middle school together.

A few days later, the man convinced young Suleiman to continue his studies at night. 'Goodness me, you've got free night schools, after all!'

Suleiman began to take night classes at the Farouq Secondary School, and his admiration of this lovable Jordanian began to grow. Then came the day he stopped seeing him. Given the job of supplying boxes of newspapers and correspondence to various ministries and institutions, Suleiman would dump the newspapers very early indeed and go on his way.

Finally, Abu Essam caught up with him before he could disappear, reproaching him for his absence and for not dropping in to see him. The pair became more than friends and one morning Suleiman thought the time was right to ask for his daughter's hand in marriage. What could the Jordanian do but welcome the offer and salute his self-sufficiency and self-confidence?

But Suleiman felt that he had been far too hasty, and now found himself vacillating before his two obligations: the first, to inform the kindly gentleman of his imprisonment and former membership of a religious group, and the second, to inform his family, even though he believed that no one else had the authority to question his decisions.

'Haven't you made inquiries about me, Abu Essam?'

'What are you talking about? I've known you six months and your character speaks for you.'

Suleiman was standing in the kitchen of Abu Essam's house in Khazan Street and he fell silent.

'Is there anything you want to tell me that I don't know about?'

Stammering, Suleiman told him the tale of his involvement with the Divine Reward Salafist Group seven years before, his four years in prison, then his return to his family and search for suitable employment, up until his arrival in Riyadh.

'Prison is no shame for a man! What concerns me is what Suleiman has become and how he thinks now. I don't care what he used to be.'

Relief washed over Suleiman and he looked over to Soha, with her laughing face and bewitching dimples and her accent that blended her family's dialect with the Saudi vernacular she had learnt during her nine years at school. Neither Suleiman's features nor his cultured speech gave any clue that he delivered newspapers, an unskilled employee with a mediocre education. He was neat and well-groomed, his light moustache was carefully clipped, and he wore spectacles with clear, round lenses. Of medium height, his face was golden brown and serene. From the very first he set his heart on Soha and loved her dearly, not just as a wife but as a mother, a lover and a friend and for all their time together, the way he looked at her never changed.

And then, what no one could have predicted: Suleiman's own brother, the imam, turning up out of the blue fifteen years later to take his wife into his bed, the same brother who had threatened that he would empty three shotgun cartridges into Suleiman's head when he found out he was marrying a foreigner. That's what Saleh had written in his letter: he would take his bird gun and send his brother's head flying because he had brought bad luck and scandal upon them. And here he was, after all that, marrying a destitute foreigner of whose background and breeding he knew nothing at all.

It had been more than just a threat. Taking a party of men from Buraida to Riyadh, Saleh had met the head of the press distribution company at their headquarters in Malaz and demanded that he lean on his brother, bewitched by a piece of Jordanian immigrant trash of dubious background, and give him a choice between divorcing his wife or getting fired. In this way, they imagined, they had left Suleiman with no way out, but without realising it they had in fact created a huge opportunity for a young driver who was just one of a vast contingent of Sudanese and Egyptian drivers.

The head of the company asked to meet Suleiman and struck up an acquaintance with him, because when Suleiman was calm he was reasoned, persuasive and well-spoken, a manner he had learnt first studying with the sheikhs and then from his time in prison. Suleiman spoke of the hard times and crises he had been through and told him that the very Jordanian they were so set against had led him to rediscover himself and convinced him to go back to the classroom to take night classes and literature lessons at secondary school and pursue business studies at King Abdul Aziz University.

After that Suleiman abandoned his little delivery van and worked first as an accountant and then as head of the accounting department, before finally being placed in charge of the company's book distribution operation.

Suleiman was supported not only by Abu Essam, but also by Soha, his loving wife, who relieved him of the burden of the children, packing his suitcase when he was due to take his examinations in Jeddah and removing herself and the little ones to her family's apartment in Khazan Street by Jawhara Mosque. There, Fahd could get some relief from long periods he spent indoors. He messed around with a ball in the building's wide entryway with Rami and Mohammed the Egyptians and enjoyed playing with his grandfather, Abu Essam, dressed in his short-sleeved *jellabiya* and open-work skullcap, who would lift Fahd on to his shoulders, the boy pulling on his hair as they made their way to Nisma, the supermarket at the bottom of the building. Held aloft he would look down at people and feel proud whenever he saw Rami or Mohammed. They looked so small as they shouted and hopped around him.

Occasionally Soha would consent to her parents' request to take Fahd out and he would leap on to the back seat of the Caprice to fiddle with the plastic dog on the car's rear shelf. When they reached the shops in Sulaimaniya selling Palestinian and Jordanian delicacies, Abu Essam would pick him out a Jordanian olive, fresh, green and pickled, and a piece of salty white cheese and make young Fahd try everything to decide whether it was good or not, fighting back loud laughter along with his wife and the salesman when they saw the boy wince at the sour and salty flavours.

Soha was stunned by their effrontery, and the effrontery of Ibrahim, who not only had taken their side in such a matter but had accepted the idea despite the still-present trauma of her husband's unexpected death. Though Fahd was pleased at his mother's rejection, he knew how unpleasant his Uncle Saleh could be. He still remembered the first days of mourning when his uncle would visit them constantly, stroking his head and hugging Fahd, speaking humbly and warmly with Abu Essam and shamming respect, refusing to take his coffee before the old Jordanian. He would even open a jar of dates and press Abu Essam to take one, talking about free trade in Saudi Arabia, the entry of foreign companies into the country as a positive influence on the private sector, and inquire about opportunities for trade and new projects in Jordan. Had he been laying a new trap? Was he wanting to erase his old image, his extremism and his enmity with his brother, just to get closer to Abu Essam and leave the way open to asking for Soha's hand in marriage?

12

TWO MONTHS AFTER THE death of his brother, Saleh
dusted himself down and travelled to Amman. He met
Abu Essam and showered him with insincere smiles and gifts
and sacks of preserved dates, packets of *klija* from Qaseem and
date cakes which filled the back of his Toyota Land Cruiser;
all that effort and ambition in order to claim Fahd's mother,
on the grounds that he alone had a duty to protect his brother's household and two teenage children. His words were
convincing, caring and compelling enough to wear away at
Abu Essam's heart and mind, or perhaps it was the money that
weakened his resolve.

Saleh was known to the congregation at his small mosque
in the East Riyadh neighbourhood of Quds as Abu Ayoub,
after the Prophet's most militant companion. He was fat but
light on his feet with a beautifully combed beard and a *thaub*
that was always spotlessly clean, while his *shimagh* sent out the
scent of incense and agarwood oil wherever he went; you only
had to embrace him for the smell to linger on you for days.

When he entered the mosque he would bring a censer with
him and hand it to the man at end of the row of worshippers, or humbly carry it past them himself, though at the same
time he was skilled at sniffing out any new congregant, greeting them attentively and tenderly and welcoming them to the
mosque. Sometimes, when the prayers were done he would

turn his plump frame towards the line of worshippers behind him and peer at them, muttering invocations and fingering his prayer beads as he searched for a new victim. As soon as he spotted a newcomer he would send him his charming smile or a nod of the head in greeting, leaving the worshipper doubting himself and wondering, 'Does he know me, or is it just that I look regal and majestic?' at which instant he was snared.

The worshippers came to his little mosque from most of the neighbouring districts of East Riyadh, from Riyan, Roda and Khaleej, and the building's parking spots and the surrounding streets were filled with their cars. They claimed he had a wonderful voice, that his recitation brought on humility and tears, and in Ramadan they came like raindrops because he could wrap up the night prayers in fifteen minutes: anyone praying behind him who didn't know him would lose track at the end of the Qur'an recitation as he ran on in a single breath into the exaltation of the *rakaa*: ...*forGodistheonewhoseesandhearsallthingsGodisGreat!*

He attacked the prayers like a startled crow hurriedly pecking at the earth before flapping back into the sky.

Many of those who called him Abu Ayoub had no idea that his eldest son was called Yasser and not one knew the secret of his extensive contacts and influence, nor how he had convinced the country's leading sheikhs and *muftis* to come and pray behind him, nor how he was able to announce that one of them would be giving an address at his humble mosque. This won him considerable renown; men such as these were the unsullied of the earth, their honesty and purity doubted by no one. So not one of the congregation could find it in themselves to take Abu Ayoub to task if he missed the odd prayer or made use of the mosque for his agarwood oil and incense business.

He put a door in the room that led to the mosque's court-yard and after prayers he would open it to welcome his guests. Brushing the back of a worshipper's hand and suffusing his *ghatra* with the fragrance from the sweet white smoke, he would make him a gift of one of the minute vials that held less than three grams of oil, while the Bangladeshi mosque guard served coffee and preserved dates.

Abu Ayoub and the Bangladeshi guard had perfected the art of stalking worshippers and running them to ground. After the free gifts Abu Ayoub would leave it until another day to show his wares to the victim, who would be forced to buy more oil or quarter of a kilo or more of fragrant agarwood sticks, either because he liked them or out of a sense of embarrassment and good manners. Guests were impressed by the fact that Abu Ayoub had taught the Bangladeshi to wear a pressed white *thaub* and new red *ghatra* and to comb his sparse beard exactly like a Saudi; he even spoke their dialect. 'Greetings, by God! Wonderful to see you. A cup of coffee in God's name. Taste these dates, God grant you Paradise.'

Abu Ayoub, who invited the great sheikhs to his mosque, had so spun and extended his web of contacts within the Call and Guidance Centre that he had secured a fully subsi-dised annual trip to India and Eastern Europe. His ostensible purpose for travel was to call non-Muslims to Islam, but it was there that he obtained large quantities of agarwood oil jars and boxes full of huge, high quality incense sticks to sell in the mosque. His motto: 'Go on pilgrimage and sell prayer beads while you're at it.'

He would be gone a whole month and sometimes longer if there was a wife to marry. 'Marry women of your choice, two or three or four.' He would mutter in front of others (and argue to himself) that he married women from East Asia, Eastern Europe and the impoverished villages of India for two reasons: to safeguard himself against the more heinous sins such as adultery and to educate the unenlightened bride in matters of the Faith—how to wash before prayer, pray and fast and the other tenets of Islam—so that she might teach other women, not to mention the man who would marry her next. His evangelising mission complete, he would return to his mosque in Quds having divorced the Indian, the Ukrainian or the Filipino.

He was careful to marry young girls because they were quicker to learn than older women, but he never claimed, as others might, that they were more passionate or that they restored his lost youth. He would instruct them how to lie back and open their thighs and repeat with him the prayer of copulation. 'In the name of God. God keep us from Satan and keep Satan from what you have provided to us,' he would say, as he knelt to enter them.

He would teach them the correct way to wash themselves, taking great pleasure in coaching them on how to clean the vagina then, unable to control himself, would leap on them again. Such moments presented him with no great difficulties. 'There is no shame in the Faith,' he would say, pointing out the sentence in the translated text then leading them to the bathroom to become conversant with the method of achieving true cleanliness in Islam, his hands playing ceaselessly with their chests' ripe fruits like an Indian gardener assessing the yield on the mango tree.

Abu Ayoub had no qualms about taking two new wives at once. All the better to teach them simultaneously and thus transmit his knowledge to the greatest possible number of future husbands, and so that the men in these foreign countries might understand that Islam permits multiple wives, he would point out the relevant Qur'anic verse in translation. How skilfully he convinced these new converts to Islam! He would distribute blessings on these benighted individuals then return to his house in Quds to boast to his first wife, Umm Yasser, that more than 120 of these foreigners, men and women, had joined Islam at his urging.

And so it was that in a few short years he became the owner of seventeen agarwood outlets in Riyadh. His Abu Ayoub Agarwood and Eastern Perfumes chain enjoyed an irresistible appeal and credibility amongst the public. The Bangladeshi guard no longer manned the shop on his own, but was assisted by a large number of Indonesian employees with long, light beards whose individual hairs hung down separately, and gleaming white *ghatras* on their heads, the sort whose toothsticks only left their mouths when they slept.

13

O CCASIONALLY, SOMEONE WOULD ASK why Abu Ayoub was so keen on marrying his brother's widow. Was it out of spite? Was it because all his deceased brother had salvaged from the wreck of this world was a beautiful wife whom he loved, leaving Abu Ayoub dreaming of adding her to his possessions, like the hundredth camel in the story of the two brothers, one of whom owned ninety-nine of the beasts but could not rest until he had taken possession of his brother's only camel to make a round one hundred?

One summer evening Fahd and Lulua clapped for joy and shouted when Abu Essam and his wife knocked on their door, bringing with them gifts from Amman and spreading laughter through the sad house. But the laughter died away when the two young ones discovered that their grandparents had come to tell them that one day they would grow up, marry and have homes and children of their own to distract them from their mother, that this was life, and it was their mother's right to look to her own interests. So it was that Abu Ayoub slipped in, a wolf dressed as a pussycat, who later tried to win Fahd over by buying him a new car.

Just a month later and Abu Ayoub was ready to usher angels into the home that his brother—God rest his soul—had made a dwelling place for devils and infidel demons. By degrees, life started to change: the still-grieving Soha began setting the dial on her kitchen radio to play the Holy Qur'an all day long, and then the cassettes of Fairuz, Umm Kulthoum, Khaled Abdel Rahman and Ahlam vanished to be replaced by taped sermons. In one a sheikh screeched away as he recounted the terrors of the Day of Resurrection and the sins committed by the heedless, such as giving an ear to slander, gossip and song, coveting that which God had declared forbidden, adultery, sodomy, prostitution and filth. He spoke of the righteous path: hotter than burning coals, more slender than a hair, sharper than a knife-edge, more elusive than a fox, with Paradise at one end and hellfire beneath it and no way forward but along its back. Another sheikh spoke of death, when they place you in the grave and the two angels, Munkir and Nakeer, come to judge you; then he wept and wept and with him wept Soha and little Lulua.

A few months later and the uncle started urging Fahd to enrol at the College of Sharia Law, promising that he would come top of his class and get a job as a judge or court clerk. Despite the overpowering influence of his uncle, Fahd never even considered it. His loathing of the man had grown after he took down his father's portrait from the living room wall. Fahd took the picture to his bedroom where he was now confined, when in his father's time the whole house had been his. He hung the picture facing his bed, but his uncle surprised him in the room one day and screamed, 'You're in need of some re-education. Pictures are not to be glorified, don't you understand?'

His uncle took the picture down and flung it to the ground. 'I don't want to see any pictures in this house after today. Pictures are forbidden. You just don't get it. Angels won't enter a house where there are pictures. God protect me from you!'

He went out and Fahd froze, the fingers clutching his ruler and open biology textbook suddenly numb. He got to his feet, the needle stitching its thread through his chest. He lifted up his father's smiling portrait, the one taken at Studio Zamani in Thalatheen Street with its painted backdrop of books on a shelf. Sobbing, he kissed it and then hid it behind his clothes in the wardrobe. When he went to bed at night he would lock his door, take it out and sit talking to his father, reproaching him:

'Why did you betray me, Father? You had no right to run off and leave me to face life on my own. You had no right letting this person meddle with my life. Have you noticed that the only thing left of you in your own house is inside my wardrobe? All of this because of your brother, with his belly, his beard and his stink like the smell of the dead. Sometimes I think that he really is dead. He smells like a corpse as he climbs the stairs to the house. I don't know, I just smell dead men climbing the stairs. I even feel that you're alive, sometimes, that behind my clothes you're more alive than him.'

Nor did Abu Ayoub find it easy to accept Saeed, the family friend, coming into the house. This young man, raised by Suleiman as a favour to his fellow inmate Mushabbab, who had spent happy days as one of the family and often travelled with them to Sharqiya and Ta'if, was now banned from their home.

'I'm not worried about your boy other than from that Southerner,' Abu Ayoub shouted to the back of Soha's head one day as she stood silently before the stove making his bitter coffee. 'His father was a terrorist, one of Juhayman's group, and his family are a bunch of degenerate Zero-Sevens. Come into this house? Not a chance. I've bumped into him in the *majlis* a few times wearing a T-shirt and underwear and nothing else.'

One evening, when the uncle was with his first wife, Umm Yasser, Saeed called Fahd up to invite him out to Yamama College.

'We'll catch a play and get a break from studying.'

Fahd agreed and told him that he would wait at Tareeqati Café, to avoid the possibility of his uncle surprising him outside the door as he got into Saeed's car. He had no desire to bring the man's rage and ranting down on his mother. When it was time for the sunset prayer he put his *shimagh* over his shoulder, told her he was going out and hurried off.

Saeed was sitting in his car outside the café. Before getting in Fahd motioned with his hand to say that he would fetch some coffee. Saeed nodded. When Fahd pushed the glass door he found that it was locked. He peered inside where the dim lights glowed but saw no one. He rapped his knuckle against the glass. Saeed got his attention with a soft honk of the horn and held his hand in front of his mouth like a megaphone, indicating that it was a prayer time. Inside the café a little sign dangled down above the door: *Closed for Prayer*.

Fahd got in and Saeed told him that he had been to the college the evening before and there were cafés and restaurants by the main entrance. They set off towards Qaseem Road and as they approached Quwa al-Amn Bridge, Saeed moved to the right lane and turned left, heading back to Riyadh on the service road. At the corner of the college's outer wall he turned right and they passed through the northern gate, finding a parking space some distance from the main building. It was still early but they walked until they had almost crossed the courtyard in front of the entrance.

'Some coffee or tea?' Saeed asked.

'Ummm … There's a poetry evening that should be wrapping up now. Let's go and watch some.'

'Fahd, I don't feel like modern poetry, and anyway I don't understand any of it.'

'Fine, we'll just take a look. It's still half an hour till the play. Enough time to get a tea or coffee. What do you say?'

'OK.'

They entered the half-full auditorium, found a place in the centre and quietly sat down. In front of them were four bearded young men. One had long hair that flopped down over his shoulders despite being covered by a *shimagh*, while in the front row the other three sat wearing brown *mashlahs*.

'I want to try and understand this,' whispered Saeed.

'Concentrate and you will.'

The words were not difficult, emerging slowly, precisely and rhythmically from the mouth of a poet in his sixties who waved his right hand as he looked out at the audience through his spectacles, his intonation staccato as he pressed on the words to mould and shape them. After him there was a younger poet who recalled his time in prison and coming home a stranger, the kisses of his friends and girlfriends …

'Girlfriends? What? The kisses of his girlfriends! In front of these people, in a city like Riyadh?' It was the bearded man in the brown *mashlah*, rolling his eyes so the whites showed as he tried to interrupt the poet. 'This is not permitted. This is promoting disgusting behaviour!'

But the audience were applauding the poet enthusiastically and the extremist began muttering, 'God suffices me and is my best provider. God suffices me and is my best provider,' as one of the others, a sparsely bearded teenager, shouted, 'Peace be upon you!' into a mobile phone in an attempt to create a distraction.

Fahd gave Saeed a kick and gestured towards them: 'They're going to wreck the show. Trust me.'

Saeed drew closer and whispered with bitter sarcasm, 'I'd be worried if they hadn't already wrecked the country a long time ago.'

The men in the dark brown *mashlahs*, some of them with their *shimaghs* pulled back to leave their skull-caps half exposed, were being joined at regular intervals by groups of teenagers with shaven temples, who took their heads and kissed them to break people's concentration on the poets and draw attention to themselves.

As soon as the reading came to an end they tried to mount the stage and hand out advice to what they saw as the sinning, misguided poets and guide them to the path of righteousness. But the security guards in their sky blue uniforms smoothly blocked their way, asking them to remain calm while the poets were led off backstage, and so the event ended peacefully.

Fahd left the auditorium followed by Saeed and got a plain, black coffee, while Saeed had tea. They found an empty table and sat down, parking their paper cups. The smell of fried chips filled the air. By the entrance the young extremists huddled around the men in *mashlahs*.

'Don't they look like football players gathered around the coach at half-time?' Saeed said.

'Well they're certainly playing with the country. I get the feeling we'll have problems tonight.'

Squeezing a Lipton teabag around his spoon, Saeed said casually, 'No. They're all talk. Trust me.'

'You're wrong, Saeed. That's what you think.'

'After all the terrorism they've lost their hold over people.'

A cold northerly breeze had made the coffee cool quickly, though Fahd drank black Americanos no matter how cold. He took a short sip: 'Believe me, they're not done yet. They're like locusts. We've got them at school, my friend: they lure the students into the Islamic Awareness Society or the Islamic Club.'

Crushing the paper cup powerfully with his hand, Saeed whispered, 'OK, then, do you know what those two groups are?'

'They're terrorists.'

Saeed laughed and winked. 'Don't turn into a *takfeeri* and declare them all infidels! Islamic Awareness is the Muslim Brotherhood and the Club is the Surour Group.'

'Surour my arse. Listen Saeed, that lot are the furthest thing from happy and carefree. They're always scowling. It's like the whole world is wrong and they're the only ones who are right.'

'No. Listen here Fahd: it's nothing to do with *surour*, the word for happiness. I've read a lot about them online. They're called Surourists after Mohammed Surour Zein al-Abedeen from the Syrian Muslim Brotherhood. He fled Syria and came to Saudi Arabia and preached among you lot in Buraida until he got together a group of young acolytes. They became teachers and sheikhs and that's how a number of tributary organisations branched off, known as the secondary Surourist parties. They've split from the Muslim Brotherhood; there's disagreement between the two, I mean.'

'I don't think these types have real disagreements; they're all cut from the same cloth.'

'On the contrary. They get into serious quarrels and they fight dirty. Take the Islamic Awareness Society and the Islamic

Club at school: if you look closer you'll find there's a hidden conflict between the two, and sometimes it comes out into the open. The students think that every teacher is trying to increase the number of students in his club, but in reality he's recruiting for the parties that lie behind them.'

Saeed jumped to his feet. 'All the seats will be taken.'

Fahd hurried after him and the pair entered the huge theatre. The audience had crowded towards the stage and they could only find space in the high seats at the back.

The lights dimmed and the stage curtain parted to reveal a white plastic board displaying the name of the theatre along with those of the author, actors and playwright to a subdued musical accompaniment. Suddenly, sandals began to fly through the void of the hall, sandals that emerged from the darkness and clattered against the illuminated whiteboard, followed by many more shoes, until a figure in the shadows stood up and shouted, 'Stop up the pipes of Satan! This is not permitted.'

Two more rose up with him and they headed to the three steps that led to the stage. At first, some of the audience assumed that this was part of the play, *A Moderate without Moderation*, which addressed the issue of a middle ground in Islam. After all, modern plays were prone to incorporate such scenes. But the auditorium lights came on and security guards struggled to hold off the vandals, who were trying to get on to the set and rip up the pictures of women. Then others clambered up on the left and the destruction began. Whenever the security men managed to block one of them, another would pop up on the opposite side of the stage and smash whatever he could lay his hands on. One man, with a short beard like pubic hair, was pulling the bulbs from the light emplacements beneath the stage and smashing them against anyone who got in his way. Another strongly resembled Yasser. He was in a rage, his open mouth disgorging curses and obscenities.

Fahd watched as the fundamentalists smashed up the set. Some tussled with the actors and members of the audience jumped up in protest at their behaviour. In the back row sat an American critic who had come to speak about contemporary American poetry at a literary festival. He was dumbfounded, his eyes moving between the stage and the upper circle where some female audience members, sitting in a designated area separate from the men, had started to scream. This was true theatre, performed on life's stage. Chairs started to be raised on both sides, light fittings hurled like swords on some Islamic battlefield of yore, and in one depressing scene punches were exchanged, while the American followed proceedings with the camera in his mobile phone.

After an hour of active combat and struggle to control the rampant extremists, one of the security guards fired two shots in the air, and everyone stampeded for the exit in alarm.

Fahd looked around for Saeed but couldn't see him. He sat down between two rows of seats high up at the back, waiting for the hubbub to die down and a few minutes later made his way down to the exit. One of the men had been arrested and Fahd watched as he was forcibly led off to a security vehicle between two security officers, who then returned and fetched another detainee. Most of them had fled at the sound of the gunshots.

Outside stood three young men. One was wearing a track-suit and had his hair drawn back and fastened with a rubber band. His voice was loud and angry: 'What do they want? If they don't like the theatre then they shouldn't come!'

He was answered by a second youth, whose *thaub* pocket was ripped: 'A theatre outside the city and they still won't let us be. Cafés outside the city and they follow us there. Where are we meant to go exactly? God curse those vampires.'

Fahd searched for Saeed with flickering eyes. He examined the café outside and saw tables full of young men passing around a phone that showed clips of the stage assault.

'Send it to me on Bluetooth!' he heard one say.

'Just a second,' said a man studying the video. 'I'll give it a filename.'

'The Yamama Raid,' a third shouted sarcastically. The names of Islamist military operations always included the location where they took place: the Manhattan Raid, the Alhambra Raid, the Granada Raid, the Badr al-Riyadh Raid …

A hand suddenly clamped down on Fahd's arm and he spun round in fright to find Saeed laughing, sour and sly: 'Hah! You were scared, coward!'

Fahd took hold of him and led him away. 'Let's get out of here. This place is stifling.'

As they headed towards the car, Saeed said, 'All this open air and pleasant weather and you call it stifling? My friend, don't be so ungrateful.'

Laughing hard he said, loud and mocking and speaking in classical Arabic, 'What ails thee, Akrama? Wilt thou cede the matter to sinful Quraish?'

When they were in the car, Saeed said that he had received a text from his work colleague. 'It's Rashed, the guy I told you about. He's the one who encouraged me to read up on these groups: a strange person, mysterious and never smiling. You think he hasn't been following what you're saying, but when he speaks you realise he was with you all along.'

They drove to Musafir, an old working-class coffee shop tucked away inside a petrol station and frequented by students, the unemployed and truck drivers. When they reached the entrance a solitary figure in the far corner waved his hand, his beard sprinkled with a little white and an incipient bald patch on his head; he had placed his *shimagh* and *aqqal* on the ground beside him and was gripping the hose of the towering *shisha* pipe. Saeed shook his hand and introduced him to Fahd and the man smiled, his eyes narrowing further.

Saeed ordered apple tobacco and strong black tea. His expression had completely altered; his cheeriness, the laughter and derision, was gone, and he seemed sad as he stirred the coals on top of the tobacco plug.

'Something's ruined your mood today. Everything OK?' Rashed asked.

Saeed recounted what had happened at the theatre while Rashed, eyes like slits, listened intently. When Saeed had finished and silence had descended, Rashed puffed out thick white smoke, coughed a little, and said, 'Look Saeed, that lot didn't appear out of thin air. We made them, us and our grand-fathers before us, from their first flowering before the Battle of Sabilla finished them off, through to the bombings and armed confrontations of recent years, by way of the assault on the Grand Mosque and the Afghan Jihad, or the Awakening as they call it.'

Saeed interrupted to make the point that Saudi society could not bear sole responsibility and Rashed nodded in agreement, stating that society, the government, America and the entire world had played a role in feeding and propagat-ing their movement: 'That's right. There are those who fatten them up then get sucked in themselves.'

He took a short drag on the pipe and exhaled skywards. 'They're a cancer, my friend. Whenever people think the malignant cells have been cut out a new one suddenly appears.'

Despairingly, cursing everyone around him, Rashed unburdened himself. His grief rose to his throat and a long-suppressed tear rattled in his chest as he started to talk about his wife, who had abandoned him years before after a sheikh had given her a ruling that if her husband didn't pray in the mosque then she wasn't permitted to live with him in the same house.

'They brought my roof down, friends. They destroyed my house and my family.'

On the way home, Fahd seemed obsessed with Rashed's personality, so vengeful that he now spoke openly without looking about to check. Saeed changed the subject, and talked about the preparations for the cup final. They chatted about the match between Hilal and Ittihad and through his familiar, sad laughter, Saeed said, 'There's nowhere left but the stadium, my friend: it's the only place the beards don't go.'

– 14 –

A GLOOMY, ENDLESS EVENING. FAHD sat in the bedroom that had become his home. There was a gentle knocking at the door.

'What?' he snapped.

'Can I come in?' asked Lulua in a pleading voice.

She came in carrying a white sheet of paper and colouring pens.

I know this little scamp. She can be as polite as you like when she wants something, he thought as Lulua said with the playfulness they both missed, 'Best brother and greatest artist and sketcher in the world?'

He didn't answer and she added, 'It seems the prince of men is closed for the night.'

Hunched over his desk reading, he said, 'What do you want, Lulua?'

She took her piece of paper and spread it out on the floor and he began to write out a prophetic *hadith* along with the meanings of the words, while she fetched him a black Americano and a piece of vanilla cake. When he had finished the inscription in red and black ink and signed her name at the bottom of the sheet, he sat down to try the coffee and cake and asked her if she wanted to play Monopoly.

'Let's play in the living room,' she said.

'The only place I like in this house is my bedroom.' Then: 'I even hate my room.'

Although she did as she pleased, Lulua wasn't stubborn. She never fought with anybody, readily complying on the surface while secretly doing the very opposite of what others wanted from her. When their uncle took over their house in the guise of a husband, gradually imposing his own rules and interfering in the way Lulua dressed, she stopped wearing jeans despite being thirteen years old. Even the regular *abaya* wasn't enough, her uncle forcing her to wear a black *abaya* without any decoration or embroidery, and never as low as her shoulders.

'Can't you see what her chest looks like, woman?' he demanded of Soha as he bullied her into making Lulua wear it over her head.

After a few months he declared that Lulua's hands were extremely white and were attracting and seducing men, so he fetched her a pair of black gloves. Her mother tried to object, but faltered, feeling that it was inevitable that the man who had entered their house would impose his laws on them, that his word would be the only one heard and everyone would just have to do as they were told.

He even interfered in Fahd's appearance and forbade him from growing out his hair; he went so far as to insist that Fahd shave it down to the scalp, a demand he had never encountered in his father's time.

Fahd couldn't recall his father interfering in the way he looked or ever making any demands of him, except that one time, a few months before his death, when he took him to the Office of Civil Affairs in Washam Street to get a new ID card.

'Would you mind cutting your hair for the photograph?' he had said in that lovely, persuasive way of his and Fahd had happily consented.

What a wonderful moment for a boy: to walk out of the gate of the Civil Affairs building beneath the high bridge having attended the afternoon prayer with his father in the small mosque on the street, tucking his new ID card into his pocket as his father ruffled his head, smiling, and said in the manner of teenagers, 'Sweet. Now you're a man.'

Lulua came in carrying the Monopoly and laid it out, arranging the Community Chest, Chance and property cards in their places, dividing out their share of cash and putting the rest in the bank beside her. She said she would go first, and took the dice and tossed them in the air. She moved her piece and counted out her cash and Fahd chased after her as he chased after his endless anxieties.

When the uncle came in through the front door, life and joy leapt out of the windows. The satellite receiver vanished to leave Saudi TV channels One and Two, the news and sport. He regarded the Playstation as a time-wasting frivolity and they hid it from him so they could play when he spent the night with Umm Yasser or Umm Mu'adh; two nights of pleasure then a night of misery when he came back.

And suddenly there he was, poking his head and paunch round the door, eyebrows knotted like Nimrod: 'There is no strength or power save with God. You don't get it.'

He told them to throw the abomination in the bin.

'This is just a game; it's for fun,' Fahd responded.

'A game with gambling and wagers. This is what you call entertainment? I seek refuge with God.'

'But uncle, there's no money involved. It's just a game.'

'That's beside the point: it's a snare of Satan and a distraction from true worship. It serves no good purpose.'

The children packed away the game. Fahd knew he would revenge himself on their downtrodden mother who for the past three years had been afflicted with a mysterious illness. Following the death of her husband she had stopped visiting the hospital's specialist clinic; she used to go with Suleiman once a week.

Fahd heard his uncle growling in a low voice to keep his words from reaching the children. He looked into Lulua's eyes, unsure whether she had heard him, and if she had, whether she had understood what was said.

'You don't fear God.'Then, shaking his hands in Soha's lovely face: 'How can you leave them together? The Prophet says, "Keep them apart from one another in the bedchambers!"'

'My dear man, they weren't sleeping together; they sleep in their own rooms.'

'Even so: they're adolescents and they mustn't be left alone together. Is the ewe safe with the wolf?'

Damn you, Uncle, Fahd screamed in silence. *What ewe? What wolf? You'll suffocate my sister behind some imaginary wall. Even my orphaned sister's childhood won't be safe from your interference. You'll have us living like wolves and farmyard animals. You lot fool everyone with your studies and qualifications, but the real destruction is burrowing through your innards.*

His mother had closed the subject. There was the sound of coffee pouring from a pot while his uncle muttered, praying that God keep the country safe and secure. Then he began talking about the village that had been blessed with great bounty yet showed no gratitude for its blessings, and so God brought down famine, fear and poverty upon it.

Broken-hearted, Lulua closed her brother's door and silently made her way back to her own room, while Fahd returned to his books, though he was unable to concentrate or understand a thing. He could think of nothing but the night his mother had woken him, worried because he had fallen asleep on the floor between his bed and the wardrobe. Before he dropped off he had been sitting facing the wardrobe door on which his clothes dangled like corpses and lying behind them a stupidly grinning Suleiman. He had been telling him what had happened and recalling the song he used to sing to his father on those evenings long ago when his mood was fine:

An evening of goodness, fine feeling and kindness,

An evening that none but my loved ones deserve!

Fahd would sing alone at night in his bedroom, worn out by tears and uncertain if his father could hear him concealed behind his clothes. But he did know that Suleiman couldn't do as he used to long ago and take him, singing, into his arms to finish the song against his chest.

No, he didn't hold me to his chest that night. I just slept, drowned in tears and misery and longing for a childhood lost and gone, until my terrified mother woke me.

15

A SUMMER'S NIGHT LONG AGO. In undershorts and a light cotton T-shirt, hair wild and beard unkempt, Suleiman squatted by the head on the bathroom's broken shower hose, trying to switch off the mains lever so he could replace it. His voice sounded loudly, accompanied by the echoes from the tiled floor: 'Fahd, bring the toolbag.'

Fahd came, six years old and struggling to drag the green bag in which he had kept his first books and paints for Zuhour Nursery School, before it had become home to the plumbing and electrical tools his father used. He passed him the bag and sat cross-legged at the bathroom door, propping his face in his little hands.

'Dad?' he burst out innocently. 'Are you a criminal?'

The pliers clattered on to the tiled floor of the bathroom and father turned to son. 'No, old man. Why?'

'Just asking.'

'Who said that to you?'

'Aunt Hissa's son, Faisal. He told me, "Your dad's a crook because they put him in prison." Why did they put you in prison?'

Suleiman smiled. 'Because …' He fell silent for a moment. 'I'll tell you when you're older.'

'I'm older now, look.'

Fahd leapt to his feet to show how tall he was. Suleiman left his work and went out of the bathroom carrying the boy on his right arm, kissing him, and shouting, 'I love you so much, God curse the devil inside you!'

'Wiser than your years, little Fahd,' he chanted in a loud, joyful voice, then sat him down on the sofa and tried to explain that he had made a mistake and they had punished him to ensure he didn't do it again.

'Who are they?'

'The government.'

'And what is the government?'

'Well, if you made a mistake, for example, and broke the vase your mother bought last month or took the iron and burned her new dress, then Mum would punish you, right?'

'Mum's the government?'

Suleiman shook with laughter, shouting out to Soha who was making coffee in the kitchen. 'Come and see the little madman of the family!'

Fahd angrily broke in on his laughter and mockery. 'Fine, so you broke something when you were a boy and they put you in prison?'

Suleiman's hand froze on the child's neck and his eyes reddened. He got up and went back to the bathroom, closing the door behind him. Fahd heard a confused sound, like water pouring into a basin or sobbing.

All of this came back to Fahd now. He felt that his father had wanted to tell him that the thing he had broken was his heart, and with it those of his own parents. For Ali, loyalty to the government was of a piece with devotion to God; obedience to God's appointed was a duty and to turn against him was the most evil act a man could commit.

Suleiman had wept bitterly in front of the bathroom mirror. Had he cried because he was thinking of his time in prison and the sorrow in his father's eyes when he came to visit him in the last three years of his sentence? Was it from a private grief at leaving prison only to enter the prison of this melancholy country, having twice failed to commit suicide and put an end to his existence? But his marriage, settling down and the pleasure of his two children had caused him to look at life through new eyes.

Fahd was no run-of-the-mill event in Suleiman's life. He took great pleasure in the upheavals of early childhood. He worried about the boy's precocious, grand ideas. He never forgot the time that Fahd surprised him by asking, 'Dad? Who was it that occupied Saudi Arabia?' as he turned at the end of Urouba Road on their way home from Al-Ahnaf Bin Qais Primary School. He laughed delightedly while his skinny son said in exasperation, 'Don't laugh, Dad.'

'That's a political question, Fahoudi.'

'What do you mean?'

'It means,' answered his father as he pulled away from the junction of Urouba and Layla al-Akheliya, 'that it's a tricky question. Look,' he explained. 'In the beginning there were the tribes.'

'What are tribes?' Fahd asked.

His father answered hesitantly. 'Tribes are people who lived together in groups, in Riyadh, Qaseem and Ha'il and so on. Then King Abdul Aziz came along ...' He suddenly fell silent, without adding, '...and occupied them.'

As they drove past the arcades, Fahd shouted, 'I wish I were a king!' He stretched out his hand in a military salute. 'I'd tell them, "Knock the schools down."'

Suleiman burst out laughing, then Fahd asked, 'Dad? If you were king, what would you ask for?'

Suleiman was quiet for a bit. 'Maybe I'd resign!' he said.

'How do you mean?'

'I mean I'd say that I don't want to be king.'

'But why, Dad? You could ask for any toy you wanted.'

There was nothing more beautiful than those distant childhood moments. The only thing that could wreck their happiness was the presence of Soha, who sometimes tried to curb the generosity and child-like lunacy Suleiman displayed around his son, claiming that he was spoiling him and making him unfit for polite company. Even after Suleiman was lying in his grave she continued to reproach him for not raising his son properly, for being unable to refuse Fahd anything and ruining him.

A Sudanese artist called Kamal, whom his father once met in an art gallery on Thalatheen Street in Ulaya and whose pictures, with their searing African palette, had gripped Fahd's gaze and mind, said of the boy as he stood pointing at the canvases: 'The soul of a great artist sleeps in his depths and it must be awoken.'

Fahd's father gave full credence to this myth—or insane lie—and bought him sketchbooks, watercolours and oil paints while his mother, irritable and seething, muttered that it would distract him from his studies not to mention that the fumes from the oil paint gave Lulua asthma attacks. How Fahd missed him.

Possibly in exchange for penetrating and pleasuring her last thing at night, Fahd's uncle chivvied his mother into ambushing her son and nagging him to put a stop to this outrage with oil paints that his late father had involved him in. But was it his father who got him involved, or had Suleiman himself been drawn in by the chance remark of a random Sudanese artist?

Stretched out on his bed, Fahd pondered: *How can I become an artist, Father, now that you've betrayed me and left me all alone? How is it, my dear Kamal, that you managed to embroil both me and my father in your prophecy? If only you knew how my pores open and the hairs in my nostrils quiver when I smell the oils; how dizzying it is, how fatal. How worked up I get at the brilliance of the artists I love; how I flow into the tumult of their colours. Do you even realise, painting away so creative and conceited, that I have had to rip the sheet from my sketchpad into pieces no bigger than a postage stamp so that my mother does not find them and lose her temper as she warns of my uncle's rage? I draw trees or birds on those small shreds. I love birds when they're circling in the heavens with rare delight, but I hate them too. I fear them approaching me; I'm scared to touch them. I really hate their feathers: I gag when I see an abandoned feather floating on the water's surface. I can feel them moving over my tongue, the scratchy tip creeping to the back of my throat and I choke on it, like it was a clinging hair, so much so that sometimes I almost throw up.*

16

T HE AFTERNOON OF THE following day Fahd told his mother that he would be going to the stadium with Saeed. She tried persuading him to watch the match on television, then started in with her old lament that he would never do well at his studies and wouldn't get the marks he needed to go to study a respectable subject.

'Look at Yasser studying medicine. He's going to be a doctor one day.'

He hurried down the front steps cursing Yasser and Abu Yasser as her voice came from the living room: 'Don't be late.'

Wearing his *thaub* and his team's cap, Fahd walked until he came to Tareeqati Café. When he turned off Urouba Road he didn't see Saeed's Honda and he went into the café and started leafing through a copy of *Riyadh*. He read the provocations and challenges exchanged by the two coaches and club presidents and a few of the statements by former players. His mobile blared out Fairouz's *Remember the Last Time I Saw You?* It was Saeed to say he was on his way, and minutes later Fahd saw the car through the café window. He went out and got in.

They were very late and the stadium was full of spectators. They went in but could only find space in the South End next to the Hilal supporters. As they climbed the terraces the loudspeakers were playing the national anthem:

> *He who walks barefoot over coals is worthy of you,*
> *And he who waters your seed with sweat, tears and blood is*
> *worthy of you…*

'… is worthy of you,' echoed the swaying crowd, entranced, while Saeed galloped up the steps gleefully and audibly singing, 'He who waters your soil with the filth of murder and blood is worthy of you …'

Once they had passed the soldiers at the top of the steps and were sitting down, panting and trying to catch their breath, Fahd gave him a thump. 'You're crazy. The place is swarming with soldiers and cops.'

'Men, let nothing you dismay,' said Saeed, then joyfully held his arms aloft and shouted, 'Smile! We're in the pearl of stadiums.'

'Your father occupied the Grand Mosque and it looks like you're about to take over the stadium,' Fahd whispered in his ear.

Down below the soldiers were drawn up in ranks and the band members were sitting in an area by the back of the goal. The bandleader looked around at his men and gave instructions in readiness for playing the national anthem as the king entered the stadium at half-time.

Opposite the rear entrance to Hammadi Hospital lived Muhannad, Fahd's friend from middle school. One evening, as they played on the Playstation, Muhannad had suggested that Fahd come to the stadium the next day to watch a match along with him and his elder brother. He asked Suleiman's permission, who reluctantly gave it, though he wavered over whether to go with him or not. At the last minute he backed down and gave Fahd one hundred riyals so he wouldn't have to rely on anyone else.

'Watch out for yourself, and don't get separated from Muhannad.'

Half an hour before kick-off the three of them spotted a crowd of supporters rushing to the edge of the terraces overhanging the tunnel entrance to lean their heads out and watch the players stride out on to the pitch of Malaz Stadium. Muhannad's older brother, Mansour, suggested they go and see the players up close and in the flesh and the two younger boys were delighted and noisily sprinted off. The crush of people was frightening, everyone striving to wriggle through to the edge of the terrace and hang on to the low cement barricade in order to get a view. Mansour was behind them, guiding and pushing them forward, and they almost suffocated from the lack of air.

As al-Daie and al-Jaber emerged before the screams of the fans, Fahd felt Mansour press up painfully behind him. When he continued to press forward, Fahd tried to step out of the way and shifted a little to the left only for another man to barge into him. He looked round in alarm to find a man with his head swathed in a *shimagh* showing nothing but his eyes, and he swivelled about and dragged Muhannad away, saying, 'Let's go.'

The episode brought back memories of the incident with the feather from his childhood and he felt very guilty for going to the stadium with someone he didn't know well and for not taking his father with him. It also reminded him of the time he and his Iraqi friend, Muwaffaq, had climbed on to the tables in the passage that ran past the classrooms during break time, to watch a football match through the curtains of the second floor windows. Muwaffaq was getting very close to him; Fahd understood what he wanted, backed up a little to make room. Muwaffaq slipped between Fahd and the wall like a tame ginger tabby. Fahd pressed against him from behind and the two of them laughed until they were surprised by Nasser, the class monitor, who climbed up on the table to harrass them, putting his hand on Muwaffaq's shoulder and pulling the boy towards him, saying, 'You can see better from over here.'

Frightened that he might take his revenge, Muwaffaq went with him.

The game began and the crowd roared with one voice, the stadium's terraces transformed in a vast unruly vessel. Suddenly Fahd felt that it really had become a ship, rolling through the swell, and he became almost dizzy.

Every pass drew a shriek from the Bedouin youth in front of them with his long hair and blue shawl wrapped around his neck and shoulders, while the ground beneath three men next to him had become a sea of shelled sunflower seeds. In the dying minutes of the first half, as Fahd stared distractedly at the people around him, everyone started shouting and scream-ing and jumping up and down and he leapt up with Saeed. He hadn't seen the ball enter the net but he saw Hilal's players running after Sami al-Jaber. It was a moment of overwhelm-ing happiness.

Fahd's eyes were raised heavenwards towards the floodlights dispersing the darkness, fixed along the rim of the soaring white concrete awning where the pigeons flew over spectators' heads, hovering around the powerful lights then settling down beside them on the massive steel crossbeams. Every now and then a feather broke free and slowly drifted down, gently rolling back and forth as Fahd tracked its progress until it came to rest in the crowd or landed unnoticed on someone's shoulder.

At half-time, Fahd asked Saeed if he wanted anything from the cafeteria. Descending the steps and going outside, he was taken aback to find a large crowd around the cafeteria's high counter, their cries unanswered by the bewildered Bangladeshi employees. Fahd dithered: to return without bringing Saeed any water or sunflower seeds would be pretty feeble, especially if he claimed the crowds as his excuse.

Saeed's more than friend, he thought to himself. *He's a brother, if not my final support now that my father's gone, just as my father supported him in obedience to Mushabbab's wishes. So how am I going to cope with this lot?*

He approached tentatively. In front of him a man sat his child on one end of the saddle-shaped counter and screamed in vain at the Bangladeshi. At the other end were four young men. One was wearing a long frizzy wig, another the football shirt of Barcelona's Brazilian star Ronaldinho, while the remaining pair shouted at the employee who was handing out bottles of water and juice cartons and ineptly counting change. When one of the employees went into the small storeroom at the back leaving his co-worker alone at the front, the man in the Ronaldinho shirt plucked up his courage and, vaulting the high counter, took four water bottles out of an open box in front of the astonished employee.

'Take the whole box!' shouted the one in the wig, so he snatched it and set it down in front of his friends amid cries of encouragement. The remaining employee made a run for it, dodging a water bottle and a volley of loud curses, 'Bangladeshi animal.'

Fahd returned without water or roasted seeds and climbed the terraces to find the band on the pitch, ready to play, and the loudspeakers blaring out fervent patriotic anthems. Suddenly they fell silent and the stadium announcer proclaimed the arrival of the king. The king waved his hand and the crowd went wild, whistling noisily, and then the national anthem started up accompanied by the players and fans.

Now that the king was inside the guards began conducting intensive searches at the entrances to the terraces. Fahd had his pockets carefully patted down by a national guardsman with a thin, stern face who located his wallet and asked him to take it out and then went through his pockets one by one before handing it back. He asked Fahd for his ticket stub; he took it out of his top pocket, and the man silently waved him through.

Why did the soldiers always have the faces of embittered Bedouin or the inert masks of villagers, dead planks devoid of all expression, anger, hatred or joy? Were they always like this, even at home? How did they greet their wives? Did they hug their children like normal people?

His father would turn tail in terror whenever he encountered one of them. He was once riding in his friend's car when they pulled over outside a Tamimi supermarket. Suleiman got out and was chatting to his friend through the open driver's side window when he heard the traffic patrol's loudspeaker give a sudden squawk and felt the red and blue lights slap his face. Stopping in mid-sentence, he took off in a comic sprint, clearly terrified, as though he were yet to cast off the anguish of his years in prison and his fear of prison guards. In fact, the older he got the more frightened, anxious and confused he felt at the sight of any man wearing military uniform, even if it was a lowly rank.

The match came to an end. Fahd was already worried about being late home while Saeed wanted to watch the cup presentation ceremony. Patting his pockets and pulling out his phone Fahd was startled to find five missed calls from his mother and a couple of text messages. He read one: *Your uncle's come home and he's asking where you've got to. I'm begging you, my son: don't you be late!*

17

F AHD´S FATHER NEVER INSULTED him. Even when Suleiman was angry he tried to ensure that he spoke clearly and to the point. Fahd's mother had never pulled him by the ear, other than that awful time he had gone out on to the roof of his uncle's house in Buraida when she had twisted it after finding the a white feather clinging to the bottom of his green winter *thaub*.

Moreover, his father followed his progress at school and made sure that nobody upset or belittled him, even if it was no more than mocking or hurtful words in front of his classmates. How shocked Suleiman had been to discover the marks of the Qur'an teacher's beating on Fahoudi's fingers. He had accompanied him back to the school that same afternoon. Only the duty master was around, but Suleiman threatened to make a complaint to the board of education the following day and expose the school in the papers if the teacher didn't offer him a written apology and a promise never to do it again.

To Soha he would say that he didn't want anyone to hurt Fahd, not even to treat him roughly, so that he wouldn't grow up broken inside, but it didn't always happen like that. Despite himself, he had to sit there the time Umm Yasser caught Yasser, Fahd and Hissa's son, Faisal, climbing on the kitchen table and hurling eggs on the ground until the kitchen floor became a sticky yellow. Or rather, she had caught Fahd and Faisal, while

Yasser ran into the street. She packed their eyes with table salt until their wails filled the living room, then Aunt Hissa took them and roughly rinsed them clean with water while Soha, the foreigner, stayed silent and still. Fahd bolted for his father in the men's *majlis* and fell asleep in his arms as he fought back his groans: 'The old woman in there put salt in my eyes.'

His uncle gave a boisterous laugh and said sarcastically, 'All the better for you; now you'll see properly.'

It was past midnight when Fahd returned from the stadium, a blue shawl across his shoulders. Opening the door in the wall he went inside and found his uncle sitting on the steps leading up to the house. He gave him a fierce look and Fahd froze in shock, fearing the worst. They were like two wary cats meeting by a rubbish dump, circling one another with their hairs pricked up like thorns in anticipation of battle. His uncle didn't look up again, and his voice came heavy through the midnight air: 'Where have you been, you wretch?'

'I was with my friend.'

'With that Zero-Seven bum?'

'Saeed Bin Mushabbab, my friend, the son of my father's friend.'

'A good-for-nothing bum and the son of a criminal.' Then: 'Where were you?'

'At the stadium.'

'So, with all the other bums and dropouts and scum?'

A vision of the presentation ceremony suddenly flared in Fahd's mind. 'Even the king was there,' he said.

His uncle leapt from his place and Fahd lifted his arm to block the wild blow. His uncle's powerful grip fastened on his raised wrist while his other rough hand crept out and twisted

Fahd's earlobe. He tugged hard and spitefully, gritting his teeth with suppressed rage. 'Don't provoke me you animal! You and your sick mother have lost me time and business.'

He grabbed Fahd's hair and pulled him closer. The stench from his mouth was foul as he shouted, 'I swear to God, if I see you in the car with that Southerner again I'll get you both locked up! Do you understand?'

Then he shoved him towards the tall flight of stairs and Fahd ascended, fighting a violent desire to cry and a powerful urge to run from the house. No longer could he bear to live under his uncle's rules. Ever since Abu Essam had handed over the marriage certificate that allowed him into the house he had been despotic and domineering, running the place according to his habits and beliefs.

Throughout that long night, Fahd contemplated running away and experiencing life for himself, as his father had done.

I'll make my own way. I'm not Lulua; I don't have to be ruled by my uncle and his delusions. I'm a man. I'm sixteen, I've got an ID card and I'll be getting my driver's license soon enough. I'll be able to run my own affairs free of that animal!

As was his habit, Fahd kept finding fault with himself and the way he had handled his uncle just a short while before.

I'm bigger than my fat uncle. When he stretched out his hand towards me, why didn't I grab it and push him back? When he pulled at the shawl round my neck why didn't I take it off, wrap it around his neck and squeeze until his beard quivered and his great gut wobbled? He'd raise his hands in surrender and I'd see his eyes bulge and his slack tongue lolling out, then I could shove him off the third step and his fat head would crack against the stone planter. He'd lie there twitching for a moment then his soul would fly down to hell!

Fahd was sitting by his wardrobe and listening to the muffled sound of his father's voice from behind the clothes. He always felt that the voices of the dead would sound strangled, as if bubbling up through water. His dead father was telling him off. 'And then what, my young Fahd? You kill your uncle and they haul you off to prison for years, until your uncle's youngest son has come of age. Then they charge you with murder and you'll find yourself in Justice Square before the black-clad executioner, sharpening his long sword and sending your head rolling away like a football. You will die and leave your mother and sister grief-stricken not just at my loss but at yours as well.'

Fahd rolled over on to his left side and spoke to his father from his depths. *'It makes no difference, Dad. Kill him and be killed for it or not, I'm going to run away. I'm going to leave this house. I'll take your picture with me and hang it on the wall of another house without fear. I'll arrange my canvases and easel in the middle of the living room and fill the house with the smell of oil paints, just the way you remember it. I'll have no more of the stink of agarwood and incense that my uncle has filled the house with, so that I feel I'm living in a morgue or graveyard.*

'I swear to you, Father: I'll have satellite channels once again, and I'll watch the nine o'clock news on al-Jazeera just like you used to do. I'll follow the investigative reports on al-Arabiya and I'll enjoy the weekly movie. Fairuz's voice will wash through the chambers of my heart and the walls of the house where I live, as it used to when mother and you would play it in the early morning. Do you know that even Mum has changed since you've gone? She's forgotten Fairuz and the long-handled pot she used to make Turkish coffee. It's lying upside down and neglected in an unused kitchen drawer. Maybe she'll use it as a piss pot for my uncle when he's too old to reach the

bathroom. There are religious cassettes scattered through the house. I can't understand how this tyrant got my sister to memorise religious anthems and simple-minded myths.

'Everything has changed so much. Our life has turned completely upside down. Lulua's childhood has been brought to an end; now she's a woman who wants only to be a good, pious little wife when once she dreamed of being a television presenter. Do you remember her seventh birthday, when she went with you to Toys "R" Us and you bought her a pink tape recorder with a keyboard and microphone? Do you remember how she'd switch it on in the living room and you'd ask us to listen to her? How she once sang, I loved you and forgot to sleep, I'm scared that you'll forget me and read out a made-up news report? How you laughed in delight as you clapped and the report became crazier and crazier? That's all dead now, Dad. Now she dreams of being a corpse washer, or one of those female preachers, doing the rounds of gatherings and get-togethers and delivering Islamic lectures, telling women to fear God and the torment of the grave, to set aside the sinful habits of those who have fallen by the way, to invite them to organise themselves. Sometimes I imagine her joining some militant Islamist group. If the terrorists changed the way they worked and brought in women as partners and operatives, they'd be enthusiastic fighters for the cause, strapping on bomb belts to blow away anything they regarded as sinful and become martyrs, flying straight to Paradise.'

'Is that what Princess Lulua has done?'

'No, not that bad! I don't think she's ambitious enough for death!'

18

T HE FIRST PHOTOGRAPH: A husband and wife, spreading out a plastic mat beside a small white car. Between them sits a boy of two, playing with a plastic bag. His mother lets down her luminous red hair while his father gives a fleeting grin between his heaving breaths, having placed the camera on a box, set the timer, and run back to his wife and child. On the reverse of the photograph a flowing hand has written: *Suleiman and Soha – Nisf al-Qamar Beach, Sharqiya, 1986.*

The second photograph: a pedalo, licensed to hold two adults only. The husband and wife and their two children all wear yellow lifejackets, inflated and tied around their chests. The father looks worn out by his exertions as he pushes pedals with his feet. Next to him, his wife holds her one-year-old daughter in her arms. The father has his arm around the boy, who looks scared, as though he wants to cry, or has just stopped. There are traces of chocolate ice cream around his mouth. On the back: *Suleiman, Soha, Fahd and Lulua – The Jeddah Corniche, 1989.*

The third photograph: a pretty little girl sits in front of a cake with four candles on top. Next to her is a laughing boy with his arm flung round her neck, his other hand moving as though to grab a candle or snuff it out. Behind them children laugh, boisterous and gleeful. On the back: *Lulua (4), Fahd (7) and Saeed – Lulua's birthday, Funtime, King Fahd Road.*

The fourth photograph: a frightened boy on a little pony, his hands nervously placed in front of him on the animal's back, peers towards the camera with tearful eyes. On the back of the picture: *Fahd in Thamama, Riyadh, 1990.*

The fifth photograph: a groom with his *ghatra* hanging self-consciously down over his face and resplendent in a white *mashlah* with wide, horizontal stripes, stands alongside a bride in her wedding dress, her white, rose-embroidered veil over her face. On the back: *Suleiman and Soha's wedding – January 6, 1984. May you have a long and happy life together!*

The sixth photograph: a young boy stands on a white blanket next to another boy holding a bunch of roses; both are laughing at the camera. On the back: *Saeed after the operation with Fahd – King Abdul Aziz Hospital, 1992,* and then in a shaky hand in green ink: *Memories of an appendix.*

The seventh photograph: three boys bashfully stand behind school desks, one of them shyly ducking his head. In the background is a wall decorated with blue paper and flowers and the edge of a row of lockers beneath a high window. Written on the back: *Fahd in middle school with Muwaffaq the Iraqi on his right and Ziyad the dwarf on his left – Second year, Middle School, Class 2/2.*

The eighth photograph: a boy belted into a high chair. To his right is a man with a carefully clipped moustache, its red hair mixed with a little white, sitting back with a beautiful smile. To his left is a woman wearing a *hijab* who laughs as she puts a potato chip dipped in ketchup into the little one's mouth. On the back of the picture: *Fahd with his grandparents, Abu and Umm Essam – Abu Kamal Restaurant, Thalatheen Street, Ulaya.*

The ninth photograph: a husband, his wife and their two children, with a handsome young man in a jacket and tie alongside another youth with an open collar and an old man with a white moustache. On the back: *Suleiman, Soha, Fahd and Lulua with Essam, Kamal and Abu Essam – Sham Restaurant, Amman, 1995.*

The tenth photograph: a small picture, 6x4 centimetres, of an eager-eyed boy, his red hair combed backwards, fighting back a grin. On the back: *Fahd Bin Suleiman al-Safeelawi, 1992.*

This last photograph Fahd remembered well. He recalled his father and the Yemeni photographer in Studio Zaman on Thalatheen Street laughing together at the boy's eagerness. He had held his breath before the lens to hold back his laughter and appear a man, for a man does not laugh.

It had been after this picture was taken that Suleiman had grasped his son's hand, and the two of them had walked the length of Thalatheen Street and gone into an art gallery, one of whose pictures Suleiman liked. He had spent a long time arguing with the salesman over the price, then they had walked out without buying it.

Pictures then more pictures, memories coming to life in the photo album Fahd kept in a wardrobe drawer. It felt to him as though they were his memories and his personal history, his whole life, in fact. Nothing took him back to his beautiful past like this album and the songs that summoned up those moments to which they were bound. For Fahd, these photographs were life itself; he had no idea what he would do if one day he couldn't find them. Would he put an end to his existence? Commit suicide? What would he do if, all of a sudden, he became a person without a past? Was the past only present in photographs? Didn't memory inevitably lead back to the past? It did, but memory needed a spur to stir its cells awake; like a horse pulling a cart uphill it needed someone to apply the whip.

Some nights after the football match, Fahd was sprawled on his bed thinking back to his early childhood, until the memories and his own oppressive longing led him to his father's features and the picture of them together, his father playfully pulling his head towards him in front of the ice cream cart in Thamama.

Suddenly panicking he opened the wardrobe door, then pulled out the drawer looking for the album. He couldn't find it. Maybe his mother or Lulua had taken it to gaze on days that would never return. He rifled through the chest of drawers and bedside table but to no avail. Frantic and frenetic he remembered that he had put it beneath a large suitcase on top of the wardrobe and he mounted a small stepladder and lifted the case. A great cloud of dust billowed out, filling his eyes, and in a single movement he sprang backwards off the ladder and fell on his rump.

Standing before the basin in the bathroom to wash his face and eyes he almost burst into tears. He went out in search of his mother and found Lulua in the living room.

'Where's the album, Lulua?'

'What album?' she said coldly as she wrote out her homework.

'My album. The photograph album in my drawer. Who took it?'

She didn't answer, just shrugged and frowned. He went into his mother's room. She was in the bathroom. He waited and when she emerged, her wet head wrapped in a white towel, he attacked her with questions about the album. She replied that she knew nothing about it. He hunted through the house like a wounded wolf, inside which other wolves lurked and howled. He didn't know who he was any more. What was his name? Where had he come from? Where would he go and where would he stay? Who were these people, moving around all about him?

The next day, having searched the yellow rubbish bin without finding anything, Fahd came back inside, his head bowed and miserable, and sat on the entrance steps with their covering of artificial green grass. He was looking up at the neighbour's window where a pigeon fluttered and perched. He turned his eyes right towards the wall, then left at the basketball net hanging on the long water pipe outside the bathroom; he had gone head to head with his father trying to get the ball in that very net, and sometimes, when Suleiman was asleep, he had played against Saeed. He looked to his left, at the unfrequented space next to the low wall that separated off their neighbour's ground floor, and spotted a scrap of paper tumbling as if propelled by an invisible breeze. He stared at it for a moment then rose and picked it up. It was a deep shock when he turned the paper over to see Saeed's eyes and waving hand at Lulua's birthday party. It was a scrap ripped from the complete photograph. Searching for others he found another piece showing his father's coy face and part of the white *mash-lah* that he wore on his wedding day. He hunted around but could only find these two pieces. So. One of them had shredded his photograph album, destroyed the lot then taken it out to the street, and these two scraps were all that had escaped the bundle of shredded paper.

He went up the steps, crying and shouting, 'Who's the bastard, the dog, the son of a dog, who ripped up my album?'

His mother took fright, murmuring prayers and trying to calm him as he ran blindly about the living room, weeping in anguish. 'God curse your fathers and your forefathers.'

He was insensible to his surroundings; he could not see in front of him. He didn't know how he had acquired this vast strength as he tore the pocket of his house shirt, and kicked at the wooden partition until it shook. He threw himself down the steps shouting, 'I want to die!'

His mother and Lulua rushed after him trying to stop him. The girl handed her mother a yellow infusion from which wafted the smell of saffron, and Soha began sprinkling it on his face as she chanted, 'In the name of God, the Compassionate and the Merciful …'

A *jinn* had possessed him, she assumed, and it was the *jinn* that had rolled him down the steps.

The next day Fahd found out that his uncle had asked Lulua to tear up the pictures in her folders, because they were *haram*: they delivered their owner to hellfire and prevented angels entering the house. The Prophet, he told her, had said, 'No angel shall enter a house in which there is a dog or a graven image,' and had cautioned her about the punishment awaiting those who create pictures: '"Verily, those who shall receive the severest torments on the Day of Resurrection are the makers of graven images."'

Then he had chatted away cheerfully to her until he discovered where the album of photographs was kept and ripped them up one by one.

When he learned of this, Fahd lost his temper and finally resolved to leave the house.

Bit by bit he started to bring his possessions over to Saeed's rented flat, and when Saeed urged him to stay by the side of his mother and sister, Fahd told him he would go somewhere else if he didn't want to have him as a guest. So Saeed let him have his way until the day came that Fahd told his mother: 'I hate you, and I hate your damned husband. I even hate this house now: it's got no soul now my Dad's gone.'

'My husband is your uncle, like it or not,' she replied. 'No angel will enter the house if there's a dog or a picture in it, and anyway … we don't need pictures to remind us of anything.'

He picked up a new sketchbook that he had left behind. 'Fine, so if he rips up the photos the angels will troop in, will they?

As he scuttled down the steps like a wolf, he added, 'And shouldn't the dog leave the house before the pictures?'

Part 3

Love, fear and darkness

Starve me,
So that I become a lioness of discontent in the wildness of the
*   night thickets,*
So that I tease your bulging hide with my tooth's keen edge.
                    Akl Awit, *The Freeing of the Dead*

19

APPROACHING BISHOP'S STORTFORD THE train slowed. A few people got aboard and passed by the ticket inspector with his small handheld device that stamped the day and date on the tickets of new passengers. The old lady offered Fahd a piece of gum. He took it and thanked her. His mind was a little calmer. He looked through the window at the empty wooden seats on the platform and the policeman who stood holding a big dog on a lead.

The train set off and Fahd's memories galloped in its wake, wild and panting. He was thinking that it was no easy matter to rebel and to take risks with your life but if you didn't do it when you were a teenager or a young man then you never would. That is how it had been with him: there had been nothing worth fighting for, nothing worth preserving. He hadn't rebelled like his father. He hadn't done what Suleiman had done and clashed with government and society. His father would have taken up arms, had he not slowly withdrawn, using Imam Turki's mosque as a way to escape the Salafist Group, going to listen to the blind sheikh's speeches and sermons at sunset prayers every day until he dropped out of the reckoning altogether.

Fahd's decision to leave the family home forever was painful and devastating. Even if initially it was not on a permanent basis—spending first one night away then two, then more—it still saddened his ailing mother. What would she do at night? Would Lulua wash her forehead using water infused with the saffron ink from Qur'anic verses inscribed on white paper? Would she take three small gulps then rest her bandaged head on the pillow in search of sleep? Would she take a sleeping pill in order to drift off like the dead?

Fahd and Saeed had gone out together many times, loafing around Tahliya Street and Faisaliya Tower and pursuing the frisky girls who drew their admirers after them like panting dogs. They chased their lusts in a trance, like children chasing brightly coloured birds or butterflies, bewitched by a beguiling glance from behind a *niqab*, by eyes painted with kohl and maddening eye-shadow, by laughter, by shoulders jostling as the girls swayed, lascivious and lustful, and pointed mischievously towards the two young men.

Saeed become another person when girls teased him. Whenever he got the chance or came across some sheltered spot he would almost rub up against their *abaya*-clad bodies. He was indifferent to the presence of Indian and Filipino vendors and tried to avoid the looks of Arab street sellers—the Lebanese, Syrians and Egyptians—but when he caught sight of a Saudi walking behind his wife he would keep his lunacy completely under wraps. Alone with a girl, however, he would become demented and reckless.

One night he surged forward like a tiger towards two juicy morsels standing by the elevator and giggling in his direction and took them both in his arms. One of them hit him on the head with her handbag and he came back over to Fahd out of breath and laughing. 'That bitch. She's the one who gave me her number.'

Fahd could never match his wildness. He would follow after a girl full of trepidation but if she so much as glanced at him he would retrace his steps, stumbling like a bunny rabbit.

'Your problem is that you take life seriously, even though it's not worth it,' Saeed would always tell him. The truly incredible thing was that Saeed's extensive culture and learning could coexist with this demented pursuit of lust. When Fahd questioned him about the contradiction he'd laugh. 'There's no contradiction: it's all culture.'

One girl, Noha, was exceptional but Fahd was not in love with her. For her to leave the house meant mobilising the 'Armies of Christendom' as he put it; she was unable to go out without being accompanied by her entire family, and so he steered clear, until he discovered some comfort for his own misfortunes in her voice and past. She started calling him every day on the landline in the flat (the 'den' as Saeed called it) then got hold of his mobile number.

One day she left home in the company of the horde, all their vast baggage and retinue in tow, and arranged to meet Fahd at Mamlaka Tower in the afternoon. He stood staring nervously at the Rabei flower shop until she appeared before him and, flustered, shook his hand. Fahd grew increasingly disconcerted as she closed her eyes behind the *niqab* and trembled like a madwoman. He left her after a few minutes. Later, she confessed that she had nearly taken him in her arms: 'I just love your eyes! she said, then added, 'Not to mention your golden moustache.'

He chuckled. 'Golden, or ginger?'

Saeed always said that the girl who wouldn't go out with you after the second phone call wasn't worth your time. 'Love is business, my friend,' he would say, before delivering his famous line: 'Do you think a businessman would put all his capital into a project that wouldn't turn a profit for a whole month?'

'Of course not,' Fahd would laugh.

Profit, in Saeed's eyes, meant holding a hand, giving it a squeeze (sometimes a kiss), a playful slap on the buttocks, a breathless embrace, a deep, long kiss and so on. To call moans and heavy breathing down a phone line 'profit' was ridiculous, hardly worth the effort. Why? Because watching porn and doing the job yourself was a sight better than the self-deception of bringing yourself off to a panting, moaning voice.

Fahd didn't answer the missed calls from his mother and sister but, lifting the receiver of the phone in the flat, he was startled to hear his mother weeping and reproaching him for ignoring them. He gave a deep, tragic sigh and said harshly, 'It was you who decided where your interests lay. Everything my uncle did was designed to get me thrown out, and you just tried to keep him happy. Perhaps he wasn't the only one who wanted me out of the house!'

Through her tears she said, 'You should be ashamed of yourself, Fahd! I'm still your mother and Lulua's your sister.'

She wouldn't hang up until she had persuaded him to come round on those days when his uncle was away, especially now that her illness had become of serious concern. She said, 'No one knows how long they've got, my son.'

It pricked his conscience and he made up his mind to stop by on the nights when his uncle was sleeping with his other wives. They settled into their routine. Sometimes his mother would beg him to stay the night and despite the appeal of life in the 'den' he would agree. Everything that was outlawed and

135

forbidden in his uncle's kingdom was freely available in Saeed's lair. In Ulaya, there were no satellite channels, no glossy magazines or daily papers, no pictures, music or songs, no computer and no Internet; in the flat, there was all that and more.

Soha spent most of her time resting but only slept in her bedroom when her husband was at home; during the day she dozed in the dining room next to the kitchen, a small envelope beside her pillow full of folded strips of paper on which were written Qur'anic verses in yellow saffron. Without opening it she would take one and dip it straight into a glass of water until the liquid changed colour and then she would drink, wetting her chest and stomach and intoning prayers to God on behalf of her lungs that trembled like a pair of birds: 'Oh God, Lord of mankind, send me strength. Heal me, for You are the Healer, who alone has the cure, the cure that never fails.'

Her view of life had changed and become more religious. Had her illness done this, or was it her new husband, the imam, who had turned their life in this house upside down? The marriage was not contracted to protect his brother's wife or his brother's children. These hadn't even been fleeting considerations. It was done for divine reward in return for making devout a home that had once been immodest, wayward and sinful.

'How do you feel?' Fahd asked her.

'It's women's troubles, my son; don't bother yourself about it. Just stay close to me.'

One afternoon, Lulua placed a pot of mint tea before her mother and brother in the dining room with its bolsters and their colourful wool covers. Fahd poured his mother a glass and she asked him to fetch the phone book on the dressing table in her bedroom so she could call a technician to come and fix the air conditioner in the living room, which had started pumping out hot air.

'Maybe it needs filling up with Freon,' he said as he went to her room.

Searching on the dressing table and bedside table for the phone book he spied a small religious pamphlet, the kind that were given away free with cassette tapes in mosques and waiting rooms. The glossy cover carried a picture of a tree's branches against a sunset and the title: *The Efficacy of Charms and Herbs in Treating Cancer.*

He skimmed through and read a few lines from the introduction that declared that the best treatment for the most dangerous disease of our times—cancer—was prayer, Qur'anic amulets, incantation and blowing. The pamphlet provided testimonies of cancer victims who had turned their back on the lies and fabrications of medical doctors and placed their faith in God. It claimed that one doctor, an American, had been rendered speechless with amazement when scans showed his patient's body entirely free of tumours, and when he asked, 'Where were you cured?' the man pointed heavenwards, the smile of true faith on his lips. Fahd quickly shut the booklet, returned with the phone book and called the repairman, who promised to pass by the following afternoon. The van wasn't available at the moment.

As he was leaving, his mother embraced him and pushed a note, either two or five hundred riyals, into his breast pocket. Then she kissed his head, prayed that God protect him from all devils, human and *jinn* alike, and when he objected to her gift, saying that he wasn't looking for charity from anyone, she was blunt: 'It's your money,' she told him. 'God rest his soul, your father's money is your own.'

137

Since accepting a job as an editor for the Kanoun website's art section, taking contributions and reviewing articles and comments, Fahd would spend long hours online back at the flat. He was no longer interested in Noha's phone calls. He had met her again at the Paper Moon in Mamlaka Tower, hurriedly shaking her hand as she uncovered her small painted face and handed him a present wrapped in lemon-yellow paper, and placed in a carrier bag. On the card he read:

My darling,
    For your eyes, your mouth and your little ginger moustache:
    I give you my scent and my femininity.

Back at the flat, as Saeed laughed and shouted 'To hell with romance', he broke open the wrapping paper and pulled out a bottle of Givenchy perfume. Giggling, he sprayed it at Saeed.

20

N OHA WAS YOUNG AND mischievous. Fahd wasn't her first or last, and he wasn't her only one, either. She gathered men about her to bathe her long nights with their rough voices and suggestive banter. Fahd enjoyed getting to know her and hearing stories about her family.

Her mother, a strong personality, would flip over from the Showtime movie channels whenever Noha came into her room and was desperately worried about her daughters. Noha told Fahd that she could remember her mother forbidding her to ride the horses at the funfair, even bicycles. She was not to jump around or play too energetically in case she broke her hymen.

'A girl's a matchstick!' she would tell her.

When she was older and understood the implication of this sentence, she would lie beneath her blanket in the bitter Riyadh winter and ask herself, 'A matchstick? Who will strike me, and when?'

Noha still recalled those moments as a young girl when she would hide beneath the bedsheet and send her little hand to grope around. She felt no pleasure, just the thrill of discovering this buried treasure. One day her mother walked in on her unexpectedly and Noha snatched her hand away in confusion.

'What are you doing?' her mother asked, sensing the child's confusion and panic.

'Nothing!' Noha answered in terror.

Her mother wasn't sure of what she had been up to, but she started dropping hints that it was a sin to play with oneself: 'If you put your hand there you'll never have children!'

It was absurd that a mother should threaten her child with the inability to bear children. So what if she did? What does being a mother mean to a girl of seven?

The next time she fiddled with her hand and moved it around down there, she was doing so for two reasons: first and foremost out of curiosity and secondly because she enjoyed its the way it felt. It was at this moment that her mother surprised her again, coming into the room and fully exposing her by uncovering the blanket. She moved closer and questioned her and Noha was stammering that she had been trying on her new underwear when her mother's hand, burning and heavy, landed on her face.

Although Noha only left the house very rarely all her friends were men. She absolutely never went out without her mother and an army of brothers and sisters. Her mother would never let her go with children or the driver, nor with any of her relatives. In her mother's absence the only person who could accompany her was her father.

Being accompanied by her father felt like a moment of wild rebellion to Noha, and it was the same on those rare occasions that she was allowed out with her friend. Her mother took her to her grandmother's house, her mother took her to university, her mother took her to her doctor's appointments, and so on, so much so that Noha would sometimes feel sorry for her, wrapped up in her daughter and neglecting her husband.

'It's wonderful that she's done this,' she would tell herself from time to time, 'because otherwise I would have slept with lots of the men I've met. It's true that I've done the deed with three to date, but that was only on the phone. If Mum had let me be for just a bit of the day I'd have done so much …'

It was imperative that Noha dispose of her sister, Nadia, with whom she shared a bedroom and bathroom. She did her best to upset and annoy her. Exploiting Nadia's fear of the dark she started switching the light off early, leaving her sister quaking with fear. The two of them bickered until at last Nadia moved her books and bed in with her younger siblings, and the little bedroom became the kingdom of Noha's secret love affairs.

During her first year at secondary school she was pursued by a boy two years her senior. He made her come, bringing her to a climax with just his voice and groans, as happened in the movies. Noha was amazed that her mother never heard her back then. She eventually took care to close her bedroom door and then, as a further precaution, to shut herself in the bathroom. How embarrassing it had been when one of her friends, hearing the echo bouncing off the ceramic tiles, asked her, 'Are you in the lavatory?'

'Yes,' she had said, explaining that the insulation in the bedroom walls muffled his voice. He never found out the truth: that she was trying to keep her voice from the ears of her mother, who hovered in corners like bats in the dark.

A girl is like a matchstick, her mother would constantly remind her: she could only be used once. She meant that Noha should hold on to her virginity. The thought that Noha's fingering might lead her to a sticky end terrified the mother, and her fear grew when she saw her playing blind man's buff

141

in the dark with her cousins. Whenever they caught each other she was convinced they must be canoodling.

Her poor mother.

Noha remembered the time she had been asleep or, to be exact, pretending to sleep, lying on her stomach as her cousin Samer, stretched out beside her playing his Game Boy, threw his hand across her and brushed up against her.

'What a fool,' thought Noha.

Noha had a male friend who she found out was gay. More worrying to her was that either he hadn't realised it himself, or was unsure, or even that he went both ways, with women and with men. He would sometimes say things that would never pass a man's lips: 'Ha ha. Someone lift me up.'

She felt that the manliness of any young fellow in the habit of saying such things was open to question. Maybe the trickiest moment came when she sent him a risque image of herself, and pleaded with him to reply in kind, only to receive a photograph of his bottom, taken in the lavatory of a fast food restaurant.

Discussing his relationship with his last girlfriend he told Noha of peculiar moves that could only be of interest to someone with homosexual leanings.

Noha sent Fahd an intimate picture of herself, which she had saved on her laptop. One day she was with her sister Nadia, browsing through the picture folder where she kept images of the latest fashions. The girls were getting ready to attend their cousin's wedding. The laptop was perched on the revolving chair in her bedroom and her sister was busy talking about the girls at school. She quietly spun the chair round before Nadia could catch sight of the shot, her heartbeat rising and her face colouring as she imagined her sister seeing it, not that she was sure she hadn't. What would she tell her? Either that it was of her, in which case she had no reason for keeping it unless she had sent it to somebody, or that it was of someone else, which opened up another can of worms, and implied she had lesbian tendencies.

21

FAHD DIDN'T STAY WITH Noha, the Paper Moon girl, for long. Saeed was right: it was too much trouble waiting to get free of her armed bodyguards and easier to take oneself off to another, riper girl, who was easier to talk to and meet.

One evening Fahd paid a visit to Faisaliya Tower where he had organised a group art exhibition in the mall's central hall, which allowed women strolling around the shops to stop and take in a picture. He was looking at a beautiful canvas entitled *Daughters of the Rain*, an abstract depiction of village girls cavorting beneath showers of rain, when he was startled by a woman in her late thirties standing next to him and looking at the same picture. Flustered, he moved to the next picture, only to find her next to him again, examining it through her *niqab*.

'The brother's an artist?' she asked boldly.

'Yes,' he answered.

She talked to him about *Daughters of the Rain*, why the artist had given such prominence to the colour blue when the rain clearly brought such joy and pleasure. He was on edge and anxious as he spoke to her, looking about in fear lest one of them dropped down from the top of the tower clad in his light cotton *mashlah*. Little did he know that his time would come later, one melancholy morning as he sat with his lover Tarfah in Starbucks, from where they would lead him away to face charges not merely of illegally consorting with a female, but also of using feigned affection and black magic to exercise his influence over the hapless girl.

The woman, whose name he later learned was Thuraya, was talking knowledgeably about the picture in the delectable, adorable lisp of the Hejaz, with her striking embroidered red headscarf and the perfume that filled his nose and mind. Were it not for her telling him that she was a mother of six, the oldest of whom was about his age, and her faintly husky voice, he would have been unable to guess that she was in her late thirties.

She had married young to a man from Qaseem and left the Hejaz, a place which made her coo like a pigeon whenever she mentioned it: 'You're fine and soft like a Hejazi!'

All that was beautiful, fine and wonderful in life had its origin in the Hejaz; the vulgar and barbarous belonged to the Bedouin. Thuraya was fiercely partisan towards her place of birth. Unembarrassed, she brought up her age and claimed that as a woman from the Hejaz her years didn't show and that her eyes were still young and passionate: 'The eyes of our women speak.'

Two days later she called him on his mobile on the pretext that she had some preliminary sketches for paintings she wanted to make. 'Just a bored housewife's feeble efforts,' she called them, with an exaggerated laugh that sounded like racing cars speeding past. She hoped to get an opportunity to give them to him and get his opinion. They agreed that he would take them from her on a Monday, when she went to the Dr Shablaan Clinics to get her son treatment for his speech defect.

On the Monday he stopped the car in the dusty square next to the building and went inside, going up to the second floor, inspecting the signs of the individual clinics, then leaving again. He called her and said that he had gone back to the car and wouldn't be coming up because it was difficult to see her there. She came striding out in high heels and almost fell on the uneven ground as she made for the car. He suppressed a malicious laugh and as soon as she got in, he noticed her confusion and the trembling of her hand. He shook it and she quickly freed it from his grasp. Her carefully ironed, soft black headscarf hung loosely over her *niqab*-rimmed eyes. She was extremely shy. Fahd could see no part of her save her hand and a ring of white gold. She only stayed three minutes. Saying she felt confused, she handed him a large envelope and left.

The next time they spoke she said, 'I'll see you at Uthaim Mall opposite Atiqa market. Turn right as soon as you're inside. There's a little bookshop beside the escalator; I'll be there before the evening prayer.'

After sunset prayers he took a stroll in the mall. He went up the escalator. Children were stampeding towards the games arcade, wearing green bracelets on their wrists that allowed them to play all day long. He went back to the bookshop and looked through the books. Most had an Islamic theme. He picked one out by Sheikh al-Qarani and read on the cover: *The book that has sold a million copies*. He put it back and searched for some poetry or novels in translation. He sensed someone breathing nearby and a penetrating female perfume tightened about his throat. He turned to see a young woman drawing a headscarf across her mouth. She fixed him with her eyes, the eyeliner applied with exquisite care and the eyeshadow a light pink that matched the smooth pearls covering her handbag. From the opposite direction he received a sudden kick. It was Thuraya. He hadn't noticed her come in.

'Surrounded by admirers I see!' she said, gritting her teeth and handing him a coloured paper bag as she looked about warily.

In the car he found a box wrapped in gift paper at the bottom of the bag and opened it quickly and eagerly. A bottle of cheap aftershave. He laughed.

A few days later as he was cleaning out his car he picked up the bag to throw it away and discovered a card with the silhouette of a man and woman embracing while the sun set into the sea behind them. On the back he read: *I love you Fahd, but I'm scared that you'll reject my love and my crazy passion because I'm older than you, maybe the same age as your mother!*

Fahd felt remorse that he had been ignoring her, claiming that he was busy, that his studies took up all his time and that his friends wouldn't leave him alone.

Haha, she would chortle in her text messages. *Your friends, or your little girlfriends? I admit it, see? I know you've got girlfriends. Just give me a little of your time!*

When she sensed that he wasn't interested in her, she turned her conversation to art, and asked him about the sketches. Had he liked them? Very politely and extremely embarrassed he answered that she had conveyed her ideas very directly, and most of them were highly romantic and sentimental.

22

F OR THEIR NEXT MEETING Thuraya asked if they might sit together a while longer, in other words that she come out in his car and the two of them take a little drive. It would be easy, she said. 'I'll get in at the hospital entrance at evening prayers and we'll go anywhere we like or just drive around in the car.'

He was hesitant and unsettled. Saeed hooted when he heard him prevaricating, and when he hung up, gave a wild laugh. 'The classic case of the village boy who falls for an older woman. My friend, she's the same age as your mother.'

Fahd smiled and blushed. He took the bottle of Givenchy cologne, tipped a few drops into his palm and rubbed his hands together.

He borrowed Saeed's car and as he got in his phone was hit by a message. He headed out for the Eastern Ring Road. He had no idea where Iman Hospital was and was embarrassed to ask, so he called telephone inquiries and got the number. A Sudanese employee answered who gave an awful description of the route.

'I know it's in the South, not the East,' he said, then handed the receiver to a young colleague who gave Fahd precise directions.

Ten minutes before the appointed time, Fahd was there. He passed through the Medical Institute's gates with its domes like wind-filled sails, assuming it belonged to the hospital.

I'll take a look around and get to know the neighbourhood in the few minutes that are left, he said to himself.

Worshippers were pouring into the mosque next to the hospital. Fahd felt that his bladder would burst. He looked around for another mosque. There was a large one facing the hospital, with Pakistani, Indonesian and Sudanese workmen clustered around the entrance to its toilets. He passed a Sudanese worker who had raised the hem of his *thaub* to avoid getting it wet as he sipped water from a palm cupped beneath a large cold-water tap. The droplets flowed in a long line along the bottom of his arm and dripped from his black elbow.

He pulled up at the domed gateway.

'Where are you?' she asked. 'I'm at the gate.'

'Look to your right!'

But the woman in the embroidered *abaya* did not turn round.

'The gate's the one with the domes like tents, right?'

'No, you're at the Medical Institute. Keep going.'

He started the engine and found her looking out through her *niqab*. She got in next to him.

'At last. Those kids were hassling me.'

She took a large bottle of scent from her bag and sprayed away at her chest and hands for a few seconds, then put it away and held his hand between her palms. Her hands were soft and finely lined, her long nails untended and untouched by red or silver nail polish. His fingers were curled to form a ring that she mischievously poked her thumb in and out of until he heard her moan.

He grew bolder and reached for her chest. Her bra was the rigid kind and he couldn't tell if what it concealed was sagging or firm. Not firm, he guessed, or else why wear this horrible contraption?

She said that she had had her children young.

'Married at sixteen and here I am with six kids. The oldest's at university; he might be your age or older.'

She laughed. 'But as you see, I'm not old.'

She had an adorable, seductive roll to her 'r' when she spoke.

'Want to see me?' she asked. 'Just go down any dark alley.'

She raised the *niqab* and turning her head to the window on her right she shook out her short hair and ran her fingers through it. She looked like a lustful young boy. Then she turned to Fahd and fixed him with a lascivious gaze. Her eyes were Javanese, eloquent and eager, while her red-painted lips were large and full, as if bruised by lust. The streets were slightly darker now but what few cars there were still passed them at every turning inside the alley.

'Forget it, I'm covering up.'

She put the *niqab* over her face.

'Khanshlaila neighbourhood scares me. They might know me,' she said, then added, 'I want to see your face!'

Fahd turned towards her. Their eyes met for an instant and he realised that she was mewing like a cat on heat. She extended her leg into the small space between them. Its smoothness shocked Fahd. Braver now he went a little further and then forced himself to stop.

'It doesn't bother you that your mother's Jordanian?'

'Not at all! Does it bother you?' he said, laughing.

'On the contrary! Here you are, white and sweet and the way you speak drives me crazy!'

They passed the end of Batha Road and stopped beneath the flyover at the lights for Southern Ring Road. Thuraya spotted a pink neon sign and pointed: 'Furnished flats! What do you think?'

'No. It's not safe.'

'To hell with you, you beast. It's me that should be scared, not you.'

Thuraya ordered him back to the dark alley. He went in and saw her fiddling with something in her lap. Then she guided his hand down. Her moans were loud and startling and he was scared some passer-by or passing car would notice, especially since his upper body was leaning conspicuously over towards her.

She loved this, she said.

'All I've got at home is an animal that can't get it up.'

'Have you thought about how I'll drop you off and where?' he asked anxiously.

'No. I'm just thinking about being with you.'

Though nearly forty, she was terrifyingly irrational. She never thought with her brain, but rather with her emotions or even her lust, which she described as her 'mood'. Speaking like a sensible adult he told her: 'You have to think hard about this so you don't get discovered and destroy your family.'

She stroked the back of his hand and answered like a reckless teenage girl. 'Great! Let it be destroyed. Then I can be yours and yours only.'

'So I can take you all the way home?'

'No, maybe I'll take a limousine even though my perfume stinks to high heaven. Maybe the driver will think I'm a lady of the night!'

Fahd stopped at an entrance to a ladies' hairdresser and spotted an ambulance some way off, its lights doused and a man sitting inside, waiting, as though on the lookout for something.

'Get out by the hairdresser's. Go inside for a bit and when I'm gone come out and take a limousine.'

She got out and he drove his friend's car away with a sigh of relief. Half an hour later he called her. She said that she had taken a limousine driven by a young Saudi, alarming him with the quantity of perfume wafting off her body. He had given her his mobile number and told her that he was at her service. Fahd laughed as he said, 'So why did you take his number?'

She answered that it was just a business card. 'The man makes his living from the passengers. Why, are you jealous?'

'Never,' said Fahd, cheerfully.

After two days, when Fahd had failed to answer her repeated calls, Thuraya sent him a text threatening to talk to the limousine driver and give him a chance to woo her. When he answered her call on the third day she said that the driver had told her she was lovelier than all those young girls and that he was ready to drop by, take her off in a Mercedes 'Viagra' and install her in her own flat.

'So that's your level, is it?' Fahd asked.

'No. I just want you to be jealous.'

'Jealous of what? That you want to be a whore?'

She cried and hung up.

When Fahd lost his temper, he spoke with his mother's accent. His mother had done the same. Whenever she had been irritated with him as a child, her speech would transform into a Palestinian-Jordanian dialect like that spoken by the inhabitants of the West Bank.

23

FAHD MESSAGED THURAYA TO say he wasn't prepared to meet. It was Wednesday and the week's end sent the Committee's cars roaming the streets of Riyadh like venomous snakes.

'I can't shake this fear,' he told her, and she replied that he hadn't made his mind up about having a relationship with her. She kept insisting that he, a young man in his twenties, wasn't interested in her because she was nearly forty, even though she had taught him so much and he had certainly enjoyed their last meeting.

He ignored his mobile for a while then found three unanswered calls and a couple of texts that he hadn't noticed. He explained that he had spent an hour trying to call her but her phone was off. She had been in the bathroom taking a shower, she replied, and hadn't wanted any of her sons and daughters to open her message inbox and 'see the scandals'.

'So … what do you say? Shall I make a move?'

'Where?'

'You're such an idiot, Fahd,' she said. 'Didn't I tell you last week that I was invited to a wedding in Suwaidi? Will you come and pick me up there?'

'OK. I'll need half an hour at least.'

'Oh, that's so long! Where are you at the moment?'

'Maseef. Up north.'

He started his friend's car and sped off. He took out the little bottle of cologne from the side pocket and poured a little into his palm, dabbing his neck and behind his ears. He took King Fahd Road. It was eight o'clock exactly, which meant he had taken the wrong road for rush hour. The cars flowed slowly along like a river. His phone rang.

'Shall I get going, Fahd?'

'No, just bit longer. Wait until I'm at least halfway there.'

Five minutes later she called again. Then a third time. 'Where are you?'

He looked out at the skyscraper alongside him. 'Past Faisaliya.'

Then he told her to come out of the same hairdresser's as before. After waiting with the Bangladeshi limousine driver for seven minutes she called and said, with an air of issuing instructions, 'Look. I'll wait for you at Haram Mall on the ring road.'

When the southbound King Fahd Road came to an end, Fahd took the Southern Ring Road heading east and, passing the first exit, he turned right off the slip road for Ha'ir and Batha. At the lights beneath the flyover she told him that she had left the mall on the ring road and taken the Iman Hospital road heading north. Before he reached the end of the road, she told him, 'look left and you'll see a hairdresser's. I'll wait for you in there.'

He jolted over the speed bumps without noticing and saw a police patrol car, lights flashing, race past in the opposite direction. Turning at the end of the street he pulled over at the World of Dreams hair salon, then called her. She only answered after it had rung five times.

'Hold on a moment and I'll be out,' she said quickly.

He looked to the right, where a Bangladeshi workman sat on the kerb outside the newsagent's that was next to the salon. Pulling himself together he turned left and noticed the patrol car pulled over in front of a van.

Thuraya emerged and hurriedly climbed in. Her eyes were rimmed with kohl and he was unable to make out what eyeshadow she was wearing because her *niqab* was tilted slightly forwards.

'How come you were so late?'

Tenderly, she took his hand. Her palm was hot and its surface so fine that the yielding, silken skin almost sloughed off when he rubbed it with his thumb.

He set out for the Southern Ring Road, but the street didn't continue on ahead and only two directions were available: right towards Batha Road and the jaw-dropping traffic by the lights beneath the flyover, or left, past the beauty salons, spare parts suppliers and the new district with its stench of overflowing drains.

He went right and looking over at the other side of the street she said, 'Don't go back! Just look at the traffic!'

The tunnel took him by surprise and he turned right, then turned again and re-entered the neighbourhood they had just left. Passing World of Dreams he decided to take the left-hand road this time in the direction of the new district where he could do a U-turn under the bridge and take the Southern Ring Road heading west towards Shamaat al-Amakin event hall.

In the new district there were open plots of land and whole floors of translucent darkness despite the putrid stench that crept through the air conditioning vents.

'Fahd? Shall I uncover?' she drawled.

He nodded, and she struggled to unfasten her head covering from behind, then looked over at him, a wanton catamite. She moved closer in the darkness and the car swayed slightly. She brushed his lips with a kiss that was fleeting and timid, as the darkened road had now come to an end and other cars suddenly appeared. Fahd decided to return to the ring road, turn beneath the bridge and head west.

'Well, I don't know where I am!' she said. 'The most important thing is to get me away from Khanshlaila!'

She took his hand and laid it on her chest.

'See how hot it is?'

The small potholes in the road were filled with filthy water that gave off an acrid smell. Fahd tried to avoid them in the soft gloom.

On the ring road the cars raced crazily. He tried keeping to the middle lane, avoiding hassle from the lunatics to his left and the influx of new cars on the right. He was not that skilful a driver yet, and cars in Riyadh moved as chaotically as blind ants fighting over crumbs.

'Do you love me?' she asked.

He nodded. 'Of course, and I desire you.'

'Ahhhh!' she sang with the madness of a forty-year-old child.

Her middle finger was toying with his fingers and every time he looked at her he saw her staring hungrily back.

'Will you marry a Jordanian or a Syrian?' she asked and he laughed out loud, then suggested she marry him to her daughter in middle school.

She remembered her husband and her mood suddenly clouded. He was a dog, she said: He beat her!

'No one does that without a reason ...'

'OK then, I'll give you an example and you be the judge: the last time I caught a slap from that bastard. For twenty years I've been trying to get him to buy us a house. Not for my sake, it's for his kids, not that he ever cared about them! He always refused and asked me whether I lacked anything? This one time I decided to call his best friend and ask him to persuade my husband and help him buy a place, but on the condition that he mustn't say it was me who called. More than once I told him: "Please don't say that I called to ask you!" He gave me his word, but unfortunately he lied and told my husband about the call. My husband returned home like a raging bull. He came into my room, chucked the kids out and closed the door, then he flogged me with his *aqqal* until I wept.'

'You're in the wrong because you got his friend involved,' said Fahd, boldly. 'If you can't persuade him yourself then that's the end of the matter.'

'Well of course, that's not all that happened.'

'Sorry for interrupting … This is Exit 25. Shall I get off here?'

She was silent and he turned towards her to find her devouring him with her gaze.

'So, you're going to leave me so soon, are you, Fahoudi?'

She glanced at her imitation Charroil watch. 'Tell you what, let's make a plan about where we're going first, then we'll drive. I want to see it and try it out, too!'

As she spoke she put her hand in his lap and he shrank back like a cat.

He took the exit and turned left at the lights. The area was all brightly lit hotels and cars. Children clustered at shop entrances and the women sold toys, nuts and fizzy drinks stored in blue and orange ice-filled refrigerators.

Thuraya resumed her story. 'Later, I called my husband's mobile when he was at work and his dirty little pal picked up. When I heard his voice I told him, "You'll come to a bad end, mark my words," and I hung up on him. When my husband got home he beat me again. I ask you, does anyone beat his wife for a friend?'

This time round, Fahd tried to avoid angering her. 'I don't know, I've never been married.'

She punched him in the chest and in her beautifully flawed accent said, 'My little idiot. So silly and soft. You're just like the smooth men from the Hejaz: they love women and appreciate them.'

Fahd was heading south, and before the side road gave out he turned right and saw a rose-red neon sign proclaiming *Shamaat al-Amakin*. He pointed.

'There's the spot, see?'

She said he had to get out of the hotel district so they could drive around one of the new neighbourhoods until her friend turned up, because she didn't know anyone else at the wedding.

24

F AHD NAVIGATED A NARROW path through the rows of cars, worried that he might hit one. A Honda stopped in front of him. The boot opened, then the doors, and two women got out of the back as a fat youth emerged from the driver's seat and began pulling out white tubs of food. The tubs looked heavy and the youth hunched forward as he walked over to deposit them by the women's entrance to the hotel. He closed the boot and moved off, and Fahd followed him to the ring road.

Fahd was forced to mount the pavement and come back down on to the road. Then he swerved across to the far left-hand side of the street and without stopping at the lights, kept to the left and turned into a newly built neighbourhood. Its buildings were of average height but its streets were fairly broad. In the darkness Thuraya's hand reached out for his lap. Fahd's breathing became uneven and rapid. Excusing herself she turned to look behind her then raised the armrest and leant towards him, snapping open the safety belt and entering the virgin forest.

Unable to drive Fahd stopped at the end of the road facing an old wall made out of breeze blocks. He hesitated. Should he switch off the car's lights in the middle of the street, or would that leave them at risk of a car careering along in the dark? He kept the lights on and maintained a lookout for any headlights approaching from either side or from the rear. Bolder now, his right hand began caressing the softness of that realm of irresistible pleasure.

His phone rang in his pocket and Thuraya grimaced, saying that she'd told him more than once to switch off his mobile as soon as she got in beside him.

'Seems you're scared of Mummy!' she added in vexation. 'A Jordanian, to boot.'

Fahd laughed openly as he patted her thigh. He checked the number and saw it was Saeed. *At a time like this, you bastard?* he said to himself.

'Don't let it bother you,' he whispered and they continued their tour of the quiet streets.

'Go back to that street by the wall!' she said with relish, but he found a wide road that was more or less dark and stopped the car by a high marble wall. He doused the lights, keeping the engine running and Thuraya surged forward like an enraged tigress in pursuit of its prey.

She was more skilful this time, calmer. This time he didn't close his eyes but stayed on the lookout. An Indian labourer shot past them on a motorbike then a speeding car whose driver didn't turn their way. Suddenly a car came swerving right up behind them and Fahd gripped her boyish crop and held her still so she couldn't rise. Frightened, he snapped, 'Don't move.'

Her body stiffened.

'Don't be scared,' he said soothingly, 'but don't lift your head up just now.'

Her body stopped moving and became cold as a corpse. The thickly bearded driver crossed to the right-hand side of the road, drove past in his old blue Ford Crown Victoria, then turned left across their car, pausing for a moment while he pressed the remote control for the automatic gate. He was the owner of the house next to whose high marble wall Fahd and Thuraya were parked.

The car mounted the cement ramp in front of the garage door and went inside. Fahd watched the red glow from the rear lights reflecting off the wall until the garage door closed, then switched on his lights and drove away.

'You're done?' she asked.

'No, but you need the right mood and a bit of peace, not anxiety and fear.'

He entered Aisha Street, always crowded at night, then went straight across at the ring road traffic lights, heading back to the cluster of hotels and passing the old, black women stacking up cans of Pepsi and Seven-Up in front of them, their *niqabs* hiding eyes that brimmed with the sadness of long years of toil and hardship. A white Toyota Camry estate stopped in front of him and two young black women got out and stared at them.

'Good God, looks like the whole street's black!' said Thuraya.

'Look's like you're a racist,' said Fahd in a bantering tone, but she replied sharply, 'Get out of here with your "racism" and your silly slogans.'

He laughed, embarrassed by her aggression and whispered that song he had once heard in the house of his grandfather, Abu Essam: '… from the red spirit of the revolutionaries …'

'"We have set you in ranks, some above others …" she said, then, 'God, Lord of the Worlds said that, not me.'

Thuraya hunted for a cassette. She found an old tape, blew on it to clear off the dust and put it in the machine. Suddenly, Fahd stopped outside the hotel's entrance for women where a southern Egyptian was posted in a sky blue *jellabiya*, his turbaned head lolling forward over his cane. He was overrun by children trying to get past him to the women's section.

'I can't get out unless I'm sure my friend has really arrived.'

She pressed the buttons on her mobile and started talking, waving at him with her left hand to lower the volume on the cassette player. Her friend appeared to have asked her a question, because she said, 'It'll be quarter of an hour before I get to the wedding.'

She was lying. She hadn't told her that she was outside the door at that very moment.

'Let's take a quick spin,' she said.

'It's tricky to get out of this area because of the traffic. I don't think there's anything stopping you going in and waiting.'

She sensed he wanted rid of her and in a broken, faltering voice said, 'You still haven't taken that money out of the bank for me. I told you my sister was coming from Jeddah and I need to go shopping with her.'

Fahd was carrying no more than one hundred riyals in his pocket. His bank balance was in good shape but he found it hard to swallow that a woman his mother's age should be exploiting him. True, she was in need, he told himself, but it was unpleasant to be begged from so brazenly. He took her lined hand and kissed it in something like apology.

'I'll bring the money next time, before your sister gets here.'

As Thuraya prepared to open the door with a defeated air, he said, 'Just a minute, I'll set you down right outside the entrance.'

He wanted to atone for disappointing her; he hadn't brought the money and he hadn't found a quiet spot where they could sit together and she could see him properly.

'I want to see you facing me,' she had said. 'The whole time we're in the car I only see you from the side and you're concentrating on the road.'

He didn't really understand what she meant by seeing him properly. He thought of inviting her to Saeed's flat but he kept having second thoughts, worried that some disaster might occur and he would put his best friend into harm's way.

He left Thuraya and drove Saeed's car to Maseef. He told himself he had to get a hot mocha and stopped at Coffee Day on King Fahd Road. Most of the seats were taken. He went to the bathroom, washed his face and looked at his eyes in the mirror, rinsed his mouth out repeatedly, then finally took a seat in a far corner, parallel with the road outside and raised his hand when the Filipino waiter looked his way.

He thought of when she said to him: 'I was a Hejaz girl, coddled by my family, until circumstances dictated I marry that man from Qaseem. Miserly and filthy. My friend, that man never washes or puts on scent. He doesn't seem to know that there even is such a thing as scent. I'm the complete opposite. I was always clean and nice-smelling. To this very day I take care of myself and my clothes, and that's after half a dozen kids. One time I called this sheikh and told him that I couldn't bear living with my husband and that I didn't sleep with him at all. "At all?" he asked. "No, but every couple of months or more and I need a man who's always there and tender." The sheikh suggested straight out that I ask for a separation. How could I ask for a divorce when I've got no job and six kids to look after? And what did he tell me? That he was worried I would fall into temptation and sin!'

Her voice became dreamy: 'I'm with you now, Fahd. I want you but I know that you won't marry me, that you're a young

man and I'm a married woman with six children, the oldest
only a year younger than you. Remember how I told you at
the start that I wasn't one of those girls who spends her nights
in hotels on the outskirts of Riyadh or in furnished flats, that
I was scared to weaken before you, your good looks and your
youth? Well now I'm ready to open my heart to you. I'll open
everything.'

They were parked outside a stall selling mango juice and he
asked her, 'OK, and what about Fadwa?'

She became agitated. 'Please don't speak about her ever. I've
become jealous of her. When I first told you about her, I said
it was because I was looking for some warmth. It's not as easy
for women to meet men as it is to meet women. I got to know
her at a wedding in Jeddah. She was leading the band: brown,
with a strong yearning voice. I was utterly bewitched when
she sang,

O my desire,
My solace,
I love you, how I do,
Why turn away,
Why leave me,
When I love you,
I love you, how I do!'

Thuraya sung in her throaty voice, and that night, Fahd sang
along with her. She laughed. 'It's like you lived with female
wedding singers all your life. Like you listened to their drum-
mers and memorised their songs.'

He told her that it was an old and famous song, and that it
had been recorded by Abdel Muhsin al-Mahanna, Ahlam and

Asala. He had a nice voice, she said, then continued, 'Fadwa sang in that voice of hers looking dazzlingly in my direction, so I smiled at her and she smiled back! My relationship with her began then. Of course, my three sisters were with me and they think I'm very pious and strict, mainly because I've lived most my life in Riyadh with an old man from Qaseem, so it wasn't easy to go up to her and talk or get her mobile number. But her looking at me encouraged me to smile. She was watching the bodies of the dancing women as she sang, then she'd steal a glance at me. I'd smile and she would smile.'

Thuraya sighed.

'My sisters asked me what I thought of her, and I said her signing was incredible, that her voice was wonderful, strong and expressive, that she chose sad, romantic songs, but I didn't tell them that she had a face like a child, or that her hand slapping the drum was sublime. I wanted to press her to me in a long embrace and smell her breath. Oh Fadwa! My poor Fadwa!'

She turned to him, pressing her lips together.

'You know, Fahd, I'd love to be with you and her together.'

Her wish took him completely by surprise. She desired Fahd and in the same instant longed to have Fadwa for just one night.

'I want to see her in front of me, smoking and blowing smoke in my face. I love her voice, her face, her body.'

Fahd put the mocha on the café table. His troubled train of thought, uninterrupted by the al-Arabiya report on Saudi stocks and shares on the television, came to end and he left.

25

Fadwa was a young woman in her late twenties with the features of a boy. Thuraya was captivated by her eyes and brown skin and loved her firm breasts.

'Lovely and feminine,' she told Fahd, adding that she had pursued her until Fadwa had finally consented to meet at a café on the Corniche in Jeddah.

'She ordered a grape-flavoured *shisha* and said, "Shall I order you one?" I apologised saying that I didn't smoke, even though I'd like to, and she took a packet of Marlboro Lights out of her silver handbag and handed me one. I hesitated, but her wink and captivating smile hypnotised me into taking it. She changed her mind and took it off me, putting it in her mouth, swiftly lighting it with her silver lighter and blowing a thin stream of smoke into my face.'

Fadwa's eyes were grave as she handed her the cigarette. Thuraya saw her lipstick on the filter and put it between her lips with pleasure, feeling dizzy as she tasted the butt that had been in Fadwa's mouth. She drew in smoke, filling her chest, and coughed violently, resting her head on the table until Fadwa was almost dead from laughter and her eyes wet with tears. She came over and sat next to Thuraya and pulled her head to her breast.

'I caught this scent that left me light-headed. She was stroking my head and saying, "Seems you're too old for these games."'

She was on the verge of tears as she looked at Fahd.

'Must I lose what pleasure is left to me just because I'm thirty-seven? You can't imagine the risk I'm taking with my sisters and family by going into that café, the fear I feel when I'm wiping my face with a handkerchief covered in rose-water and spraying heavy Oriental perfume until the smell goes away.'

Was she missing tenderness and warmth? She wasn't looking for relationships with women, but she needed intimacy and love, to be held tight.

'What can I do with a man whose entire life is hotels, *shisha*, friends and satellite TV? Shall I look for another man? "Thuraya," I tell myself, "at least avoid committing a sin!"'

'What do you mean?' asked Fahd. 'What sin?'

She looked out of the car window at a fat white cat that leapt off a rubbish bin and scurried off as a Yemeni emerged from his room in a loincloth and white T-shirt and threw the leftovers of his chicken ribs in its direction.

'My darling Fahd, you know a relationship with a stranger is considered adultery and my relationship with you hasn't gone that far, but I'm scared.'

With a happy childhood and troubled youth in the large family home in Jeddah, Thuraya had been pampered by her late father. In year two of secondary school she had loathed mathematics but the woman who taught the subject, Miss Awatef, gave her such looks of tenderness and admiration that Thuraya followed her lead and passed with flying colours despite knowing nothing at all.

In middle school she had been very interested in her cousin, the son of her paternal uncle. Her brother had married this cousin's sister, and she assumed she would marry the boy. She went to the house next door, where they lived, and set about ironing his clothes when he was due to travel to Cairo, but she lost hope and consented to marry her husband.

In the beginning her new life was fun. 'I admit he was handsome. At the start of our marriage he'd drown me in presents but everything broke down after the first year. I remember the time I made up my mind to leave him and go to my family in Jeddah, that thing my mother used to say to me and my sisters came back to me: "What doesn't kill you makes you stronger, my girl."'

Thuraya told how in a modest, working class home in the East Riyadh neighbourhood of Salehiya, near Salehiya Roundabout on the right-hand side after the petrol station, there in the house where her in-laws lived, her husband lay sleeping in the dining room. He was due to get up and attend Friday prayers at the mosque with his brothers, and Thuraya, in obedience to his mother's instructions, laid out the food in the dining room and woke her husband, who opened his eyes with difficulty and then went back to sleep. When she woke him for the third time he sat up on the floor-cushions scowling and sent his meaty palm flashing out towards her. Her soft ear rang and a wobbling tear descended. It was the first time he had laid a hand on her and it wouldn't be the last.

Thuraya stopped and murmured at Fahd, 'I wish I'd known you ten years ago, back when I had my strength and my desire to take revenge on him. I would have betrayed him and bedded you whenever I liked.'

She married a year before her cousin. When she gave birth to her first son at her family home in Jeddah, and while she was in her forty-day seclusion, she went to the window of her second-floor flat to watch her former sweetheart's wedding procession. She laughed as she remembered the scene: 'I was peering from the window like in those television dramas and weeping with grief while my firstborn wailed on the bed. Can you imagine?'

Thuraya spent long years virtually untouched in bed. She imagined her life to be a good one, settled and safe, but from a woman in the neighbourhood and the wife of one her husband's friends she learnt that they had sex more than once a day. One of them said that her husband would come home exhausted and couldn't have his afternoon nap without one; the other confided that her husband used to rouse her when she was fast asleep at night to take his pleasure. Looking at them both Thuraya asked herself, 'What makes them so special compared to me? Their dark skin? Their ugliness?' But though she might tell herself these things she went through a period devoid of self-confidence, which she gradually began to regain with the adolescent Fahd, before he, too, eventually left her.

Once, she said to him: 'Don't go thinking that I'm telling you about my problems and his neglect just to excuse my betrayal or get you to sympathise with me. It's not that at all, Fahd. You might not believe it, but ten years ago my husband and I abandoned each other. We don't do any of the stuff that married couples do. My six-year-old girl was a whim of mine. I wanted a little boy or a girl so I went in to see him all covered in perfume, even though he doesn't deserve it, and that was the last time he did it.'

26

FAHD'S TIME WAS DEVOTED to the art pages of the Kanoun website, his exhibitions, and his worn-out mother and sister, turned in on herself in their house in Ulaya, never seeing anyone and never seen. Her time was divided between caring for their mother, her schoolbooks and writing precocious Islamic anthems. For fun, Lulua would invent rhymes and riddles, raising her voice to make herself feel someone else was in the house as she waited for Fahd to take her out to Cone Zone in his new car to buy toffee ice cream. Their uncle knew nothing about their excursions. They would steal ten minutes to go to some nearby shop in Ulaya Street or Urouba before their uncle returned and so as not to be late back to their mother who had aged painfully quickly in the last two years.

'Is something wrong with Mum?'

But Lulua never answered. She would dodge the question by starting some new topic of conversation. 'Have you seen what my uncle's arranged …?'

Once, as they stood waiting for cream cheese *fateer* from the Damascus Fateer House on Layla al-Akheliya Street, he cornered her. 'You throw me out of the house and hide everything from me, even my mother's disease.'

She told him that their mother had had a tumour in her colon for the last four months. 'Seems that it's benign.'

'Seems!' he shouted in anger. 'What do you mean, "seems"? Listen to me, Lulua, I have to know: is it malignant or benign?'

Gradually she told him and finally conceded that it was malignant, though, according to the doctor, it was in its early stages and a cure seemed likely, God willing. But the uncle said that cures came from God and even Yasser the doctor said that the treatment would be painful and psychologically damaging; herbs were healthier and more effective.

After sunset prayers each day their uncle would open the street door and come inside with his bulk and muttered incantations. The cat would flee from the entrance with her kittens, and he would climb the long staircase panting loudly, short of breath and searching for Lulua, who would prepare a glass of water into which she had dipped a strip of fine Hejaz paper dyed with saffron. Having blown over the water for several minutes he would sit down next to Soha, give her three mouthfuls and start blowing on her as he held her forehead in his right hand, tugging at her roughly while reciting Qur'anic verses and puffing at her face and chest until at last she gave a sigh and forcefully thrust his hand away. His strong grip hurt her and no sooner did he desist than she would slump, her eyes drooping, and sleep with the calm of the dead, as though she had run vast distances during his recitation and now he was done she was seeking out the nearest bench in a public park to stretch herself out to nap.

On their way back to the flat after picking up the *fateer* the message tone sounded on Fahd's phone.

I love you, the sweetest man in all of Sham.

His conscience painfully unfurled, tree-like, until his limbs trembled. He thought back to how Thuraya had made a fool of him, making him drive to a strange and filthy flat, throwing her small handbag, patterned like snake skin, on to the living room sofa and embracing him.

Burying her head in his chest she had lifted it up to face him, her narrow, ardent eyes turned towards him. Though he had responded, he was tense and frightened. She pulled him to her by his hair and he surrendered like a suckling infant, led on like a masochist who needs a firm hand to proceed. She gasped and thrust his head down but at the critical moment he leapt up like a cat sensing danger and fled to the kitchen where he opened the tap over the sink. The long stream of water made a loud sound as it struck the bottom of the zinc basin, drowning out the gurgling of the water in his mouth as he tipped his head back then ejected the water in a single spurt, spitting as if hawking up his guts. Thuraya didn't immediately understand what had happened but he motioned to her that they should leave.

Slumped in the living room at Saeed's flat, the smell was still in his nostrils. It had the scent of agarwood oil, and though not in and of itself unpleasant, the sudden image of the dark oil that his uncle had scattered on his father's white casket made him gag. Was this the reason why, to Saeed's astonishment, he had abstained from food for two whole days?

'Come on man, she'll come right in the end, God willing!' Saeed said, assuming his fast had been precipitated by his mother's illness and recent decline.

For two days the smell of oils never left him. He squeezed the paint tube, moving the rough brush distractedly over the paint and staining the canvas the purest black then suddenly attacking it with red, sketching out a small bird hovering in the top left corner that almost escaped the edge of the canvas to fly around the living room ceiling. When Saeed asked him if he wanted anything from outside, he handed him the wrung-out, empty tube of white paint and told him they could be found at Maktaba on Ulaya Street or any branch of Jarir. He returned to the painting. Along the bottom edge he painted a bunch of hands, just hands held aloft, impossible to tell if they were pointing to the sky, bearing witness to something, threatening someone or raised in supplication to the bird in the top left corner.

By dawn the next day the paint had dried a little. With Saeed still sound asleep, Fahd opened a small tube of white paint and selected a one millimetre brush with a rounded, tapered point. Very delicately he swept up the white paint and in the centre of the canvas, right in the eye of its stormy blackness, began to draw exceptionally fine white lines, bunched together and bowed like swords. At first he imagined he was painting palm branches, bent and flying through the air, but after an hour spent hunched over the canvas in the quiet of the hateful city the outlines of a little feather started to appear, rocking in the heart of the painting; a bird's feather falling from the lofty heavens to a sickeningly silent city. It seemed to be swaying between two skyscrapers, but it was bigger than both of them, the artist's lens held close against it, rendering the vast towers no more than a distant backdrop to the scene.

Fahd painted with precision and perfection while in his mind an old memory unfurled of his Aunt Heila's house in Buraida, of the wood fire in the coffee room where one cold winter's night he had been playing with cousin Faisal, Hissa's son, and Heila's daughters, Shareefa and Lateefa.

The elder daughter, Shareefa, ordered them to all place their hands on the floor then suddenly lifted hers: 'The car has flown!'

They kept their hands on the floor, alert and repeating warily and suspiciously,

'It has not flown …'

Whoever got it wrong and raised their hands saying, 'It's flown,' was out of the game, and so on until there was a winner.

'My mother Noura's flown.'

'She hasn't flown …'

'The cat has flown.'

'It hasn't flown …'

'The pigeon's flown.'

'It's flown.' and everybody raised their hands as one, while Fahd wavered for a moment before lifting his own.

'Fahd, you're out,' screamed Shareefa.

'No I'm not,' he shouted angrily.

'You didn't lift your hands fast enough.'

'Pigeons don't fly!' he said, swaying.

'Pigeons fly, you idiot!' said Lateefa, laughing.

'Fine, Fahd gets a let-off,' said Faisal sympathetically. 'Let's carry on.'

Sharifa thought for a bit then shouted, 'The palm tree's flown!'

'It's hasn't flown …'

'The feather duster's flown!'

'It hasn't flown…'

'The feather's flown.'

'It's flown,' said Fahd.

'It hasn't flown,' shouted Faisal and Lateefa together.

The children began arguing in the still of a night broken only by the chirrup of cockroaches on the tall palms in the courtyard. Shareefa said that feathers don't fly and Fahd objected loudly and angrily, saying that feathers flew.

'No, no. Wrong,' yelled Faisal and Lateefa. 'Feathers don't fly. It's the pigeons that fly.'

Did pigeons fly? In his friend's flat in Maseef, Fahd peered at the painting and thought back, spreading the wings of his memory and flying away to where the velvety pigeons in his uncle's yard in Buraida scuttled on red legs, pursued by Yasser or Faisal. They dashed about flapping their clipped wings, tipping forward on to their breasts and righting themselves, then continuing their scampering and pecking at the tacky earth floor.

He remembered an old folk story from Buraida that he had heard as a child, about a young carpenter whose mother lived with him in a house with a yard where a large thorn tree rested against the top of the wall. The young carpenter sat in its shade all day making doors and windows, until his mother grew sick of his constant presence, which prevented her from meeting her lover and being alone with him. She wracked her brains for a way to make her son go to work outside the house. One day she summoned up her old woman's cunning and came up to him, mumbling and mortified, to complain that the birds in the thorn tree were watching her naked and that the only way to get rid of these peeping fowl was to cut down the tree. She got her wish and her son lost his cool shade. He left to work beneath a distant tree and she, free of his constant company at home, could have her lover visit whenever she wanted.

27

A FTER PASSING GHABEERA ON Manfouha's main road, Yasser stopped the car outside a dilapidated old building below which were shops for pots and pans and a cheap goods emporia (*Everything for 2 Riyals*). He adjusted his spectacles in order to dial the Egyptian sheikh's number.

'Peace be upon you, Sheikh Mohammed.'

In stately tones Sheikh Mohammed Abdel Muati informed him that he would be down in a few minutes. Yasser stared out at the road ahead: the female street sellers, the Egyptian women in their *hijabs* out shopping on the high street, two Egyptian youths waiting outside a stall selling sugar cane juice, municipal buses parked by the roadside, Bangladeshi labourers carrying buckets full of water and car-washing gear on their shoulders, Pakistanis in Punjabi dress driving their motorcycles next to the kerb, Indians, Afghans and children queuing outside the Temees Afghan bakery on the other side of the street, an old beggarwoman, black, hunchbacked and tapping on his car window. Yasser pointed his thumb to the sky and his lips moved: 'God is generous.'

There was a tap at his other window and he swung round in irritation only to find the Egyptian sheikh smiling at him. His face was round and pink, rimmed by a reddish beard, a dark prayer-bruise on his forehead. He wore a pristine and well-pressed white *ghatra*, slightly raised to reveal a sieve-like string prayer cap, while his collar hung open where he had forgotten to button up his *thaub*. This he now did as the car left Old Manfouha for Ulaya and 'the Jordanian woman's place' as Yasser called the house of his father's third wife.

The Egyptian was talking about corruption in Manfouha and the Bangladeshis who traded in alcohol, prostitution and other banned commodities.

'God suffices me and is my best provider!' he exclaimed, combing his fingers through his beard while Yasser expressed his agreement. Then he changed the subject and asked if Abu Ayoub was well. Almost playfully he said, 'Wouldn't it be better if we found him a jolly young Egyptian girl, Sheikh Yasser? A real salt of the earth type, instead of the hassle and problems of a sick woman who needs her kids, not a husband.'

Yasser nodded, 'Just as you say, sheikh.'

At home, Lulua was in the dining room with the green bolsters, changing the foam mattress for her sick mother, while Soha walked slowly and listlessly to the kitchen and from there to the bedroom, where she put on a long-sleeved shirt and a black headscarf. Then she wrapped herself in a blue, spotted prayer robe and faced towards the *qibla*, raising hands tattooed with henna and imploring her Lord to treat her kindly or take her to the side of Abu Fahd, who had left one morning never to return. Whenever she thought of Suleiman and their outings in the Riyadh night a tear sprang to her eye and a sob grumbled in her little chest.

The steel gate at the bottom of the stairs creaked and the sound of the Abu Ayoub's coughing and incantations grew louder as he mounted the stairs, a plastic gallon jug of *zamzam* water in his hand, which he set down by the entrance to the kitchen from which wafted the smell of fried eggs.

'This *zamzam* water's been blessed,' he said to Lulua.

She poured a glass and handed it to her mother, who staggered towards the dining room. Minutes later the doorbell rang and Sheikh Mohammed Abdel Muati entered accompanied by Yasser. The pair of them waited in the men's *majlis* for the five minutes Soha needed to dress herself in her prayer robe, over which Abu Ayoub placed her black *abaya*.

The Egyptian sheikh sat facing her, reassuring her that God had great compassion for His servants and that He, praised be His name, would cure her of what ailed her. From time to time he tugged at his white *ghatra* as it slipped backwards. Then he approached her, and laying his heavy hand upon her head, began to recite *surat al-najm*—'"By the Star when it goes down, your Companion is neither astray nor is he misled …"'—first chanting, then muttering, then reciting in his head and blowing so hard that her *niqab* almost flew off.

Soha felt no relief. She sighed to herself, resisting the rough hand that weighed upon her. It was heavy and his breath stank of rotten eggs, but for twenty minutes she kept her composure until he mixed some oil with caraway seed, stirring them together with his thick thumb. He left, having first prayed for her speedy recovery and told her that to show resistance and steadfastness in the face of God's test made amends for any sin committed by man.

Part 4

The elephant's last dance

– 28 –

T wo guards, one bald, the other short and slender, both wearing the uniform of a private security firm, stood outside Entrance Three of Le Mall inspecting the men and women entering the mall complex through the sliding glass doors. Outside, Fahd reduced speed but instead of turning left at the roundabout by the entrance he continued along beside the wall of Ibn Khaldoun School, then stopped and called Tarfah's mobile. Tarfah, wandering around a shop next to Entrance Three and exchanging a pair of earrings, suggested that he circle the roundabout and stop directly outside the doors. She had taken precautions and entered via Entrance Two on King Abdul Aziz Road and the guards here wouldn't be the same.

Tarfah, or Scarlet—the name she used in the message boards of Kanoun's art page—had got to know him two years before but neither had thought of getting any more intimate than interactions on the site's discussion threads, emails or Messenger.

A phone call had never been an option, despite Scarlet being an active member of the site and her many charming contributions and astute observations. Fahd had even sent her a private message when she first registered, suggesting she change the signature line that appeared at the bottom of her posts—*Suwaidi and Falluja are the two eyes in the face of terrorism*—and explaining that the website was an art forum and did not permit discussions of security issues and politics. Despite all this irregular correspondence they had never held a conversation until the night he found a request from her to be added to his Messenger contacts. He consented and in the excitement of their late-night exchange she had sent him a mobile phone icon. He paused for a few seconds, unsure whether to write his number.

Forget it! Don't bother! She wrote, but she had him hooked. He sent the number only for her to respond with a winking smiley.

She was in her thirties, with wide eyes, extraordinary dimples that appeared whenever she smiled, whether shyly or seductively, full lips and a round face of golden skin tinged an olive green. Her hair was black and soft, set in place with the hot air from the blow dryer that never left her room. Her hands, to which Fahd was addicted, were smooth, small and dark with beautiful thumbs; he had once told her that he dreamt of painting a picture made up entirely of thumbs like hers. Always calm and measured, she had an aura of hidden glee about her which hid a profound sadness that lay within her, manifesting itself through bouts of misery and anxiety that surfaced whenever she looked back over her short life: two failed marriages leading to an unshakeable phobia of matrimony, then three relationships, the latest of them with Fahd. During each affair she told herself: this one's my true love; he's the most beautiful; or, this one's my love, he's the most honest. But after months or years the love, or the sexual desire, would start to fade and die, until, finding herself neglected, she would begin all over again, cocooning herself in the affections of another man.

Fahd had teased her. *Why do you have a picture of an elephant in your Messenger window?* he'd written. *Don't tell me you're the size of an elephant!*

His taunts provoked her. She started playing a guessing game with him, first putting up a photo of a large eye painted with kohl and eyeshadow, then a pair of plump lips, then a small nose, then an earring hanging from her earlobe and finally her whole face, stunning despite being touched up with Photoshop. Then she restored the little elephant.

In the course of a first phone call full of laughter and noise, she told him she dreamt of riding an elephant and in the madness of the moment he replied, 'I wish I was an elephant!' She laughed at his indecency, and he laughed at her laughter, and so the hours passed, first in intimate confidences then in debate over the various artists showcased on the forum and the exhibitions scattered throughout Riyadh, at the Shadda Hall outside the Aziziya branch of Panda in Murabba, the Sharqiya Gallery north of the Takhassusi Hospital and the Faisal Bin Fahd Centre at The Capital Model Institute. She didn't paint in oils and wasn't obsessed with buying paintings; she was fond of many pictures but didn't have the extra cash, so her only option was to collect images of these pictures from the forum and save them in a special file.

At first he was scared and unsure. There were signs that Thuraya wasn't going to leave him be. She never stopped threatening him for his failure to create an opportunity for them to meet somewhere alone.

Strange, he thought to himself, the smell of her still in his nostrils. *Young men are usually the ones who blackmail and threaten girls, so how come this woman's threatening me?*

Although Tarfah had been an acquaintance of his on the website for two years now, doubts continued to attend him, cawing crows hovering over a corpse. Had she been sent by Thuraya to exact revenge? Was Thuraya already online? Was she somewhere in the list of the last ten members to join? He looked over the pseudonyms and found nothing hinting at her name, her personality or the Hejaz origins she boasted about constantly, but still he asked himself why Tarfah had appeared in his life at this moment in particular, just as he was slowly extricating himself from Thuraya's curse. Why had she only now begun writing to him and trying to get closer to him, when both of them had been around since the website started?

As he stopped by the guards in their sky-blue uniforms outside Entrance Three, Fahd caught sight of a woman, walking with excessive self-confidence and lethal and magnificent composure, swathed in a black *abaya* with a small white bear swaying from a loop on the side of her black handbag. She opened the car door and got in beside him.

'Good evening,' she said shyly, shifting her body and hitching up the lower half of her *abaya*.

Once the car had started moving, she looked at him with alluring eyes. His heart gave an unexpected lurch and he stretched out the fingers of his right hand so they rested between her succulent palms and the cocoon of her own, dark-brown fingers.

'Go right,' she told him and he turned north into the neighbourhood of New Wadi, with its protective cover of darkness that left all living things suspended in mid-air, raucous and honeyed.

Through his laughter he asked her, 'How come you know the backstreets of North Riyadh when you live in Suwaidi?'

She giggled and said that her older sister Asmaa had nick-named her Google and now all her relatives either called her Google or Tarfah.com; even the men of the family, young and old alike, were aware that she knew the lanes, main roads and shops, as though a comprehensive map of the city, its roads, buildings and neighbourhoods, slumbered in her little head.

29

T ARFAH'S VOICE WAS THE same as it had been on the phone, perhaps a little riper and more musical.

It was noon when Fahd first phoned her, anxious and uncertain, and after three rings her drawling voice had come down the line. A woman's voice in every respect: supremely feminine, pleasant and welling with coquetry and refinement. When she spoke it was like a reed flute sounding sadly in an abandoned palm grove. Powerful and fluid, her voice could detonate passion in anyone's heart. It was nothing like the throaty maternal utterances of Thuraya, or Noha's unintelligible mumbling. More than just her voice, it was the warmth and searing honesty of what she said.

From their second phone conversation it seemed to Fahd that they had been friends since childhood. She told him how she had married a relatively unknown actor and separated after two years of suffering and disagreement. He had developed schizophrenia. Before the divorce she had travelled with him to Jeddah, where he forgot to take his medicine and started riding camels and horses on the corniche, screaming dementedly at her, 'Take my picture!'

Back in their room her ex-husband had put on swimming trucks, crooning with furtive delight, 'If only the gold market were lined in silk …' and snatches of famous songs. Pointing from the high window at the swimming pool below, he said, 'I'm going fishing.'

Tarfah was astonishingly warm and bubbly. She stole Fahd's heart and made him feel exceptionally close to her, only rarely asking him questions as she told him of her childhood in Dakhna. She only mentioned her first name. He wanted a family name to feel more at ease, and despite her initial hesitation, she gave to him, making it clear that any similarity with the owners of a well-known commercial centre was pure coincidence. 'Tribesmen!' she called them.

With her chin resting on her fingers, she was beautiful. Her eyes were splendid, defying comparison with Thuraya's Javanese slits, and likewise her tender, angelic voice, utterly dissimilar to the husky tones of the older woman. Even the things they talked about were different. Tarfah spoke like Scheherazade of her life, and that of her family and friends, filling Fahd's heart and memory in the course of single week, while for months on end, Thuraya continued to ask after him and his Jordanian mother, giving him nothing of herself and shielding her life with a man's caution.

He was eager to meet this angelic voice, and he turned his mind to a close comparison of the three: Noha, Thuraya and Tarfah. Which was to be his Mona Lisa? Tarfah of the wide eyes and the beautiful hands that supported her chin like faces in Salvador Dali's paintings, propped on sticks and branches so as not to fall? Was it to be Tarfah's face, burdened with the sorrow of angels, alert and tender and mournful all at once? Would it be Noha with her delicate sidelong glances, snatching fleeting moments to flick out a furtive look from between her Praetorian Guard, single-mindedly marching along the path by the wall of Prince Sultan University? Or Thuraya's face, bewitched by Fahd's, and perspiring with the force of her desire for oblivion?

These were the questions that attended Fahd as he met Tarfah at Le Mall. This time he was prepared for a romantic assignation of a completely different sort: a divorced woman of about his age who shared the same hopes and jokes and cultural references. Her text messages had brought them even closer and encouraged him to leapfrog the standard preliminaries.

When will I see my dear elephant? she asked, to which he mischievously replied, *With the trunk or without?*

The mall was close to the flat and he called her to say he was just setting out.

She whispered down the phone, 'I love you!' and there was the sound of a ringing kiss planted on the mouthpiece. Brazen as always he asked, 'Where does that go?' and she laughed.

'On your mouth, my little lunatic!'

When he arrived he called her. She didn't pick up, but sent a text telling him she was with her brother Ayman and would let him know when she was on her way.

He drove past the mosque in Ghadeer as the sound of the imam chanting the first *rakaa* of the evening prayer swelled from its speakers. He got out and went inside. The smell of Pattex glue filled the mosque's interior and offcuts of new carpeting were scattered about the floor. Prayer, he felt, might summon God's protection from the troubles he faced. *How will He save you and deliver you from sin, O man?*

He left the mosque and returned to the car, his phone ringing ever louder.

'Listen: don't come from direction of the main entrance.'

He stopped and doused the headlights. A few cars were stopped outside the entrance and he took a space by the wall of the Ibn Khaldoun Schools.

'Give me a ring just before you come out,' he told her. 'I'll be outside; it's a blue Hyundai.'

When she called he did a U-turn and stopped right outside the entrance. A young woman emerged, wrapped in an *abaya*, walking steadily, neither hurrying nor dragging her steps. She opened the door and got in: 'Evening.'

She was breathing rapidly, panting, as though she had been sprinting over the gleaming porcelain tiles inside the mall, her high heels rapping at the lamps reflected in the floor like stars.

Fahd noticed her hand: the living image of the one he had seen on Messenger, resting on the keyboard with rare splendour. He reached out his hand and enfolded her long, slender fingers. Raising her hand, he kissed it passionately and she let out a muffled groan.

At the traffic lights next to the mall he turned left down King Abdul Aziz Road, passing the Leen furnished flats, and as he approached the lights by the Panda supermarket in Maseef, he asked, 'Shall we look for somewhere dark and quiet so I can see you?'

Her enchanting eyes watched him from behind her *niqab*. In contrast with her boldness over the phone she hardly said a word. When he asked her, 'Which of these three roads shall I take?' at the Panda lights she pointed with her hand held low, concealing it below the level of the window:

'This way?'

'Why are you pointing in that furtive way?' he asked.

She gave her wonderful laugh. 'My brothers warned me not to lift my hand when I point so people in neighbouring cars don't see it!'

'I don't blame them!' Fahd said mildly through his laughter. 'If you were my sister I'd make you wear black gloves.'

She said that her mother and older brother, Abdullah, had once tried making her wear black gloves so men wouldn't see the naked flesh of her hands, but she had fought back and refused.

She knew the city very well. Perhaps her knowledge of Riyadh's more recent roads and neighbourhoods came from rides with her former lover around the new residential zones of North Riyadh, but she was reluctant to direct him there for fear he would find out about her past adventures, despite the fact that he had said on a number of occasions that he respected her openness and honesty.

After half an hour aimlessly circling Maseef and Murouj she said, 'Go back towards Le Mall.'

So he went back, crossing the traffic lights heading north then turning left into the residential zone where the road twisted round and driving on a little further until they entered the darkness. He looked over at her and she unfastened her head covering. Her face bore the promise of eternal Paradise: round and full with soft cheeks, a small, pretty nose and a mouth that hinted at breathtaking lechery. She would smile and her amazing eyes would become more alluring still. How had her eyes acquired such magic, such splendour?

When he praised her she smiled and taking his hand between hers, kissed his knuckles one by one, then the tip of his thumb, and he felt the dampness of her saliva. Each looked at the other

189

in the same instant, as though her eyes were calling out to him, and he leant towards her, pulling her head over with an audacity that would later amaze him when he remembered it and caressing it with infinite delicacy. He didn't understand how he had been liberated from his old fears and he descended on her passionately until the wheel slipped from his hands and the car veered right and left.

The unlit road came to an end and he emerged on to a brightly illuminated main road. Gathering himself, his attention was caught by a car following behind them. No sooner had it drawn level, than the driver flicked on his headlights.

She laughed. 'That's a well-known signal between us roadside romantics.'

'What do you mean?' he asked.

'Nothing serious. It means, take it easy, you've been busted. Go back to the road we just came out of.'

He turned around and headed north, then took a right, passing a petrol station on his right and a wedding hall on his left. He saw a number of hotels spread out in the darkness.

'Take any road to the right and go into the dark,' she said.

He turned in, proceeding eastwards until the road gave out at a packed earth barrier, giving him the choice of going right or left. He went right, the illuminated hotel buildings and the main road now to his left and switched off the car's lights, leaving the engine running in case of emergency.

She lunged and embraced him, kissing him roughly as she murmured: 'I love you … I love you …'

He returned to the main road. She sat up straight and put her *niqab* over her face. But they weren't silent for a single moment, both of them chattering away, full of joy and the desire to discover one another.

'I forgot to pull your hair!' she said.

He lifted his *shimagh*.

'God knows I've got enough.'

She laughed and said that young men these days aged quickly. They got treatments for their depressing bald spots and took Viagra, and despite it all: nothing. He smiled.

'And what about me, then?'

She unfurled her thumb. 'Like this!' she said then tugged at his hair, screaming, 'Oh God, I love you.'

He asked if women liked baldness, or if it had become fashionable. How else to explain those football players who shaved their hair off with a razor?

He returned to Le Mall.

'Where's the poster of the Klimt painting?' she asked.

Turning behind him he pulled out a sealed cylinder and said, 'Forgive me, sweetheart. I was going to pick out a nice frame, but I didn't like to weigh you down.'

'So what? I'll put it in my room without a frame.'

She pointed. 'Don't drop me at the Basic House entrance. Entrance Two, I mean. Look, Entrance Three is close by.'

After he left her he grabbed a hot mocha and set off, distracted by the echo of her anxious voice asking, 'So, how did you find me?'

30

S AEED WOKE UP AT eight the following evening. He glanced at the clock on the wall opposite. His thoughts drifted to his distant childhood and the days spent in his grandmother's house in Khamees Mushait, recalling that evening five years ago when she had told him the story of his father, Mushabbab.

Mushabbab had taken her and Saeed's mother, Aida, on a trip to perform the *umra*. This was nothing but the flimsiest of pretexts. The goal was to take over the Grand Mosque and proclaim the coming of the Mahdi at the dawn of a new century, rebelling against the government and its troops and awaiting the sally of the infidel horde from Tabuk that God would swallow up into the earth.

Saeed turned his face to the ceiling, knitting his fingers over his forehead, and his ever-active memory started roaming mournfully over the past. Fahd moved on the adjoining bed. His eyes were open and he gave a languorous yawn. 'You look like you've been up for a while,' he mumbled in a muffled voice to Saeed.

Saeed's memories flowed on unchecked as he answered, 'Know something, Fahd? There's this very strange story that took place a couple of months before I was born. I keep thinking about it.'

Fahd snorted, his eyes puffy with sleep. 'Don't tell me you remember everything that happened before you were born!'

Unfazed, Saeed said, 'Seriously, Fahd; my grandmother told it to me, and my mother confirmed it. While I was still in the womb and my father was in prison with Suleiman, my mother got up one morning at dawn to make Arabic coffee for my grandmother: weak coffee without cardamom. While she was busy washing the pot out over the sink her earring fell out and she cried out. My grandmother took fright at the harsh sound. You see, it didn't resemble my mother's voice, or to be exact, it wasn't a voice that came from my mother's throat but the throttled voice of a *jinn*.

'My mother told me that my grandmother became alarmed and got up to help her, the two of them walking slowly towards the coffee room where the tongues of flame were dancing in the pot of coals. She was weeping and groaning and my grandmother was muttering, "What God decrees is good ..." But that morning, my mother sobbed as she told my grandmother that they had killed Mushabbab at dawn, cut off his head with a sword, and as she patted her other earring, the one in her ear, she laid her hand on her belly, crying and repeating over and over: "God preserve my only child!"'

Saeed's body bent at the waist as he propped himself up on his elbow and went on. 'At that very moment your father was in prison, having bid Mushabbab farewell with a final glance as he put on the leather sandals they took turns wearing when one of them went to interrogation. But the sandals didn't return after that final interrogation. There was no interrogation when they woke him on an early spring morning, in the final hours of the night. That night was the only one, your father told me, that he didn't pray the voluntary late night prayer, but slept instead, troubled and ill at ease. As they led him away at that early hour, Mushabbab said, "Don't forget my last wish, Suleiman!" This is what he said as he walked out, without turning round or stopping to say goodbye. That night he felt the chopping block. I was that final wish. I still remember the first time you came with your father to my grandmother's house in Khamees. Do you?'

'I remember you showing off!' Fahd said, smiling.

'I remember you being scared and hiding behind your mother's *abaya* while I strutted around in front of you, acting like I didn't fear a thing. Do you remember me running towards the fig tree in the courtyard, trying to climb it and flashing my skinny legs? After several attempts I remember falling on my back, which made you laugh and brought you out from behind the *abaya*. I still remember those first moments. I remember your father coming, laden with presents and food. God have mercy on your soul, Suleiman!'

He paused briefly.

'You know what, Fahd? Your father was like a man who runs a child over in his car. For years his conscience keeps him up at night, and all the time he's trying to bring some happiness to the little boy he paralysed. It was a rare instance of loyalty on your father's part, and you know there's no such thing as loyalty in this country and its conscience has been asleep for a century.'

Fahd lay there listening.

'I still remember my paternal grandfather's death five years ago. Can you believe that a retired army general, a man who led a battalion in the Yemen war, defending the southern pass into the country tooth and nail, died at home like an old dog, forcibly ejected from Khamees Hospital to free up a bed? Think of him vomiting up blood while myself, my two uncles and my relatives looked on. No one cared. How could they, when they were busy separating those twins who had been brought here from the ends of the earth to have their photos taken and splashed on the front covers of local newspapers beneath the headline *Medical Miracles*. How could this happen to my grandfather, whose bones had been rattled by whining bullets in the seventies, who was almost killed by a stray round, but could find no one to tend and care for him?'

Fahd turned on his right side and peered at Saeed, who had fallen silent for a moment, staring at the ceiling.

'If my grandfather had twins, my father and my uncle I mean, shouldn't the government have taken care of him?'

Fahd gave a noisy laugh and said slyly, 'But they were local twins. They don't count: you have to be a foreigner. Unless your father's eyes were blue, that is, that might work. It's so our country becomes global and can pass on its scientific achievements to all the countries of the world.'

Saeed sat up in bed.

'Anyway, it's nine already. That was a nap and a half. Shall we get some fresh air in Tahliya?'

Fahd lifted his silenced phone from the table between the two beds and looked at the screen. There were seven messages waiting for him. Alarmed, he said, 'Seven messages. Some good morning that is.'

Saeed cackled from the flat's only bathroom. 'What do you mean, morning? People are getting ready to go to bed.'

When he emerged, a nervous Fahd played him one of the messages:

'So you're not happy with me, as you put it ... Well, some day I'll settle my account with you ... It'll be savage, because I'm out of my mind and wounded and betrayed and I'm sure you know what happens to a woman when she feels betrayed ... She becomes a lion!'

'Who's that?' said Saeed anxiously. 'Don't tell me it's the Hejaz one?'

Fahd nodded his head.

31

A S FAHD CLIMBED INTO the Committee's vehicle that morning he wondered whether Thuraya was behind what had happened. On several occasions she had threatened to take her revenge if he didn't respond to her desires. Had she reported the sea-blue Hyundai Accent? Had she told them that it was a car like a blue wave adrift in an arid desert? Had she taken down the number plate when she came out of the entrance of Iman Hospital that time, or as she left the World of Dreams hair salon? Had Tarfah's old boyfriend wanted to revenge himself on her and been stalking her, his mind filled with suspicion? Had it been the uncle who hated him and thought of him as a shameless sinner?

He often thought of his arrest as he walked out alone along Great Yarmouth's sandy shoreline and saw the lovers stretched out beneath the little bushes, whispering together, or embracing, still as stones, for hours on end. How hard it was for him to recall a passage from one of the three books his father had left behind in his bag, which discussed the societies of the *jahiliya*. The passage described how the writers, journalists and novelists in these societies openly told their young women and wives that … *there is nothing morally repugnant about conducting free relations. Immorality is when a young man deceives his girlfriend or a young woman her boyfriend and does not keep her affection solely for him. Indeed, it is immoral for a wife to remain celibate once desire for her husband has died down, and virtue is when she seeks out a friend to whom she can safely entrust her body! There are dozens of stories with this message at their core and hundreds of educational programmes, cartoons, jokes and comedies that promote it...*

Had the hand that drew the wavering blue line beneath these words in *Milestones* really been shaking as it seemed? Was it his father's hand? Was it some sign, something his father wanted to keep before him at all times? Was it really some precocious and successful attempt at prophecy?

In recent days Fahd had opened the leather satchel, stuffed with documents and diaries, stories and memories, specialist books and picture books, secret pamphlets, pens, the olive stone prayer beads and a picture—how it had been taken and by whom he had no idea—showing his father and fellow inmates in the prison yard. These mementoes of his father had yet to claim his attention, with the exception of the green volume, a black line across the middle of the cover and on the first page a title in *thulathi* script that read *Milestones* with the name *Sayyid Qutb* in beautiful *farsi* typeface in the top right corner, then the words *Dar Dimashq Publishing*. The handwriting inside was in his father's hand, notes in the margins written long ago.

Back then his father, or perhaps just the author, believed that all societies existed in *jahiliya*, a state of godless ignorance, and were either ... *atheistic communist societies, pagan societies in India, Japan, the Philippines and Africa, or Christian and Jewish societies that followed their deviant creeds.*

Within this definition of *jahiliya* societies he included those that professed to be Muslim, but in fact submitted to an authority other than God. It was as though the words in the book Fahd leafed through were being uttered by his cousin

Yasser. Was this the well from which his father, his uncle and Yasser had all drunk? The common source for all those that followed the call to wage war on society, to the extent that some of them abandoned their normal lives and took up residence in ghettos for their kind?

Haraa Sharqiya on the outskirts of Mecca, the neighbourhood where the families of the Divine Reward Salafist Group lived, was little more than a chaotic assemblage of houses and buildings, between which ran exceptionally narrow alleys like cattle pens, scarcely wide enough for two people to pass at the same time. Their homes were ferro concrete structures with three doors. The rear entrance of each house led directly to the front door of the house behind it, and was commonly used by the women to meet, hold whispered conversations and swap favours and cooking ingredients—they were also the doors through which many of them fled during the raids carried out by the security services shortly before the occupation of the Grand Mosque.

Suleiman al-Safeelawi was brave and reckless, returning at night with rare courage to a neighbourhood under surveillance and making his way inside via the back door that opened on to the whip-thin alleyway, to rescue his bag containing his proofs of identity—his ID documents and certificates from primary and secondary school—before slipping away while the detectives and soldiers stood watch over the front doors.

He could hear his own heart thudding as he crept to the house of the group's leader, silent as a butterfly as he passed through the darkness to the men's *majlis* where he slept at night, to find his bedding folded up as he had left it and beside it his black leather satchel. He picked it up without opening it and, fleeing to the cattle pen behind the house, made his way out of the sprawling district, most of whose modest dwellings housed members of the group—Brothers as they called themselves—along with a few students from the Islamic University.

That moment, back at the time of the second wave of arrests and now sunk in dread and silence and forgetting, did not permanently distance young Suleiman from the group. Even so, he began to attend lessons with the blind sheikh at Imam Mosque in Deira in the company of a young man of a similar age, before being joined by a third student, then a fourth. The group's military commander sent a messenger to warn against keeping company with government sheikhs lest they draw attention to themselves, unaware that the young men had grown impatient with the group and its impetuosity. Nevertheless, when Suleiman met Mushabbab that afternoon outside the Kutub Watania publishing house he almost flew with joy to learn that the leader was asking after him and expected him to arrive on the tenth of Ramadan; joy, because the leader's eye only singled people out if he had confidence in them, when their abilities and talents set them apart from the rest.

So Suleiman travelled to see him at a farm in the village of Ammar, west of Riyadh, where some of the Brothers were gathered. The leader took him by the hand and led him to a long narrow room like a corridor and showed him the red string onion bags packed with yellow pamphlets that bore the title of his first message to the *umma*: *Correcting Confusion over the Faith of he whom God Has Made Imam over All People*. It was only once Suleiman had driven the bags to their destination that he actually read the contents of this message, at a little house in Mecca, where the leader of the Meccan Brothers, entrusted with handing out the pamphlets in the Grand Mosque, was staying. It was the night of the twenty-seventh of Ramadan.

That first message, sent fluttering into the skies over Mecca, Riyadh, Ta'if and Qaseem by Suleiman and his zealous companions, made reference to part of a prophetic *hadith* that contained the following saying of the Prophet, upon him be the blessings and peace of God: 'The religion of God shall only be established by he who is secured on all sides.'

Or, as the pamphlet explained: *The story of this hadith, for whose sake we have come to divide ourselves into groups, is that the need to keep aloof from those who deny the oneness of God, to expose their enmity and cleave to the truth, was seen by some as an embarrassment and a hardship, an obstacle to spreading the faith that repelled the common people. Some were lax in applying this principle, while others abandoned it entirely. But we say that it is not as they believed, for God has lifted the embarrassment from us and adjured us to this principle, for if there were any embarrassment in it he would not have so commanded us. Listen to His exalted words:*

'And strive in His cause as you ought to strive. He has chosen you, and has imposed no difficulties on you in religion; it is the faith of your father, Abraham. It is He who named you Muslims, both before and in this revelation; that the Messenger may be a witness for you.'

If God Himself has commanded us to strive and made it clear to us that there is no embarrassment in it, and that this is the faith of Abraham, then know that adherence to this principle—striving and following the faith of Abraham—is what sets the true Muslim apart from the pretender.

And so in their eyes all people were pretenders and hypocrites, and it was their duty to exhort them, unembarrassed, to wash their hands of those who denied God's oneness, for if they did not, they were of them. The faith was not to be established through sycophancy and silence but by cleaving to the truth and forbearance in the face of suffering.

The initial wave of arrests sent Suleiman fleeing into the desert in the company of the group's leader, the two of them wandering the wastes for two weeks living on lizards captured in their burrows. Forty days later, after most of the group's members had been released from prison and after the second wave of arrests prior to the assault on the Grand Mosque, Suleiman decided that things were now in deadly earnest. No longer was this a matter of a pellet gun puncturing the heart of a loudspeaker, as his brother had done in Muraidasiya, nor was it a handful of boys demonstrating outside the governor's palace in Buraida. It had gone beyond mere jail terms: they now faced execution by the sword.

So Suleiman began to shun the group. Like black hawks, accusations of neglecting his duty to the cause eventually caught up with him, but he had vanished from sight, returning to a tiny burrow in Umm Sulaym before deciding to escape to Buraida. He would never leave again, he decided; he would be buried there. That was before the two security agents took him away from the Jurida marketplace to lose four years of his youth in a cold-walled prison. Yet this was certainly more forgiving than standing in Justice Square, waiting for the rattle of a sharp sword.

And so Suleiman's fear saved him. He did not join the Brothers in their assault on the Grand Mosque at dawn on the first of Muharram, the first day of the fourteenth century after the Prophet's flight.

32

T HE NEXT TIME AROUND Fahd set the alarm on his phone to six o'clock, but only came to when he heard Saeed's shout beside him, as though issuing from the depths of a cave.

'Your mother called on the landline. She says your mobile's off.'

Fahd quickly washed his face, put on his robe and throwing his headscarf over his shoulder said, 'I'm late, I've got an urgent appointment. If she calls, say I have a meeting at the university.'

Before closing the door he looked back in. 'Saeed! Tell her I've gone to enrol in a summer course.'

'It's almost sunset, you lunatic!' Saeed shouted. 'What university?'

He shut the door behind him, started the car and set out for Granada Centre in East Riyadh, towards the heavenly face of his beloved, the face that had shaken his weak and ever-eager heart to the core.

Switching on his mobile, he found three messages.

From Lulua: *Mother's asking for you. Where are you?*

From Thuraya: *All I ask is a word, to say you're mine and you miss me. Answer me, Syrian!*

From Tarfah: *Where are you? I've been waiting an hour for your call. Shall I head out? It's a long journey from Suwaidi, sweetheart.*

He called Tarfah and told her to set off. 'Sorry baby, I overslept.'

'So, shall I bring anything?' she asked with delicious playfulness.

When he burst out laughing she cut him off. 'No, really. What do you long for most?'

'Your heart!' he replied passionately.

'Trickster. Hustler,' she cried in exasperation. 'You leave me no way out.'

'Your mouth, then.'

She sighed deeply and contentedly. 'Now I believe you.'

When he started the car Rashed al-Majed was singing *Oh, Don't Keep Me from Him!* on MBC FM and he thought of Noha, her tears and her choked and hesitant voice. He stopped at a petrol station and asked the attendant to fill his tank while he rushed into the little shop and bought a box of *Fine* tissues and a couple of bottles of water picked from the back of the refrigerator.

Tarfah described the different entrances to the vast Granada Mall: 'Come to Entrance Two. Turn in off the Eastern Ring Road and it's next to Dr Keif. You'll see the main entrance in front of you with a picture of Marah Oasis hanging over it.'

'I know the Extra Café at the end on the left,' he replied. 'Is it before that?'

'Well, of course it is, and before Paris Gallery. I'm not talking about Entrance One, OK? That's the one by Costa Coffee and Espresso. I'm talking about Entrance Two. You turn in off theEastern Ring Road and if you look right you'll see Dr Keif. The entrance right next to it.'

As he turned at the traffic lights at the Imam Street exit he looked left and saw the green Dr Keif sign. It was nearly eight o'clock. He took a right, then another at the small roundabout facing the main entrance. Passing Entrance Two he saw that it really was a forgotten spot: nobody was about.

He called her before he stopped the car and she answered eagerly. 'Where are you?'

She had gone in via the main entrance then headed into the VaVaVoom Beauty Salon, walking out again a few minutes later and going for a wander that took her past the family section of Starbucks, where she ordered two small cappuccinos. She walked to the main hall and turned right as if towards the up escalator, but marched straight past it in the direction of Etam. Her black bag swinging, she emerged from Entrance Two.

He took the Starbucks cups from her and slowly moved off. He asked her about the unusually heavy crowds around the main entrance.

'Maybe because it's a Wednesday,' she said.

They crossed the small roundabout and doubling back to escape the congestion around the mall, headed out to the highway.

Two days earlier, she said, she had gone with her family to an event at a hotel along Qaseem Road in a part of town full of vast building developments, hotels and small farms. She fell silent then suggested they go there. He drove on, past the petrol station on the Medina Road and past Musafir Café and Half Moon Café, then as Yamama College came up on the left he turned right off Quwa al-Amn Bridge and they entered the moonlit night. There were high, long walls with massive locked gates.

'If only we could go inside one!' he whispered.

'All this sky to ourselves and you're looking for walls?'

The car crested a rise heading east and descended. To his right he saw a small tarmacked road into which he turned without noticing the barbed wire and open steel gate at its entrance.

'I don't know this place,' she said, cheerful as ever, 'so I'm not responsible for it!'

'Should I go back?' he asked her nervously.

She smiled. 'No, keep going!'

It was a very narrow, tarmacked farm road, just wide enough for a single vehicle. On the left sat a small cabin, a yellow lamp suspended from a cable over its door, and next to it a white tent and concrete latrine. Beside them was parked an ancient and dilapidated Hilux pick-up that looked as if it hadn't been driven in a long time.

A kilometre and a half further on, the road ran out at a barrier of packed soil. A right-hand fork led to a muddy open space. There was a large piece of agricultural machinery for extracting well water and what appeared to be towering walls of dried alfalfa bales. The tarmac curved to the left and he followed it round until he came to yet another left turn that looked as though it returned to the highway.

'You're going back to the main road!' she said.

'We'll stop here.'

He found a track cutting across a field of alfalfa and drove in. He switched off the lights and the engine and an awful silence descended. He raised the armrest between them and pressed her to him, breathing in the perfume on her neck. Gasping, she pulled him towards the foot space beneath her. The smell of the fields came in through the windows, a sudden breeze pushing the scent of the purple alfalfa between them. The fragrance was strongest as they reached their peak.

He plucked out some tissues, handed her the box, opened the door and poured water from a small bottle.

He got to his feet and bared his chest to the mild breeze. Up on the highway the trucks' headlights moved slowly and steadily.

'You like the field!' she teased. 'You know, I don't like fields.'

He laughed as he canted the last drop of water from the bottle. 'What field? You mean your field?'

'Idiot!' she drawled, her voice languid and embarrassed.

He told her that the sky here had its own fragrance, that the crescent moon being wooed by a star above them was waiting for her to perch on one of its points like a child, her legs dangling down: an image inspired by some place or picture he had seen.

She laughed. 'Seems the artist inside you has woken up!' she said. 'But there's not much for you to work with: no morning, no light, no harvesting women with sickles in their hands.'

'Tarfah!' he cried suddenly. 'I've just had the most wonderful idea for a picture: a couple making love in a field beneath a rustic straw awning. I'll call it *The Lovers*. What do you think?'

Then he remembered Van Gogh's painting of the peasants resting at noon in the shade of a haystack.

He got in.

'Shall we go?' he asked.

She was trying to wind her *abaya* about herself and muttering, 'I seem to have put it on wrong.'

He turned away from the door. She was gazing intensely at him, gratitude in her extraordinary eyes, and a tentative smile forming on her face. He kissed her forehead and she pulled his face towards her and kissed him on the nose.

She urged him to get going so that she wouldn't be late for her brother at the mall. He started the car and turned the wheel. Instead of taking the left that would lead them past the cabin with the lamp, through the gate and on to the highway, he went right, guessing that this road ran parallel to the one that brought them here. There was no need for them to go back the same way.

At first the road was good, then the smooth surface gave out abruptly on to a track through the fields, two straight lines, evidence of where cars had gone before. The crops were high but he decided to risk it and pressed on at a moderate pace so as not to get stuck and sink into the soil or sand. Suddenly the field ended and he emerged on to a bumpy track. Concerned that the car might stall he kept going. Then he realised they were on the wrong road. Tarfah, who had been enjoying his devil-may-care approach, began to show signs of anxiety.

'Why don't you go back to the other road?'

After a few minutes spent circling around, lost and panicking, he said, 'I don't think I can find it.'

He parked the car on a patch of firm and level ground and looked over at the nearby road and the barbed wire. His heart beat faster.

'Take this road,' she told him. 'We came from here.'

And though he knew she was pointing in the wrong direction he did as she suggested, telling himself that her encyclopaedic knowledge of Riyadh's roadmap must cover even this wilderness. All of sudden he found their way blocked by a vast expanse of ploughed earth and coming to a halt next to the huge furrows he slipped the car into reverse and stepped on the accelerator. The rear wheels spun but the car stayed where it was.

'We're stuck.'

He tried again, pressing harder on the accelerator and the car sank deeper. Getting out he bent over the rear tyre. When he touched the soil it was soft as paste. *Damn.* What was going on?

He glanced at her face. She seemed pensive. Was it fear that rendered her speechless or confidence that they would get free? Did she expect him to blame her for getting them into this situation? His first thought was how to get her out of here, how to return her to her brother now they were stuck in some remote agricultural area fenced in by barbed wire. Then again, how was he going to free his car from this trap?

Terrifying scenarios began wheeling through his head. What if he walked to the highway and flagged down a car?

The car stops; the driver is bearded. He's suspicious—some guy hanging about in the middle of nowhere with a frightened girl—but he seems concerned and pulls over.

'You go back to your sister and I'll find a shovel so we can clear the earth around the car.'

He moves away and conducts a whispered conversation on his mobile. Is he calling the police? The men from the Committee? Either would cause a scandal beyond Fahd's worst nightmares.

'Let's dig!' declares the man, his eyes on the road. Damn him; he's waiting for one of Committee's SUVs.

He'll see it signalling with its brights from a distance, then two men will approach and take Fahd to one side, calm and reassuring: 'Who's that with you? Don't be scared: just tell us. If you're honest with us we'll make sure you're OK.'

He admits that she's his girlfriend. They question her and suddenly she bursts into tears.

Those wonderful eyes; how can they shed tears?

His feverish contemplation was interrupted by Tarfah.

'Why don't I call my friend Nada? Get her to send her driver?'

'It's an idea … At least I'd be able to concentrate on getting my car out without having you on my conscience.'

'You mean you wouldn't come with me?' she said, her eyes welling. 'I have to go with the driver on my own? Perhaps you could come with me to the mall,' she added. 'Find someone to tow your car.'

He cleared some of the soft earth from behind the rear wheels then returned to the driver's seat. 'Have you called her?'

'She's not answering!' replied Tarfah dejectedly.

'Her phone's switched off?'

She gazed out at the furrowed horizon. 'No, it's on. She's just not picking up. Perhaps she's asleep.'

Leaving his door open he tried pressing gently on the accelerator and leant his head out to watch the wheels. The car moved a couple of metres backwards then the wheels spun in place, digging into the dusty ground.

Tarfah's mobile rang and she picked it up, thinking that maybe Nada had noticed her missed calls. But when she looked at the screen, blinking on and off in the darkness, her face fell and she didn't answer. 'What does he want now?' she spat.

'Who is it?' asked Fahd nervously.

'My brother, Ayman.'

'If you come back to the mall with me,' she said, 'I could tell Ayman that you're a brother of one of my friends and that you need help. What do you think?'

He breathed deeply and went back to digging. His heart began to beat faster; his white robe was smeared with dust.

He noticed a gaping hole next to where he was digging in the dark.

What if a huge snake suddenly slithered out from that burrow and bit him while they were all alone in the middle of nowhere?

Then he noticed the place was full of burrows. This city was all burrows—burrows upon burrows—and you never knew which burrow would swallow you up next.

With the long nail on his little finger he squeezed the valves on the rear tyres and the air rushed out. Deflated tyres gripped better in sand. He set the car in reverse: a metre backwards then the wheels spun again.

What was this? Was this the curse of Thuraya, with her fever-ish, miserable messages? She had already threatened to expose him as an artist who led women astray. Was it his mother's, from whom he had fled and failed to call? Perhaps her health had reached breaking point and she needed his help.

He was about to open his mouth for the thousandth time to tell Tarfah, 'I was worried about this ploughed land; it's cursed for sure!'

Suddenly he stopped. If he walked into the field now he would never return.

He asked her about Nada. 'She answered yet?'

'I sent her a message,' she replied in a soft voice, low with fear.

He stripped off his robe. His body had begun to sweat. A short while before this body had delighted in the paradise of alfalfa blooms as it gazed at the smiling, playful moon. Now the field had become a ploughed wasteland, empty and deso-late, and the moon the brow of a wrathful demon gazing down gloating and mocking at a puny, isolated, powerless human being trying to extricate himself from disaster.

As he dug away and smoothed the ground behind the car her phone suddenly rang. It was her brother and she didn't answer. Fahd tried to shift the car again, opening the door and watching the wheels as he repeated, 'Oh God, oh God,' over and over. The car moved a further two metres and sank again. This time, he felt despair take hold.

Her phone rang and she answered, smiling.

'Listen, I'm in this place miles away. Get your driver to take Qaseem Road to Quwa al-Amn Bridge. He takes a right at the flyover then goes straight until he sees lights from a car.'

She fell silent and listened. 'I'll tell you later. Now's not the time.'

Nada must have asked her what she was doing there.

By his efforts he had succeeded in moving the car backwards a total of seven metres.

'I'm going to try going forwards,' he said to Tarfah. 'If the car gets free I'll turn right and drive off.'

He put the car into first gear then stepped on the accelerator, wrenching the wheel left and right and screaming in English, action-movie style, 'Come on! *Come on!*' It moved slowly, then surged and he pulled the wheel to the right, straightening out and rocketing towards the highway like a lunatic until he reached the field of harvested alfalfa, where he proceeded calmly along the firm ground at its edge, unable to believe that they had escaped.

'O wholesome harvest girls!' he bellowed. 'How great thy charity, harvesting this crop that I might proceed along the path to deliverance …'

And Tarfah, aping his pomposity with magnificent derision, cried, 'What ails thee, Abu Jahl?'

33

T HE WHITE PICK-UP TRUCK, stuck in the sand a quarter
of a century before, on 30 July 1979, was nothing like
the sea-blue Hyundai that Fahd drove with Tarfah beside
him. In this vehicle sat a man, his *shimagh* wrapped into a
filthy red-and-white checked turban around his head, driving like a lunatic through the dark of the night to escape the
border guards, now dousing the headlights and proceeding on
instinct, now guided by the light of his passenger's small flash-
light that prevented the guards tracking their Datsun. They
were waiting for gunshots to catch them from the rear but the
onslaught of the demented sand was swifter than any bullet; it
held them firm, the pick-up's lights suddenly froze and they
fled in opposite directions, each man panting as he laboured
to pluck his feet from the sand's snare.

The passenger got furthest and when he heard the sound of
the border guards' pursuing vehicles and the powerful lamps
begin sweeping the desert in search of them, he ran for the
cover of a small and straggling *ramth* bush and lay still, his heart
straining. He was like a bird grazed by a rifle, that flees flapping its one good wing, bleeding and hopping as it hunts for
the shade of a tree or rock to hide from the hunter's gaze.

The guards stopped their vehicle by the pick-up in the soft,
paste-like sands. Their voices were strident in the night and
the searchlights' beams wandered about like cudgels cocked

over bare flesh. They fanned out in three directions, away from the route they had come, and like swords drawn for the kill, four beams of light circled the desert.

The passenger trembled, hiding his head between the branches to appear like a tarpaulin abandoned in the scorching midday heat, but the light fell suddenly into his gleaming eyes and one of the guards cried out to his companions: 'It's him.'

Pointing a pistol at him, the guard shouted for him to get up with his hands behind his neck. Exhausted, his face filthy and holding his hands behind his neck, he rose to his feet. One of the guards came up behind him, patted his pockets, and securing handcuffs around his left wrist first, then his right, he steered the man away. A few minutes later they had found the other man and they took them both back, together with their truck, to the Ruqai Centre on the border with Kuwait.

The pick-up was impounded with seven other trucks, their loads concealed beneath green tarpaulins held in place with ropes wound round the brackets on the vehicles' sides. After stepping forward with two other officers and cautiously uncovering one of the trucks, the border centre's commander ordered the detention of the drivers and their passengers.

They were carrying stacked bundles of small pink pamphlets, on their covers the title: *An Address on the Subject of the Emirate and the Swearing of Fealty and Obedience, and a Judgment on the Duplicity of the Rulers towards the Scholars and the Common People, and the Proper Position with regards to the Rulers in Particular, and People in General.*

The duty commander at the border post sat at his desk, a copy of the pamphlet in his hand. He leafed through it rapidly, reading some of the Qur'anic verses and *hadith*, the first of which was Ibada Bin al-Samit's report of their pledge of allegiance to the Prophet on the grounds that '… we must speak the truth wheresoever we be, for we are with God and so fear not the censure of critics.' Flipping the pages with his thumb he read out loud to the two officers:

> *Know that some of those who fawn over kings and rulers excuse themselves by pointing to the* hadith *recorded in the Sahih Muslim, when a man addressed the Prophet, saying, 'O Prophet of God have you not perceived that when princes are set over us they look to their own rights and deny us ours? What do you command us to do?'*
>
> *To which the Prophet replied, 'Hearken: they must bear their burden and you, yours.'*
>
> *But this furnishes them with no excuse, for the* hadith *is concerned with rights of the individual: the rulers' monopolisation of booty and plunder and the like. Religion is not one of the rights of an individual, where forbearance in the face of preferential treatment is urged. In the* hadith *the man says, '… and they deny us our rights,' but when the right is that of God, then no: the duty then is to reject the legitimacy of those who fail to implement God's law.*

The commander tossed the pamphlet to one end of the table.

'God preserve us!' said one of the officers. 'That's outright sedition!'

The commander nodded his head in agreement. 'Planning a coup, it seems.'

The third officer remained silent, averting his eyes from the others. Then he excused himself and left the office.

Seven impounded vehicles in a military post on the Kuwait border, were laden with vast quantities of pamphlets churned out by the Vanguard printing presses in Kuwait and destined for remote villages and farms around Riyadh and Mecca, where they would be handed out to members of the group who, with precisely coordinated and pre-arranged timing, would distribute them through major urban centres such as Mecca, Riyadh, Qaseem and Ha'il.

Suleiman led his own small group, delegating tasks with the spirit of a practised leader of men, his abundant vigour some-times beguiling other worshippers into helping his compan-ions and himself distribute the booklets, blissfully unaware of the incitement they contained against the government and what they termed *jahili* society.

Seven years later, by a strange twist of fate, Suleiman al-Safeelawi was transformed from a distributor of clandestine literature into a distributor of newspapers for a major company.

He had descended ravenously on newspapers after being denied them during his first period of incarceration. He had often thought of writing his memoirs in prison, believing his time as a member of the Salafist Group had been far superior to the childhood memories recorded by Taha Hussein in *The Days*. Yet despite his love of reading, his writing and his powers of description, metaphor and composition were no match for the great wordsmith. It was as though the *Alfiyya* marked the division between reading for pleasure and enforced study.

Running from Ibn Malik, he had fallen, seduced and thrilled, for Sayyid Qutb, al-Albani and Hamoud al-Tuwaijri, and then, having emerged from prison, taken a job at the newspaper distribution company, married and enrolled at King Abdul Aziz University, he sequestered himself away with a new series of books, dividing his time between classical

Islamic works such as *The Unique Necklace*, *The Book of Animals* and *The Delicacies of the Caliphs and the Jests of the Refined*, and the Russian classics, getting hold of Dostoyevsky's complete works. *Crime and Punishment*, *The Idiot*, *The Adolescent* and *The Brothers Karamazov* transported him to another world, far from petty doctrinal quarrels.

After he had been promoted and his street level wanderings were behind him he would read all the time, even during office hours. At home, he would steal an hour to himself after sunset, though he still maintained his habit of dropping everything half an hour before the daylight disappeared and driving westwards over Urouba Bridge. It was as if he needed to satisfy himself that the sun had gone down to its resting place, as if he wanted to remember that distant sunrise over Jurida Square, when they escorted him away to be interrogated and from there to a series of long and arduous adventures in prison.

34

JUST BEFORE SUNSET THAMAMA Road was relatively crowded, the ice cream vans scattered eye-catchingly either side of the road as Fahd drove along, suffering beneath the yellow disc of the sun.

Every sunrise and sunset that passed before Fahd's eyes wrung his heart and reminded him of his father on that final morning, a memory that led him back to thoughts of his two uncles and Yasser. He remembered his childhood, when his uncle took them all to a nearby farm to learn to swim. The pond was deep and shaded by the tops of tall palms and verdant trees. His uncle said that swimming in shady water would strengthen their young hearts, as if he intended to turn them into black rocks, unbreakable and incapable of bringing light to the world.

Whenever Fahd thought of them he wished that one day they would all go on a trip together and that the family car would swerve and flip over repeatedly or smash into a stray camel crossing the road, leaving no one alive. How wonderful it would be to celebrate their deaths! Of course, nobody's death should be a matter of celebration, even those they called 'infidels', the ones al-Qaeda slaughter like sheep. The time he had opened a video clip on an Islamic website to find members of al-Qaeda butchering a terrified foreigner had terrified him and left him nauseous and he had fasted for a whole week.

He sometimes felt that those around him were the true heirs of al-Qaeda. The only difference was that out there they first trained in arms and laid waste to the West, then turned their attention to their own homelands, claiming they were in thrall to the infidel. In Riyadh and Qaseem, meanwhile, they merely supported their deeds and cheered.

Fahd still remembered September 11. He was in Bassam on Ulaya Street looking for a cheap microwave oven and the televisions were aglow. His attention was drawn by a group of middle-aged men gathering to stand astonished in front of the screens, watching the aircraft as they detonated into the twin towers of the World Trade Center. Three of the men were applauding gleefully. Two were clean-shaven and the third had a slight beard and they clapped as though following a video game or some movie where good triumphs over evil. Later, Fahd would think of them and ask himself: where are those joyful men now? Were they amongst those who blew up the Muhiya Compound or the Hamra Oasis Village? The Civil Affairs building in Riyadh, perhaps? Are they in Iraq? Were they amongst those who joined the Fatah al-Islam Brigade in northern Lebanon, their corpses sprawled out in the Nahr al-Bared refugee camp?

It terrified him to think that people here were in crisis, hostile to anything advocating progress. When you explained that progress was the inescapable destiny of all things, then talked to them of their errors—from their rejection of the telegram and the radio on the grounds that they were sorcery and devilry, to their refusal to accept television and women's education, to their repudiation of the latest innovations such as identity cards for women—they would shut you up, using force if necessary. They would end the debate on the grounds that your faith was weak and your doctrine unsound and then, without any hesitation, inform you that you were a secularist preaching degeneracy or a filthy liberal, maybe growing aggressive enough to declare you an apostate whose killing was permissible by law.

He still remembered that episode of *The Other Direction*, a programme he sometimes watched despite hating it for being contrived. On one side of the debate was Sayyid al-Qamani, who opined that there was no democracy anywhere in Islamic history. How could there be, when the Emirate of the Muslims passed from one Caliph to another by means of poisoned dagger or cup? The other guest wore a turban and was called al-Sebaei. Provoked, he roundly abused al-Qamani, describing him as a monkey and an apostate from religion, and all this live on air in front of millions.

The speed monitor began to tick steadily as Fahd exceeded 120 kilometres per hour. He decelerated and his attention was caught by an Egyptian labourer at the side of the road, who was setting out upturned chrome bowls along a board lying across the tops of four barrels. Next to him was a camel pen surrounded by barbed wire and a gaggle of motorists handing over the price of a bowlful of fresh milk. He would squeeze out a bowl in front of them and they would gulp the milk down until the foam filled their noses and covered their moustaches, then continue on their way, belching as they inserted a tape of Islamic songs hymning the former glories of the Muslim world and extolling the Kalashnikov, the grave and the life hereafter.

Summer had begun, he supposed. Ice cream vans were scattered about, along with sellers of Wadi melons, pomegranates from Ta'if and dates and milk from Qaseem. People straggled down both sides of Thamama Road into the early hours, searching for a cool breeze in the Nejd nights whose like was to be found nowhere else in the world.

His mobile rang and it was Tarfah, promising to wait for him. He had assumed that she was at Granada Mall but she said she would wait for him at a clinic. 'When you get to Abraj Street call me, and I'll come to you.'

He was returning from a weekend place belonging to friends and had taken Abraj Street heading south in the direction of the Knowledge Clinic where Tarfah was waiting. He drove past it, then turned right down a side street as she had requested, so the people by the door and the receptionist wouldn't notice that she had got out of one car (her brother Ayman's) and left in another.

She got in and they set off for Quds then doubled back to the eastern extension of King Abdul Aziz Road. When he reached the traffic lights by Jarir, his face to the east, she signalled to him, her finger concealed from the eyes of other motorists, that he should turn back in the opposite direction. He turned, driving past Panda then Jarir, and they took the southbound Eastern Ring Road.

On their left, in Quds and Roda, they noticed a number of furnished flats on offer, and picking a complex, Fahd parked the sea-blue Hyundai outside the entrance as the street filled with people emerging from the sunset prayer.

From the glove compartment he took out a folded copy of a forged marriage certificate that Saeed had procured for him that day: 'This is for you to use in emergencies!' The Sudanese receptionist pretended to inspect it without moving his eyes from a card game on his computer screen. The price of an apartment was 250 riyals, he said. Fahd handed him the money and he began to enter their details, continuing to click on the mouse and move cards across the screen as though locked in a life or death struggle for victory.

'Go and get your luggage,' he said, desperate to carry on with his game.

'I don't have any,' Fahd said. 'We've only come for a wedding in Riyadh.'

The receptionist returned the certificate and handed him the key to the flat. Fahd went back to the car then they went together into the lift, embracing passionately as he said apologetically, 'Sorry sweetheart, there are no lights in furnished flats!'

She laughed out loud as he opened the door and they crept into flat 101. Like any nosy woman she headed for the kitchen and opened the cupboards, then the fridge, and inspected the dark brown sofas in the living room.

They went to the bedroom. She removed her *abaya*, revealing her uncovered shoulders and gave her familiar smile, that delicious grin both coy and impudent. Her hair was soft and her breasts were alive with anticipation; part of her bra was visible, an elastic strap covered in striped red satin. As always she rushed to his mouth, devouring it hungrily as she pulled off his *shimagh* and whispered, 'That's better!' then let out an unexpected laugh as she threw her body on to the bed.

He asked her why she had laughed and she turned her face away, 'It's nothing!' and busied herself with stroking his chest. He stopped her. Taken aback, he asked her why she had laughed like that. He remembered Thuraya, who as he departed after their first meeting had told him that he looked funny naked, scampering into the bathroom like a rat making for a drain!

He felt unexpectedly irritated. His mood clouded as he insisted she tell him. She laughed and explained that she was too embarrassed to say. Summoning a strained smile he coaxed her to speak.

'I'm worried you'll be angry,' she said.

He hugged her, kissing her neck and earlobe and whispering, 'How could I be cross with my Taroufi?'

'My friend Nada saw a picture of you on the forum standing next to one of your pictures at a group exhibition ...' She roared with laughter, her hand clamped over her mouth, and said, 'I can't ... I can't ... Fahd, please don't embarrass me ...'

'Come on!' he said impatiently. 'Tell the story!'

Still laughing, Tarfah told him that Nada had said that he had looked ridiculous standing next to the website's owner; his pale skin, red hair and *shimagh* had made him look like one of the *darfours* in the Lipton Tea adverts: a whitey. He frowned slightly, and laughed to humour her. Why *darfour*? How had the word first found its way to this racist society? If you came from the Eastern Mediterranean, that's what they called you. They had said it to him at school when he was little, even though his father was Saudi, he had Saudi nationality and he had been born here. The teachers at Al-Ahnaf Bin Qais Primary referred to him as 'son of the Jordanian woman', as though he didn't have a name. Even the website's owner, whom he took to be a cultured man, had once referred to the fact that his mother wasn't Saudi.

'You know,' he'd said offhandedly, 'you can tell you're half-grilled from your red hair.'

Fahd sat up all night thinking about the phrase 'half-grilled'.

'Damn it! Was he trying to say that I'm not fully Saudi? Why would he talk about me as if I were a lump of cooked meat? Or did he mean that the sun hadn't tanned my face properly, that I hadn't been seared brown by the heat of the Nejd or the desert and my hair turned black as night?'

He could still recall the decision he had taken in the summer holidays before starting secondary school to dye his hair, angering his mother who said, 'Ever since you grew up your heart's been dyed black!'

How he had hated her at that moment.

Tarfah threw herself at him, hugging him and whispering, 'She's an idiot, anyway; she's never experienced the taste of that red-haired madman in her mouth, or had it flog her!'

Her brown hand had descended and started fondling him and it awoke, uncoiling like a snake. In a teasing tone she said that she loved lollipops and that a year ago she had been handing them out to some women and children who were guests at her house when a woman in her fifties asked her what they were.

'They're lollipops!' she'd answered. 'You suck them.'

The woman had laughed and said, 'Well thank God I've got my own special lollipop at home. It's black, true, but it'll do.'

She was pointing over at her dark-skinned husband, and Tarfah murmured, 'My lover's lollipop is red. The imported kind.'

Whenever Tarfah mentioned her surname she would add that she didn't come from the family of the same name who owned a huge shopping centre in Riyadh. 'We're not tribesmen!'

It was the distinction people drew between tribal types, nicknamed '110 volts', and the brighter '220 volt' bulbs from the cities: a bit like she was reassuring him that he wasn't obliged to think of marrying her. Once, he said to her, 'I don't

224

know why people here are always turned into numbers. When a guy's a farmer or a tribesman you call him "110 volts" and sometimes no more than 60, not enough to power a light bulb! Southerners are Zero-Sevens after their dialling code, and loads of those of mixed birth from our parents' generation and before had their birthdates recorded as 7/1, as if the whole lot were born on the day the welfare budget's announced. You even retire from a government job on 7/1. The government would love it if we all dropped dead on 7/1. It would make their job easier!'

Tarfah moaned, his madman plunging in and out, a famished polar bear switching back and forth between two darkened caves, and her beautiful wide eyes rolled up in ecstasy as though she had fallen into a coma of everlasting pleasure. He cried out at her, cursing and clutching himself with his slippery hand and she embraced him with an intoxicated whisper: 'I love you!'

Returning from the bathroom he was surprised to see the light from a pair of candles wavering over the two tables beside the bed. His bewilderment showed, and she told him that she had brought them in her handbag, thinking of furnished flats with no lights! He embraced her and kissed her nose, which reminded him of the pliancy of cotton wool or young girls' rosy cheeks. It was slightly broad and squashy, as though devoid of cartilage and bone.

Fahd opened the wardrobe, took his cigarettes from his pocket and before lighting one from the candle flame, asked her, 'Do you mind?'

She shook her head coyly and he blew white clouds into the room's murk, the smoke rings rising like dancing demons.

'Have you ever smoked?' he asked.

'Twice, when I was working at the clinic. Nada, my friend in reception, she's a smoker.'

He handed her his cigarette and she hesitated, then took it, saying that she would only try it 'because it tastes of your mouth'.

As she exhaled he said, 'I get the impression your relationship with Nada is a strong one. There's nothing else going on between you, is there?'

'Oi,' she shouted. 'Don't come near me.'

She would talk about relationships between women, how in crowded bathrooms at wedding functions you would see each pair of friends enter a cubicle together for ten minutes or more, to emerge in disarray and make a hasty stop in front of the mirror, taking their lipsticks from their purses and restoring colour to their lips.

'What about you, then? How do you know all this if you haven't tried it?'

'Want to know the truth?' Tarfah added. 'Lots of people are convinced that Nada and I must have some history together, because we've been friends for eight years and because Nada is really fair and soft and has a small body, while I'm dark and taller than her. They always assume I must be her man and she's my sweetheart. I just can't imagine myself ever being in a relationship like that.'

She wrapped her leg around him and began kissing him slowly, savouring it, as the hot breath from her mouth whispered, 'How can I think of woman when I've got a lover like you? Huh? Tell me. How?'

When they were as hot as two coals she assumed the position like a cat awaiting her tom, her voice growing gradually louder and louder until he ordered her to put the pillow in her mouth. She was grateful and giddy, her long lashes shading her wide eyes, and every so often she would press her fingers against her lower eyelids, feeling a faint pain run through them.

From time to time she would talk about the old boyfriend who had left her after five years together. In their final year, she said, he had tried persuading her to marry, on the grounds that he was married and settled and that she, too, had the right to expect marriage, security and children. He was plotting to get rid of her politely, ostensibly looking out for her interests but really looking to end it.

She said that Nada had told her she dreamt of marrying a Saudi man who wouldn't betray her. They were in Sahara Mall together and she noticed a handsome man sitting on a bench in the main plaza, playing catch with a little girl and waiting for his wife to emerge from a shoe shop.

'That's the one!' Nada had cried in delight and Tarfah had pulled her away by the hand, saying, 'You moron. If you show you're keen what's a guy like that to do? They're all acting, sweetheart!'

'And what about you lot?' said Fahd. 'A man only cheats with a woman who gives him the chance. Don't you think wives cheat on their husbands?'

She smiled, thinking of Leila.

With a little sigh of annoyance, Tarfah pulled the bed's white blanket over her exposed buttocks and told him about Leila, who claimed to be religious, ruled her *majlis* like the head of a sect of dervishes and interfered with what other girls wore, and how she had discovered her betrayal. Tarfah and her sister had stalked her as she wandered around the hotel looking for an unlit spot to continue her secret telephone conversation.

'My sister pointed at her. "She's asking her sheikh for guidance!"' she said cattily, and let out a loud laugh.'

Fahd laughed, drawing her soft, moonlike face toward him and kissing her nose and mouth. Her lips formed a cocoon around him as she gathered in his face with unhurried pleasure. She wanted to sweep the sheet off but he prevented her and abruptly got out of bed, picking up one of the candles and placing it beside the other. He looked at her breasts and the shadow on the side of her face that leant against her palm was extraordinary. The folds of the bedsheet, rising and falling from light to dark, lent a compelling beauty to the composition. She laughed and let her face fall from her palm.

'You look like you're drawing me.'

She would make an amazing subject for a new painting, he said. He could see it in his mind, along with all those paintings of nude reclining women, and he thought of *Les Demoiselles d'Avignon* and another of Picasso's paintings, *Femme Nue au Collier*.

'Should we go?' he asked.

She screwed up her face as she laughed and told him, 'You're an idiot. You've got it all wrong. It's the woman who says she's late. For example, you should ask me, "Aren't you late?" so I get the hint in an indirect way.'

He apologised with a kiss and she started to get dressed while he went into the bathroom to wash his mouth. He heard the imam reciting the second *rakaa*—'Does he not know, when that which is in the graves is scattered abroad and that which is in human breasts is made manifest…'—and for a moment considered going out to pray to mislead the receptionist, but he didn't.

Emerging from the bathroom he asked her the name of the old wedding hall opposite Uwaida Palace on King Abdul Aziz Highway.

'You mean the Malakiya?'

He nodded and talked her through a credible way of leaving the key with the receptionist so he didn't have to return the next day just to hand it in.

Before she went out she covered her head. In the living room she stopped him and kissed his head. He laughed.

'You're the first person to fall in love with my head.'

Lifting her *niqab* she pulled his face to hers and kissed him, then let it fall as she giggled and said, 'You've had your final kiss from me.'

He had left the key in the door after locking it in case anyone tried opening it from outside with a spare set.

Before opening the door he replayed a scene in his mind, based on a dream she had recounted to him earlier, which had left him terrified though he hadn't revealed his fear lest he ruin her mood. Before they had met that afternoon, she had told him, she had been asleep and dreamed of him lying on a bed in a room that resembled her own while she sat beside him, stroking his face with her fingers and gazing at him lovingly. Every so often out of the corner of her eye she would catch a glimpse of lizards' tails, with their thorny scales, poking out of the space beneath the wardrobe. As she toyed with his face she grew afraid and thought of how she could suggest they go somewhere else without alerting him to the presence of the hideous reptiles and frightening him. At that very moment she heard the sound of her brother coming out of his room and she woke in a panic, staring over at the wardrobe but seeing nothing.

Turning the key he remembered the door of flat 102 across the hall and the shoe rack outside it, crammed with six or more pairs of shoes. Was this the explanation of the dream, that the shoes were the fat lizard tails seen by Tarfah? Or were they the bearded men of the Committee, lurking behind the door in their hair *mashlahs* and waiting to pounce as soon he opened up? They would lead him away to the GMC, pulling his lover behind him as she wept and pleaded. 'Silence, whore!' they would say, and enter a case of illegally consorting with a female against him at the Committee's headquarters in Roda and turn him over to the police.

Quietly, apprehensively, he opened the door. The shoe rack was completely empty: the flat's occupants had left.

They took the lift down in silence and he led her out to the car before returning to the Sudanese receptionist and asking him, 'Do you know the Malakiya wedding hall?'

The man shook his head apologetically.

'They told me it was on King Abdul Aziz Road. Do you know how to get there?'

'Leave here and take a right on to the service road leading to the ring road. Then at the lights at Exit Ten take a left and you'll be on King Abdul Aziz Road.'

Fahd handed him his secret treasure—the key—and brought his carefully planned conversation to its conclusion. 'Great. Look, we're going to a wedding and so long as the hall's near Qaseem Road and we manage to get out early we'll drive directly to Majmaa. Keep the key and if we're not back by two then you can free up the flat.'

The receptionist took it gratefully and said that if Fahd wanted he would hold the flat for him until tomorrow.

Tarfah said she wouldn't go back to the clinic because it had locked its doors half an hour before. Instead of Le Mall or Granada Mall, she chose Sahara Mall at the intersection of King Abdul Aziz and King Abdullah.

He drove west along King Abdul Aziz Road, the tape player drawling out the song she loved—*My sweetheart, so far away from me, I long for your eyes*—nodding her head in quiet rapture. After the lights he turned right into the King Fahd quarter, swung behind the mall and stopped at the main entrance.

Tarfah said her goodbyes, got down and he went on his way, rolling down the windows and breathing in the warm breeze that blended with the cold air from the air-conditioner.

The following day she told him that a Bedouin had chatted her up after she had got out and in front of the security guards had started chanting, 'The sure of step walks like a stunner,' unable to recall that the last word of the proverb should be 'king'. Were women being truthful, or were they making it all up, fantasising that their femininity could arouse a man's lust? They might be being honest after all; men here were maddened by desire, hunting women any way they could. Many women had lived harrowing, painfully blighted childhoods, their formative years swinging back and forth between violence and tyranny, between psychological damage and physical harm. There was little Noha, surrounded by an army and with a mother who counted her breaths even as she slept, Thuraya who spent her days with a neglectful, filthy husband, and mischievous Tarfah who refused to accept the favouritism shown to her sisters.

35

T ARFAH'S CHILDHOOD HAD BEEN painful and never peaceful, from her name, a sacrificial offering to her deceased grandmother, to its endless, depressing days.

One afternoon, in Class 2/3 at the Twenty-Sixth Middle School in Suwaidi, the gigantic school monitor, Halima the Ethiopian, had come to the door and asked for Tarfah. The grammar mistress standing in front of the blackboard motioned for her to go to the headmistress's office and as a terrified Tarfah crept out from behind her desk Halima added, 'Bring your bag with you!'

The teenager froze, then snatched up her bag and went outside, cocking her head to the left. In the corridor leading to the headmistress's office Halima said to her, 'Tarfah, your father's waiting for you at the entrance.'

Pulling the monitor's hand to make her stop she cried, 'Has something happened to my family?'

'No. You're suspended.'

'Why?'

'What, you don't know?'

At break time a sheikh had come to give the girls a religious lecture. He sat in the security guard's room, took the microphone and began addressing the girls who were drawn up in orderly rows in the playground.

Tarfah was rebellious and domineering and held sway over a little gang made up of Amani, Amal and Jawaher. The girls were sitting next to each other for the lecture and Tarfah started making fun of the sheikh's speech, waving her hands and waggling her head, a living representation of the bewildered old man hidden from view behind the four walls of the guard's room. Her friends, almost dead from laughter, buried their faces in their arms.

The headmistress had been standing on the edge of the playground, and she walked up and pointed with her stick, calling out Tarfah's name. Tarfah stood up and the headmistress signalled for her to move to the end of the row. When the lecture was over and the pupils scattered back to their classrooms Tarfah went to see the headmistress, who hadn't even had time to sit down at her desk.

'Why was I moved during the speech?' Tarfah asked boldly. 'They were all laughing!'

'That is correct. However, moving one girl is quite sufficient and in any case you were the cause of the disturbance. Everything quietened down after you left.'

'Or maybe it's because they've got connections ... teachers or monitors or ...'

This was a reference to Amani, whose sister taught maths at the school.

'That's quite enough insolence!' broke in the headmistress, waving her stick threateningly.

'I'm not insolent!'

'Get out of my sight before I beat you.'

The headmistress shoved her.

'Insolence!' said Tarfah, her mouth twisted in contempt.

'Come here, you little bitch!' the headmistress shouted.

Tarfah turned towards her, her eyes throwing out sparks and her hands trembling with rage, then spat at her in disgust as she shouted, 'You're the bitch!'

The headmistress drew up an order for three days punitive exclusion, then called her father and asked him to come over immediately and collect his daughter who was being suspended for misbehaviour.

As the monitor accompanied Tarfah to the exit, Tarfah begged her to let her apologise to the headmistress; she might change her mind. Knocking on the steel gate to make the guard open up, the monitor said, 'The headmistress has given an order. It's been signed and sent.'

She gave Tarfah a superior, vicious look. 'Try behaving yourself next time.'

The fourteen-year-old Tarfah went out, tripping over her *abaya* and holding her school bag and the suspension order. Her father took her away. Her mother was in hospital, having given birth early that morning to a little girl, Ilham. No sooner did he reach the house than he dragged her inside like a piece of livestock and pelted her with blows without knowing why he did so himself. He was panting, hitting and shouting,

'You want to show us up in front of other people? God destroy you!'

He left her crumpled up in her grimy *abaya* and went out, locking the front door and Tarfah burst into noisy tears, wailing, 'God curse you! May He bring you death! Please God, let me die and leave this life.'

She hated her father very much; she hated living with him. It tormented her that the only reason she had spat at the filthy headmistress was for his sake. The woman had called her a bitch, which made him a dog. She'd been defending him!

After she had calmed down, having woken from a nap that lasted the whole afternoon, she stood in front of the mirror and said to herself, 'The headmistress is right: I am a bitch!'

Giving a sigh, she added, 'And my father's a dog, too, a dog sixty times over!'

They were taught in their lectures that flirting was a serious matter, one of the greatest sins: *a disgrace in this world and in the world to come an exceeding torment*—words that fell heavy on the soul. Just considering the possibility (i.e. of talking with a young man) would strike the young girls not only with fear, but with outright terror.

After that day, however, Tarfah longed for the chance, if only to defy her father, though she was not in need of a man, or a woman for that matter; she needed to speak and spill it out, if only to a mirror, so she might bring a halt to the oppression that had begun to eat away at the edges of her two beautiful hands.

Her father was troubled by her. Her mischief and insubordination made him anxious. She wasn't like his other daughters, who were utterly calm and cold. There was a hidden fire within her. She loved people, mixed with them and made friends with all the other pupils. Everyone knew her for her rowdiness and good humour while at her sisters' schools their fellow pupils were scarcely aware of their existence.

It was a shameful day for her father when he first introduced a telephone into their house in Suwaidi, where the family was at that time going through something of a crisis. Nobody was to answer when it rang except him, or their mother if he was away. Having taken the caller's name and handed the receiver to one or other of his daughters, he would remain next to her, listening in. The reason for all this angst over the telephone was a mystery to the girls. Of all of them Tarfah was the most resentful of her father and mother; how she longed to leap up at the first ring and answer!

The only thing that recommended her to her father was her excellent marks at the end of each year, which made him happy. Neither did he have any worries about her gang of friends at primary school—where they were taught by a paid tutor who was known to the family and who also gave lessons to the daughters of neighbours he knew—most of whom came from villages around Riyadh such as Sudair, Huraimla and Thadiq or from the traditional city neighbourhoods of Old Shamesi, Sabala, Umm Sulaym and Jaradiya. But when he registered her at the Twenty-Sixth Middle School he became uneasy. It was an excellent government-run establishment, part of a complex that included primary, middle and second-ary schools, but its pupils were utterly different to those at her fee-paying primary. They were fearless.

Tarfah gradually grew apart from her village friends and extended the circle of her acquaintances until she came to lead a small gang of her own. She was in charge, the one who performed all the most daring missions. Hearing stories of girls' relationships with boys, she was amazed and aspired to do likewise. She would see the secondary school students, with their clothes, their sexiness and their shameless gestures, and returning home would be shocked by her mother's refusal of her reasonable requests:

'Mum, I want to cut my hair.'

'Mum, all my friends are dying their hair.'

But her mother refused and refused until she grew weary and thinking of a way to shut Tarfah up, told her to ask her father, at which point Tarfah's demands instantly ceased. That wasn't so important, however; the difficult part was how to broach the subject of her teachers' demands with her father because he would meet them with abuse and invective until, resolving to have done with his insults, she made her older sister Asma ask in her stead, at which he responded instantly.

Tarfah hated them all, starting with her own name, which had been given to her in memory of her grandmother. Her sisters, Asma, Amal, Ahlam and Ilham, had modern, pretty names that started with vowels, while hers stood out like a mark of shame. Why Tarfah?

'A curse on my grandmother and my grandmother's father!' she would say to herself when the intoxication of her rancour reached its peak. 'Their names all begin with A or I—soaring, confident letters—and I get a T, squat and heavy as a toad.'

'It's enough that you have the honour of bearing your grandmother's name and keeping her memory alive,' they would say and she would weep.

'Damn her and damn her memory! Who is she, Lady Diana and no one told me?'

Despite the strong, undaunted image she presented to her sisters, Tarfah's existence was fringed with tears. The thought of running away had often got the better of her as a teenager, but to actually take off? Where to? Not to mention the fact that the idea was insane and extremely difficult to pull off. It was perhaps her greatest fantasy.

She would be the last person in the house to go to sleep and she found herself in the grip of a strange habit: she would make her way to the front door and, opening it, would look up the street in both directions, though mostly peering to her left where the street stretched furthest with a mysterious turning at the far end.

For several nights she went on opening the door and looking left, as though waiting for someone or something, until one night she felt the sharp edge of a leather sandal strike the top of her head, then a meaty palm twist her face round and a savage kick to her body. It was her father, beating her and swearing at her, biting his tongue to muffle his voice for fear of waking the household or creating a scene.

She ran to her bed and crept beneath the blanket, stuffing her sleeve in her mouth to silence the sound of her sobs. Catching up with her he stood before her body interred in the blanket, then kicked at her foot.

'Cut it out! Understood?'

She cut it out and fell silent and in the morning he came to wake her up as usual, with a sudden prod from his foot.

Whenever Tarfah remembered those times she would ask herself, *Why was I standing there at the door? And even if his suspicions that I was waiting for someone were correct, why didn't he ask me who it was?*

Two days after the incident her father brought it up again. He hadn't told her mother, but he impressed upon her that she had better watch out. His attentions became so oppressive that if he sat to sip his cup of coffee at sunset and Tarfah wasn't there in front of him he would dispatch Amal or Ahlam to find her and report what she was up to.

Sometimes, she would watch their neighbour as he stood outside the door to his house, patting the head of his young son or even sitting him on his lap, though he was really too old for it. Occasionally, he would take the boy's hand and laugh and play with him. Whenever Tarfah saw this she either

238

laughed or felt scornful. From her parents she had learnt that patting on the head was a sin; it was a form of sexual harassment and molestation, even when it was the father himself that did it.

Now, grown up, with her second husband gone and her only daughter, Sara, sharing her bed, she still woke every morning with the feeling that any moment a foot would strike her where she lay, even now, a full ten years after her father's death.

Her father had been so tender and jolly with his brother's daughters. She would be consumed by jealousy to see him laughing and joking with her cousin Maha, who openly prayed that God grant him a long life instead of her own father.

'If only God had taken you with him!' Tarfah would mutter to herself.

36

If only God had taken me with him!

FAHD HAD REPEATED THESE words to himself many times through his endless misery in the week that followed his father's burial beneath the soil of the Naseem Cemetery. He said them again after his mother's marriage, against his wishes, to the uncle he couldn't stand, and after learning of his mother's death by torture. And, finally, he said them as he sat there in the detention cell of the Committee for the Promotion of Virtue and the Prevention of Vice, where he was merely a rich joke in the mouths of the bearded men who brought him for interrogation: the hawk-eyed man and with him a muscular fellow, cheerful and mocking, and a third individual with an uncovered head and an incipient bald patch at the front of his pate.

They sat him on a chair at the far side of the room and the hawk-eyed man scattered his belongings on the table, tipping the bag and letting them fall: his wallet, a gift from Tarfah with the Givenchy logo, a cheap pen, the 3G Nokia mobile phone, various bits of paper (mainly receipts from Maktaba), a fob in the form of a small silver elephant from which hung the keys to his Hyundai, Saeed's flat and the inner and outer doors of their house in Ulaya, and the primitively-worked olive-stone prayer beads.

'Goodness!' the balding man said sarcastically. 'All this in your pockets?'

'Yes, sheikh.'

'The brother is a Saudi?' he asked, scrutinising Fahd's features.

'Of course! The ID card's in front of you!'

'I know that. I can see it. But you don't look right.'

'Maybe your mother isn't Saudi,' said the strongman with the massive face.

'That's right, she's from a Jordanian family.'

'So you're a mongrel?'

'Half Saudi, then!' he said, chuckling happily.

Staring at the papers and receipts the balding man said, almost in a murmur, 'Half a man, in other words …'

Fahd sat there, trapped by the three men. One of them studied his ID card. 'Which branch of the al-Safeelawis is this?'

'The Qaseem lot.'

The balding man peered at him mistrustfully. 'Where in Qaseem?'

'My family is from Muraidasiya.'

'Do you know Abu Ayoub?'

'Sheikh Saleh …' the hawk-eyed man said by way of explanation.

'He's my uncle!' He almost added, 'And my mother's husband!' but a lump rose in his throat and he fell silent.

'Blessings!' said the hawk-eyed man, then added offensively. 'On him, not you.'

'As for you, who cares?' said the strongman.

Pips of sweat had started to appear on the bald patch of the man with the uncovered head. He drew a pen from his pocket and sliding the point beneath the string linking the widely spaced prayer beads he lifted them towards his nose and gave a tentative sniff, his eyes blinking rapidly and anxiously, then slowly moved them across to the hawk-eyed man and lifted them to his nose. The hawk-eyed man sniffed twice, moved his head back, then leant forward and sniffed again, his eyebrows raised. The balding man slowly transferred them to the nose of the strongman.

'What's this?' he asked Fahd.

'Prayer beads.'

'Why are they all coloured like an African necklace?'

After a period of silence Fahd replied, 'I painted them. I'm an artist.'

The balding man slowly raised his eyes towards him. 'You draw human beings?'

'Everything.' Even nudes, he almost added.

An Indonesian entered carrying pots of tea and coffee, placed them on a table in the corner of the room, then poured coffee for the three men. Having put the prayer beads into a small envelope, the balding man rose to his feet and tipped a few drops of coffee on to his thumb, unwilling to wet it with his tongue after it had touched the beads lest the black magic pass to his mouth, then into his body, and he die. He wiped the moistened thumb on to the glued flap on the envelope and pressed it shut.

The strongman whispered a few words in his ear and he nodded in agreement. The hawk-eyed man, who had heard nothing of this but clearly understood the secret message, nodded in turn.

Fahd stayed staring towards them anxiously. He remembered a newspaper report he had read a year back about a witch who had been seen by the men from the Committee, fleeing her flat on a broomstick after they had raided it and discovered prayer-beads, amulets and charms.

Witch arrested in Medina; Den of black magic raided
Ukaz, *29 May 2006*

Yesterday morning (Monday) members of the Committee for the Promotion of Virtue and Prevention of Vice received a surprise when they raided a den of black magic in the neighbourhood of Ard Mahbat, near Seeh in Medina, and found more than twenty women in the company of an African witch, naked as the day she was born.

The real surprise was not her refusal of the blanket provided to cover her nakedness, but that she flew from the room like a bird and disappeared from the flat to the amazement of more than twenty members of the Committee who were present.

A terrifying landing
The chase was on.

Committee members set out in pursuit, hunting for the witch through the upper and lower levels of the four-storey building, the sorceress having vanished from the second floor. During their search they came across a citizen in his pyjamas with his children behind him, appealing for help from his fellow residents. The citizen informed them that a naked African woman had dropped from the bedroom ceiling into the middle of his sleeping children, terrifying them and setting them screaming and wailing.

'When I went to see what was going on in the bedroom,' he added, 'my children told me about the bizarre scene they had just witnessed and when I realised it was a witch we all fled from the flat.'

Witch hunters

Ascending to the fourth floor the Committee members located the completely naked witch in a citizen's flat and loudly recited the call to prayer and the Ayat al-Kursi to paralyse her. One Committee member then threw a blanket over her until her clothes could be recovered, and once dressed she was arrested.

A source at the Committee stated that the operation to arrest the witch and her accomplices was led by Sheikh Faheed al-Oufi, head of the Committee's centre in Harra Gharbiya. Recovered from the witch's room were prayer beads, amulets, written charms, magical knots, instructional videos for the practice of black magic and a belt of the sort worn around the skirts of female primary school pupils, indicating that a schoolgirl had been bewitched. A Qur'an was also found beneath the witch's chair.

Part 5

An old black bag

37

IN THE MONTHS THAT followed his father's passing Fahd discovered drawing in pastels and for some time afterwards he stayed devoted to the technique. At that time he didn't use an easel.

Closing the door to his room he opened the box of colour-graded sticks and with lunatic preoccupation pushed the pastels in every direction over the paper; at times he even felt that the pastels were moving of their own accord, guiding his hand about. Here a long road, shadowed with a storm cloud, there a solitary bush, an old upturned cart and a murder of crows wheeling at the top of the sheet.

He laid the pastel aside and used his thumb to smudge the road's far end into the darkened sky. The horizon merged. His fingers became tinted with colour until they almost turned into pastels themselves and he was unable to judge which was his forefinger and which the chalk. He was eager and felt that he was panting as he pulled and pushed the pastels.

Just before dawn he grew drowsy and his heavy head slumped over the page. He came to mid-morning, his drool spread out over the sheet in the shape of a rectangular trunk, a *jinn*'s smoky body sprouting from the upturned cart.

After giving up pencils, then pastels, Fahd became addicted to oil paints, brushes, easels and palettes, but here he was, sketching away with his pencil as he sat at the Tea and Coffee Pot Café, across from Carrefour in Granada Mall.

He had chosen a seat next to the window, its opaque plastic film shielding the customer inside from the mall's bustle. By the chair he had selected this film had split, a small gap through which he could spy on the shoppers.

He ordered Turkish coffee and water, took from his pocket a piece of paper and a 0.5 millimetre gauge pencil and surveyed the scene through the window. Women in *abayas* that failed to hide their jeans, some pushing trolleys that were empty or contained a sprawling, playful child clutching the string of a helium balloon, others trailing an Indonesian maid pushing the trolley after them, while yet more clustered around the ATM machine by Samba Bank, ringed with mischievous children.

The Filipino waiter set down a small brass pot on the table and as Fahd gripped the handle to pour the thick coffee the waiter peered at the page and said that it was beautiful. Fahd thanked him, and sipping at his green porcelain cup he stared at what his hand had made.

A small car stopped at revolving door number four and Tarfah got out, walking calmly and confidently and gazing at the drivers sitting on the small square plots of grass near the security office. She walked inside.

To her left were the shops whose layout she knew well, while on her right lay Carrefour's open doors and the khaki-clad security guards chatting to each other through the crowds of shoppers. She passed the women gathered around a cash machine and glanced over at the café, walking straight ahead until she reached the spacious court next to the escalators, then doubling back to let her see more easily into the café's curtained-off men's section and look for Fahd. She didn't want to call him; she wanted to catch him unawares.

Walking past, Tarfah saw Fahd busily smudging the pencil with his thumb and swung right, approaching the exposed patch of glass and rapping suddenly at the window with her ring. As Fahd turned she withdrew a little and all he saw were her eyes, smiling through her *niqab*.

He hurriedly drained the water from his bottle and walked outside, accompanied by his mobile's message tone. He opened the message:

Beware of the following phrases if uttered by someone older than you:

1. *Let's go bird hunting.*
2. *Would you like me to teach you how to wrestle?*
3. *What do you say we go up to the roof and look at the pigeons?*
4. *Would you like me to teach you how to drive?*
5. *Let's go and find some jerboa in the desert.*
6. *Today, the bill's on me.*
7. *Let's open the wardrobe.*
8. *Let me show you my stamp album.*
9. *Let's stay up and watch a video.*
10. *Let's see how a gecko suckles her young.*

Compliments of the Committee for Fighting Sodomy, Qaseem

Fahd closed his eyes and sighed, clinging to Tarfah's hand for several minutes and then releasing it as they traversed the mall's wide central passage and passed Carrefour. Noticing that he seemed a little put out she asked him what the matter was, but he told her it was nothing. Where were they going, he wanted to know. Her molten eyes gave her answer, but she added that if he was preoccupied or not in the mood they could grab a coffee and just go for a drive. They stopped at the Starbucks inside the main entrance.

Saeed was just fooling around. Whenever he got a message making fun of Qaseem and its inhabitants he would pass it on to Fahd, who would respond with sarcastic remarks about southerners.

As they bought their cappuccinos, Lulua's mournful voice reproached him: she and her mother had been trying to get hold of him for two days, and their mother was exhausted, worn out trying to track him down. He tried making the excuse that he had been painting for the next spring exhibition and promised that he would visit them both that night.

As soon as they drove off Tarfah's phone rang and she began hunting fretfully for it in her bag. Fahd was miles away, staring up at the advertising hoarding at the traffic lights while she giggled to her friend Wafaa, but he paid attention when she glanced over at him and said, 'There's a friend of mine who's been doing "short time" with this guy but so far, no action. Looks like she'll end up paying him for it!'

She ended the call and her laughter trailed away as she put the phone back in her bag. 'She's completely mad.'

'Who?'

'Wafaa, my friend. She worked on the programme for eradicating illiteracy for nine years. She studied psychology. And now they've cancelled it; they've cancelled the contracts of more than eight thousand female teachers … Imagine! Just like that!'

'God! And what did she do?'

'Nothing. They thought of staging a demo at the Department of Education in central Riyadh.'

'If they tried that they'd end up wishing they were at home unemployed.'

'Now she tells me that her friend in the programme suggested they form a troupe of wedding dancers, so Wafaa told her there was a much more enjoyable, easy and quick way to make cash.'

'And what was that?'

'Work as a Friday girl. "Short time" for a thousand riyals in furnished flats and in hotels for two and half. Amazing!'

'Are you serious?'

'No, I'm joking, you maniac. Did you believe me?'

'Why wouldn't I? Anything's possible in this country.' Fahd lowered his voice as though speaking to himself. 'The women are turning into Friday girls and the boys are off to Iraq!' Then: 'Friday girl! I like that!'

Tarfah laughed. 'That's what they call them. We once asked Wafaa about her man and she said he was going to Bahrain. We really thought he was travelling, but she laughed at us and said it was code for a guy who drinks too much!'

He didn't spend long with Tarfah that evening. They roamed the darkened neighbourhoods of North Riyadh for a while and he gave her a half-hearted peck. She felt hurt and asked him to go to his mother's; they would meet tomorrow if they could.

38

'SAY SOMETHING!' SAID LULUA.

'Who to?' Fahd answered, setting down the bag containing bread and three cartons of yoghurt that he had bought from the supermarket and the bakery next door.

'Anyone on planet Earth would be nice.'

'You mean the *jinn*?' he said, smiling.

'I know you don't believe in those things but I swear to God I heard it. Its voice was completely different …' Then: 'I swear it wasn't Mum speaking!'

He wasn't convinced, but when he took his seat beside his mother, prostrate on her bed in the dining room, he handed her a glass of *zamzam* water. She took three sips, then sprinkled a few drops into his right hand and he stroked her brow and head as he muttered a Qur'anic verse.

It came to him that there was a spiritual cure that might save this ravaged body; even holding her hand, still beautiful, warm and soft, could give her new impetus. She adjusted herself and began to tell him about his childhood, then his father. Her tears flowed and she was silent. She had remembered the bag, maybe. She asked him to call Lulua.

'I'm making tea, Mum. Just a minute.'

'Your father bequeathed it to you.'

She grabbed Fahd's hand and squeezed it.

Choking back a sob, Fahd said sternly, 'Let's have none of that talk; it's no good.' Then he added, 'God give you a long life. You'll be there for my wedding and you'll see your grandchildren.'

Wearily, Soha described to her daughter where the old black leather bag was kept on top of the wardrobe. She would need the little stepladder behind the kitchen door.

39

T ARFAH SENSED THAT FAHD'S usual high spirits were dampened; she missed the touch and tenderness she had come to expect. He was going through a crisis, she felt, but wasn't telling her. Wasn't she the queen of trauma and tragedy? How many dreadful things had happened to her, and she hadn't gone under, rising phoenix-like from the ashes every time and telling Fahd in lavishly sarcastic tones: 'Smile! You're in the Kingdom of Human Kindness!'

She thought of the despondency that sometimes overwhelmed her when she was with him.

She was sitting in the dark of her top-floor bedroom in Suwaidi listening to the sunset call to prayer from a nearby mosque; it was the first time she had listened to it in such a downcast state: how could it be calling for peace of mind when she felt such hopelessness? As a child, whenever she'd felt sad or a strong urge to cry, she would creep into her wardrobe like a cat, closing the door on herself, shutting her eyes in the dark and letting her tears flow unchecked until her soul was purged and she could emerge to play and stampede about crazily.

All she remembered of her childhood was the bad and the sad, starting with being named Tarfah and, perhaps too, the superstition with which her immediate family and relatives poisoned her early years: that any woman called Tarfah was destined for bad luck in life. Though she hadn't believed it, the years that followed had proved them right.

It was a mystery to her why her entire family should prefer her older sister, Asma. Was it because of her utter docility, the very opposite of Tarfah's naughtiness? Or because Tarfah excelled at school while her older sister failed and had to repeat one year after another until they ended up together in the fourth year at primary school, before Tarfah overtook her and went to middle school first? Tarfah relied on her own talents, while her sister received assistance from private tutors, all to no avail. Was that really sufficient to make her family hate her, so that as a girl she often felt that she wasn't their daughter at all, that she was in the wrong family? Neither their ideas nor their way of life tallied with her own and comparing her dark skin to her four fair sisters only made her more doubtful. When she was older and her father had died she would ask herself, 'Did Mum sleep with someone else?'

Not a day passed without her being beaten for some reason, or for no reason at all, by her brutal father and her brothers. Even her youngest brother took pleasure in hurling his sandals at her when she walked by, as though she were a cat in the doorway that he wanted to drive off.

Nor was this confined to the immediate family; even her aunt preferred Asma. Yet despite her father's harsh treatment he would call no one else when he wanted food, drink or clothes. Was it because she was more scrupulous than her sister, or because he wished to put Asma at ease and have the little servant girl Tarfah perform her tasks for her?

Her father had not loved her mother. She would complain about him, never letting him alone and always suspicious. One morning, months after his death, she told Tarfah that he had cheated on her, and the whore he'd cheated with had borne him a child.

'That's enough, Mum!' Tarfah had cried. 'Please, stop it! God rest his soul!' Then added in a subdued tone, 'Speak well of your dead.'

But the terror she felt at night as she looked back over her long life and her sense of alienation while surrounded by her family only grew stronger. She remembered that it had been her father's dream to be blessed with a daughter who mispronounced her 'rs' to sound like 'ls'. Maybe his lover had had this flaw of speech and he had longed to see it embodied in front of him at home. Tossing and turning in bed, Tarfah whispered to herself, 'So why did he hate me if I fulfilled this dream of his?'

She never won his love and was helpless before her siblings' mockery whenever she uttered a word that contained an 'r'. They would mimic her and one would always shout: 'I dare you to say, "Rabbits run right to rocks"!'

Tarfah was exceptionally brave and had a sharp tongue, but she never had it in her to tell her mother what she went through as a child for fear that she would punish her and step up her surveillance. She couldn't find the courage to tell her about her cousin, some five years older than her, who had asked her to come to his house to see the hawk his father had bought. She went off with him and he had shown her a hawk of his own.

For days afterwards she felt irritable and guilty and when she saw him at the door would hate and blame herself, as though he had been perfectly within his rights and it was she who had done wrong. She was scared that he would tell on her; the sin was her own.

Tarfah neither hated nor loved her father, though by rights she should have loved him because he was her father. Whenever she grew angry with him and whispered to herself that she hated him she would quickly become flustered and fearful of divine retribution, even though she couldn't remember him ever holding her or hugging her or stroking her hair; the very opposite of her uncle, who adored her, showering her with praise in front of her family and his own daughters, too, and never hesitating to give her a hug every time he saw her. In his tender embrace she found all that she lacked in her family home.

When her father died, Tarfah wept dementedly and cried in silence for a whole month, so that the women who had come to pay their condolences pitied her and called back later to ask after her. She cried like a child, repeating over and over, 'Bring back my father!' But with the passing of days she grew reconciled to circumstances and on the final day of her mother's mourning period, as she sat with her in the still night, her mother told her what had never been told: how he had once made accusations against her honour, how he had done her wrong and abused her.

She talked of the girl he had loved before he had got married and how his family had refused to let him wed her, forcing him to marry her mother because she was a cousin and an orphan and his financial circumstances were weak enough that only his cousin, cheap and no bother, was within his means and he within hers. She told Tarfah how he had betrayed her with the girl he got pregnant and Tarfah had been unable to stop her until she had convinced her daughter that it had really happened.

Her mother had shattered that dazzling aura, the barrier of sanctity surrounding her father. What disappointment Tarfah felt! How she hated her mother for destroying the image of a strong father that she carried inside her! Yet she hadn't blamed her.

To this day, Tarfah was amazed that her mother had observed the mourning period and carried out his last instructions (for the woman who observes the prescribed period of mourning shall make for her husband a dwelling in Paradise), continuing to give alms on his behalf and refusing to remarry. If his name ever came up she would praise him and perfume his memory before her sons and daughters, who came to feel proud of him.

Tarfah almost wept when she learnt of his betrayal and the pride felt by her brothers and sisters never touched her. She would laugh to herself to see them squirreling his portrait away in the wallets they carried in their pockets. She was the only one who didn't keep a picture of him; she wouldn't even look at one. She feared herself and she feared him. She sensed she would catch a look of reproach in his eyes, a reproach that would seize on the doubts that swirled inside her, stirred up by her revulsion at what her mother had told her.

These things kept Tarfah awake at night as she grew older and the passing of time eroded her hostility towards her family. She began to draw closer to them, to live alongside them in peace, until she married Sami and divorced two years later to return with quite different feelings. The gulf between them had grown and she felt more estranged than at any time before. Her room became her refuge and her world. True, her brothers certainly appeared to treat their sisters with kindness, alarmed and jealous for their well-being, but Tarfah thought them selfish and fake.

Over the years she tried to bridge the chasm dividing them. She was, undeniably, disobedient and foolish with an ungovernable tongue. She was incapable of keeping her counsel for anyone, answering back fearlessly. For that is how she saw herself: fearless and restoring what was rightfully hers. They, meanwhile, regarded her behaviour as vulgar, as a shamelessness and insolence that contrasted with her calm, well-mannered sisters. Tarfah thought them naïve idiots, mocking their staggering stupidity and laughing herself silly when they failed at school, and so nobody was ever happy for her when she did well.

40

I N SPITE OF HER relationship with her father, Tarfah still wished that he had been there when she got engaged to Sami.

She wanted to marry Sami, but something told her that her father would have refused the match because she was yet to finish her studies and also because he evaluated men quite differently than her brothers, unmoved by material concerns and never flattering anyone. He hoped to see every one of his girls at university and in the best departments. He had no patience with absenteeism from school and would turn into a tyrant whenever his wife asked him to let Ahlam or Ilham take a day off. But after his death, anyone who wanted to go to school could go and if they couldn't be bothered than no one would blame them. The house was transformed into a little city of chaos within a city beset by chaos.

One night, Tarfah read the little advertising slogan blinking on the ATM screen, which described the country as the Kingdom of Human Kindness. Putting the notes in her wallet she thought to herself, 'Incredible! They're calling it the Kingdom of Human Kindness! Wouldn't the Kingdom of Chaos be better?'

'Find out about him? He's our child! We've known him since he was little!'

This was her brothers and sisters, speaking about Sami. They were delighted whenever he came over, sitting beside him in a fever of excitement like someone having a photo taken with a minor television star. Only Ahmed, the second oldest of her brothers, remained unimpressed. Actors, singers and sports stars, he said, led dissolute lives and were unsuitable for marriages; that went for Sami, too, regardless of the fact they knew him.

Ahmed wasn't extreme in his beliefs but he observed the daily prayers at the mosque, the first and only person to perform the dawn prayer in their neighbourhood mosque for many years. He disliked gossip, hated nobody and was affectionate and devoted towards his family, his sisters and his widowed mother.

Before her father passed away, Tarfah's cousin, son of the uncle who lived in Khobar to whom, or to whose family, she was partial because she felt that they were more civilised, asked for her hand in marriage. Her father refused on principle to countenance an unemployed man, even though his family were only suggesting an engagement, and gave them to understand that her future would never be linked to a man who couldn't tell how long he might be waiting for a job.

As for Sami, Tarfah knew no more about him than the average television viewer or what could be gleaned from his photographs in the press, but she was quite certain that she disliked his inquisitive, vulgar family whose general manner and way of speaking lacked sophistication and breeding. When his mother and older sister came to present her with the offer her reaction had not been good, but his maternal aunt, who happened to be Tarfah's cousin, spoke with her and managed to convince her, telling her that he had confided his love for Tarfah to his sister, recalling the lovely eyes she had had as a child before she had covered up.

If he couldn't marry her, he declared, then he would never marry.

She didn't have a clear childhood memory of him. She had seen him in the flesh just once, a few months back when he had visited her uncle's house. With her cousin Samia, Tarfah had spied on him through the opening in the tent. She had thought that he was just a vain young man, inordinately proud of the pair of curls that flopped across his brow. He was talking to his aunts and moving his hands about confidently, maybe arrogantly.

Their phone conversations after the engagement never went further than his television appearances, his minor stage roles and his friends in the industry. They never touched on any relationships with other women. He was just an actor playing supporting roles, who got his break on Channel One, in instructional slots that advised the viewer not to waste water, to exercise financial prudence, and to show respect to the disabled and assimilate them into society, and so on.

Tarfah didn't take the business of marriage terribly seriously. She sat watching a foreign film with subtitles at noon on her wedding day while Asma shouted, 'From now on you'll get him in the flesh!' from outside the room, assuming that she was gazing at Sami on screen. This lack of excitement on her wedding day left her family in shock. Her appearance didn't change until after the evening prayers in the wedding hall. She wore a blouse and skirt and her hair was carelessly tousled; in the end Abdullah shouted at her, bewildered at her indifference and lack of emotion.

No one understood that Sami needed her to be able to show her off at events, while people whispered, 'That's Sami's wife!'

'He cared about my dresses and how I looked, not for my sake or his, but for those women whose comments he always looked forward to.'

She was led to him by her gossiping sisters who spent the time comparing Tarfah to her cousin or her aunt, and despite her happiness to see her family gathered together in one place, especially the women, her mother-in-law began to isolate her bit by bit from the rest, claiming to be worried about the jealous eyes of the other women.

Sami travelled a lot for work, moving with various camera crews around Egypt, Syria and Jordan where the studios were, but he missed her and at night he would woo her endlessly down the phone. He bought her gifts and beautiful antiques on which he inscribed poetic sentiments and the words of favourite songs expressing how he felt inside. Indeed, when he came home he would bring scraps of paper on which he'd recorded his longing: receipts and bills, a ticket stub from a bus or train, film and theatre tickets. Every scrap of paper he kept in his jeans was a blank page for the words and thoughts he addressed to his beloved Tarfah.

The strange phone calls didn't bother her at first either when Sami answered and told the caller it was a wrong number or the times she answered and the caller hung up. It didn't make her angry, but doubt took root in her heart, especially when he would lower his voice during phone calls he didn't want her to hear. She ignored it, though, because she trusted him.

All this she let pass without a fuss, but not so his peculiar attempts to isolate her from other people, to keep her as far as possible from his relatives and in particular, his aunt and her cousin Samia in whom she had discovered two new friends. He didn't like her calling them when he was away, as though he wanted to hear every word she said to them and they to him. It got to the point that on entering the flat he would immediately ask her who had called and what they had talked about, even sneaking a look at the list of received calls on her phone and rampaging about the house, enraged and consumed by suspicion, if he found that the list had been deleted.

Yet at the same time, returning to their flat after taking Tarfah to see her family in Suweidi, he would spend hours on the phone with his aunt. He was uneasy about his aunt's manner and he was worried about her influence over his wife. She had something on him. His surveillance of Tarfah reached a point where instead of checking her incoming and outgoing calls he felt the need to place a small listening device beneath a couch in the men's *majlis* that sat alongside the table where the phone lay. So suspicious was he in fact, that before they went out together on some errand or other he would wait for Tarfah to go to the bathroom, then rummage through her handbag.

Sami was paranoid, but life went on, slow and unchanging, until the day he returned unexpectedly early from Amman, before the end of a shoot for a new soap opera. The production manager had fired him for molesting a young Palestinian make-up artist. As she bent over him to apply cream and make-up at the start of each day he would start praising her eyes and mouth. Then he went further, sliding his hand along the armrest, to make the movement look accidental, and letting his elbow brush her thigh. She finally screamed at him one day and everyone gathered round, the actors, the director, the assistant director, the set designer and the wardrobe master, to find the girl in tears, casting her powder brush aside and refusing to work.

After this, Sami was forced to accept the minimum wage for soap actors, and remained without work for a year; they even had to give up his flat and go and live with his family. A new and painful episode in Tarfah's life began. She argued with his mother over trifling matters and Sami would stalk out of the flat in a temper and be gone for a day or two, while Tarfah stayed behind in the family home, mistreated and downtrodden as a slave. She grew to hate his selfishness and poor behaviour and his running away infuriated her.

Around this time another a major change took place in Tarfah's life. One day she came across a small, blackened spoon on top of the shade for the bathroom light. Naturally enough, she threw it into the kitchen bin. Two days later she found another spoon, slightly singed. She suspected that he was on something, what she didn't know, and then she noticed brown crumbs scattered on the carpet beneath his side of the bed. The carpet was light in colour and the crumbs that darkened it she recognised as hashish. He was rolling joints.

She had never noticed the way he smelled before, but after the first year she began avoiding his embraces; he stank and every time he took her to bed it was as though she were a virgin. It felt like rape.

He had no real money, just a modest sum he earned from bit work in television, no more than 3,000 riyals, not even enough to cover his secret budget for a single week. Though they were living with his family he began harping on at her that she should take her expenses from her family and his refusal to shoulder any responsibility caused her irritation to peak.

Then his mother started to unleash her arrows at Tarfah, attributing every new incident, crisis and sudden disappearance to her failure to give birth. She said that if Tarfah had had children Sami wouldn't leave the house after every argument, as though he wasn't running away from her sharp tongue and their swapped insults. In order to stop his mother's crazed assault Tarfah was forced to make repeated visits to a gynaecologist, until after numerous examinations and consultations he threw her out, saying, 'If your husband isn't with you next time, don't come!'

Sami kept promising to come to the doctor with her, and didn't. He kept promising to start over with her in a flat away from his family, and didn't. He tried summoning up the spirit of the happy times they had spent together in the flat in Wuroud but she had become a wife in name only and in the end she went back to her family in a rage.

He tried to get her back, making up stupid excuses for why his life had turned out so badly: there were people conspiring against him in television, people in production companies who hated working with him and people plotting to abort his promising start on stage. It was these people who had got him hooked on the delicious giddiness of hashish cigarettes. Even his family hated him for his success and his popularity with the public. With this he lost possession of Tarfah's respect and her soul. Unable to bear being shut up with him in one place for longer than half an hour she returned to the family home in Suwaidi to put her old room in order, a tiny space more like a cupboard, no larger than twelve square metres.

Though she missed him and longed for him for the first few months, Tarfah eventually got used to living on her own, despite her brother's badgering her to go out and see her friends. Her brother Ahmed, meanwhile, felt that his unshakeable conviction that artistic and celebrity circles were filthy and depraved had been vindicated and whenever there was slightest problem at home he would chastise his sisters and mother for casting Tarfah into such iniquity.

41

S TOPPED AT THE UWAIS Mall traffic lights on Ulaya Street,
Fahd tried opening the bag and discovered that it was
secured with a combination lock. He entered a few guesses.
Three numbers wasn't difficult, but nor was it easy. The year
of his father's birth, minus the millennium: 956. No response.
He put in 985, the year of his own birth. No response. After
a few more failed attempts, the year of the mosque's occupation occurred to him, 979, but it didn't open to that, either.
What if he tried a nice round number? Fahd asked himself,
like the *hijri* date of the same incident: 400. To his surprise, it
opened.

He was parked in Ruman Street just off the Northern Ring
Road, beneath the building where Saeed lived. The smell of rot
spread through the car's interior, masked by the reek of cheap
perfume. His nostrils twitched and he started to sneeze, then
he switched on the light and gazed upon the bag's secrets.

He began to leaf through the documents and diaries, the
books marked with their date of purchase from Mecca's bookshops and the pamphlets containing Juhayman's addresses,
one of which his father had distributed that Ramadan to
the worshippers in the Grand Mosque. Fahd read the titles.
A weighty tome turned in his hands: *Apprising the People of
the Signs of Discord and the Portents of the Hour* by Hamoud
al-Tuwaijri. He opened it and a light cloud of dust rose towards

his face. He closed his eyes, opened them again, and on the page before him read:

Concerning the man of Qahtan

Qais Bin Jaber al-Sadafi relates a hadith *handed down from his grandfather, by way of his father, that the Prophet, the blessings of God and His peace be upon him, said:*

'After me there shall be Caliphs, and after the Caliphs, Emirs, and after the Emirs, Kings, and after the Kings, Tyrants. Then shall come a man of my House, to fill the earth with justice after it has been filled with tyranny. Then shall the man of Qahtan be made Emir. In the name of He who sent me the True Word, it shall be no other.'

This account is given by al-Tabrani; Al-Haithami said of it: 'In its chain of transmission are names I do not know.'

We also have the account of Abdallah Bin Amr Bin al-Aas—may God be content with him and his father before him—in which we find the following:

'Then shall come the Zealous Emirs. Six shall be born of the line of Kaab Bin Luay, one shall be a man of Qahtan and all shall be righteous and without equal.'

Abu Harira, may God be content with him, relates that the Prophet, the blessings of God and His peace be upon him, said:

'The Hour shall not arrive until a man from Qahtan comes forth and drives the people before him with his staff.'

Fahd shut the book and hefted another, which he recognised from the cover: Sayyid Qutb's *Milestones*. He took a number of small pamphlets and read some of their covers: *The Emirate, The Oath and Obedience, Exposing the Rulers' Deception of Scholars and Men* and *Sincere Advice and Justice in the Life of Man.*

He lifted a small, yellow booklet of only a few pages, whose cover proclaimed: *A Vindication of the Religion of Abraham, Upon Him be Peace.*

In the margins of these pamphlets he read the comments in his father's shaky hand: *The position on civilisation … peaceful evangelising … jihad … compliance … the Religion of Abraham … obedience …*

Lifting these books up, Fahd came across a series of letters to his father, a small folder with diary entries and a number of documents. One was a *fatwa* dated 20 November 1979:

> *In the name of God, the Compassionate and the Merciful, Praise be to God alone and Peace upon His Prophet, His family and His companions:*
>
> *On Tuesday, the first day of the month of Muharram in the year 1400, we, the below signed, were summoned by His Majesty King Khaled Bin Abdul Aziz Al Saud to attend him in his office in Maadhar.*
>
> *His Majesty informed us that directly following dawn prayers that day a group had entered the Grand Mosque bearing arms and demanded the oath of obedience be given to one they called the Mahdi. They swore the oath and prevented people from leaving the mosque, fighting those who opposed them and opening fire on people both within the mosque and outside.*

Fahd replaced the document and took up another yellowed sheet of paper, which he realised was a long poem in the classical style. He read the opening:

> *Through a dark night a servant ran,*
> *With his piety, fleeing the faithless,*

Fleeing the feuding that beset him round,
The warring of happiness and woe.

He scanned the page and turned it over: there were more than forty lines of verse.

Closing the bag he switched off the car's overhead light and got out.

He turned the key in the lock. The flat was dark. Saeed hadn't returned yet, and he decided to open the bag again, picking out the small folder of diary entries. He read on, wide-eyed.

42

Mecca, 1979

*A fter two days of questioning I was transferred from Buraida to
Riyadh accompanied by a soldier who stuck to me like my own
shadow, leg irons at my ankles and handcuffs about my wrists. The
bolted truck drove down what I think was the old airport road until
it entered a gate at the back of an old building and I was placed in a
cell no more than 1x2 metres in size.*

*Fifteen days deprived of sleep. Whenever my head nodded they'd
hammer on the cell's steel door and I would jerk upright in panic.
These desperately cramped cells were laid out along a narrow corridor
where I was brought, first descending four steps into a room full of
soldiers and guards then dragging my leg irons down another four
steps to the grim cells themselves.*

*After they locked me in I amused myself by reading the graffiti on
the back of the door: names, dates, a calendrical table for one of the
hijra months written by a prisoner to count off the days, a variety
of contradictory political slogans reflecting the prisoners affiliations,
penises and arses, sexual positions and obscenities. Pushing it in to
enter, the cleaner hadn't noticed what lay behind the door, while the
cell doors that opened outwards were subject to constant scouring.*

*After two weeks I was transferred to Jeddah and from there I was
taken to Mecca in a jeep. They bound my eyes with a blindfold made
of fabric and did not remove it until I had been sitting in the cell for*

three hours. When at last I could open my eyes, I saw an old friend of mine, a fellow student from the Grand Mosque Institute.

The cell was about 6x4 metres and was home to five of us. Its walls were covered with a white paint that gave off an acrid smell. It was the new prison in Mecca and I stayed there for five months knowing nothing, without the faintest idea where I was, nor whether I was above ground or below, with no book, newspaper or wristwatch to indicate the time, day, or date. It was as though time had stopped on the first day of Muharram, 1400 AH.

After what seemed like an eternity, I finally saw, one day at noon, some books in the possession of the young prison guard Daghaylaib, who had brought them to the cell. My heart fluttered with joy at finding a window through which it could peer out at a world other than those hateful walls.

Daghaylaib stood there reading out our names in order and handed each of us a Qur'an. After he had gone one of the Brothers noticed that the cover bore a picture of the Holy Kaaba, on either side of which was something like the figure of a man. These were depictions of living creatures on the Noble Book, he told us; God protect us, they must not be permitted to remain there. Three agreed with him and decided to strip off the covers, while myself and my friend begged to differ. We saw no harm in it.

The next morning the guard called out their names, and the three of them were taken out and lined up between the cells. Three troopers came with special clubs and began to beat them, the whistling of the staves stirring the still air of the prison, their voices rising and falling.

In prison emptiness towered as tall as the minarets in the Grand Mosque and we had nothing save the dream of books and newspapers. I amused myself breeding cockroaches. Whenever a particularly fat one *came near me I would hit it with my sandal until it lay flat and a small sticky sack burst from its rear. I would peer at it for a while then lift the sack in my hand and put it in an empty yoghurt carton and a few days later I would enjoy the sight of tens of tiny cockroaches pouring out of the sack. I'd bore a hole in the carton's lid for ventilation and the cockroaches would keep growing and growing and with them grew my sadness, until one day I decided to kill them all.*

Later, I wanted a string of beads to count out my prayers, or the members of my family lest I forget them, or the Brothers who had been executed. Asking for a luxury like prayer beads was difficult and so I began saving up olive stones until I had enough to fill my palm. I grated the stone's tip against the cement floor so the hollow centre showed, then turned it over and did the same to the other end until I had a pierced bead. I then cleaned out the core, and when I had thirty-three beads I pulled a thread from the matting, arranged the stones along it and tied the ends together.

Was I in such dire need for prayer beads or had the emptiness driven me to find something to entertain myself, to disperse the endless hours, coiled like a hibernating serpent?

After a year had gone by they asked us what books we wanted and I asked for a collection of al-Mutanabbi's poetry. I was full of joy as I soared with the verses of vainglory and wisdom. I memorised half the collection as well as fifteen juz'a of the Qur'an.

One man memorised The Delight of He Who Longs To Journey *and after they took it back he decided to write it out in its entirety upon the white walls. Using the metal tabs from fizzy drink cans he inscribed it with the utmost care. The oldest man in the cell, an old illiterate fellow who had saved up the drink cans, could not understand the words, but he took his pleasure from the beautiful lines and the man who had written them decided to teach him the alphabet.*

The walls told us tales of times past and we told them of our sadnesses, our loneliness, and our great fear of the unknown. After they started allowing us family visits, one man's relatives brought him cologne. He gave it to Daghaylaib, who was a kind man, and he perfumed us all. He sprayed the cheap shimaghs we had been given after a year inside. That night I wrapped the scented head cloth over my face and no sooner had I fallen asleep than I saw nightmares, the like of which I had never seen and never will again. I saw them take me, blindfolded, to Justice Square. They stood around me and one read out my sentence: one of the corrupt of the earth, to be beheaded by the sword. Hearing the sword slither from the scabbard I trembled and recited the shahada. Then, without warning, the executioner pricked my side with the point and I hunched my back in fright, my neck stretched out like the scrag of a bird. The briefest instant, then the unsheathed blade split the filthy air and cut into my frail neck. My head flew off, rolling like a football while my eyes stayed open, looking out at the crowds.

I woke up, sweating and afraid, and opening my eyes I stared at the cell walls until the cramped chamber seemed a shady Paradise. It was truly the happiest moment of my life to find myself breathing evenly and to see the beautiful prison walls, a happiness only to compare with the instant of my release.

For my first visit, my father and Ibrahim came. They were happy that they had found me at last and that I was still alive. The time after that it was my mother with my father and brother. The trip from Riyadh to Jeddah was sleepless and exhausting for them, and so it went on until the order was given, three and a half years into my sentence, to alleviate these hardships by distributing the prisoners according to their home regions.

I returned to the Ministry's prison in Riyadh where I lived among new cellmates, before they moved me to Ulaysha Prison. I *sensed that they would release me, then. It was wonderful there: we read newspapers, listened to the radio and knew what was going on around us.*

I found it hardest to sleep at Eid and just afterwards, because the release orders were issued towards the end of Ramadan and when the list of names was published, ten or fifteen prisoners, or sometimes just one, and I did not find mine among them, I would enter a state of severe disappointment. At the end of a year's hardship, injustice, tedium and anticipation, I would be hanging on the small and nebulous hope of the Ramadan to come.

They let me go at the end of Ramadan 1404 AH. The head of the prison's investigations unit sent for me. I was asleep. My cellmates woke me and I sprinted for the bolted door in my underwear.

'Put your robe on, idiot!' one of them shouted, so I dressed and Daghaylaib led me to the office of Lieutenant Saoud.

'God willing, this is your chance!'

That's what he said. They were always mysterious, even though they had become our friends through long acquaintance. He said nothing more, even though my father and Ibrahim were in the room next door finishing up the paperwork.

There was a detective who was supposed to be standing in a hidden location behind the chair where I sat, studying my features through this mirror-like panel. He was meant to familiarise himself with me, tail me in the first months following my release and write reports on my conduct. Instead, he came straight into the room. The lieutenant shouted at him, threw him out and smiled.

'This lot just don't get it!' he said in his Hejaz accent. 'Idiots, I tell you.'

Then he explained to me that the man who had just come in had been given the task of following me and warned me at length to keep

275

clear of suspicious activities that might do me harm and to ensure my behaviour was irreproachable.

'Suleiman, you have to prove your good behaviour. Invite the man for a cup of coffee or something!'

Then he laughed, and I laughed with him.

My father, my uncle and my brother came to collect me. Walking out with them was a wonderful moment, delightful, but at the same time terrifying. I came out in Ramadan to find my family home transformed into a scene of great celebration.

Scarcely a month passed before I was swept by nostalgia for my time inside. There, the days had all been alike, but that serenity and calm and one's reliance on others just did not exist in the city outside. There you were required to work, to scrabble and lie and cheat and dissemble, to get married, to be a good father, to own a house, to…

My brother said I should travel in order to shake off my depression, but I had no passport; they had confiscated it when I was arrested. I went back to the prison investigations unit and asked the lieutenant if I might have it back. Through half-closed eyes he looked at me and said, 'You need to go to the Interior Ministry and present a request for reconsideration.'

'A request for reconsideration!' I whispered within myself.

As though I had been lost and created anew with no passport or memory.

I went and wrote out a letter in which I begged them to recreate me as a human being. They are the Creator and we their dependents.

I forgot to tell you: when I came to use my identity papers they told me, 'You have to renew your civil status and get a new ID Card, instead of using the old papers.'

No objections. We're their dependents, my boy, dependents in every sense, from our nationality to the choking air that we breathe.

A month after submitting my request for reconsideration I went back to the lieutenant in prison. He rebuked me, 'You're the strangest, stupidest prisoner I've seen in my life. Prisoners never show their face around us once they've left!'

To myself, I said, 'I've been longing for the days of loafing around, sleeping, reading, writing and having fun inside. It's an extraordinary blessing to be found nowhere but in your venerable prison.'

Every five or six months I would go back and ask what had happened to my request for reconsideration, to which the answer would be, 'Your letter hasn't come yet.'

Where has it got to?

One year and two months later I was informed they had consented to my request and a week after that I made my way to the pass- port office and entered the section for Saudi citizens. I stood before the official and submitted my request, which he examined for a few seconds then asked, 'Is this your first passport, or have you owned one previously?'

With the innocence for which my brother envied me I answered, 'I had a passport before!'

He raised his head from my documents. 'Where is it?'

'You've got it!' I said, stupid as only I could be.

He frowned and shook his head. 'How do you mean?'

I explained how I had been a political prisoner and he indicated that I should go to the special desk: the desk run by the security services. Off I went and found myself standing before an alert young man with blazing eyes who told me, 'Your passport has been placed in the archives; it can't be recovered.'

I was anxious and almost wept.

'Well, what's to be done?' I asked.

'My good fellow,' he said casually. 'There was no need for you to say you'd owned a passport. If you'd asked the official for a new passport

he would have searched the computer and your name wouldn't have appeared. Your old one predates the computer system.'

'What can I do now?' I asked him.

He was dismissive. 'Come back in a week. Maybe he'll have forgotten your name and what you look like.'

Just two days later a colleague of mine at the distribution company suggested I apply at the passport office in Sharqiya and put me in touch with one of his relatives there. I did so and when the passport came through I left the building almost flying. The green passport was paper wings that could take you anywhere in the world. It was my key, my first revelation of the beachfront in Bahrain where the low, gentle waves broke before a bewitching sunset and the sun's golden rays scattered and tangled in Soha's hair. There was nothing more beautiful than to stand surrounded by waters that stretched endlessly away. It was as though life itself had no limits, as though the cell no longer surrounded me, though I sometimes had the feeling that it was pursuing me, embedded within me like a tree I could not chop down or break away from.

Part 6

No one picks the lock

He did not turn;
He did not see any of us,
But stared at the doorstep and the door
And surrendered his gaze to the plants on the balcony.

Bassam Hajjar, A Few Things

43

THE ⁵HUBRA DAWN SEEMED calm and mild: a street stretching away east and west, twenty metres wide and lit with
dim yellow lamps, a plastic speed bump midway down its
length outside Fantoukh Mosque.

Out of the north door that opened on to the street came
Abdel Kareem, the end of his *shimagh* wrapped about his neck,
unable to conceal his anarchic black beard. He descended the
steps in his sandals then turned right into the backstreets.
Halting at a water fountain by a *zawiya*, he cupped his hand,
took three gulps and went on his way. He greeted Ahmed
al-Sameetan in a voice surrendering to sleep and the two
of them walked home. Ahmed entered first and courteously
invited his friend in. 'Please do …' to which the other, passing
on, replied, 'Too kind…'

They had come together years before, first at Fantoukh
Mosque's Qur'an school and then at Sudairi Mosque where
they attended a study circle memorising the Qur'an. Later,
they would go in the afternoon to the public library in
Suwaidi, borrowing books by al-Albani and perusing the
bound volumes of *The Meadows of the Righteous* and *The Guide
for the Fortunate*. For years now, Abdel Kareem had taken part
in meetings and trips with other large groups and his proselytising activities had increased, while Ahmed had begged off,
preoccupied with family affairs, his sisters especially, following

the death of his father, Ibn al-Sameetan. He often alluded to his virtuous sisters in front of his friend and to his desire to ensure their well-being with an upright husband who would appreciate them and keep them safe.

The matter of Tarfah's failed marriage was no trivial matter. Her brothers had got her involved with a failed actor deficient in morals, humour and manners, but the victor in all of this was Ahmed. He felt his view of the matter had been correct, that here was a world of degradation and filth, which encouraged Ahmed to speak directly to his friend after a number of hints and intimations. He took the plunge: 'As our forefathers said, "Arrange your daughter's engagement not your son's."'

And with that the offer of his sister Amal was broached. He affirmed his brotherly love for Abdel Kareem and his faith that with him, Amal would be in the hands of one who feared God and sought His reward.

It wasn't Amal that Abdel Kareem sought, however, but Tarfah. He wished to deliver her from Satan's wiles into the kingdom of God and His justice, to bring her back, after two whole years spent astray, to the right guidance of the Creator and His servants who feared Him, His punishment and His vengeance. He would be rewarded twice over: once for his own sake, for completing his religious duty through marriage, and once again for offering protection to a weak woman ensnared by the devil Art.

So he took her and the three months she lived with him were some of the loveliest of her life.

Calm and self-possessed, he never hit or betrayed her. It was only that he sometimes felt he was betraying his religion and neglecting his work: his evangelism and his *jihad*. On warm evenings he would tell her that he appreciated and respected her but feared that growing used to idleness and comfort would divert his attention from spreading the word, the summer activities and retreats, not to mention his long-standing ambition to commit to *jihad* and not just with financial contributions.

Three times he took her to Jaffal Centre on King Fahd Road and once she persuaded him to go to Faisaliya Tower, but emerging at the end of a tense half hour spent wandering about he informed her it was her duty to remove herself from temptation and that he, too, must shield his sight from those ornamented women.

During the first two weeks he ploughed Tarfah twice daily and showered her with such great passion that she fell in love with him and gradually began to change, dressing as he wanted, placing her *abaya* over her head instead of her shoulders so that her breasts were no longer visible to the naked eye, and replacing her *niqab* with a full face covering lest her beautiful eyes be an enticement to the weak hearted. After two months of this affectionate relationship, without him asking anything of her or making a single suggestion, she bought black gloves and thrust her hands into them whenever she left the house.

Following afternoon prayers Abdel Kareem would stay behind at Sudairi Mosque on Sudar Street in Shubra to study with some of the Brothers, observe the sunset prayers and attend a lesson or lecture at the mosque. Then he would return to his flat, in the same street as the mosque, bringing *tames* bread and either stewed beans or bean paste. These he would eat with his wife after she had brought him stewed tea, two sprigs of mint, a wedge of onion and a couple of slices of lemon. He would fondle her as they ate, then he would take her to bed.

Returning one evening as usual he came across a copy of *Riyadh* in the little living room. He glanced at it and asked, 'Who was here?'

'My brother Ayman.'

'I don't like that guy. Anyway, you know I don't like newspapers and magazines in my house.'

Tarfah asked his forgiveness and kissed his head. He smiled and stroked her cheeks and round face.

Everything about him was wonderful: his delicacy and playfulness, even his anger was serene and self-possessed.

His lovemaking was neither too short nor too long, a delightful balance, yet he wouldn't take her from behind. She had once shifted around during their drawn-out preliminaries, but he had backed off and returned to his familiar missionary position. Tarfah had got in the habit of doing it with her previous husband and learned to relish its pain, knowledge she would pass on to her lover, Fahd, when she slept with him.

One afternoon, talking to Nada on the phone, she said that she had found the perfect man. True, he was an extremist and very conservative, but he loved her and worried about her. Nada laughed and said, 'You idiot, he's an insecure paranoiac!'

In Nada's eyes, men might act in various ways, but they were all paranoid. Tarfah would not accept this.

'Abdel Kareem's not like that!'

That's what she thought: that she would live with him forever.

44

T HE MODEST HOUSE WAS melting into the darkness as Lulua buzzed about on her own like a bee, lighting the oven in the kitchen, putting a kettle of water on to boil and listening out for the sound of bubbling. All of a sudden a fly began circling about. Lulua had no idea why she became so terrified whenever she saw flies and ants swarming together as if about to feast on a corpse.

Two days earlier she had made a dash for the can of insecticide and sprayed it at a column of ants marching beneath the skirting board of the wall separating the kitchen from the dining room, telling herself that they were trying to devour her mother, whose body had become as lifeless and limp as an autumn leaf. And here she was now, hunting through the kitchen drawers for the plastic swatter and pursuing the fly like girls in fairytales who chase butterflies through the forest, slapping at it as it perched on the upper door of the fridge. The fly exploded, sticky blood and splayed wings, and Soha's voice piped up, asking about the noise.

'A fly, Mum,' Lulua replied. 'I was only killing a fly.'

Trying to remove it from the white of the fridge door she felt nausea flip her guts, the opposite of the great satisfaction her father had felt in prison as he executed his cockroaches en masse.

Fahd was taken aback to discover that Lulua had swapped her ring tone for a prayer.

'God, I am Your servant,' said the humble voice, 'born of Your servants, man and woman. We are guided by Your hand, Your judgement carried out, Your verdict just: we beseech You in all the names that You possess.'

Lulua was silent for a moment then said, 'This is my business. Prayer is a comfort and brings one closer to God. Mother needs prayer, Fahd, not Fairouz and Khaled Abdel Rahman.'

Her impersonation of their uncle irritated him. 'He's made fools of you and ruined you. He's wrecked every loving and affectionate relationship that my father ever made.'

She sighed. 'For your information, my relationship with my mother is better than it's ever been. Prayer and being close to God increases people's love for one another, but you're stubborn. You've got a head like a rock because you hate my uncle.'

Lulua opened the lower half of the fridge and took a sealed plastic container from inside the door. She had undone it and smelled the mint's green leaves, then plucked off a chilled sprig, washed it in lukewarm water and slowly lowered the leaves into the teapot, before swaying over to the dining room where the forty-year-old body lying on the bed had shifted upright. The woman smiled at her daughter.

'Fahd hasn't called?'

'He called yesterday. He asked after you; he says hello.'

'Do you know if he was able to open the bag?'

'I didn't ask him. I forgot.'

'Fine, so you've no idea what's inside?'

'Treasure maybe? Gold?' Lulua laughed.

45

Fahd drove the car down University Road, inspecting the shops on either side. Tarfah said she didn't like tunnels; despite the dim red lighting she sensed that she would die in one.

He laughed. 'Don't tell me you're not Tarfah any more. You've turned into Diana without my knowing it!'

Her laughter died away as she moved her head to his right shoulder and whispered flirtatiously, 'I love you, Dodi!'

He had bought her a mocha from Dr Keif and a Turkish coffee for himself. He didn't like Turkish coffee in paper cups, he said, because Turkish coffee was all about creating the right mood, and that meant somewhere to sit, a porcelain cup and his mother's wonderful laugh as she whispered in his father's ear at sunset in their home on the top floor in Ulaya. The coffee's aroma would steal out of the living room and enter his room, fashioning a warm and intimate atmosphere from his parents' love. Two cosy lovebirds, until King Death, idly circling over Qaseem Road and searching for a victim, had swooped down on two drivers, one sleepy, one fiddling with his mobile phone, and his father had crashed, his soul flying up into the distant skies.

In the last tunnel westbound tunnel before King Saud University she told him to take Takhassusi Road. She examined the shops on the side of the road and told him that this road had a history: her cousin Umm Samia had lived there. Running south to where it hit Mecca Road at the Aziziya branch of Panda, the street began with construction supply stores and travel agencies and ended with interior décor shops and the offices of the Bin Baz Marriage Project, before running on into undeveloped plots, the very plots where the Committee once ran into her friend Nada.

'Just imagine, the stupid girl goes for a morning drive down Thamama Road with her boyfriend and on the way back they decide to go into the new developments and suddenly the Committee's vehicle is right behind them.'

As she said this Tarfah little realised that a few months later, on a street near Takhassusi Road, she too would fall into the hands of the men from the Committee and would weep and plead to no avail.

They passed a luxurious décor store and she said the owner's son had proposed to her through her brothers before she married Abdel Kareem, her brother Ahmed's friend.

No one in the family said anything when Ahmed insisted on Abdel Kareem. Tarfah had become a guinea pig in her brothers' experiments and she loathed them all with the exception of Ayman. He was sweet and calm; nobody felt his presence in the house and nobody called him by his name.

'Come here, goat!' they'd say. 'Go there, goat!'

Anyone sitting with them for the first time would assume they were mocking how tractable he was with his mother and sisters; any one of them could set him trotting ahead of her like a goat.

Their older brother Abdullah's fabricated story was another matter. He claimed that when their mother, Qumasha, gave birth to Ayman her breasts had dried up and his desperation for milk had prompted her to hire a black woman as a wet nurse. Unable to continue paying the woman, Abdullah would say, Qumasha had finally let her go after her older brother came up with an ingenious solution: he took the two-year-old and gave him a she-goat's teat, from which he drank until he became so inoffensive and pliable that on first acquaintance anyone would think he was mentally ill.

But Qumasha, who smiled whenever Abdullah told this tale of his, said that when Ayman's uncle found out that he was the only one of the children to be raised on powdered milk, he started calling him 'son of a cow'. This became 'son of a sheep' and the children took up this nickname and toyed with it like a lump of clay until it turned into 'son of a goat'. His siblings almost forgot his real name, and he became 'son of a goat', until his mother became exceedingly cross at the indignity of being described as 'the goat' and his name changed again, becoming simply 'goat'.

Ayman had left her by the Paris Gallery entrance of Granada Mall and she went in, giving the impression that she was late as usual for her two friends, Nada and Fatoum. But instead she snuck out of the mall: going into a couple of shops then leaving via the main entrance where her lover waited for her. She took great care that no one recognised her. Though enveloped in her black *abaya* and veil, there were those who might guess it was her from the way she wore her robe, from her slow, funereal steps, from the exaggerated confidence with which she looked about her and from the plump white hand which Fahd was addicted to kissing.

Fahd switched on the car's secondary lights as she walked out, happy that there was no security guard at the entrance, not that he would have noticed that she had arrived in a black Camry and driven off in a blue Hyundai Accent. Given her fear of the average security guard's keen powers of observation she was careful to go in by one entrance and leave by another; when she entered by the Paris Gallery she would go out by Carrefour, Extra, the main entrance, or the rear door that led to the neighbourhood of Granada.

'I worry that my aunt and her daughter might drop by the house, decide to join me at the mall and call me on my mobile to find out where I am,' she had said, but the only call she got was from Ayman, which she answered immediately, convincing him that she would be late and would give him a ring as soon as she'd finished walking with her friends.

Fahd was parked outside the mall's main entrance and he started the engine as she approached. She walked slowly over, her handbag in one hand and a pink carrier bag in the other. Climbing in she said that she didn't want to do anything with him, they would just talk, but his hand mounted hers and she took it, bringing it beneath her black veil and slowly kissing it. In no time she was sucking his fingers one by one.

Fahd slowed outside the entrance to some furnished flats and saw a fat, young, bareheaded Saudi sitting on a chair in reception. He didn't stop. Saudis scared him because they were more curious than Sudanese or Indian receptionists. He might co-operate with the Committee or inform for pay and turn them in.

They entered the bedroom of another furnished flat like a pair of thieves. She started to kiss him as usual and, intoxicated, he surrendered. She took a red rose from the pink carrier bag. It had no cellophane wrapping, as though it had been freshly plucked from a garden. She said that she had taken it from a flower shop inside the mall. He handed her a small, container and a carton slightly larger than a matchbox. Smiling shyly she opened the container and looked at the strip within: three bubbles sealed with tinfoil. He told her to rip one open and smell it. She broke the seal, sniffed and said, 'Oh! Wonderful!'

It was the smell of fresh strawberries.

She took hold of him by his head and as though it might be their last time together, moved over every inch of him until every pore in his body came alive and his mouth sprang forward searching for the rain cloud. Her rain cloud. She rained torrents, he would tell her, and her soul laughed lightly as she mischievously asked, 'Even in summer?'

He chuckled and whispered in her ear, 'Even in summer: no rain dance needed. Just passing next to it makes it pour.'

On her way home she talked to Fahd on the phone as she sat alongside her brother, telling him he hadn't given her the hand cream or her gloves. Then she laughed. He only realised she was sitting next to Ayman when the steady blip of the Camry's speed monitor sounded. Hastily, he said goodbye— 'When you get home, call!'—and hung up.

She was certifiable, he told himself; how could she speak so brazenly next to her brother? Her innuendo was transparent: hand cream was the lubricant and gloves were the rubber sheath.

'Gloves. What symbolism! Completely crazy!'

Her recklessness called for revenge, he told himself. The next time they met he found a choice spot behind the front door to the flat where he hid and held his breath, with some idea of singing her hair with his lighter. She called out his name repeatedly and he didn't answer, so she punched his number into her phone and his mobile rang suddenly in his pocket. He emerged from his hiding place laughing, 'Damn you. It was too late for me to put it on silent!'

She embraced him, her head encircled in her *hijab*, and passionately received his mouth.

In the lift he moved closer to hug her and lifting her veil she snatched a final kiss. 'I'm really worried for you, Fahoudi.'

She feared loss, loathed it: the loss of the father who had hated her and never stopped beating her, the loss of Abdel Kareem who left without telling her he would never return, the loss of Khaled who had slept with her for three years until his wife had discovered what was going on from his mobile phone and he had decided to abandon Tarfah and never see her again.

Tarfah took Fahd's hand and laid it on her cheek. 'Promise me you won't leave me, Fahd?' she whispered fearfully.

He nodded gratefully, lost in the ripe tenderness of her cheek.

46

O NE NIGHT ABDEL KAREEM didn't return from Sudairi
Mosque.

He called Tarfah to say that he wouldn't be back until
tomorrow: he was going on a trip for two days. But he didn't
return after two days or three days or a week or a month.

After a fortnight of waiting and weeping in the flat she
went back to her family. Ahmed avoided looking at her.
At first he accused her of tiring Abdel Kareem out with
her demands. Withdrawn from the world, pious and god-
fearing, Ahmed believed that life held nothing worth fighting, boasting and struggling for. His life was the life of the
soul and required no hardship or suffering. Yet after two
weeks of searching and questioning friends and family and
the worshippers at the Fantoukh, Sudeiri and Sanei Khairi
mosques, Ahmed discovered that Abdel Kareem had made a
clandestine trip to Syria with two acquaintances from Eid
Mosque in Suwaidi.

His mother wept for a long time, as did Tarfah, who had
assumed that God was compensating her for the suffering
of her bitter childhood and two years of a failed and bloody
marriage, with a man worthy of sacrifice and love.

But he had betrayed her and she hadn't fully realised it at the
time. In the second month of their marriage, Abdel Kareem
had received a young man at the flat in the most mysterious

manner. His phone rang once and he jumped to his feet and went down to see him in his *jellabiya*.

Rushing over to the window of the men's *majlis* that looked over the street, she switched off the lights and spied on them from behind the drawn curtains. On the other side of the road she saw a tall young man with long hair reaching nearly to his shoulders, talking away as he sat behind his open car door with the engine running, and at the same time she saw the back of Abdel Kareem, absorbed in their discussion.

At first, she asked her husband who came and went like that without being invited up to the *majlis*, to which he replied that he was one of the Brothers from the nearby Eid Mosque. When she began asking closer questions about his name and his job and how Abdel Kareem had first met him, he said, 'He's a childhood friend, from primary school,' and she understood that he didn't like her asking about things that didn't concern her.

He locked his phone with a password and grew jumpy whenever the message tone sounded. He persuaded her that this was men's business and that she had no right interfering and prying. 'Do you lack anything?' he asked her and when, unsmiling, she said she didn't, he added, 'Do I deny you anything?'

But she would smile again and change the subject. 'Can I make you coffee?'

When he stripped and went to the bathroom to take a long shower before the first call to Friday prayers, Tarfah tried to open his phone, entering all the numbers she thought might work and give her access to his inbox, but she never succeeded.

She was amazed by how much time he spent on the Internet in that second month. One evening his friend called him from the street and he hurried out, leaving the computer on. She ran over and jogged the mouse before it could close and leave her needing a password to open it. Opening a few files on the desktop she found maps of Syria, Northern Syria and the region around Raqqa and Deir Azzur.

'Is he thinking of marrying a Syrian?' Tarfah thought to herself, before coming across a map of Iraq. She closed the file quickly. She noticed another labelled *Expelling the Infidel from the Arabian Gulf* and then some documents: *Training Regime for the Mujahid* from the *al-Battar* online magazine, various texts from the Maqrizi Centre's website and *fatwas* from The Voice of Jihad. She opened the favourites file in his web browser and quickly scanned the list of sites that Abdel Kareem had saved there: The Maqrizi Centre for Historical Studies, The Islamic Media Resource, The Minbar of Tawheed and Jihad, al-Battar, The Voice of Jihad.

Suddenly she heard his key slip into the keyhole in the flat's front door and she came back out.

'Why are you so late?' she asked with loving concern. 'I hope nothing went wrong.'

Put on the back foot he said something about the mosque needing help with its library and replacing the air-conditioning units. Would he like coffee or tea, she then wanted to know, or would he wait for supper?

Going into his little office he noticed that the screen hadn't shut down. He had been gone for more than twenty minutes and it was set to switch off if left inactive for two minutes. It must have been her; she had spied on his things, Abdel Kareem whispered to himself.

She came in and set a cup of tea on the table. He looked at her. 'Tarfah, where were you a moment ago?'

'In the kitchen,' she answered, pretending not to understand.

'When I was downstairs with my friend, I mean.'

'I was here,' she said, and pointed. 'In the living room.'

He rose from his chair, went out into the living room and sat on the sofa, where he picked up a little book. To make a mistake was no sin, he told her, but lying was. 'Don't lie, Tarfah!'

'You keep everything from me!' she shouted, losing her temper. 'I don't go near your computer or your phone. People I don't know come and visit you and when I ask you who they are you dodge the question. It's my right to know. I'm your wife.'

'My life isn't your personal property, woman, understand? Don't stick your nose into things that don't concern you.'

He slammed the door on his way out and two hours later returned carrying bread, milk and a box of sugared dates. She rose to greet him and kissed his head. Then they went to bed.

When Abdel Kareem vanished, Tarfah stayed in the flat, waiting. Every time she heard a car stopping in the street outside and a door slamming she would peer around the curtains. When she heard the footsteps of the man who lived in the flat next door her heart would stop beating for whole seconds, waiting—longing—for Abdel Kareem's key to slip into the lock and turn twice, for him to push the door slowly open and come in, weary with travel, or from some long and arduous retreat. She would kiss his head, remove his rumpled *shimagh* then undo the buttons of his *thaub* and take it off so he might go into the bathroom and stand for long minutes beneath the pulsing spray while she dashed to the kitchen to make him supper and prepare two pots of tea—one with red tea, the other ginger—and pour some honey into a little dish with a few olives. Overjoyed, infatuated, she would wait for him in the living room and consider whether she should phone her family to breathlessly inform them, 'Abdel Kareem's back!' or call his mother first.

But no one opened the door.

No car came quietly to a halt outside the building.

No voice called from a strange number to tell her he was all right.

Nothing at all, save the longing that gnawed at her limbs and filled her nights with loneliness.

47

I T WASN´T JUST THAT Tarfah sensed the cooling of her relationship with Fahd; lying on her bed at night and examining her life her intuition would bother her. She began to
lose hope of ever seeing Fahd without having to beg him.
What was at first a mere impression had become undeniable
fact, had become a sort of pleading on her part. There was
some mystery she didn't understand. Why was he avoiding
her? When she spoke with him he seemed almost tearful with
longing for her.

There was a mystery in their relationship that Fahd barely
understood himself. He wanted to meet her, to hold her, to
sear her mouth with kisses, but he kept going to the bathroom to wash his mouth out, gargling and spitting, sniffing
the air almost, as if his very breath smelt foul. It got so bad that
when she dragged him down there he almost vomited. How
many times had he lingered in the bathroom dousing himself
with blisteringly hot water, watching the steam rise up as he
scrubbed away?

That evening his directness surprised her, and maybe himself
as well: 'Will I see you today?'

She didn't moan lasciviously, but, coquettish and sly, replied
that he should give her an hour to see how she felt. Then,
because she had already made up her mind to agree, she
became impatient.

On his way over to see her he was eager and full of longing. He was listening to MBC FM and the voice of Abdel Majeed Abdullah streamed sweetly out. As soon as he got close he asked her where he should pick her up.

'Entrance Three,' she said.

'Facing the schools, right?' he asked to make sure. 'The one opposite Nada Alley?'

He called again to tell her to come outside and she took him by surprise, swaying slowly over. Arrogantly, he thought.

She got in beside him, in one hand the olive green hand-bag embroidered with knights holding lances and arrows and in the other a plastic bag whose shop logo he couldn't make out. She said that she had been going to call him but he had surprised her by stopping the car outside the entrance. There were no shoppers about, just a pair of security guards lighting their cigarettes.

'It's evening prayers,' she said to him. 'That's why no one's outside the entrance.'

They drove along together.

He asked if they should take a hotel room or a flat, or hide out in one of the unlit building lots since it was nearly nine and there wasn't enough time to settle down for a long session.

'Don't mind,' she said. 'You decide.'

They drove north, searching for a building plot. They passed the first unlit dirt road. She uncovered her face and he kissed her quickly. They decided to look for a flat. She suggested they head over to Fahd Crown Hotel on the airport highway and he explained that there wasn't enough time to enjoy a place like that. They ran through the names of furnished flats they had visited and settled on a new flat in Nuzha that they hadn't used before.

He parked the car, consumed by the worry that Tarfah would search through his things. He always did his best to stop outside the entrance to the flats so he could see her body move if she bent down to have a rummage.

The reception area was spacious and luxurious but no one was there. The door to a side room was ajar and he knocked gently, calling out, 'Friend?'

An Indian emerged. From his broken Arabic it was clear he was a recent arrival to the country. He rapped out the usual question—'Family section?'—then picked up the key and Fahd followed him to the second floor. The corridor was clad in expensive marble and the doors on either side gave the impression that the flats within were clean and respectable.

His first impression on opening the door to flat 18 was that it looked like a room in a highway motel. He looked at the bedspread, worn through from repeated washing. In view of the time, which was flying through their fingers, he decided to take the flat and handed over a photocopy of their forged marriage contract and one hundred riyals to an Egyptian employee who had arrived that moment. Tarfah was sitting in the car. He signalled to her that she should come over but she didn't move. He phoned her and asked her to get out.

Taking the key he walked ahead of her to the lift and when the door slid shut she threw herself into his arms. He told her the place was run down and filthy but searching for another and wasting time wasn't an option. Her heart fluttered as did her delectable breasts, a photo of which she had sent to him on the phone that morning, showing two currants, pricked up behind the pink stretch top that pressed against them.

This is me just woken up … she had written. *Fresh as a daisy!*

He had spent half an hour enlarging the area over her breasts in an attempt to read the printed English slogan: *Let's dance the Hula-hula!*

He opened the door and shut it quickly behind them. The flat was pitch black. He tried turning on the lights but without success, flicking the switch by the door, in the bathroom and the bedroom, even the button for the air-conditioner. It was no use.

'Lock the door,' she said. 'I'll light the candle I brought last time.'

They needed the air conditioner, he said, and lifting the receiver dialled reception. The Egyptian answered. 'Look on your left, sir. Flip the big switch.'

He opened the grey fuse-box and pressed the large rocker. Everything in the flat lit up. He slid home the bolt on the front door and she rushed into the bedroom. Taking off his shoes, his socks and his *shimagh* he went into the bathroom for a short while and when he came out found her doing herself up in front of the mirror on the dressing table, lightly spraying perfume over breasts that quivered beneath the perforated black satin.

He hugged her hard and squeezed her sinuous hips. She kissed him and he let his hands creep over her. Besieged by fear of failure he attempted to arouse himself.

Her moans grew louder and she pulled him towards the bed, but he was slack and limp and he turned on to his back beside her, staring at the ceiling. She rolled on to him, laughing, doing her best to make the moment light-hearted, but she couldn't erase the fact that she was handling a flaccid piece of meat. She sat on the edge of the bed and heard him say, 'The place is disgusting!' then, 'The filth in here makes

300

me feel sick!' as though searching for something to excuse his failure.

He noticed that her back was half-naked and shivering and her head, with its exceptionally soft, exceptionally black hair was trembling violently. He tried to comfort her and stroked her back but she went over to the dressing table as though she were drugged, picked up her head covering and spread it over the dirty pillow. She laid his head back upon it and said, 'Relax!' then added with a strained smile, 'Don't let it bother you. Everything will get back to how it was, and better.'

She sat next to him and told him a joke, but Fahd was still dwelling on his failure. At last he got up, got dressed and gave her a sad smile.

'Shall we go?'

Going over to the dressing table she took a pack of slender Davidoff cigarettes from her handbag and lit one, blowing the smoke into the room. She handed it to him and he took a single drag then returned it to her, saying, 'Sometimes I think about what's changed in our relationship: how I start to feel afraid before we even touch, how even as we're fooling around and kissing I'm worrying I won't get it up … and then I end up failing for real.'

Tarfah didn't fully understand what lay behind this but she worried that their love really had begun to wither, that one day, not long off now, she would lose him. Who would fill his absence? She laughed to herself, remembering that she had the same thoughts about Khaled, who had devoured her body for fully three years, and now here came Fahd al-Safeelawi invading her life and making her forget her former lover.

The life she led with her four-year-old, Sara, was so much lovelier than time wasted with these wretches, she thought to herself, *But what can I do when my instincts take over? How can I quench the flames? I'm tired of taking care of myself and I don't want another woman in place of a man. How I hate that! Whenever Nada comes close to whisper in my ear, or puts her arm about my neck and pulls me towards her to say something, or presses herself against me it disgusts me more than I can say. 'I don't like girls rubbing up against me!' I shout at her and she and cousin Samia laugh and Samia, that idiot, says, 'So you like boys doing it, then?'*

Sometimes Samia's stories astonished her, like the time she told Tarfah about those everything-for-two-riyal stores crammed with junk where the only floor space left were narrow passageways just wide enough for a single person. In the crowds that came during festivals and at the start of the school term young men would squeeze past her and bump against her on purpose. She paid no attention and did nothing.

'Let them have their fun, poor things!' she would say, shaking with laughter.

Tarfah embraced Fahd by the door and he pulled her slim hips violently towards him then lifted her plump hand and gave it a chaste kiss. In the lift there was only enough time to raise her veil and snatch a quick kiss between the second and ground floors. Handing her the car keys he issued rapid intructions. 'Walk straight out to the car and wait till I've finished with him.'

Handing over the flat after just two or three hours was tricky, and he launched into his oft-repeated lie, this time asking about the Nuwara wedding hall. When the Egyptian receptionist professed his ignorance, Fahd told him that it was on Qaseem Road; did he know it? Shamefaced, the Egyptian shook his head and said that he was new in town, all he knew was this building, to which Fahd, bringing the conversation to its natural conclusion, said, 'We're off to a wedding. If we're not back by one, consider the flat free and the deposit's yours.'

The Egyptian grinned gratefully and thanked him.

On Tahliya Street the luxury vehicles coasted slowly by, blaring music as they went, and young men sat chatting in cafés. When he reached Coffee Day he asked her if she wanted an Americano or a cappuccino. She declined. He took out a rose and sniffed gaily at it, but it only made him feel intensely sad. He nearly wept as he thought of his life.

After he left her at the mall, she didn't call him for an hour. He showered and switched on the television and then phoned her and asked, 'Where are you?'

She was yet to leave the mall. Her brother hadn't come. This time he felt her reproach more strongly. He hadn't given his lover what she needed; his soul wasn't what it was, his heart was just a witless blood pump. After switching off the light he wept and told himself it was a good thing Saeed wasn't there because this was a golden chance to make fun of him.

Tarfah rang. She was doing her best to sound cheerful but her voice was sad. She was practically certain that there was another woman in his life and that he, so sensitive, didn't have it in himself to break her heart. He tried convincing her that he was going through a tough time with his sick mother, but gave none of the details about his personal life that she was looking for. Their conversations were about love and longing, or about the scandalous friends she described with sweet sarcasm, or about his problems with painting, his ambitions and his negative views of Saudi artists.

48

F AHD HAD HAD NOTHING all day except a dried-up donut taken from the fridge and a cup of filter coffee. He had been wholly absorbed by his painting, *Mecca.* He was wired. In his mind sat Pablo Picasso's *Guernica,* and facing it, an image of an uncovered marketplace in the small Basque town with warplanes overhead pouring down fire and obliterating the strolling citizens.

He painted a rooftop, broad as a desert and surrounded by minarets, and corpses sprawled all over the canvas, heads riddled with sniper rounds and trucks transporting the dead like crates of aubergines and tomatoes.

Fahd sometimes wondered what had caused him to love art so, to become addicted to the heady reek of oils. Was it a true passion, a hidden need to express what lay within him? Was it a response to the prophecy of Mustafa, the Sudanese artist he had met as a boy with his father in Thalatheen Street? Was it merely a stubborn, perverse desire to crush his uncle, always bellowing that on the Day of Judgement Fahd would be asked to breathe life into his creations?

He started to make a preliminary sketch for the painting, laying down pencil lines angrily and sadly. Then he threw the sketch away and began another until, with the tragedy and drama of Guernica in his thoughts, he made the decision to paint in only two colours, black and white. He drew widely scattered circles, heads like fat melons in a big field with small holes from which black liquid ran out to the earth.

He was working away, sighing from time to time with suppressed exasperation, when it suddenly occurred to him that a painting finished in anger would turn out excessively sentimental and he had better calm down a little. Taking a cup of coffee he went over to his father's bag.

He opened it and rummaged through the books and papers, taking out the olive stone prayer beads and turning them one by one between his thumb and index finger, before returning to his chair beside the canvas.

He picked up a brush and painted one stone white then another grey. This pleased him: a fresh distraction that lifted his burden of worry. Squeezing a tube of red he deposited a quantity the size of a small bird's talon on a stone and with his thumb smeared the paint over its surface until it was bright red all over. He did the same with another stone in yellow, then another in green, and so on until the dull loop had been transformed into an African song, warm and pulsing with life. It was as though he had restored the prayer beads to life.

His phone's message tone trilled. He made no move to get up and ten minutes later it sounded again. Laying the prayer beads on the palette he slowly made his way over to the pocket of his *thaub* and read the two messages, one from Tarfah and one from Lulua: *Fahd, Mum's been asking for you since yesterday.*

He went back to the canvas hanging on the easel and contemplated the corpses, sprawled chaotically and absurdly. He heard the door of the flat slowly open then close, and measured footsteps proceed to the kitchen that opened out on to the small living room. Water poured into a cup and glugged into a thirsty body. There was the light tap of the glass on the kitchen table, then Saeed's voice a few paces away: 'Superb, Fahd! You really are a great artist!'

Fahd turned to him with raised eyebrows. 'Huh! How did you get in here?'

Saeed laughed pointing at the canvas. 'The door, but it looks like you need to get away from this picture!'

Saeed went inside to sleep while Fahd worked on. The features of masked men and soldiers started to appear. As the time approached one in the morning he felt his chest constrict, as though twenty soldiers had thrown him down and were sitting on his heart. His breathing became irregular. He washed the brush he was holding and quickly cleaned the palette knife, then doused his face in a continuous stream of water at the kitchen sink. He put on his *thaub* and left without his *shimagh*. He started the car and drove away, directionless.

Paralysis crept through Riyadh's body, slumbering like a mysterious woman. The streetlights were faint as they fought against the columns of dust laying their fire over the city. In the murk of the heavy dust the bridge by Mamlaka Tower was invisible, likewise the crystal ball atop Faisaliya Tower. Cars driven by high-spirited young men waited at traffic lights. He pulled up beside one. On the back seat three heads bobbed uproariously as the voice of Rashed al-Fares split the dust of the night. Fahd looked over at them with a smile. In the front seat was a young man, his hair tied back in a ponytail, gesturing at some girls who sat behind the smoked windows of a pearl-grey Cadillac Escalade. One of them opened her window and made an obscene gesture with her middle finger. They erupted with a loud yell accompanied by the squeal of tyres as they chased after the girls' Indian driver, well-trained in these night time excursions.

Fahd glanced in the direction of Shoe Palace and considered paying a visit to his mother and sister. It was late, though. He took a right on to King Fahd Road and opened the window—perhaps the twenty soldiers slumped over his chest might be swept away—but the surging dust, like a wild squall of rain, whipped at his face and hurt his eyes. He reconsidered his need for fresh air and closed the window.

If he wept softly now, he whispered to himself, it might ease his cramped heart and the smugly squatting soldiers would fly away. Opening the glove box he took out the first tape he found, then pushed it into the slot, and Fairouz's voice emerged, wounded and sorrowful:

I yearn for you and cannot see you, nor can I speak with you;
From the backstreets, from behind the shutters, I call out to you.

He thought of the nights long ago, his father reading in his room and Fairouz's voice melting softly in his ears.

He didn't go over the bridge over Imam Road, but stopped on the far left, by the Abdel Lateef Jameel traffic lights, and looped back round to the petrol station on the corner, stopping in a parking bay outside a Coffee Day kiosk. He ordered a medium-sweet Turkish coffee and a small bottle of water and drove slowly along Qaseem Road sipping his coffee as Fairouz summoned up a sad memory of his father, drawing his final breath on this accursed stretch of road.

When he returned, having driven some seventy kilometres, he wasn't breathing calmly as he had hoped.

A completely jinxed night, he told himself.

In bed he tossed and turned and drank water until the daylight came and he dozed off, discontent.

Part 7

The *jinn*'s deadly laugh

A settlement bleak as a buckler's back
About whose edges sing the jinn *by night.*

Al–Asha

49

T HAT DISTANT MORNING IT was not the cries of his mobile's message alert that woke Fahd, but a repeated ringing, like weeping. Very sluggishly he opened his eyes, his head weighed down with sorrow, and saw the number of a landline blinking on the screen. With a sense of foreboding and disquiet he pressed the green button and his uncle's voice, which he hadn't heard since leaving home, informed him that he was at King Khaled University Hospital: Fahd's mother was very ill and they were waiting in the emergency ward.

'What happened to her?' Fahd shouted frantically.

'She's in a coma at the moment,' his uncle said, 'and we hope that God will deliver her from harm.'

He hadn't said that she was dead, but the tone and numb quality of his voice hinted at something dreadful.

Fahd rushed into his *thaub* and *shimagh* and drove recklessly to the hospital. At the second roundabout just before the exit for the university, the car swerved violently and he lost control, though luckily there was no one on the internal road except for him. He pointed the car in the right direction and drove calmly on, muttering prayers, until he reached the lights, where he took a left then went right into the bays opposite the emergency ward. He parked and sprinted off, shooting past the parked ambulances like a sand grouse flapping over the desert.

Behind the glass door, his uncle and cousin Yasser were standing with the doctor. As soon as he opened the door and went inside his uncle greeted him and kissed him on both cheeks, then led him to a seating area near the trolley beds by the door. He eased Fahd on to a wobbly leather chair, then sat down beside him and said, 'May God console you. What God gives and what He takes belong to Him alone.'

He began to talk about his mother's virtues and piety while Fahd raised his bare feet, which he had freed from his sandals that lay on the tiled floor, and placed them on the edge of the chair in a squatting position. He gripped his head in his hands and his slender body started to shake silently as his uncle consoled him, 'Weeping cannot help the dead. What she needs from you now is prayer and patience. Umm Fahd was a true believer, a godly woman; she lived like a companion of the Prophet, may God have mercy on her.'

When he had recovered from the fright and shock of the situation, the doctor came over, offered his condolences and told him that she was lying in bed three if he wanted to see her. Fahd instantly recalled standing with Saeed before the receptionist at Shamesi Hospital's emergency ward, the receptionist suggesting they go to the morgue to examine the body and see if it was his father.

Fahd stood up, disoriented and nervous, and went in, sweeping back the white curtain that hid the bed from the corridor with trembling hands. His uncle came in with him for a little while and Fahd burst into tears as he kissed her head and the golden hairs that spilled from beneath the bed sheet. The doctor gestured at the uncle to go outside and leave her son with his mother. He was kissing her, imploring her, trying to assuage his suffering, his sorrow and his tortured conscience.

Where he got the courage to expose her white brow and kiss it he didn't know. He searched for her hands, kissed them humbly, then kissed her feet. He noticed that her feet were swollen and saw that the ends of her legs were blotched and bloated with water. He lifted the cover from her glowing face and looked at her neck and shoulders where there were clear signs of bruising. He started shaking and rushed out to the doctor, taking him by hand and steering him to an out of the way spot. He asked the doctor if he had seen the bruises and injuries on his mother's body. The doctor nodded and stated without being asked that he didn't believe they had been the cause of her death. But who had beaten her like that? Fahd wanted to know and started yelling down the corridor, 'My mother's dead! Someone killed her!'

The doctor calmed him down and his uncle and Yasser came over with Ibrahim, who had just that moment arrived and now embraced Fahd and offered his condolences.

They took him to an empty waiting room. The uncle explained that ten days previously an Egyptian sheikh had blown on her and diagnosed that she was possessed. Moreover the infidel *jinn* inside her had spoken aloud in a voice heard by Yasser, Lulua and himself; the sheikh had even held a conversation with it, and it had promised to leave her, but yesterday it had reneged on its vow and defiantly refused to come out from her body. The sheikh had been forced to beat it until it did. He kept beating her until the *jinn* fled and its voice fell silent, then asked them to let her sleep so she could rest. She had slept, her eyes like clouds that couldn't rain, and failed to awaken for dawn prayers the following day.

She had slept with her face covered completely with her prayer robe, only her reddened feet showing. Pill bottles lay beside her; the voice of Imam al-Sudais faded away from within her mobile phone as he read *surat Maryam*, the *sura* that she loved so much. There was a bottle of *zamzam* water, bundles of paper inscribed with saffron, a slip covered with Qur'anic verses written in saffron and steeped in a cup of yellowed water, her Qur'an with an ostrich feather marking *surat al-hashr*, a small booklet of prayers, and grief suppressed, soaring on wings of pain, tears cocooned in the hanging curtains and the angel of a tormented death gathering up his things and bestowing a last glance on her before departing through the window. Outside there were men by the dozen, girls from middle school in Khazan Street. In Fouta Park playful children tumbled gleefully about. Employees of Jordanian and Palestinian eateries stood on the pavement as she passed by, flying, robed in white, face smiling despite the cloud of sorrow hovering round her eyes.

Fahd stood up and made for the doctor, then turned, bewildered, towards the emergency ward's entrance. Grabbing the arm of the dark-skinned security guard he said in a harsh voice, 'An Egyptian beat my mother to death. Call the police.'

The man moved away and made a call, speaking for several minutes as he took notes on the table by the outer door. Fahd's mobile barked and, choking on the horror of the situation, he explained to Saeed what had happened: 'My mother's been killed, if you can believe it.'

Alarmed, Saeed said that he was on his way and advised him to investigate. 'You have to find out what happened, Fahd. Aunt Soha was as much my mother as she was yours.'

313

50

F AHD PACED LIKE A wolf outside the emergency ward, passing back and forth before the glass door as though it were
an iron cage standing between him and freedom.

He saw his friend Saeed rushing down the west-most steps
from the uncovered parking bays, looking bewildered and lost
as he advanced. Saeed hugged Fahd to his chest, pulling his
head towards him and kissing it as he muttered in distress, 'May
God console you and give us strength in times of trouble.'

He began comforting him with commonplaces: this is the
road we all must travel, maybe her passing gave her relief from
the suffering of her illness.

'But it's murder, Saeed, not natural causes.'

'Fine, so what now?'

'I've brought in the police and the detective's here now.' He
pointed inside. 'He's interviewing my uncle at the moment.'

They went into reception. Yasser was leaning against the
corridor wall looking right to where his father sat before the
detective, talking to him with intensity and conviction and
gesturing with both his hands, tugging every now and then
on the *shimagh* as it slipped to the back of his head. Yasser was
watching his father but couldn't hear him.

A fat man next to Fahd suddenly rose to his feet, the bottom
half of his plump calves showing beneath the hem of the white
thaub. 'Peace be upon you and the mercy of God.'

Raising his head, Fahd saw a stout-bodied Egyptian with a pale, round face beneath which a carefully trimmed black beard lay coiled, and a *miswak* that he chewed continuously and anxiously on both sides of his mouth. Fahd answered without holding out his hand. The man went over to the glass door and spoke to the security guard who pointed towards Fahd. The Egyptian sheikh came towards him, breathing unevenly, and warmly shook his hand, extending his condolences, invoking God's mercy on the deceased and insisting on the inevitability of death and fate.

Throwing his hands up in the man's face Fahd screamed, 'How could you kill a sick and frail woman, you criminal?'

His rage and wild cries were met with calm and dignity.

'God grant you the best reward,' the sheikh intoned, crushingly emotionless, until the guard intervened and took them both outside. Fahd continued to call down eternal torment and hellfire on his head while the sheikh kept his features as impassive as the dead. 'God guide you,' he said, his glassy eyes staring into space and avoiding looking directly into Fahd's face.

After Fahd had calmed down a little and asked him why he had done it, the sheikh embarked on an explanation that the Prophet, too, had performed Qur'anic readings, then informed him that her husband, Fahd's uncle, had also taken part in the assault. He described it in detail. When the demon's harsh voice was first heard, Abu Ayoub had shouted at Lulua to fetch him a heavy stick: 'Give us the broom handle.' She had searched the kitchen and found it behind the door. She asked him what was the matter and he replied that the *jinn* had begun to speak and that the sheikh would now flog it until it left Soha's body. As he explained this he was rushing over to hand the broom to the sheikh, who requested that Soha's arms and legs be held down and started to beat her, first on her back, then upon her shoulders, since the demon was known to stand on the left shoulder. She was wailing in a voice eroded by exhaustion and effort until it sounded like the lowing of an ailing cow, the sheikh thrashing at her savagely before handing over to Abu Ayoub, who beat her calf muscles then her feet. Finally, with Soha cursing him listlessly, the Egyptian whispered to Yasser to hand him a scalpel, which the latter took from his pocket as if prepared for this very moment. The sheikh sliced her thumb and out flew sticky black blood, the blood of both the infidel demon and Soha's spirit, after which she slept peacefully.

The sheikh said that she would wake the next day a different person, her health transformed; all they had do was cover her face with a light blanket until noon the following day.

But she slept forever.

Invisible birds swooped down over the body stretched out in the dining room, while Dr Yasser, his eyes as round as an owl's behind his glasses, gazed at the corpse with pride: all the knowledge and learning he had accumulated over the course of seven years at the College of Medicine in King Saud University had failed. The only true medicine, he now knew, was the Qur'anic cure.

51

A BU AYOUB'S FACE HAD darkened, either from grief or from his anxiety over the investigation and the questions about death and crime. Yasser trailed him like his shadow as the detective summoned the Egyptian sheikh, who handed over his residence permit. The detective jotted down a few pieces of information and began questioning him about the events of the previous night.

How painful for Fahd to recall the previous evening: dust settling thick over Riyadh, the city swimming in heavy layers of dust that clogged eyelashes and flew up nostrils to enter the brain, dust caking the heart.

He thought of how he had gone out after midnight and begun gloomily circling the streets, unable to sleep or breathe. He remembered stopping at the traffic lights at the junction of the Urouba and Ulaya roads, thinking that he would visit his mother if it weren't so late. Had that been the moment, the instant her breath grew still? Had she looked at the *qibla*, towards Mamalka Tower where Fahd sat, and given up her soul? Had he not seen, for instance, a butterfly fly through the grime, or a blinded pigeon stagger into the lampposts by Ulaya Mall, or maybe fall at the feet of the security guards by the entrance to the parking bays of Mamlaka Tower? Might his mother's soul have been flapping away, sad, listless and content, scornful of the world, of people, of this extraordinary country?

Was her soul yet to depart, the thick staff at that very moment lifting into air full of dust and dirt to descend with the lisping whistle of a high wind fleeing the backstreets?

Through the door of the emergency ward came a man in his forties carrying documents and dressed in civilian clothes and a *shimagh*. He passed quickly inside and greeted the doctor, speaking to him for a few moments, before going to stand over the detective and leafing through the ten sheets of paper loaded with sadness and anger, where Soha's name was listed like that of a soldier struck down by a stray bullet before ever reaching the field of battle.

Yasser suddenly materialised alongside the man and appeared to discuss something important with him. Fahd approached, leaving Saeed sitting on a plastic chair like those usually found in public parks. The man in the civilian clothes, who was the senior detective, was explaining to Yasser the procedure that would be followed in this case: the body would be transferred to the morgue at Shamesi General Hospital where it would be dissected to establish the cause of death. Yasser was trying to persuade him to bring things to a close without carrying out the autopsy, since the family wouldn't permit his aunt's body to be exposed to the gaze of strangers, its sanctity and dignity violated by the surgeon's scalpels. There was just no need for it.

From beside them Fahd suddenly asked, 'Who are you to decide if we need it or not? Did you lot need to flog her to death?'

Yasser, the honorary doctor, waved his hands frantically in the face of his angry, grief-stricken cousin as he tried to explain that according to tests and X-rays her death had been inevitable.

318

'The disease had spread to her lungs and there was no hope of recovery so we tried curing her with the Qur'an. We'd heard that God had cured many people through traditional Islamic healing.'

The senior detective remarked that there had been a similar case two days previously in Dawadmi. The victim had been a ten-year-old boy who was beaten to death. He mentioned that there were many cases of people being tortured to exorcise *jinn* and demons.

As the three of them stood in the passage opposite the curtained-off beds, Abu Ayoub came over and stated that the best way to honour the dead was burial. Death was a part of life, he said: Umm Fahd's death had been decreed and might atone for her sins, for a Muslim's suffering on earth shall ease the torment they face in the afterlife. The senior detective was nodding in agreement. Abu Ayoub went on: the autopsy would delay the burial and complicate matters for the relatives who would be arriving tomorrow afternoon, travelling from outside Riyadh to pray over her.

Glancing at his father out of the corner of his eye, Yasser completed the thought: wouldn't withdrawing the case make it unnecessary for the deceased to go to the dissection table and mean she could be put straight in a fridge?

Fahd objected. 'Am I going to withdraw a murder charge? And whose murder? My own mother's! I will not.'

Fahd dripped sweat and rage, the events of his mother's final days streaming past his eyes like some endless film reel.

He remembered his mother a month before, telling him the story of his father's eldest sister, Haila, a tale she had heard a number of times from Suleiman. She'd never forgotten it: how Haila had died fifty years before out in Wadi al-Rawghani near Unayza; how the girl's father had fasted for two successive months in penance for manslaughter, or neglect of a ten-year-old child.

Haila had started experiencing frequent headaches. She took to supporting herself against walls as she walked and dragging her feet. The world around her gradually faded and bit by bit the light went out. The traditional remedies and cures offered by a woman called Moudi in Sabakh didn't help; her attempts to cure Haila's dizzy spells and loss of sight were fruitless.

Suleiman had never known his sister—he was not yet born when she died—but he could picture her perfectly from his mother's description: a beautiful, pale-skinned child with two pigtails hanging down her back, a parting that gleamed like lightening and wide eyes with a singular gleam. When she laughed her white teeth showed and she smiled with the watchfulness of a twenty-year-old, though younger by far. She relieved her mother of many of the household duties.

Her father returned after sunset prayers and told his wife that the imam from the mosque in Jurida would come to blow on her. The sheikh came twice and in a loud hoarse voice recited, "'By the star when it goes down, your companion is neither astray nor is he misled,'" then blew out forcefully from his mouth until the young girl, fed up, covered her face with a black shawl. She was disgusted now, trying to keep her covered face away from him, so he wrenched her face in his direction and recited in something like a scream, 'Say: It has been revealed to me that a company of *jinn* paid heed ...'

'Enough!' Haila said more than once, holding out her hand like someone trying to ward off harm.

Afterwards, going out to the front door with her father, the sheikh decreed that she was possessed, which is how the father came to burn a thumb-sized twist of the black shawl over the spirit stove then puffed on the catching flame. As soon as the white smoke coiled up from the glowing fabric he inserted it into Haila's nose. She cried out at the touch of the searing ember and almost gave up the ghost, pinned down by her mother's arms until both tiny white nostrils had been trans-formed into something resembling a stovepipe, rimmed with black and open sores.

A few days later her father and his wife drove the old red Ford south out of Buraida, carrying the blinded, woozy child with them. The road to Unayza was unforgiving and rough, the vehicle lifting and dipping through the potholes. Near Urouq al-Nafoud they had to dig and tamp around tyres that had stuck in the soft red sand. At last they reached Wadi al-Rawghani and breathed a sigh of relief.

It was night and exhaustion had left them drowsy as the dead. There were tents for hire in the wadi but the father stopped the car and got out, dragging the box of tea and coffee-making implements from the boot. Opening the wooden crate he took out a long-stemmed brass coffee pot and hunted in the dark for matches and a scrap of cloth which he stuffed in the spout. He took a match from the box marked *Abu Shuala* and illuminated the darkness with a small flame set at the wick of the spirit stove, which immediately gave off a smell of gas. The father needed to set his head straight with a cup of bitter coffee before he slept. In the Ford's cabin nothing disturbed the sound of the mother's snoring save an occasional wail from Haila.

One still summer's night, a few days before her death, Fahd's grandmother revealed that she had put snuff in the water and made Haila take seven swallows in a row. On the third day of living in the tent and being treated with the dusty-smelling snuff, in the early morning while her father was out negotiating with some men about buying a cow, Haila died in her mother's arms.

Having purchased the cow and tied it to a tent peg the father returned and went in to see his wife. They washed their little girl's body, placed her in a coffin and said the afternoon prayer over her with the other worshippers, then they buried her in the Taeemiya cemetery outside Unayza. Father and mother returned to town with their cow. When his grandmother told this story, she felt a rage and bitterness that robbed her of her voice as it had done every time she had told it over the past fifty years.

Had Soha died the same way? Haila had died at the hands of a sheikh in Wadi al-Rawghani and now Soha had perished at the hands of an Egyptian sheikh. Back then, his grandfather had paid penance for his sin, an admission of guilt, but Fahd's uncle and cousin avoided taking responsibility for killing Umm Fahd. In their eyes they had used their initiative after modern medicine had been unable to cure her.

'Dear God! Had mother ever imagined for a second that she would die one day beaten with a stick and unable to breathe, drowned by drinking water until she vomited? Can it be that science and the study of medicine have had no effect on my cousin with his big, close-set eyes, like an owl lurking in the dark?'

Yasser withdrew from the heated argument, rapidly punched the buttons on his mobile phone and conversed in a low voice. The senior detective was explaining that the right of Soha's descendants to withdraw their case was their right as individuals, but that the state's right to pursue the charge remained with the police. In other words, the Egyptian sheikh would not escape punishment just because they withdrew their accusations.

Fahd insisted that he would never back down where his mother's rights were concerned and he would sign nothing to that effect. Abu Ayoub returned to the subject of fate and how Fahd didn't believe in it—'My brother, fear your Lord'—as though laying the ground to accuse his nephew of being a secularist, an infidel and an atheist.

The phone rang in Fahd's pocket. He looked at the number and saw Tarfah's name blinking insistently. He refused the call and noticed an unread message from Saeed: *Fahd, don't surrender your mothers' rights to these dogs!*

He turned and saw Saeed sitting on the white plastic chair, one leg crossed over the other and jiggling to a jittery, remorseless rhythm.

Escaping the suffocating atmosphere, Fahd went outside to the ambulances' covered parking lot to light a cigarette between two of the vehicles. He blew out smoke and wept bitterly. A gentle hand fell on his shoulder. It was Saeed, comforting him and urging him on.

52

F AHD'S EYES WELLED. SAEED held his arm and tried to
comfort him as he burst into tears and rested his head
against the driver's wing mirror on the side of the ambulance.
He wept aloud: he needed to be outside in the fresh air, to
light the tip of a cigarette, to receive comfort from someone
other than the killers: the Egyptian sheikh, his uncle and
his cousin. To not only lose his mother, but to lose her in
such awful circumstances … His father had never hit her,
yet some stranger had flogged her to death with his son's
assistance. What gall his uncle had! For that matter, what gall
his sister had to snatch the broom from behind the kitchen
door and hand it to Abu Ayoub as he galloped up in a fright
at the voices of infidel *jinn. Has your little heart died, Lulua?*
Heartbroken, anguished, sad and tearful, Fahd muttered, 'The
best way to honour the dead is to bury them, and I don't
believe a man can honour anyone in this world more than
his mother!'

Back inside, Abu Ayoub spoke at length, standing with
Ibrahim, Fahd and Yasser and directing most of his words at
Fahd as he rolled the toothstick in his mouth and clicked
prayer beads over his thumb with a rapid mechanical motion.

'"When it is their time to die they shall not delay the hour
nor shall they hasten it,"' he said. 'Her day has come, may God
have mercy on her, and her hour has struck. It falls to us to

keep faith in fate and divine decree. Brothers, everything we are doing now is the work of Satan and will not restore the dead to life.'

'But it will restore her rights!' Fahd broke in. 'Otherwise, we might as well be living in the jungle! My mother was murdered, never mind if she was ill. Even if the doctors said she was going to die in a few months, or a year, no one knows how long she would have lived.'

'I know,' said Abu Ayoub, his eyes fixed on Saeed who was standing on the other side of the glass. 'But the sheikh means well and follows the *sunna*, and he who forgives and makes peace will be rewarded by God. That's one point, the other point you seem to be forgetting, Fahd, is that transferring the corpse of your mother, God have mercy on her, to the dissection table and the tender mercies of the surgeons will cause great pain both to her and to us. Do you not mind—can you even imagine—your mother being subjected to the surgeon's scalpels after her death?'

'No!' said Yasser. 'We do mind!'

'Don't talk of what doesn't concern you!' Fahd said.

Abu Ayoub grabbed Fahd's hand and led him out of the ward. 'But it does concern me, Fahd. I was her husband. Then there's the fact that we're in mourning at the moment. And don't imagine that anything will happen to us: each one of us gave her the traditional cures with the best of intentions. Even your sister played her part. In a case such as this sacrificing an animal or a couple of months' fasting should be enough if our approach was in error.'

Yasser, who had caught up with them, now interrupted. 'We weren't wrong. The sheikh is well-known; his books are in the Rushd bookshop!'

Abu Ayoub went on as if he had heard nothing. 'To be brief, what we need to do now is withdraw our case against the Egyptian, get that withdrawal endorsed in court and try and prevent the body being referred for autopsy. We won't sleep tonight until she's been put in the refrigerator and tomorrow we'll wash the body and say the afternoon prayer over her grave.'

It was a day as turbulent as a dream, streaking by before Fahd's eyes.

Till now, his days had been spent between the reek of oil paint, the rough, pimpled canvas, brushes of all shapes and sizes, memories of college, the corridors of King Saud University, the central library, Granada Mall, Le Mall, his friend Saeed and his girlfriends Noha, Thuraya and Tarfah. Days both uncomplicated and formulaic, sitting at Shalal Café on Dammam Road, or Tareeqati Café on Urouba Road. He loved Fairouz and Khaled Abdel Rahman, loved dancing and painting, went to art exhibitions at Shadda Hall in Murraba and Sharqiya Hall north of Takhassusi Hospital. His jaunts with Saeed never went beyond Tahliya and Ulaya streets and for food he alternated between the Damascus Fateer House in Layla al-Akheliya Street and Zeit wa Zaatar in Tahliya: with the exception of McDonald's, he disliked all fast-food restaurants.

True, before his uncle had taken over their home he had managed to establish some fleeting connections with people around him, like Abdel Razaq al-Hindi from the Sulaimaniya supermarket who had opened a deferred account in Fahd's name and Abu Rayyan, owner of the Sufara bakery on Urouba Road, but the contact had always been swift and evanescent. Now, he had moved beyond his small and intimate world, as if dropped from a helicopter into the thickets of a dark and untamed jungle, forced for the first time to look at the dense foliage, to hear the calls of new and terrifying creatures, to confront reddened eyes aglow with treachery.

He was in a dream. One morning he would wake to find nothing left of it save dry leaves stirring in Zuhair Rustom Alley before a light September breeze. He would stand in the street, the budding yellow sun at his back already striking the soaring bridge by the vast Mamlaka Tower, stretch his arms wide and call, 'God, what a beautiful morning!' then go on his way, slowly dragging his tattered leather sandals whose metronomic slap on asphalt lacerated the morning's stillness. He would be received by Sayyidat al-Ru'osa Street, parallel with Urouba Road, and head east, walking down from Ulaya's old police station to stand sleepily before *Fahih al-Tanawwur*, the stocky torso of Abdel Moula the Afghan baker swaying as he lightly tapped the rounded baker's peel against the oven wall and wiped sweat from his brow with the filthy towel that dangled from his right shoulder.

The hospital, the emergency ward, his mother's death by torture, his fight with Abu Ayoub and Yasser, the conversation with the detective, all the talk of withdrawing his case and of judges, courts, refrigerators, washing corpses, the mosque and cemetery: none of this was routine or familiar to Fahd, but rather the occasion for consternation and fear, as novel and intimidating as exiting the gloom of a small flat in Maseef into a void both desolate and formless, oppressive and painful, that filled him with doubt and suspicion.

Chaste and meek, he had been addicted to the smell of oil paints, had loved flowers and music and art and a life as simple and untainted as the sun itself, and he had loved Tarfah, too. Now, he had taken the first step into a mysterious and unfamiliar world that held him up to judgment and conspired against him. He had been in the midst of a warm romantic scene, part of some endless film reel, that had suddenly cut to the thunder of hoof beats, brandished blades, gunfire and battle, heads and limbs flying to all quarters.

The detective had suggested that were they to withdraw their case the autopsy would be a superficial one: there would be no deep cuts into his mother's body and it would take at most two hours. Abu Ayoub tried to get the whole matter of pathologists and autopsies dispensed with entirely 'to save time', but the detective refused, promising to hasten the process. He made a call and told them he had tried to get the doctor in Shamesi to come to them instead of taking the body to him, but had failed. Nevertheless, he assured them, he would make sure the business was wrapped up inside two hours. Smiling and unfailingly polite, the detective said his piece, took the interview file from the policeman and went on his way.

Fahd was like a five-year-old who had become separated from his mother at a wedding, looking about in bewilderment and listening to his uncle make phone calls as he tried to get hold of a judge he knew to make their retraction official. Saeed whispered in his ear, 'Why are you backing down so easily?'

Looking lost Fahd replied, 'The point is to bury the dead and honour them. At least I'll clear my conscience after neglecting her in her last days.'

Saeed raised his voice. 'But now you're neglecting her even more. You're giving up the right to take revenge on her killers.'

His hands raised in grief and helplessness, Fahd grew agitated. 'Saeed, I'm suffering enough. My conscience is eating me alive.'

328

Taking his hand, Saeed led him like a blind man to the hospital mosque next to the garden and removing his sandals guided him up the three steps.

'Pray for guidance!' he advised and went into the garden, lighting a cigarette as Fahd found a place in the far corner of the mosque beneath the tall glass window.

There was no one there except a cleaner in his yellow boiler suit, who sat at the front facing the *mihrab* absorbed in the Qur'an between his hands while Fahd prolonged his prostration, praying and invoking God. He got to his feet, eyes closed in humility and contentment and as he bent to perform the *rakaa* he saw a tiny, soft white pigeon feather on the edge of his *thaub*. He held his position, weighing up the life that was embodied by the feather. He didn't know what he had recited as he prayed; had he performed two *rakaas* or three? He sat down and asking God's forgiveness he plucked the feather from his *thaub*, moving it slowly over his faint moustache and imagining the vile pigeon from which it had fallen. He imagined the feather grumbling, muttering and rambling as it slumbered lonely and miserable on the mosque's red carpet.

53

I N FRONT OF A large palace in the Ghadeer neighbourhood of North Riyadh, the white Land Cruiser stopped and four men got out. First came Abu Ayoub, who hurriedly unfolded his bundled *mashlah*, then threw it on his back, fastening the embroidered collar about his neck so that the garment hung down over his shoulders. He was followed by the other three—Ibrahim, Fahd and Yasser—and they were admitted by an Indonesian guard with a long beard like a billy goat.

The palace gardens were breathtaking, causing Fahd to look about in wonder, lost in contemplation of the large rose bushes that bordered the lawns' vast expanse. They waited in the *majlis* where an ancient Eritrean circled with cups of coffee.

Like a man signing a death warrant, Fahd took hold of the pen and began slicing over the page as if cutting into his mother's heart, his uncle and himself signing their consent to withdraw the case against the Egyptian sheikh, Mohammed Abdel Muati. Ibrahim kissed his head as the judge spoke of the importance of Qur'anic healing and the legality of beating, though not without an understanding of the limits proscribed by Islamic law. He made reference to tolerance and forgiveness in religion and prayed that the deceased might receive the mercy of God and His forgiveness, that her torment and suffering in this life might be accepted coin for her sins. Following every prayer, Yasser responded 'Amen' with simulated sorrow, sobbing and dabbing his eyes with the edge of his *shimagh* while with his left palm he hastily wiped his leaking nose.

Fahd recalled an absurd incident reported by the newspapers in which the relatives had relinquished their rights following the death of their son.

Family of traditional healing victim in Jeddah withdraw case; Healer freed on bail
Watan, *29 August 2006*

Police sources have revealed that the family of a sick man treated by a traditional healer in Jeddah's Rehab neighbour-hood, who passed away two days ago in the evening, have submitted their waiver of rights to the circuit judge of the Bureau of Investigation and Public Prosecution to be legally ratified by the Jeddah courts.

The healer, who has been released on condition he make himself available for further questioning, told police that the man he was given to heal had been possessed by jinn since a young age. He claimed the victim had been possessed by three female jinn, giving the names of two as Mabrouka and Habeesa.

Yesterday, the North Jeddah Police transferred the case against traditional healer T.H.A. (45 years), accused of the manslaughter of patient M.A.A. (27 years) from the city of Qalwa in the Makhwa District, Baha Province, to the circuit court of the Bureau of Investigation and Public Prosecution.

The healer is charged with blowing into the victim's mouth, causing his teeth to enter his throat, blocking the airway and suffocating him. The case was overseen by the Chief of the Jeddah Police, Major Saad Bin Daajam.

*The incident had been promptly reported by the Head
of Investigations in North Jeddah, Major Mohammed
al-Khodari, and the Chief of the North Jeddah Police, Colonel
Mohammed al-Malaki. Islamic Law specialists have criticised
a number of traditional Qur'anic healers for undertaking cures
without a proper understanding of the correct procedures.*

*Sheikh Radwan al-Radwan, Imam of the Ikhlas Mosque
in Jeddah, has emphasised the need to give more powers to the
committee made up of the Mayor's Office and the Ministry
of Islamic Affairs, Religious Endowments, Proselytising and
Guidance, to enable it to pursue illegal acts resulting from such
circumstances.*

*Al-Radwan added that the profession of traditional healing
has become debased, stating that he had personal knowledge of
incompetent healers who had been granted licenses to practice.
He remarked that when the Qur'an is recited over a victim of
possession the jinn will speak on the victim's behalf, which can
have a deleterious effect on the healer. He went on to criticise
certain healers for hiring female secretaries and specialising in
treating women in contravention of Islamic law and called on
all traditional healing to be overseen and ratified by scholars
competent in the field.*

54

T HAT NIGHT FAHD VISITED Lulua, and in the dining room overlooking the street he placed his head between his hands like a man coming round after a near-fatal car crash. Lulua stood before him and consoled him, stroking his hair, lighting the stove to make him a cup of tea and telling him to give thanks to God: their mother had been a believer, she had loved Fahd dearly and he had been a devoted son in turn.

Fahd recalled his mother's enjoyment when he would lay his head in her embrace while she made a show of searching for some louse lost in the wild jungle of his hair. *Everything on the top floor carries your memory: your small bedroom facing east, your prayer mat, the blue prayer robe you bulked out when you prayed, the large Japanese radio, the seven-columned oil-fired radiator by your bed, the oil pan atop it and the small bottles of mineral water surrounding it, the Rico wafers with their thin chocolate filling, the covered tub of dates, the small silver pot filled with dried figs, your cotton shirt hanging on the wardrobe door, the head covering stuffed between the radiator's columns to keep it warm and drive the cold from your head, the new curtain in the dining room, lined to hide the light from your tired eyes, your brown handbag hung from the curtain rail, the plastic box inside the bag where you stored your lumps of bitter asafoetida, the bottles of medicine for blood pressure, digestion, inflamed bowels and migraine—your Zocor, Scopan, Coli-Urinal and Panadol—everything that forced you out of your room, out of the living room where you would stretch out your legs as you sat on the bearskin rug, the Singer sewing machine before you, whose wheel you delicately turned to patch a* thaub.

Silence filled the house while Fahd sat on a plastic chair in the kitchen remembering, his groans cutting through the awful hush.

'Take refuge from Satan, Fahd,' said Lulua.

She offered some words of consolation as she placed a cup of tea before him, then closed the kitchen door behind her as she headed to the living room.

He felt suffocated. He carried the cup of tea over to the west-facing window and slid it back on aluminium runners. The bridge by the soaring edifice of Mamlaka Tower was lit up. He took a deep breath and wept loudly and bitterly as a black butterfly settled on the peeling paintwork of the window's metal frame. It took off and landed on the chilly aluminium runners.

Silence filled the dust-choked skies. The heat spilled over and descended on people's heads. Fahd threw his body down on a bolster and resting his elbows on his knees he knitted his hands together over his eyes and sobbed passionately.

He heard the raucous message tone from his phone. *God comfort you and grant your deceased forgiveness!* The number was unknown to him and he paid it no mind.

He switched on the air conditioner and closed the window. The black butterfly flew inside, first landing on the fabric of the lampshade in the corner then upon the table's edge by the cup of cold tea.

What a strange butterfly, Fahd said to himself. *A butterfly dark as night. I remember reading once that the souls of the departed become black butterflies, roving about. Are you my mother? Come here*

334

my darling one, light upon my heart, or rather, light upon my eyelash and tell me how it happened, how they stopped your heart, how they laughed, the Egyptian, my uncle and my trickster cousin, as the heat began to trouble you and you felt the air about you drain away. You raised the hem of your thaub *and the Egyptian laughed, saying, 'This is what I want!' My uncle laughed, certain that the hands that raised the* thaub *were those of the* jinn, *for you no longer counted for anything. Here, come closer, Mother; tell me all that happened …'*

When his hand approached it, the black butterfly flew to a small bookcase by the door. Would it make its way inside a book and re-emerge as Soha?

Just think, Mother, what kind of wasteland we're living in. A few days ago the Shura Council discussed setting limits on the beating allowed in traditional healing. As easily as that! In other words, it admitted that the beating itself was legal. Just two years ago the Council turned the world on its head when a member, on a whim, proposed a vote on whether to debate a matter so trivial it never deserved debate in the first place: should the Shura Council debate the matter of women drivers, or should it not? Those religious scholars approved beating, which is forbidden by the laws of every land and religion in the world, and because of that your slender, pure body deserved to be flogged to death to exorcise a jinn! *Come here, Mother, don't fly too far. The doors and windows are sealed shut. Come here. Don't go into the book, I want to talk to you, to tell you of my pain.*

This strange country on whose soil we live in fear, at home and in the street, at work and in the car, this strange country, where we never wake without a tremor in our hands or our skin crawling: it ate your heart. It tossed you in the morgue. Wasn't there something a few days back about an African witch who rode a broomstick black and naked and flew from the second floor to the fourth a Medinan apartment block? Our newspapers printed the story—our glorious press—as if to lend credence to the statements of those moral guardians, the men of the Committee for the Promotion of Virtue and the Prevention of Vice, who saw witches flying through the air.

At times, Mother, I feel that I am not in the real world, but in a dream or film. I sense some legendary creature seated in the heights, winding the reel of some epic movie, enjoying himself at first, then roaring with laughter and thinking how, when the reel is spent, he will throw it in the bin and go on his way, while we hop about like puppies dumped in deep trenches filled with filth, while in the distance the sound of a vast tractor draws nearer, pushing the dirt to send it heaping over us.

Absent-mindedly he reached out to the cup of cold tea and the black butterfly fluttered abruptly from on top of the bookcase and clung to the mirror. It reminded him of *King of the Butterflies*, a story he had bought with his father at Jarir Bookstore in Ulaya years before. It told of the ruler of the butterflies who flew from his kingdom to find work for his young butterflies and caterpillars. He alighted on a window at the Fara Palace and was just peeping inside when the heavens thundered and torrential rain poured down. Before the servant could close the window he nipped in. He flew to the bedroom and there he found eternal love. In the mirror he saw a brightly coloured butterfly queen, looking much like himself but slightly smaller. Every time he approached her, she drew closer, too. She was his reflection, no more, and when a sudden bolt of lightening and roar of thunder shattered the mirror, the beautiful queen fled. Downcast, the butterfly king returned and told his subjects, who became convinced that the lightning, that bright light, had swallowed up their queen, and from that day forward butterflies have fluttered around any light they found.

Are you searching for the king who flew from you, my mother, my queen? Is it the fate of kings to hunt for that which might hold their kingdoms firm, until like every king in the world before them, they are swallowed by a light that becomes a burning, all-consuming fire?

In the days that followed Fahd would dwell on that night, the night in which his mother slept in the morgue.

As he lay in bed he saw black butterflies flying around him and after rising to drink cold water from the fridge he dozed and saw himself in a dream, asleep, as ants crawled over his body and face, invaded his ears and mouth, tramped over his closed eyelids until his skin shuddered. He saw himself awake in terror and turn over on his right side. Just before dawn warplanes circled above Mamlaka Tower, directing their bombs and cannon fire towards their little building. As the neighbours fled into the street he searched the roof for Lulua. There was a grey pigeon there, barely able to leave the ground, just sprinting about on scarlet legs. He flicked his hand towards him to make him fly before he could leave a feather on the roof or on his *thaub*.

55

I T WASN'T JUST FAHD'S mother who was searching for a king. All the tribes were searching for the ancient King of the East, searching for him in order to bring him down and seize his throne, flying on horseback like the wind, brandishing their swords aloft like fate, to pluck the feather from the breast of his dominion, for the feather's fall means the fall of his kingdom.

Thus have the affairs of feathered countries run their course for long centuries. Thus did the tribe of Ajman tire of the rule of the Bani Khaled and their king Ibn Urai'ar, renouncing their decades-long fealty. The king wished to discipline them and killed twenty of their number, leaving one alive to tell of what had happened. In response, when Ajman came upon seventy of his men, squatting in the desert and peacefully gathering fodder for their horses, they fell upon them and wiped them out, leaving one to tell his king what had happened. Then Ajman came to Radheema in North-Eastern Riyadh, readying themselves for a long war and sounding out the tribes that flocked to join them, for the law of the desert is such that either you attack your neighbour or, if you settle peaceably, you shall be attacked by him.

One tribe stipulated that when Ibn Urai'ar fell they should have Saman and its renowned watering places of Lahaba, Qaraa and Lasafa. A second demanded al-Sharaf, the night-dark she-camel owned by the king, while a third tribe asked for the stallions that stamped the ground like lightning. The last tribe's condition was that it be granted a feather. No more than a feather from the king's house. No more than a feather perhaps, but its seizure meant the fall of the king and its transferral to another tribe meant the transferral of pride, prestige and glory. *Umm al-Duhour* was its name, The Mother of the Ages, because, over the ages, it had ceaselessly conveyed glory from one tribe to another. It was the desert's plaything: a toy possessed by the blood that watered the desert sands and raised up the boxthorn and acacia shrubs that stand in the blazing noonday heat like hanged men, forever gazing earthwards.

A savage battle swallowed up the horses, camels and men, a battle whose contestants drew no pleasure from that clement March of 1823, its cloudless skies, a daisy growing, enticing and beautiful, a rainfall's remnant in pits and dips and fissures, the song of a bird that soared aloft into the heart of heaven then fell like a stone, heralding the coming spring. Nothing in this land could trump the gush of fresh blood, no voice could be heard above the clash of swords. There could be no gentle silent nights while the feather was denied its secure, untroubled slumber upon the door of a house where a man, cruel-featured and severe, gazed out each dawn to the horizon, ready for the first speck of dust to rise from the columns of horses stamping the earth and rolling forward with horsemen on their backs whose faith in victory is drowned out only by their panting breaths and the thrum of their wild, untethered pennants in the chill breeze of a restless dawn.

Fahd always wondered what had happened to this country, so completely changed from the land it had been two centuries before: black oil, wide well-lit streets, towering buildings and skyscrapers.

'Has anything changed here?'

He pointed to his head as he addressed Saeed. It was evening and they were watching yet another television programme on camel dressage and the 'revitalisation of the tribes' and their alarming quarrels. Saeed was scornful. 'They used to put their money on religion and now, after the terrorism and bombings could it be that they're thinking of a return to the tribe?'

Centuries ago, poems were newsletters, spreading word of a tribe's heroism and glory. Later neighbourhood walls took on the role, with local kids boasting of their lineage, challenging other tribes with tales of their bravery and magnificent deeds and signing their words with a tribal mark. The tribes entered the age of the Internet and satellite television while their worldview continued to revolve around depredation, murder and kidnap: seizing the feather and bringing the kingdom down.

56

O F THE VILLAGE ITSELF, sleeping in the embrace of the Nafud desert, its tall palms breathing in the bashful breeze, Fahd remembered a funny story his father would tell whenever the discussion turned to the banning of music. It was a story about the wanton wooden door in his grandfather's house in Muraidasiya which took to squeaking when opened and closed due to rust in one of its hinges, a gentle music to wake people from their afternoon nap.

'The pipes of al-Safeelawi are playing!' the old women would cry.

The old man felt compelled to take prompt action to nip the scandal in the bud and considered smearing the hinge in cooking oil to silence the squeak once and for all. It was as though for a century past life out here could not bear to hear any sound save that of speech. Men's speech, Fahd thought, for a woman's words were also forbidden.

A century before, the Brotherhood had unsheathed their swords and brandished their iron souls. At Mount Arafat, in poor ragged *thaubs* and squat white turbans wound about their heads, not one hesitated to wave his sword and utter from his heart, 'I am a horseman of *tawheed*! I am a Brother! Enemy of God, show yourself!' at the vainly prancing Egyptian convoy, led by two buglers with armed horsemen in their wake. No sooner had the trumpets sounded, thundering off Arafat to clear the convoy's way, than the white-turbaned men descended on the convoy with their glittering swords. One man drew his slender blade and opened up the stomach of a bugler, who stopped his blowing, the trumpet dangling from his mouth and trembling like a thorn tree's branch. The Egyptian horsemen poured fire on the Bedouin knights until some fell and those who could, fled, weighed down with the sorrow and shame of abandoning the True Word and religion's victory. Most, however, were content that the Satanic music had been stilled forever, never to return to sacred soil now that relations with Egypt were so irrevocably soured.

Years later, the grandfather would neglect to treat his wanton door.

Three Brothers stopped by carrying thorn tree staffs and knocked upon the massive wooden door to chastise Ali al-Safeelawi for the squeaking hinge which woke all Muraidasiya: a forbidden sound that must be prevented and silenced and if it was not, then Exalted God would pour molten lead into Grandfather Ali's ears on the Day of Reckoning. As they shook their staffs in his face, Ali's face grew very pale, not because of their presence or their threats, but because he had been shamed: in the depths of the house his wife was rhythmically rocking little Hissa and mournfully singing,

'How happily you sing, little pigeon,
Up there on the green palm fronds,
But how sad I'd be for you if Salama found you there,
He'd leave you moaning like he left me,
He broke my bones, may God break his,
See the bruises his staff left on my brow.'

As soon as Ali had come away from the door he gave her kick. 'Shut up woman! Embarrassing me, like that! May God shame you before His servants!'

342

The Brothers were unforgiving, ready to oppose any new invention they did not understand. Heresy, they called it—it must be repudiated!—a work of magic and the dark arts that had no place in the House of Islam. To stay silent on the matter would anger God.

From Abdallah Bin Hassan to His Excellency, the Respected and Foremost of Imams, Abdel Rahman Aal Faisal, may God relieve him of all woe and burdens and deliver him from those who seek to deceive him, Amen.

The Peace and Mercy of God and His blessings be always upon you, and with all inquiries after your good health and all due celebration and respect, and hoping that our news may bring you joy in every respect, for which we thank God, we beg leave to inform your Majesty that on the nineteenth day of Shawwal we arrived at Buraida and finding all well by the grace of God, we looked into the meeting between the Brothers and al-Ibn Abdel Aziz on the occasion of his arrival in Buraida. This meeting, however, was postponed on account of matters that the Brothers raised, seeking the response of al-Ibn. To wit: the matter of the telegraph and the cablegram and the matter of the customs offices, all of which they ask be removed after the pilgrimage.

Sheikh Abdullah and Sheikh Omar Aal Saleem sent word to them, explaining that neither they nor the other sheikhs considered these things forbidden. At this the Brothers came to them and spoke frankly, refusing to accept their judgment and stating that either these things are destroyed or the Brothers would take to the Hejaz during the pilgrimage and render it impassable. Fearful of harm befalling Islam, Muslims and the customs houses, al-Ibn, may God grant him peace, responded to their demands and asked them to defer action until the end of Ashoura, when he would decide whether to destroy

343

the customs houses himself or license them to do so in his stead and provide them with assistance.

He then set out conditions which he asked them to pledge to uphold, including that they would not rob any man nor carry out any act in the name of religion or injurious to the sovereign without consulting the sheikhs and their leaders, nor would they take up arms against any of the king's subjects, Bedouin or townsfolk, without the knowledge and express command of the sovereign. Whosoever disobeyed these conditions would have his case brought before the king, who would take responsibility for disciplining him. Furthermore, they would use neither God's Book nor the Prophet's example as justification for their actions until they have consulted the sheikhs and obtained a fatwa. Abdel Aziz Bin Musaaid was sent to them and they pledged to observe these conditions.

Shawwal 28, 1346 A.H

The appearance of the telegraph in the land of the Muslims back in 1928 was a blow to the True Faith and stirred up the Brothers in defence of their religion. The customs houses and guard posts erected along the borders with Iraq sent them flying on their horses, white *thaubs* and turbans flapping, swords bared, racing the wind that roughly flipped green pennants emblazoned with *There is no god but God and Mohammed is His Prophet*. They fasted for days and nights, their only sustenance a dried date wetted in parched throats and an unwavering zeal for the religion of God. If necessary they held up peaceful caravans, the passengers' godlessness beyond dispute.

Concerning the telegraph, this is an innovation of recent times and we know nothing of its true nature. Having seen no pronouncement from the scholars on the subject we withhold judgment, for no man may

344

speak in the name of God or His Prophet without knowledge and to declare something sinful and forbidden requires its true nature to first be understood.

Concerning the mosques of Hamza and Abu Rasheed, the Imam, may God grant him success, has advised us to destroy them immediately.

Concerning secular law, we have noted that it is practiced here and there in the Hejaz and it must cease forthwith, for there shall be no judgment save the rulings of divine law.

Concerning the entry of the Egyptian pilgrims on to God's sacred soil with arms and military force, the Imam advised us to repel them by force of arms and prevent their displays of polytheism and other abominations.

Concerning the convoy, the Imam advised us to prevent it entering the Grand Mosque and ensure that no man might touch it or kiss it.

'These people never died,' a heavily moustachioed Rashed had once said to Saeed in Musafir Café. 'They've just evolved and changed their outer appearance. The man who once wrapped a white turban around his head and accused anyone who wore the *aqqal* of godlessness is the same fellow who these days wears the *thaub* that stops midway down his calf and accuses those who wear the long *thaub* of wantonness, godlessness and hypocrisy!'

Saeed gave a small smile. 'It's not that bad,' he objected. 'They don't call someone who lets his *thaub* down an infidel, they just advise him.'

'Believe me Saeed, they're the ones that pull the rope and loosen it. Give them an inch they pull even harder. Can you believe that they cut King Abdul Aziz's *thaub* because he let it hang down?'

Saeed gave a loud laugh and said sarcastically, 'You shouldn't be so hard on them. They're brave fellows.'

'But don't you believe that times repeat themselves, that things repeat themselves, even if the names might change? Just think, Saeed. They were fighting the infidel in Iraq, then they got involved with the British at the start of the last century and now they're doing it all over again. Fighting in Iraq against the Americans and their "dogs" as they call them.'

Saeed shook his head as he attempted to light a cigarette. 'No, Rashed, you're mixing things up. There's a difference between terrorism and *jihad*. I think the Brotherhood were *mujahideen* and their intentions were pure.'

Rashed closed the conversation. 'You're calling what's happening in Iraq terrorism, but there are some that call it *jihad* and others that think of it as resistance and self-defence: the defence of one's honour and religion!'

A few scant hairs atop his head, Rashed perched on a barstool drawing on the *shisha's* tube, exhaling rising columns of smoke into the air and directing an unceasing flow of insults against everything around him. Saeed never argued with him, except when he wished to increase his own fund of knowledge. Life here was unbearable, he told his friend. Nothing had changed for a hundred years. Life spun in place. The grandsons of the ones who outlawed the telegraph and the radio had surfaced ten years ago to ban satellite dishes and receivers, and now they themselves were hopping back and forth between the very channels they had denounced: a *mufti* here, a dream interpreter there, a scholar of the *hadith*, a scholar of the Qur'an, a preacher, an expert in Islamic women's issues, and, and, and ...

Part 8

Dear Lorca,
I stole no olives

The olive tree does not weep and does not laugh.
Mahmoud Darwish: The Butterfly Effect

57

I N RAJEHI MOSQUE ON the Eastern Ring Road, in the room where the corpses are washed, Fahd's mother slept on the slab, eyes closed like Sleeping Beauty. Sleeping before being readied for her final rest. Is anyone ready for death? Don't they always say that death comes suddenly? Why can't the angel come gently, alighting in the room, sitting opposite the creature and, before asking if he might pluck out its soul, talk to him a little about his dreams and what he wants from the world, give him space to get his papers in good order, to wash the dishes and clean the tea cup, taking out the sodden mint leaf and throwing it in the bin, to fold his underwear and tidy up his things, to burn his secret diaries, write a will, pen a note setting out his feelings in the moment before his passing, describing the taste of death, sour or bitter, the faces of the those who will read the *shahada* over him, the eyes of the man who will wrap his face in a flimsy white cocoon?

Abu Ayoub's two wives, Umm Yasser and Umm Muadh, came in, accompanying Lulua to the washing room, while Fahd squatted on the floor and wept noiselessly, his *ghatra* swathing his face. He felt the severe heat penetrate his eyes. The sound of cars and trucks speeding along the Eastern Ring Road ruptured the silence. A hand took hold of his wrist.

'Take refuge from Satan. God comfort you.'

Muadh helped him to his feet and led him to an area set aside for relatives of the deceased. She sat him down and asked the coffee boy to pour him a cup. Abu Ayoub and Yasser were sipping coffee and talking to Ibrahim about unemployment, the stock exchange and the chaos of Riyadh's job market.

How terrifying it is to sit next to cold-blooded killers! Fahd thought.

The phone of one of Abu Ayoub's wives rang and she told her husband that it was time for the final prayer over the deceased. He stood up, holding on to Fahd with his icy hand and they went through a side door to where Soha's body lay. The stench of ammonia filled the space, the humidity and dampness spreading out through the spacious room. Hearing voices, Lulua pulled back the white curtain and the men came in, Fahd bending over his mother's tender brow and kissing it, followed by Abu Ayoub who pecked her head and boomed, 'God, forgive her sins; make wide her path!'

Why was it that his hoarse voice reminded him of vegetable sellers?

Fahd felt a river running through his heart. He trembled all over and braced himself as a shudder threatened to shake him apart. He was convinced that they felt nothing for the dead, no different to the other objects in the room, a lump of matter that neither felt nor saw. Not one of them could see that Soha had muttered and risen to join him.

The sun is hot today, Fahd. Dying in the heat of summer's no good, but what to do? It's the only time I was able to leave my room. The other months, the cold gnaws my bones and I never leave my radiator.

Fahd had never seen his mother so strong and sure, opening the door to his car that was parked on the ring road and telling him, *Drive faster than them.*

Won't they look for your body? he said and her laugh rang out.

The body's in there. It's your mother's spirit with you now. Go to Khazan Street then take a right off Suwailam. I'll show you my primary school, so you might know that I'm the daughter of this ancient place, the daughter of this godless city. My only ties to Jordan or Palestine are roots and names. A man is the son of his present; the son of the place where he lives.'

Yes, thought Fahd later, recalling his mother's words, he was a son of Great Yarmouth now, son of the dark blue sea, son of the print shop where he worked, son of the little college where he studied, its tall windows open to the cold air and green clouds.

Saeed sent him a brief message: *Fahd, we're to the right of the* mihrab. *We've saved you a place.*

Fahd went in and sat between Saeed and Yasser. They performed the afternoon prayer then the sliding door opened on the three bodies. The imam in his cream *mashlah* walked over from the *mihrab* to pray over the dead, his bearded face stern and unsmiling, as Soha slept quietly, wrapped in a black *abaya*. Even in death she had placed the black *abaya* on her white coffin just as a bride wears it over her white dress. When the imam had finished, the worshippers rushed to the caskets and Fahd ran with them to take up one of the box's four corners, then hurried to the hearse, leaving his shoes in the mosque and making do with his white socks. Could he join his mother, thought Fahd: could he descend into her grave in his white socks and *thaub*?

Does all this whiteness mean I want to remain with you in your grave, Mother?

The men pushed the three coffins into place inside the hearse and a dark-skinned young man weighed down with grief got in, followed by Abu Ayoub. Yasser shoved Fahd from behind.

'Get in. Hurry up and take your place.'

The driver drove fast, a little recklessly, even.

As though he, too, wants to make sure you're lying in your resting place without delay. Were you awake just then? Fahd wondered. *It was as though I heard you breathing, or perhaps your muffled laughter, your hand held to your mouth. Is the laughter of the dead a little stifled? I sat between them as they recited the* shahada, *asked God's forgiveness, prayed. I heard the sound of the rough toothstick grate against my uncle's loathsome teeth while Yasser's thick fingers were busy at a string of black prayer beads.*

Abu Ayoub hitched his *thaub* around his waist and descended into the grave, followed by Fahd and Yasser. A shaven-headed man came up and addressed them. 'This grave hasn't been dressed with mud brick. Go over there.'

He stretched out his hand to Abu Ayoub, who leapt out then down into another pit. There was a group who had missed the prayers in the mosque lined up to pray over her bier in the cemetery, while Fahd waited with his uncle down in the trench, watching the sun descend into the city's heart, his head poking over the lip of the grave, his eyes melting as he faced the dreadful moment of burial.

He contemplated death's awful majesty. At the moment of death a man goes back to being a child. From white cradle to white casket; from the cot's straps that bind his body so he may do no more than cry, to the coffin, belted lest he leap back up and flee into life, as though the moment when his mother was laid in her cramped resting place beneath the earth and the bonds loosed from her bier was the critical one.

'Now fly!' they tell her. 'The layers of earth above you are nothing. Fly! Fly as a child flies: crawling, walking, running. Stir your angel's wings, beat them through the heavy, second-hand air. Fly over the city, search for some lost body in Khazan Street, in Fouta Park, in Ulaya. A man is only heavy when he's alive. He cannot fly. With death he becomes weightless, floats and rises from the earth, his feet suspended in the air!'

'Clean the grave, Fahd!' Ibrahim shouted. 'Make sure there are no dry lumps of earth in there!'

Impatient, he pushed Fahd aside and awkwardly clambered down, inspecting the grave from within, measuring the length of the brick with his hand and the width of the grave's mouth. He instructed Fahd to stagger the rows of brick inwards, but only after the first layer was laid, lest they fall on her corpse. Overhead, Saeed reached out to Ibrahim and he jumped out, knocking a small cascade of soil from the lip of the grave.

They brought you into the cemetery, Mother, carrying your casket like bridesmaids. I took your blessed head and passed it to my uncle then we descended with you to the mouth of the grave. We laid your head facing Mecca and propped your back, worn out by life's toil and hardship, against a half-brick. Before we lined the grave mouth one of the crowd reminded me, "Get the abaya!*" and I pulled it hard, until it was all in my hand and I peered up at those standing over me. I saw Saeed ready, so I coiled the* abaya *round my hand and threw it to him.*

Here is your abaya, *which I hand to Saeed, who used to clutch the seam on the right, while I clung to its left, as you took us to Central Hospital. I close up the grave with big mud bricks. I do not know how my heart can be so cruel to imprison you inside your grave. How terrifying to lay the last brick lengthwise and shut you off from air and light and life.*

I saw myself in there. There was a small glimmer of light from the last hole that remained after the clay-slicked brick had been laid. Who would put the last brick in place and cut me off from all light? It will be my uncle, for certain: he will block life's light from me. Yet what use is it for the dead to have eyes when all about them is pitch-black and dark? Dear God. I felt myself trying to push the last brick with my foot, trying to free my foot from the coffin, and when I could not I raised both my legs together and shoved the brick, whose mud covering had not yet dried. I gave a powerful scream. There was no one on hand, not even a visitor to the grave or the cemetery guard, to dig out my tomb so that I might emerge, unkempt and singed with a face full of bruises, and flee towards the sun's disc, like some hero galloping along at the end of a film accompanied by the closing music and the names of actors and technicians scrolling past in fine white font.

Someone gave Fahd a hand and he jumped out of the grave, waiting for Abu Ayoub who was daubing the bricks with clay, while further along Yasser scraped at the edge of the grave so the particles of soil streamed down like the breeze.

So now you're scraping delicately at the soil, when just yesterday you and your father were flogging my dead mother with a stick to drive out the demon? What a demon you are, and how backward.

Abu Ayoub grabbed him. He had walked away from the graveside to scatter three palmfuls of dust, escaping the crowd to rouse himself and cry. His uncle led him to the shade of a nearby car.

'Take refuge from Satan!' he said. 'You must pray, my boy. Pull yourself together and have patience. God is with the patient.'

Fahd stood with Abu Ayoub, Yasser, Ibrahim and Saeed, and the mourners began to crowd around them and kiss them on both cheeks.

353

'God comfort you!'

'God reward you!' he would answer in a choked voice.

Then they prayed for his mother as he wiped the end of his nose and muttered, 'Amen. Amen!'

A man presented him with a little bottle of water and he held it without drinking. The man opened another bottle and handed it over, and Fahd took a gulp, tugging at his *shimagh* that had slipped right back and almost fallen off his head. When he heard Abu Ayoub explain how he would hunt for customers even in the cemetery, and not confine himself to the mosque, Fahd dragged his weary body away and sprinted back to the car in his white socks. Saeed caught up with him and snatched the keys away to drive Fahd himself.

58

T HE FIRST NIGHT AFTER Soha's burial Saeed decided to distract Fahd from his sorrow and take him around the whole of Riyadh, leaving no street, no alley old or new, unvisited.

They began in South Riyadh, where they circled Badr and Shifa, then drove east on the Southern Ring Road and entered Khanshlaila and Haraj Ibn Qasem before doubling back, taking King Fahd Highway and getting off at Souq Atiqa, briefly entering Suwaidi Street and Sultaniya, and passing Muntaza al-Salam and Old Salam Roundabout. He was flying towards Old Manfouha, but Fahd, remembering the Egyptian sheikh, begged him not to go to that home of *jinn* and sorcerers. They turned north again into the city, into Old Dakhna, reaching Zaheera Street and from there, Khazan Street, where the Egyptian and Syrian women in *hijabs* were still wandering around the shops that sold fabric and off-the-peg clothes.

Saeed stopped at Fahd's request and the pair proceeded on foot between the ends of Zaheera and Suwailam streets and then, crossing the road, they walked beside the wall of Fouta Park. Fahd sobbed as he walked along, tormented and consumed with grief. Without taking his eye off him, Saeed left Fahd to wander erratically ahead. Fahd was rambling along, now and then lifting his face to the sky as if directing blame to someone up there in the heights. *Why have you done all this to me? Why bring me into being if you were planning to destroy my life on a whim? What have I done for you to make me a plaything for your enjoyment?*

He crossed the little street next to the Fouta Theatre Complex then headed towards the massive mud-brick palace, turning left towards the King Abdul Aziz Centre for Culture and Knowledge and gazing at the trees, tranquil in the dying hours of the night, and the few families in the square, the children riding their bicycles. He stopped, astonished, and looked at them for a moment, searching for someone here who might be missing him and contemplating what might befall these children in just a few short years: what black path awaits them to lead them off to hell?

He made for the expanse of Wazeer Street. Saeed was exhausted by now, panting after him, but Fahd never halted his capricious progress. Saeed wondered how they would get back to the car. Should they take a taxi? He turned left after Fahd, who proceeded down the long street towards Washam Bridge, but halfway along he stopped and looked over at a petrol station on the right, then crossed the street. Saeed assumed he was after a bottle of water from the station's mini-mart but he halted outside a framing shop and stood staring at the coloured canvases in their expensive frames. It was a place he would come with his father years before, dropping off pictures and posters to have them framed.

Was he searching for his father now?

Fahd walked away a little distance, calm as a wild beast stalking his prey. He glanced at the neon sign that bore the name of Dr Ibrahim Ruslan, his old paediatrician, and clutching at the air before him, walked on for a moment with his eyes closed. Was he holding his mother's *abaya* as she took his sister Lulua to the doctor? Saeed felt a shudder course through his body as he witnessed this alarming sight.

It was approaching one in the morning. Fahd had taken a left beneath Washam Bridge. Catching up to him, Saeed said that if he was tired they should go back to the car, but he didn't answer, silent as an unfaltering camel that knows the desert's secrets and trusts its instincts. Saeed decided to gently take his hand and take him back along the same road and when he did Fahd didn't resist, retracing his steps, inhaling vigorously and suddenly bursting into tears then looking about himself in terror.

It was nearly two in the morning. They were heading back to Fouta Park when Fahd resisted and headed north up Khazan Street, crossing King Fahd Road and passing Jawhara Mosque, until they came to the old building where his grandparents had lived before their enforced emigration in early 1991. He sat on the steps of the building, his legs exposed, and cupping his head in his hands he buried it between his knees and wept and wept. Saeed sat down beside him and tugging at his shoulder, pulled Fahd to him.

'Take refuge from Satan, Fahd,' he said, then added, 'I thought I'd cheer you up with the streets and old alleys and happy memories. I had no intention of torturing you and me with you.'

In a voice vague and choked with tears, Fahd replied, 'There's not a single place, not one corner or street in this damned city, that doesn't remind me of my father.'

Once they had got back to the car, Fahd said, 'I have to emigrate: anywhere in the world. I must leave this place and as soon as possible.'

'And the university?' Saeed asked him.

'Maybe I can start university again, somewhere else.'

'What about your sister?'

'Forget it, Saeed, my sister's become like my uncle now.'

Then, after a moment's silence: 'Soon she'll marry and be busy with her life and kids.'

He looked through the window at Television Tower. 'Maybe her husband will be like Yasser and convince her that her brother's an infidel, that his faith is in question because he draws naked men and women.'

'Maybe.'

'I just can't face any more surprises. I can't follow any more dubious dreams. If they were able to turn my mother's head— my mother, Saeed—then how do you think things will be with a teenager like Lulua?'

'You've got a point.'

'Saeed, this is a crazy country, galloping after myths and dreams.'

The message tone sounded on Fahd's phone: *Darling, I'm worried about you. Answer so I know you're fine.*

Saeed didn't ask about Tarfah and Fahd never thought of her. True, her life was much like his own terrifying existence but she would end up living with another man, like Khaled. Maybe Abdel Kareem would return one day and win her back when he discovered he had a beautiful little girl called Sara.

59

W HEN SAEED AND FAHD had returned home, the canvas that had cost him so much suffering and gloom still bore its scattered human skulls surrounded by dried tendrils of blood. The morning had begun to spill in from the living room window overlooking the street. He looked out towards the few cars on the Northern Ring Road and the Jarir Bookstore building on the other side.

Despite being utterly exhausted he thought of going for a drive. The Starbucks on the ring road would still be closed, as would the Dunkin Donuts. He tried stretching out in order to get some sleep and entered something like a coma until the ringing phone beside him snatched him awake. It was his scarlet sweetheart, Tarfah. He hesitated a little then answered, his voice excessively hoarse and hollow, as though he were rising from the depths of some painting. For a moment, Tarfah lost her composure, demanding insistently, 'What's wrong with you, sweetheart? You sound completely worn out.'

Suddenly he started crying, whimpering in a barely audible voice. Her worry grew as she tried to make him tell her what had happened. 'This is a road we must all take,' she said, but differed from the other mourners by adding, 'We have to live our lives the way we want, Fahd. We won't live twice.'

She offered to be with him for a while, suggesting that he leave his friend's flat. 'Let's take a furnished flat for a day or two until this passes.'

'I wish, darling, but it's difficult!'

'Nonsense. It's not difficult at all. I'll coordinate with my friend Nada. My mother trusts her.'

'No, sweetheart, it's difficult for me.'

He hung up, promising her that they would meet when things were a little calmer. The meeting, a week later, lasted just a few minutes, before the sheikh with the cream *mashlah* crept up on them and led Fahd to the final disaster of his short life.

He tried closing his eyes. His mobile whispered a message's arrival. Opening it he found an image file: lying on a white marble table top, a striped napkin folded into a small triangle and beside it a cup of Turkish coffee on a small white saucer. *Darling: here's your coffee, like it or not, and don't forget mine, sweetened with your honeyed lips. I really miss them, Fahoudi.*

He smiled and dozed untroubled until the sunset prayer.

He awoke enveloped in a lethal migraine. Swaying, he stood up and looked over at Saeed's open door. He searched the kitchen shelves for some Panadol Extra then took two tablets one after the other and forced them down with large gulps of water that left him panting like a dog. He went back and stood facing the canvas, staring at it in a daze.

He saw the skulls lying about and the corpses, but noticed the birds at the top weren't ravens but had turned white instead. They were pigeons flying over the bodies. Damn it, why were these white and grey pigeons here? In a choked voice, not knowing if anyone could hear it, not knowing if he heard it himself, he shouted, 'I don't like pigeons.'

He adored the life of Pablo Picasso, his creative madness, his transitions from one artistic period to another—blue, to pink, to cubist, to starkly abstract—though most of all he loved the stage that produced his famous painting, *Guernica*. However, he had no affection for the artist's habits and behaviour. He loathed his love of bullfighting and his passion for doves … Or could they be pigeons? Why must pigeons flock into everything? Fahd started forward and made to rub them out but his sight grew dim, the canvas swayed, and he sat down slowly, holding his head, before stumbling over and taking the coffee pot from a drawer. Gripping the table edge, he poured water into the pot, placed it over the flame and heaped two spoonfuls of black Turkish coffee on to the water's surface, stirring it around before lifting the pot from the heat.

He sat and drank his coffee in a dream. He raised his face to the ceiling and found that it was neither moving nor slowly descending. He rose to his feet and went over to the paint box, taking a tube without paying attention to the colour, just unscrewing the tiny lid, lifting it to his nose and inhaling deeply as he continued to drink the bitter coffee. He took a look around him: his bed over there, the kitchen in the corner, the ceiling lamps dangling over the dining table, shoes randomly scattered by the front door and the canvas unchanged on the easel, black ravens hovering at the edge, crows circling bodies cast down on a rooftop like a field of melons beneath the searing sun.

He felt that his senses had returned to him and imagined the ravens and crows suddenly flying from the canvas as he slept like a dead man and feasting on his eyes. What would he have done then? He would have woken without eyes, without a heart, perhaps.

He thought of the poem by Lorca that he loved, *The Ballad of the Moon*, and how the gypsies sought to fashion necklaces and rings from the heart of the moon that descended from its heights. He would be like Lorca's moon, dropping down to play in the blacksmith's forge, but there would be no boy to warn him of the wounding crows.

He thought of little Sara, her face unfolded like a moon, her childish laughter, her charm, as he carried her that evening in the Joy Oasis Arcade in Granada Mall, taking her back to her mother, Tarfah, and sitting with her in the family section. He wept when he imagined her warning him of the crows, without him warning her of the long nights she must live without a father, that father who was not alive that she might wait for his return, nor dead that she might forget him, for she had never seen him.

60

FAHD REMEMBERED LORCA'S POEM as they questioned him about the olive-stone prayer beads around his wrist. He remembered the gypsies sallying forth from the olive groves on horseback, kidnapping the playful moon and from her glorious silver fashioning necklaces and rings. Were the stones about his wrist from the olive trees through which the gypsies rode, flying from the hands of Spanish girls out picking, to a prison on Mecca's outskirts, between whose walls an inmate fretted, incarcerated for handing out his group's anti-government pamphlets one dawn in the courtyard of the Grand Mosque? That inmate passed the nights, the nothingness, the silence, grinding the Spanish girls' olive stones against the prison's rough cement floor, piercing them through from both ends, threading stone after stone until they became prayer beads that he would keep as a legacy to his son, the artist, who would colour them with oils and set them at his wrist like a bracelet that he might always remember his father's tragedy, never realising that he too would thread together his own tragedies and be forced to flee from the land he loved, accused of sorcery.

While they were summoning the sheikh who now sat before him, Fahd thought, *What accursed prayer beads are these? What ripe olives flew here from Granada or Seville? What olive tree in Andalusia is cackling faintly at my plight, in league with gypsies against the moon, now plotting with the gypsies here against me? Are*

these men gypsies, too, my father? Are they gypsies, too, dear Lorca?
Am I the moon who came to earth and entered the forge to play? Yes, I
am he; I have a side that glows like silver, and a dark side, too. I have
descended to this forge of a land that I might live, but I paid no heed to
little Sara's warning and I could not do as Lorca's moon and suddenly
ascend at the right moment, grasping the child's hand. No, I remained
for the gypsies to charge me with possession of olive stones. Dear
Lorca, I stole no olives, I merely kept their stored and dusty stones safe.
A week ago, I painted them to resemble the bright African skies. When
the gypsies came stealing through the forest of cars I did not hear their
drums. I did not hear them cry from their car at the frightened people
in the alleys, scampering and hiding like rats. I heard nothing but my
sweetheart's voice as she eased the burning loss of my mother. I failed
to see that Andalusia had come to Riyadh, never thought that Riyadh
would travel to far-off Andalusia.

'So shall we go for a drive in the car or take a furnished flat?'
Tarfah asked.

'What do you say to a coffee?'

'Mmm. In the car, perhaps.'

'No, let's sit at a café.'

'I think the cafés are always being watched by the Committee.
Nada says there are employees in the cafés who work as spies
for them. They earn more than their regular wages.'

'I don't think so,' he said, adding, 'Sounds to me like exag-
gerations and rumours.'

'Anyway, going into cafés in the morning is scary.'

Fahd didn't give it much thought. His grief was over-
whelming, stifling. Although a week had passed since his
mother's burial he still had the feeling that Riyadh's skies had
lowered until he could touch them with his hand. It muddled

his thinking. He was unable to continue work on his oil painting or start on another while he remembered Naseem Cemetery, Rajehi Mosque and the morgue. Perhaps the image that affected him most was the memory of standing inside the grave and looking up at the faces of the people, the movement of their lips, their outstretched hands bearing brick and lumps of clay. Whenever their faces came to mind he tried imagining them silent, that sound had been utterly abolished, leaving nothing but the image. He tried imagining that he was deaf, freeing up vast space for the image alone. How might he paint bodies circling about him, stopping to incline towards him, faces muttering, murmuring, staring, old faces, others youthful, faces wearing glasses, faces veined and worn, and all with a light coating of the dust thrown up by the ring of feet?

A scene worthy of a future painting, perhaps: *The Cemetery*.

61

FAHD REMAINED IN THE cramped holding cell, detained on charges of practicing sorcery and committing the lesser idolatry, all because of a string of painted prayer beads. Despite the kindness of the sheikh with the cream *mashlah* and his paternal air, he had now vanished and Fahd hadn't seen him again. He was like Lorca's gypsies, hiding their knives in the dust.

It was a narrow, stifling room with a fan dangling from its ceiling, though he couldn't tell whether it was working or whether warm air was shuffling in from some high window like a crook-backed pensioner. If this was going to go further, he wondered, how long would he be held here? Would they transport him to another prison? Would the court hand down a harsh punishment? He remembered the hawk-eyed man telling him that the penalty for sorcery in this safe and untroubled country was death, telling him this as his slender fingers toyed calmly with his beard. The killers' calm was agonising. Despairingly Fahd shouted that he was no magician; his father had been in prison that was all. He had passed the time with these olive stones, he had …

The man had smiled, until Fahd could almost see the cutting beak behind his mouth, and mockingly said, 'My goodness, are the whole family ex-convicts?'

Fahd was in a desperate situation, the man went on. The charges against him were solid, especially since the woman's brother had made a complaint on her behalf that Fahd had bewitched her so that she would go out with him against her will.

Damn! Fahd thought to himself. *Wasn't it she who had pursued me? Hadn't my desire for her faded? Hadn't she been the one who proposed meeting to console me for my mother's death? Now who will console me for my death, when it comes? Will I have to stand in some public square like Saeed's father, Mushabbab, wearing a hood that bears the reek of impending death before my head is sent flying? The penalty for sorcery is beheading by the sword, so kill every sorcerer, but I, sheikh, am not a sorcerer. My father was the one who got me in this fix; he was the one who bequeathed me his effects that I might be mindful of his mistakes and avoid the long imprisonment, the night-time terror of waiting for deferred execution and that was his lot. Look, Father, I've taken a short cut. I'm going straight to the slaughterhouse.*

The huge man terrified me, roughly turning the toothstick in his mouth and telling me that my file had been handed over to the Bureau of Investigation and Public Prosecution. There was no way out apart from the Indonesian bringing food and tea. How could I offer him a bribe when I had nothing? I promised him a big reward if he helped me. Not to escape: I just wanted to make a call.

His eyes flickered about as he handed me his battered mobile phone. I hurriedly dialled Saeed's number, terrified that it would be turned off or he wouldn't answer, particularly since he wouldn't recognise the number. The moment I heard his voice I quickly said that I was in the Committee's headquarters, mixed up in a serious case, to which he said in his Southern way, 'Leave it to me.' The next day the sheikh with the cream mashlah arrived and I was so happy to see him that I almost hugged him. I reproached him for leaving me, for not listening to my story and the story of the coloured prayer beads, and he smiled, patting my shoulder and telling me that I would leave once I had drawn up a confession of being alone with a woman other than a relative and signed it, pledging that I would not commit the same sin again.

Feeling that I had been set free, I almost fainted. A murderer condemned to death, out in Chop-Chop Square, and just before the sword is raised through the air to split him with its maddened whistle, just before it sinks into the flesh and tendons of his neck and sends his head flying, one of the crowd cries out, 'I release you in God's name. In the name of God Almighty, go, you are free,' and the people gathered there praise God and noisily rejoice, while the condemned man is led back to the car, his hood removed, and seeing life anew, signs away his right to appeal in the courts.

And so the worthy sheikh saved me from execution. I could have fallen on his head and kissed him and I could have embraced Saeed when he came to collect me. My eyes were flickering all over. I had no idea how he'd managed to arrange things, more easily than I had thought possible.

As soon as Fahd saw Saeed he asked him how he had done it.

'Get in and I'll tell you,' Saeed said.

'But how? How come they changed their minds so easily?'

'Connections, my friend. Connections over and above the law …'

'What connections?'

'Your uncle.'

'Damn you and my uncle!' Fahd bellowed in a rage, trying to open the car's locked door. He raised a pointed finger at

Saeed and screamed, 'I swear if I'd known this when I was back there I'd never have signed the pledge, even if they'd condemned me to death. I've nothing left to lose!'

'Fahd, listen to me. If things had been left to grow and spread it might not have been a death sentence, but you could have gone to prison for a long time and been robbed of your life and your studies.'

'What, Saeed? There's no one left to help me off their rubbish-tip except my murderer of an uncle?'

'Because your uncle has ties to them. Don't forget, he knows their top guys and most of them pray at his mosque. They've got interests in common.'

'Fine. Where is he then?'

'He came after making a few calls and finished your paper-work, then he left again.'

'He left? Really? Without saying anything? He didn't make any problems for me?'

Saeed avoided the question and turned his gaze towards the shops in the street. He would go back to the flat, he said, so Fahd could take a shower and change his clothes and celebrate his release at an expensive restaurant.

When Saeed tried to park the car outside Buhasli restaurant on King Abdullah Road, Fahd objected, remarking that he hated the whole street, its shops, restaurants and cafés. He had barely recovered from his unpleasant memories of Starbucks, he said, so Saeed drove on to Saraya, the Turkish restaurant on Thalatheen Street, and as they were waiting for their food, Fahd asked, 'Tell me. What happened?

'Basically your uncle asked me to tell you that he never wants to see you again.'

369

'To hell with him. I don't want to see my mother's killer anyway.'

'There's something else.'

Saeed fell silent, poking holes in his paper napkin with a fork and considering how best to explain. 'He took a copy of your case file at the Committee and asked them to keep a record of your pledge.'

'Why? So he can haggle with it whenever he wants?'

'No.'

'You sure?'

'He told me he was taking your sister to live with him because you are untrustworthy and incapable of looking after her.'

Fahd said nothing for a while, briefly peering out at Thalatheen Street as if he was struggling with his eyes to stop a sudden tear springing forth. He saw pigeons wandering around over the broad pavement. One of them hopped on a tub containing a wilting bush while the rest continued to circle the tightly packed paving stones, pecking away as if reading their painful life stories. He returned his gaze to the gloom of the restaurant and whispered in a sad, defeated voice: 'God damn him.'

'A week ago you were thinking of emigrating. When I asked you about your sister you said she was the same as your uncle and she didn't concern you any more.'

'She's all that's left of my family, Saeed, do you understand?'

His voice changed, becoming strangled. A grief-wracked sob rose from his chest and he cried a little. Knotting his hands on the tabletop he laid his head on them and wept for a long time, silent and full of sadness. Saeed let him be for a few minutes and then reached out his hand and laid it on his head.

'Be brave, Fahd. You're a man, you have to confront life and its challenges.'

Leaving the restaurant, Fahd saw a Starbucks on the other side of the street with its famous green sign and shouted in a mocking voice so Saeed could hear, 'Bye-bye Starfucks!'

Saeed laughed as he opened the car door. 'That's a global company. You'll find it on every corner in the world, maybe even in that village you're planning to live in in Britain.'

'Very possibly, but you know something? The difference is that there's no Committee there, nobody watching your every move and counting your breaths. No, "Where are going? Where have you been? Who's that girl with you? Your mother, your sister or your lover?"'

Saeed let out a long whistle. 'Well, I hope life over there agrees with you.'

62

F AHD DROVE HIS SMALL car towards Ulaya Street, past the
Pizza Hut in Urouba Road and into the narrow side
street called Sayyidat al-Ru'osa, from where he entered Zuhair
Rustom Alley, stopping briefly by the black door behind which
his childhood had passed like a dream. This door, from whose
threshold he had bade farewell to his father Suleiman as he
started the car and headed off to Qaseem, never to return. This
door, through which his gypsy uncle entered with glassy eyes
and a belly fat with care and deliberation, to expel not just
Fahd, but Fahd's whole life, from this contented household.
This door, through which he passed for the first time carrying
his satchel, headed for the unfamiliar faces of pupils and teachers at Al-Ahnaf Bin Qais Primary School. This door, scuffed
by the feet of his grandfather, his grandmother and his mother's three brothers. This door, from which they carried the
body of his mother, fighting for life after being subjected to
a savage beating. This door, ponderous, melancholy, scowling.
This door, broad-shouldered as a gorilla, not wide enough to
admit the dreams of one small family that began its life with an
ill-starred association with the Divine Reward Salafist Group,
the breadwinner spending years in prison for taking a risk
and handing out pamphlets inciting rebellion before returning to live his life with honour, shunned by respectable families. This door that opened smoothly and didn't creak, unlike

his grandparents' door in al-Muraidasiya, which shamed them with its vibrant squeak, reckoned a kind of singing by the local congregation, some manifestation of the Satanic pipes that must be stilled. This door, witness to a life which flew past in a demented rush, never pausing to look over its shoulder.

Fahd raised his eyes to the fogged glass of the car window: maybe he would see his sister's ghost. But he saw nothing there save silence and slow death, nothing save a pot with its withered plant.

He started the car and drove off. Turning left and passing Sheikh al-Islam Mohammed Bin Abdel Wahhab Mosque he looked out at the southern steps where the shelves for sandals stood empty. But lying on the ground he noticed a pair of tattered leather sandals like those of his father, his father's final pair that had driven him to his death.

Once past the mosque his heart thumped in alarm and he turned back and parked the car. He got out, frightened and confused, removed his shoes at the entrance to the mosque and glanced briefly at the size of the sandals by the door. He put his right foot in one—'It's my father's size!'—and reaching out to the door he felt a shiver run through his body like cold water and the hairs on his skin prick up.

Very slowly, he opened the door and in the far west corner of the mosque, next to the *mihrab*, he saw a body wrapped in a hair *mashlah* and apparently asleep, its face turned towards the *qibla*. He considered walking quietly round to see the face. He was frightened that he might wake, but he was determined and he moved forward with slow steps, alert to any rustling from his *thaub*. Reaching the *mihrab* he took a look at the sleeping man's face, but he had covered it with his *shimagh*. He thought of making a loud noise to wake him up, but instead retraced his steps to the door, turning every few paces towards the *qibla* where the man lay.

He peered at the sandals for a while. They looked like the ones his father and Mushabbab had taken turns wearing in prison whenever one of them was summoned for interrogation, until that heavy day had dawned and Saeed's father had donned the leather sandals and gone outside and neither he nor the sandals had returned. Were these sandals, lying like a witness outside the door of the mosque, the sandals that Saeed's father had slipped on a quarter of century before?

He left the alley in the direction of the street where flowers were sold and drove south until he reached Jazeera Mall, then took a left towards Iblees Street where the Bangladeshis had their shops, selling illegal satellite dishes and receivers and cards for encoded porn channels. He crept into a little street behind Sadhan Mall and, at exactly ten in the morning, carrying all the necessary forms and his plane tickets, he stopped outside a company issuing travel visas to Britain.

When he presented his papers, having passed through the routine security check at the door, the long-haired clerk asked him a number of questions, sent him to a room where his thumbprint was taken, then handed over a receipt stating that Fahd's application would be processed in two days.

Fahd left. By the outer gate he breathed a sigh of relief and wondered what had happened to Tarfah. Had they handed her straight back to her family or taken her to the women's shelter? What was her family's view of what had happened, especially that of her brother Abdullah? What had they told Sara about her mother? Good God, how merciless this country was! How exorbitant the cost of a coffee with a random girl!

374

Fahd muttered to himself as he made for Tahliya Street, where he stopped at a Dunkin Donuts to drink a cup of black filter coffee with a bear claw pastry, taking out his mobile every now and then to check that it was working and that he hadn't received a message.

The Filipino closed the long curtains as the afternoon call to prayer sounded and Fahd went back out to the car. As he was turning the key in the ignition, the mobile buzzed like a cockroach and he opened its message folder: *I swear to God I'm going to create a scandal in front of everyone, at every exhibition, at every artists' gathering, you rat!*

Selecting 'Reply' he wrote: *Screw you, screw 'everyone' and screw your country, too.*

He imagined Thuraya the Hejazi, waking late to the sound of her squabbling children, feeling the air conditioner wash against the semi-naked body that gave off the powerful, penetrating fragrance of her perfume. There was no man beside her to ravage her, and she wrote to curse the young man, the immature stranger, who failed to fill her life, who refused to surrender to her will. The phone buzzed again: *See here, Syrian. You've got the right to swear at me and other people, but I'll be saving that comment about my country. It'll get you fucked up.*

My God, thought Fahd. *How can people bear to live in a racist, conspiratorial society, a society that hates and cheats and dupes and gossips and steals and murders, a society for which I have a representative sample at my fingertips: my uncle, Yasser and Thuraya? True, there are selfless friends like Saeed, and there are those in search of certainties and absolutes, like my father, Mushabbab and Abdel Kareem, and then there are those, like me, like Lulua and Tarfah and Sami, who are lost. But just thinking of it makes me want to vomit.*

63

I NSIDE THE LOCKED OFFICE in the Committee building, Tarfah contemplated her moment of shame. She imagined what might have happened had they taken her to the women's shelter and placed her on the register, to spend the following day sitting in front of a sheikh with knotted brows who would question her about the crime of going out to drink cappuccino with a stranger. She imagined the supervisor calling her broken-hearted mother to inform her of the incident, requesting that her father come to pick her up:

Her mother is completely thrown and decides not to tell Abdullah for fear that he might lose his temper and exact revenge on his sister. She hastily rounds up Ayman and the two of them drive off, following the supervisor's directions. They lose their way more than once and Ayman pulls over to question passers-by, once by the Passport Office and once by the Girls' Education building, asking them if they know where the women's shelter is.

When they arrive, her mother goes in to see the supervisor and requests that she might take her home.

'Not allowed, auntie!'

'I'm her mother!'

'Sorry, only her father can pick her up.'

'Her father's dead, my girl.'

'Well, her legal guardian, then, and he has to bring the original of his custody document and a picture of the girl.'

'Her brother's the guardian!' says her mother, then adds, 'Her brother's outside with the security guard.'

'Does he have a court-certified custody document in his name?'

'No, her guardian's the older brother.'

'Then he has to come here and pick her up in person.'

Damn! It was as though they were arranging Tarfah's death, quite blithely and in cold blood. Her mother imagines Abdullah coming with a killer's calm taking her away—forgiving, understanding, affectionate—without mentioning the subject, as though he didn't care. Then he would drive her home, apologising for having refused to let her study at the nursing college. But not to worry, a friend of his would make sure she was accepted on to the course. On the way, he would drive her to dark parking lot in the basement of some building, butcher her with a huge, razor-sharp knife and put her body into a black bag, which he'd heave on his shoulder and throw into a large yellow skip.

Tarfah imagined her mother contemplating her fate for a few moments, thinking of a way to get out of this fix.

'Her older brother's travelling,' her mother says.

'She's stays with us until he's safely home again.'

'Listen, my girl, he's gone abroad on a study trip. Anyway, Tarfah has a young daughter at home. She can't sleep at night unless her mother holds her. God have mercy on your parents, my girl,' she pleads. 'God watch over you in this world and the next.'

Tarfah heard the rattle of a key in the lock and sat up, alert; she was in the Committee building, not the women's shelter. Wrapped in serenity, the man in the cream *mashlah* entered in the company of a lightly bearded youth with shaven temples, who was holding a sheet of paper and a blue ink pad. The sheikh told her that the Committee would protect a guilty woman for a first offence but for a second offence—God forbid!—she would go to the women's shelter and be handed over for questioning there. She might stay there for six months or a year, and if convicted and sentenced, she could be sent to women's prison.

'This is a pledge. Place your thumbprint here, promising not to commit any more offences against the law, and we will keep it safe with us, in complete confidentiality. We might need it again if, as I mentioned, you engage in any immoral act a second time.'

The sheikh turned to young man beside him. 'Brother Saad will take your confession and help you sign it. I am going to call your family so they can sign for your release.'

The sheikh went out, leaving the door open behind him. The bearded youth approached, placed the sheet of paper in front of her and pointed at a sentence at the bottom of the page: *Write your name here*. He handed her the pen and she wrote her name, her hand shaking. He uncovered the damp blue fabric of the inkpad and placed it on the table beside her, then taking her full white hand, he spread her left thumb, pressed it on to the pad then held it next to her name for a few seconds, fondling her hand until she pulled it away from him. He coloured instantly.

'So, what's fine for him is forbidden for me?' the young man said.

She scolded him, harsh and self-assured: 'Fear your Lord, sheikh!'

She knew he was no sheikh, but wanted to give him a rank he respected and would be ashamed of dishonouring. Alarmed, he ran from the room and Tarfah rubbed her thumb against the underside of the table's edge to remove the loathsome ink.

It made her weep bitterly when Ayman cried in front of her, repeating, 'This is the end of my trust in you, Tarfah! I'm the only one who respects you and does what you ask, and now you put me in a situation like this.'

Although he was years younger than her, she could pull his head towards her and kiss him twice as she asked his forgiveness; he did not deserve her deceiving him.

'You're the only one who has been there for me after Dad died. I don't have anyone but you. May God never take you from me.'

In the heat of her fervour she said, 'I swear I'll only leave the house to go to my grave!'

His mobile had not stopped ringing from one that afternoon and he eventually answered, telling his mother that he and Tarfah would be late because one of the doctors at the university had been suspended. Tarfah had called him several times from the college, he said, and when his mother asked, 'Shall I send Abdullah, then?' he had shouted, 'No! I'm right outside the college. We'll be home in a few minutes!'

Tarfah cried for a long time in the car. Ayman didn't ask her who she had gone to the café with but she was unable to raise her beautiful eyes towards him when he sat with his siblings in the living room.

64

T HE DUST WAS CHOKING Riyadh for a third day in succession. The moon's disc struggled to be seen without any noticeable success. Everything in the city cried out for a lament, for pity.

Fahd was riding next to Saeed as they headed out to the café and feeling almost as if he might fly. He had picked up his British visa and here he was, on his way to meet friends and some other people Saeed had organized as a surprise.

Arriving he found a group, some of whom he knew and others he was meeting for the first time. Saeed introduced him to them one by one: 'Firas: a friend from the neighbourhood. Saoud, you know: the general director of the Kanoun website. Omar's an Islamic political activist; he's been unemployed since he was fired for putting his name to a statement calling for political reform. Ziyad the Dwarf from middle school, the one with a woman's voice. Ali Bin Abdel Lateef, first in the *thaniwiya aama* exams at the Najashi Secondary School. And Rashed.'

They sat down and Fahd ordered a pipe of Bahraini apple tobacco and scanned the printed menu, then became aware of the earnest conversation taking place around him. They were arguing with Omar, Saeed having a go at him because he was sitting with an atheist like Brother Firas who believed in nothing. Omar was making it clear that he still believed in the drive to institute reform in the country, even if it ended up fading away or smothered in the cradle. He believed Islam was the only route to this reform, though he rejected both what he called 'Talibanised religion' and the form of the faith propagated by the Council of Ministers.

'Just because there's a brother without faith like Firas here, doesn't mean I have to agree with him and nor does he necessarily have to believe in anything himself. It's a personal matter. It concerns him, his relationship with the world and his view of religion.'

Saeed broke in to say that they had come together to say goodbye to Fahd who was travelling to Britain, perhaps to study, and perhaps to emigrate, temporarily or permanently as it might be.

As he began telling them the story of Fahd's tempestuous life over the last two years a group of bearded men entered the café, led by a portly man whose body jiggled inside his short *thaub*, the corner of his *shimagh* dangling down either side of his face. He halted in the middle of the seated patrons. Some hid their *shisha* hoses beside them while others hung them on the brackets next to the pipes and got up to leave. Fahd was on the verge of walking out when Omar gestured at him to sit down and whispered to everybody: 'Please, no one leave. I want you to witness what I'm going to do with your own eyes.'

'Brothers, the sheikh has something to say!' bellowed one of the men. Most of them were over twenty. Some carried plastic bags full of free cassettes and little booklets; others ringed the fat sheikh with his round red face and groomed black beard.

'Brothers, not one of you can claim to be a believer until he desires for his brother what he would want for himself, and, by

God, I love you all in God's fellowship and wish for you what I wish for myself! My Brothers—may God guide you—the smoking of *shisha*, and tobacco in all its forms, is among those things that are proscribed for the harm they bring, as doctors have shown, and is forbidden by the words of Almighty God, may He be praised: "They ask you what is lawful for them. Say: lawful for you are all things pure and good." And also: "He commands them to do what is just and forbids them from evil; He makes lawful for them what is good and pure and prohibits them from what is bad and impure." Tobacco and *shisha*, my Brothers, are amongst those impure things proscribed by God in His Book, for they are the cause of illness and destruction: "Make not your own hands the instruments of your destruction." And also, "Do not kill yourselves, for God has been to you the Most Merciful."'

The sheikh talked on for ten minutes amid absolute silence, some even lowering the volume of their mobile phones, giving him a feeling of great satisfaction and importance. As he finished reciting his final verse, Omar raised his hand and in a loud voice that broke the hush, he shouted, 'God reward you, sheikh! I have a question.'

The sheikh glanced at him for a moment. 'Please.'

'Truly, God reward you for that advice, but might we know your name?'

The sheikh looked him up and down sourly and one of his acolytes said, 'Sheikh Hamoud Bin Abdullah.'

With a self assurance and courage that was the envy of the silent crowd, Omar said, 'Naturally, sheikh, you would agree with me that you yourself contain both good and evil.'

The sheikh nodded uncertainly. 'Indeed …'—while his companions lifted their eyebrows in disbelief.

Omar fired his second volley: 'And of course, sheikh—God reward you on behalf of us all—you will know that there are those amongst us who will be better even than you.'

Then Omar came to the point, speaking with a crazed bluntness: 'You came here to speak to these guys, most of whom are unemployed, so that they'd give up smoking but you didn't ask yourself why they're here. Don't you know that most of them don't have work or a hope of finding it, that they're poor and struggling? Don't you think, sheikh, that standing up to tyrants, fighting for what is right before an unjust ruler, is more important than taking on the *shisha* habit of these penniless men?'

The sheikh was staring at Omar, struck dumb by shock. His face reddened and he began to mutter unintelligibly as he made for the exit followed by his bearded men, while Omar continued to scream in a blind frenzy: 'Sheikh! Don't turn your tail and run! Come here, I've got something important to tell you!'

Some of the young men in the café chuckled and Saeed shouted, 'A big hand for Sheikh Omar!'

A roar went up, the youths clapping and whistling with a delight rarely to be found in a city whose dust only cleared when a new dust storm rolled in.

'For shame, Omar,' Rashed said. 'You denied them their heavenly reward and the chance to hand out those tapes of theirs.'

'Can you believe it?' said Saeed. 'Everyone's going to hear about this little session. The minute I get home I'm going to send out the details of what happened.'

Salem agreed. 'Right. It's interesting. I reckon it will get a big following.'

Saeed became conscious of Fahd's unhappy silence and spoke to him as he pointed at Omar. 'So haven't you changed your mind about travelling? Instead of pulling out and running off, it's possible for a guy to confront that lot.'

Fahd shook his head and Saeed went on, 'I mean, you saw Omar's bravery; how it made them flee like foxes ...'

As Omar preened with pleasure, Rashed objected, 'Don't you believe it, my friend. If they could have been certain that Omar wasn't an undercover cop they wouldn't have run. They might have made a serious problem for him.'

Saeed agreed with this, as did Fahd. Sipping his tea, Omar pointed out that they were human beings like anyone else: some were genuinely frightened and cowardly, others brave and hungry for fame, well aware that their recklessness might lead to detention or a prison term, and this was what won them supporters and disciples. Some were frankly simple-minded and assumed that these lectures were a way to win heavenly reward. Some even became high-handed and tyran-nical, possessed by a need to break and subjugate those around them.

Omar believed that most of his fellow signatories to their most recent statement calling for a constitutional monarchy suffered from a persecution complex that turned them into petty dictators; petty, though their claws were cruel.

'So I have nothing to lose,' he said. 'I can dedicate the rest of my days to exposing them!'

Rashed interrupted. 'Don't forget the liberals, Omar. They need exposing, too.'

Omar laughed mockingly. 'What liberals? Bless you, they're just lambs to the slaughter. The real game is with the Taliban who are polishing off what's left of this country, if there is anything left, that is. They've invented the liberals out of thin air to justify their iron grip and lead this hapless society of ours to their final solution.'

Fahd gestured to Saeed, who made his excuses to the group, telling them Fahd didn't have a car and was travelling tomorrow, so they had to go. They went out past the men selling cassettes and CDs at the café door.

The car moved west towards the Dammam Road into Riyadh. It was two in the morning and the traffic around the café had thinned out. Saeed grimaced in disgust. 'No theatre, no cinema, no public spaces, no streets where you can get a breath of fresh air. Even the cafés have been chucked thirty kilometres out of town. But still they chase after us wherever we go. God help you, where can we go?'

'What do you expect? The people set free? Left to frolic about unmolested, no one to watch them, no laws to bind them, no rights protected and upheld?'

'Tell me: where's the law, anyway? Anyone can stop you and make accusations, force you to sign a confession, or even get you detained or sent to prison.'

Saeed was drumming nervously on the steering wheel as he spoke: 'Know what, Fahd? There's this guy at work who was talking about some woman assaulted by the Committee and he says, casual as you like, "Why doesn't she go and complain to the Human Rights Commission?"'

'The problem, Saeed, is that a lot of people are simple-minded and naïve. They don't understand that the Human Rights Commission is a government body, no different to the Ombudsman. It's not independent. It's controlled by the same people the government always employ with their salaries and bonuses.'

The car crossed Khaled Bin al-Waleed Street and Saeed suggested they stop in at a Herfy or Kudu and pick up a meal. He wasn't just disgusted, he explained, he was hungry as well.

'Don't you ever feel that this country lives just to eat and shit? The restaurants are the only places open after midnight.'

'What I feel is that everyone is panting like a dog after a couple of pennies so he can escape for a month or two in the summer and live abroad. He spends his pennies then he comes back to live like a dead man for ten months, making a little bit here and a little bit there, until he flies off again next year, and so on.'

Saeed pulled in at the Herfy drive-through window in the Panda on the north-eastern boundary of Maseef. He ordered two chicken combos and refused to let Fahd pay his share, claiming that travel and life abroad would put paid to the modest sum he had made by selling his car the day before.

Back out on the Northern Ring Road the heavy dust cloud began to drop towards the tarmac until it brushed against the two men. Fahd hid his nose in his *shimagh* as he got out by the entrance to the building. Saeed said he would stop by the grocery store to pick up a pack of cigarettes and asked him if he wanted anything. Fahd turned him down with a wave of the hand as he climbed the marble steps on his way to the second floor.

65

T HE JOURNEY FROM LONDON to Great Yarmouth was not a
long one and it would have been pleasant were it not for
the crying jags and painful memories that overwhelmed and
upset Fahd the whole way. The route was lined with verdant
nature, redbrick houses, rivers and contented livestock, but
though he stared through the window and tried to hold on
to his pleasure at this delightful journey from London, he saw
nothing but the barren desert. When he managed it, that is,
when he managed to force his memory like some stubborn
goat towards new pastures and away from his former life, he
found the threads re-knotting, weaving themselves together
until they brought him back once more to the same tragedy.

He had stood for ages before Nelson's Column in Trafalgar
Square where the Mayor of London had forbidden the feeding of the pigeons that Fahd hated, the vile pigeons whose
shit polluted the beautiful square and clung to its monuments.
Even Nelson wasn't safe from pigeons, and nor was Fahd. If
the commander of the British fleet, the man who defeated the
navy of Napoleon Bonaparte, the legendary Admiral Nelson,
couldn't keep his body free from the shit of some piddling
pigeon, then how could Fahd protect himself from the malign
effects of a feather?

That pigeon. Fahd remembered it well, asking himself over
and over: 'Why didn't it take flight like the pigeons in London's

parks? Why didn't it beat its wings and try to fly away in the courtyard of Abu Ayoub's house in Buraida?'

Fahd recalled how it had desperately scurried and hopped, yet had never left the ground. Were its wings not strong enough to fly? Had its feathers been clipped, for instance? Was it too heavy, lacking air-filled chambers in its limbs? Maybe its toes were straight, not curved; Australian biologists had discovered that in prehistoric times, birds had spent their time on the ground rather than perched on branches, and fossils showed their feet were flat, suited for walking and not flying. Was life in Buraida still stuck in prehistory?

He had returned his gaze to the pigeons of Trafalgar Square, pondering the ban on feeding the pigeons and the public outrage at the rule, particularly from environmentalists, though their cause was shared by suppliers of birdseed whose business had gone flat.

'Those birdseed merchants mean nothing to me,' Fahd thought. 'The thing that really hurts is that a great artist like Picasso could love this ugly bird and paint it into his pictures. Even Chagall painted a pigeon, descending beak-first from the sky towards two lovers. I love that wonderful painting of his, *Lovers and Flowers*. How courageous to use that powerful, vivid yellow! Yet what a miserable artist, to paint a pigeon descending from the top of the canvas towards two lovers floating above a jug of flowers. I hate pigeons. I really hate them. Not because they destroyed my childhood and perhaps my whole life, but because it's a loathsome bird, spiteful and selfish. Even the way it mates is awkward, its stupid circling, its ungainly, graceless hops. So how is it that they've proved in their studies that next to the dolphin, elephant and chimp, it is one of the most intelligent creatures after humans? Does it save people from drowning? Can it see colours? Can it recognise itself in the mirror or on TV? When I fail to recognise myself in the mirror does that make me a dumb animal? A curse on scientists, and artists, too.'

Fahd opened the bag beside him and took out an iPod, fixing the headphones in his ears.

Mmmm … Mmmm … I got wings to fly …

He awoke in alarm to the sound of the train reducing speed. Removing the headphones from his ears he looked out of the window to see the train coming to a halt. Throwing his bag over his shoulder he stepped down on to the platform and let the little town swallow him up.

YOUSEF AL-MOHAIMEED has published several novels and short story collections in Arabic and has had stories published in Lebanon, Egypt, France, Germany, Spain, and Russia. He studied English and Photography in the UK and was recently presented with an award by *Diwan al Arab* magazine and the Egyptian Journalists Union in recognition of his creative contribution to Arab culture. He lives in Riyadh.

A NOTE ON THE TRANSLATOR

ROBIN MOGER is an Arabic translator currently living in Cape Town, South Africa. He is the translator of *A Dog With No Tail* (AUC Press, 2009) by Hamdi Abu Gollayel, Ahmed Mourad's *Vertigo* (BQFP, 2011), *Women of Karantina* (AUC Press, 2014) by Nael Eltoukhy and Youssef Rakha's *The Crocodiles* (Seven Stories Press, 2014). He was the principal translator for *Writing Revolution: Voices from Tunis to Damascus* (IB Tauris, 2012) which won a 2013 English PEN award for outstanding writing in translation.